Also by Diane Burton

Switched

Switched, Too

Switched Resolution

The Pilot (An Outer Rim Novel: Book 1)

The Chameleon (An Outer Rim Novel: Book 2)

One Red Shoe

The Case of the Bygone Brother

How I Met My Husband (contributor)

The Protector

An Outer Rim Novel

Diane Burton

This is a work of fiction. Names, characters, places and incidents are the product of the author's imagination or are used fictitiously. Any resemblance to actual persons, living or dead, events, or locales is entirely coincidental.

ISBN-10: 0996637419
ISBN-13: 978-0996637411

Dedication

To my children for their continued love and support

To my grandchildren whose smiles make my day

And especially to Bob, my best friend and hero

Acknowledgements

Thank you to the members of the Mid-Michigan chapter of Romance Writers of America® for their continued support and advice. To Laurie Kuna for her editing of this work and to my critique partner, Jolana Malkston. They didn't always tell me what I wanted to hear, but their help made the story better. To Florence at The Novel Difference for the amazing cover art. Thank you, ladies.

Most importantly, I want to thank my family for all their support. Liz & Matt, Doug & Katy, I'm very proud of you. Thank you for encouraging me.

To my husband, Bob. How glad I am that our friends fixed us up on that blind date!

Dear Reader,

Welcome to the Outer Rim, the frontier of space. As wild and crazy as the American West in the 1800's, the Rim is the home of stout-hearted individuals. Pioneers eager to make their fortunes. Nonconformists who want to be left alone. Escapees from the establishment or from the law. People who reinvent themselves with new names and life histories. From uninhabited planets to primitive settlements to established colonies, the Rim is the place of fantasies and dreams.

I hope you enjoy the adventure.

Diane

CHAPTER 1

After cutting the heel off a loaf of jambor, Rissa Dix sat on a stool at her work island, closed her eyes, and inhaled the scent of freshly-baked bread. Along with her third cup of sheelonga tea, she ate the warm bread with its distinctive nutty taste.

Her Mid-Day indulgence. The only time she rested. From early morning until she closed at Mid-Night, she rarely sat. Too much to do, so little time.

The tavern had done well last night. The Winslott miners had wound down, as they usually did midway into their furlough. For the first tenday, they blew off steam, drank, and feasted. The next few days would be the same until they realized it was nearly time to return to the lambidium mines. Then they would drink more than they should and try to get in as many visits as possible to Fortuna's Pleasure Palace across the street.

As Rissa savored her treat, her comm beeped from where she'd left it on the counter near the cooler. Normally she wore the device on her wrist just not while making jambor. No sense getting it clogged up with flour. She spun on the stool and stretched to reach the comm.

When she saw Ropergor's gray face in the mini-monitor, she answered, "Hey, how's my favorite traffic controller?"

"Mistress Rissa." The Volpian's long, gray chin wobbled. *"Do you have any food or ale you can spare? A transport landed last night for repairs and they want to stock up before they leave. The mechs finished repairs on the hydraulic leak, and the pilot is ready to go. I tried Chef Nalgin, but he's in the middle of the café's Mid-Day rush."*

"How much do they want?" She and the owner of the café often supplied ships but usually with more notice.

Ropergor told her quantities. *"It must have a larger crew than I've seen."*

"No problem." As she talked, she headed toward the stairs beyond the bar. "We can be there in twenty mins."

After disconnecting, she rapped on the door to Kiran's quarters. "I need some help," she called to her bartender.

A groggy Kiran opened the door. While scrubbing his bald head, he ducked under the frame then straightened to his full height. Zeboris usually went around two meters tall. Kiran was more than two and a half. Broad shouldered, with skin as black as a manval, and teeth just as white

1

and sharp, he could be terrifying when angered. That made him a great bouncer. Not that *she* couldn't handle a drunken miner or two.

"Whassup, Boss?" Kiran voice was so deep it seemed to come from his toes.

Thank the Matriarch he'd thrown on one of his short wrap-around, native skirts—tan with dark blue Zebori symbols.

"Some numbnut pilot wants provisions. Now."

"He should have thought ahead." Kiran smothered a yawn.

Rissa couldn't believe it when he ducked back into his quarters. "Hey. I need help now."

He turned around, his hand on the closure to his skirt, his black eyes twinkling. "Figured I'd better dress appropriately."

"Uh, yeah. Hurry up, okay?"

When she bent down to reach into the storage area under the bar, her long braid fell over her shoulder. *Darn thing.* One day she'd cut it off. She pulled out an anti-grav pallet then guided it to the kitchen. Within mins, Kiran showed up wearing traditional Rimmer garb—multi-pocketed shirt and trousers in dun-colored coarse-spun. Same as hers.

She and Kiran loaded four loaves of fresh jambor, two dozen turken eggs, a large tub of frozen hican stew, and a case of Astron Ale onto the pallet. She left a note and the alley door unlocked for Sophira who could handle the few miners that might wander in. Rissa doubted many would show up. Most were sleeping off last night's indulgences.

She and Kiran made it to the spaceport with two mins to spare.

As soon as she entered the enclosed hangar, the smells assaulted her nose the way they always did. Lubricating fluid and ferranite dust were bad enough, but the cloyingly sweet odor of barzilium overpowered all. Servo-bots were transferring the bars of fuel from a stack against the left wall onto a waiting freighter.

Traffic Controller Ropergor minced up to her. "Thank the Divine One you've come. The pilot is quite anxious to get underway."

He guided her to an old freighter, its hull a shade lighter than the rust around the hatch. A grizzled Chellian in a wrinkled spacer uniform stood at the entrance to the airlock. The faded spots across his forehead and down the sides of his face indicated he was almost as old as his ship. He shifted from one foot to the other.

As she and Kiran approached with the supplies, the spacer strode down the ramp. "It's about time you got here. We're ready to get off this rock."

Rissa put her hands on her hips. "Most pilots give advanced notice for supplies."

"Yeah, yeah. Just bring the stuff aboard."

2

When he started to go back into his ship, she called out, "After you pay for it."

He returned quickly enough. After she told him the amount, she held out her credit device. She'd only been burned once by a crew who refused to pay after she'd already unloaded their supplies. She'd learned her lesson and always got payment first.

"That much? That's robbery."

"I can take it back to the tavern." She motioned to Kiran to back away.

"All right, all right." The pilot keyed in his info and the amount before slamming the small box into her hand. "I still say it's robbery."

The pilot's attitude grated on her nerves. He'd already interrupted her quiet time. Now he was complaining.

"Extra charge for rush deliveries."

While backing out of their way, he grumbled curses. Rissa had heard worse. She followed Kiran as he guided the AG pallet into the ship. Typical freighter set up. The airlock opened to a corridor. Bridge on the right, galley down and on the left. Kiran steered the pallet toward the galley.

"That's far enough." The pilot's abrupt command stopped them from going farther. "Take the boxes off the pallet and leave them on the deck."

"In the middle of the corridor?" Rissa asked.

"My crew will take everything into the galley."

All the time she and the pilot had talked—argued—two Chellian crewmen stood at the entrance to the bridge and stared at her, lasciviousness in their eyes. For the first time in ages a man made her feel unclean. The space crews and miners who frequented her tavern treated her with respect.

The faster she got off this ship the better. She and Kiran quickly unloaded the pallet. As if using mental telepathy, neither bothered to leave a walkway between the boxes and the walls. She was only too happy to let the crew do the lifting and carrying. Considering how much food they'd ordered, the rest of the crew must be working elsewhere on the ship.

"You there, Zebbie." The pilot pointed to Kiran. "Hurry up."

"You will speak to him with respect," Rissa snapped. "Or forget getting any supplies the next time you come here."

The pilot sneered. "I won't stop here again. You people are all crooks. Do you know how much they charged me for patching up a tiny leak? And you." He pointed at her. "You've got a lot of nerve gouging me for a little food."

Before she could lambaste the pilot, Kiran took her arm, steering the pallet with his other hand. "Time to go, Boss. We're done here."

They were done, all right. She'd warn Chef Nalgin and Merchant Graeson about this pilot. They didn't need his business.

After they left the ship, Rissa told Kiran to take the pallet back to the tavern while she had a word with Traffic Controller Ropergor. First, though, she needed the sanitary facility to wash off the stench from the pilot and his leering crew.

When Rissa entered the unisex san-fac, the odors made her gag. The mechanics had left their calling cards—grease and dirt smudges—in the sinks, on the counters and on the doors to the stalls. She doubted a place this dirty would wash away anything. It looked like the room hadn't been cleaned in years. Next time, she'd use the san-fac out in the passenger waiting area.

She washed her hands then realized there was no towel. Her trousers would have to do. As she turned to leave, she heard a rustle in the stall nearest the wall. When she checked under the door, she couldn't see feet. Hair on the back of her neck rose in alarm. Immediately, she looked up in case some *thing* was about to pounce on her.

She stepped back. "Pacer, you stupid space jock. You'd better not be looking over the partition."

Silence. Probably wasn't Pacer. He would've strolled out with a smart answer.

"Whoever you are, come out. Right now."

Another rustle then the sound of feet lightly hitting the floor. The lock slid open then slowly the door moved.

"Please," a soft voice whispered. "Don't hurt us."

That sounded like a young girl.

"Come out where I can see you." Rissa, too, whispered.

A tall, dark-haired teen stepped out, followed by a smaller girl with light brown hair. They both looked terrified. Their hair was matted and dirt smudged their faces. Their clothes were filthy. The smells emanating from them contributed to the general san-fac odors. Rissa did her best not to react.

Holding the other girl behind her, the tall one stepped forward, jutting out her chin. "We are not going back."

"O-kay. Back where?"

"You can't make us. We'll escape again."

Rissa had to admire her bravado. "You escaped? From where?"

"Did they send you in here to get us?"

Since the taller one seemed to be the spokesperson, Rissa kept her eyes on her. Something about her was compelling. Rissa could be looking at herself at the same age. Then it hit her hard, like a blow to the stomach. That was what Miri would have looked like at that age. Same strong Traishan features—olive skin, dark hair and eyes. Same strong will.

Rissa took a deep breath to steady herself before locking the outer door. "Nobody sent me. You asked for help. What can I do?"

"Get us out of here before they discover we're gone." Despite the strength in the tall girl's voice, she worked hard to keep her chin from wobbling.

"Who?" Rissa was afraid she knew.

"Those men. The Chellians. We can't go back. We won't."

By the Matriarch, traffickers.

Her lungs seized, her heart hurt so badly Rissa clutched her chest. *Be strong*, she told herself. *Pull yourself together.* No traffickers had ever come to Astron Colony before. Or even to Galeriana. She had to help the girls get away.

She glanced at the window on the far wall.

"We couldn't open it," the smaller girl sobbed. "We were trying when you came in. We thought you were *them*."

Since Rissa was taller, she could easily reach the window. With a shove, she got it open. "Come." She motioned to the tall girl. "You first. You can catch your friend. She's too small to catch you."

She cupped her hands for the girl's foot. "Hide outside. I'll come around and take you somewhere safe." At the girls' wary looks, she added, "I promise. Now go before someone comes looking for us."

Rissa boosted her up to the open window. The tall girl hoisted herself through, disappeared for a moment then stuck her head inside.

"The ground is higher out here. Come, Anaris." She held out her arms.

The small girl, Anaris, gave Rissa a panicked look. "You'll come for us?"

The door rattled. "Hey," a male yelled. "Open up."

Anaris gave her a panicked look.

"Gimme a min," Rissa yelled back.

"I promise to come for you," Rissa whispered then gave her a boost. Like the tall girl, Anaris disappeared through the window.

As Rissa reached to close it, the tall girl was there about to do the same. "Thank you." She shut the window and ducked out of sight.

Hoping they would wait for her, Rissa walked out of the san-fac. A mech glared at her. "Whadda mean by locking the door?"

"Didn't want you walking in on me." She glanced over at a commotion near the freighter where she'd delivered the supplies. "What's going?"

The pilot was yelling and his two crewmen were darting between ships, searching.

"Damn offworlder." The mech brushed past her into the san-fac. When the pilot saw her, he yelled, "What did you do with them?"

Rissa looked around to see who he was shouting at.

"You there." He stormed up to her. "Where are those two girls?"

She affected a confused expression. "What girls?"

"My cargo, I mean passengers. Damn you to Lexol's Fire. How did you get them out?"

The pilot's slip confirmed what Rissa feared. The girls she helped escape had been cargo. The pilot and crew were slavers, bastards who trafficked in children. A primal urge swept through her. *Kill them. Kill them now.* They couldn't be allowed to go free.

At the same time, fear that she would expose the girls stopped her from reaching into her boot, drawing out her knife, and gutting the pilot on the spot. Instead, she stared at him. "I don't know what you're talking about."

"The san-fac." He rushed past her and into the facility. When he yelled for them to come out, the mech yelled back with expletives that even a seasoned tavern owner like Rissa found offensive. She thanked the Matriarch that she and the tall girl had thought to close the window. After slamming open stall doors, the pilot returned.

Traffic Controller Ropergor sidled up to her, his long chin wobbling in distress. "Mistress Rissa, my apologies for the disturbance."

She blew out a long-suffering breath. "I don't even know what he's talking about."

At that point, Dock Master Yephos showed up. "Sir, this is a reputable spaceport. No one would take your passengers."

The pilot stalked over to the rotund Yephos. "They were on board when we landed, and now they aren't. So you tell me where they are."

"I will call Security Chief Kaminga and he will start search—"

"No!" The pilot's adamant response made Rissa doubly sure he was a damn slaver. She consigned him and his crew to the deepest level of Lexol—the level reserved for those who preyed on children.

"Are you sure they were aboard?" Yephos went on. "Perhaps they got off at your last port of call?"

"Tilfan," the pilot called. "Tell this yokel the passengers were aboard when we left Vetan."

"Uh, Boss?" The man called Tilfan edged closer to the pilot. "I'm not exactly sure about that."

"What!"

"Lindae was supposed to check. You sent me to the engine room to get—"

The other crewman scurried up. "You said you'd give them dinner while I—"

"Idiots." The pilot slapped both men on the back of their heads.

"There's your answer, sir," Yephos said with a satisfactory smile. "Your passengers must have gotten off at your last stop. What colony on Vetan? I can check with the dock master—"

"No," the pilot snarled. "We're getting out of here before we lose anything else."

"Is it all right if I leave?" Rissa asked Yephos. "I need to get back to the tavern."

"Go, Mistress Rissa," the dock master said. "This was a misunderstanding."

Forcing herself not to rush, Rissa strode through the hangar. As soon as she was out of sight, she ran outside and around to the back of the spaceport.

"Anaris? Where are you?" If she'd known the tall girl's name, she would have called her, too. "Come on, girls. I said I would help you."

Rissa raised her hand to shield her eyes from the Mid-Day sun blazing down on the planet. The wind whipped around the sand and blasted her face. Out in the open, the girls would not be safe from the desert heat. They had no head coverings, no water. They wouldn't do much better if they chose to hide in the heap of scrapped speeders, starcraft, and assorted junk. Pung rats and other more nefarious critters would make them wish they'd stayed aboard the ship.

No. Anything was better than being torn from family and sold as slaves or worse.

"Girls, I have to get back to my tavern. You have two mins to come out if you still want my help. Otherwise, I'm leaving." Not that she would. She just needed them to hurry.

The scrape of metal on metal heralded their approach. The tall girl still looked defiant. Anaris, the little one, ran to Rissa and flung her arms around her waist. "You came back. We didn't think you would."

Her emotions on high alert and still shaking in fury over the slavers, Rissa pulled the girl's hands from around her back. "The pilot couldn't find you and thought I stole you. He is very angry."

The tall girl scoffed. "He's afraid of getting in trouble with his boss. That's what he said when we tried to escape before."

The spaceport dome that kept out the constantly blowing sand from the desert to the east and north of the colony ratcheted open. She and the girls crouched next to the building so as not to be seen by the departing ship. The roar of the Chellian freighter signaled its launch, while the force of its heavy-air engine blasted sand in all directions.

7

Rissa pulled an ever-present cloth out of her pocket to cover her face. "We need to get indoors. Use the tail of your shirt to cover your nose and mouth from the sand."

She led them down back alleys until she felt safe enough to cross the main street. With the extreme temperature, she didn't think any miners would be out walking around, but she wasn't taking any chances. Better that no one see the girls. Miners were such terrible gossips. Word might reach the traffickers about two new girls in the colony, and they might return.

At the back door to the tavern, she went in first before motioning to the girls. The scent of freshly-baked bread still lingered in the kitchen. Hunger flared in their expressions. One of the crew was supposed to feed them after leaving Vetan. By the Matriarch, that had to be two days ago.

"Hey, Boss, I—"

The girls screamed and scurried behind Rissa. Obviously, they'd never seen a nearly three-meter tall Zebori before.

"Sh, sh." She tried to quiet them down. "He's a friend."

"What do we have here?" he asked.

"Stolen cargo. Help me feed them."

After telling the girls to sit at the island, she quickly sliced jambor. While Kiran retrieved butter, mongberry jam, and milk from the cooler, she set the plate of bread in front of them. When she turned around after getting glasses, they were stuffing the last of a slice in their mouths and reaching for another. *Damn those slavers for starving the girls.*

"Slow down. You'll get sick if you eat too fast. Before we go any further, we should share names. That's Kiran. He works here with me. I'm Rissa Dix. I know you're Anaris. " She nodded to the younger girl. "What's your name?" she asked the other.

"Pela," the tall girl said around a mouthful of jambor. "My name is Pela. Why did you say *Deece* when the name on the sign outside is Dix?"

Rissa smiled. "Because that's how my name is pronounced. It's a common mistake." After they downed the milk, she told them to bring the jambor. "Try to forget what you see next. I'm trusting you not to tell anyone."

She walked to the back wall and opened a cupboard door on the left. Her fingers unerringly found the hidden button. After she pressed it, the wall slid aside, revealing a set of stairs. Again she motioned to the girls who stared in disbelief.

Though Anaris came up to her, Pela hesitated. "This better not be a prosti-house."

"No prosti-houses in Astron Colony," Kiran said. "One pleasure house, across the street. This is a tavern only. Miz Rissa wouldn't have it any other way."

"All right, girls, let's go up and you two can take a bath. I'll bet you haven't had one in a while." She started up the stairs, hoping they would follow.

At the top, she pressed the button on the bottom of a black box, and the passageway opened. Light from the hall spilled down the stairs. The doorway below in the kitchen closed. As soon as the girls came up, she showed them how to close—and open—the door to the stairs.

"You are not prisoners. You can come and go as you please. A word of caution, though." She pointed to the left. "At the end of that hall is a set of stairs down to the tavern, which will soon be full of miners on furlough. It is not safe for you down there."

At their startled expressions, she explained about the gossiping miners then added, "They won't come up. But it's better for you to come down into the kitchen."

She led them to the right and to her quarters at the other end of the hall. After giving them towels and washcloths, she handed over her smallest shirts.

"I'm going to get you some clothes. I hope you'll stay here until I return. As I said, you are not prisoners. You can trust me. In turn, I trust that you will not make off with my things."

Pela straightened her shoulders. "We are not thieves."

"Good. I'll be back as soon as I can."

Downstairs, she made sure Kiran and Sophira had everything under control. Even though a few miners had come in, Mid-Day was not the tavern's busy time.

"Sit down, Sophira," she reminded her pregnant server. "You need to stay off your feet."

"Yes, Miz Rissa," Sophira said in a sing-song voice. "Kiran reminds me often."

The big bartender smiled, showing off his white teeth.

Rissa motioned both to the kitchen. "I don't think the girls will come down. Take care of them if they do. I'm going over to Fortuna's—"

"Boss?" Kiran grinned in mock horror.

"—to get some clothes for the girls. I just hope one of her girls is small."

Rissa knew better than to go into the pleasure house through the main door. Kiran's mocking would pale in comparison to the hoots and hollers from the miners or space crew waiting their turn. She rapped twice on the alley door and was greeted by the short cook who liked her own cooking a little too well.

"I'll let Miz Fortuna know you're here."

Within a min, the pleasure house owner hurried into the kitchen. "To what do I owe this honor?" The small fem laughed. "Finally going to take me up on my offer to sample my newest provider? He's absolutely delish. And what stamina."

Though her cheeks flamed, Rissa brushed aside Fortuna's offer then quickly explained her need for small clothing.

"Slavers?" Fortuna screwed up her face in disgust. "I heard rumors of disappearances in cities like Rhadaman but not in the colonies."

"About the clothes?" Rissa needed to return before the girls decided to explore. Or, worse, leave.

Fortuna led her up the back stairs to the sleeping quarters. "SeeMee isn't working right now. She's the smallest."

A few mins later, Rissa had a bundle of clothing from the generous SeeMee who was only too happy to help the escapees. "I chose this life," the tiny pleasure worker explained. "Nobody should be forced into it."

And that, Rissa thought, made the difference between pleasure houses and prostis. Choice. She had to make sure those girls bathing in her sanitary could make their own choices.

"The other girl is taller than you," Rissa said to Fortuna. "About this high." She leveled her hand near her own shoulder.

Fortuna nodded. "Wait here. Don't want to interrupt anything." She grinned.

When she returned to the tavern with the clothes, Rissa found the girls wearing what she'd left them. Her shirt hung almost to Anaris' ankles. On Pela, it reached her knees. They'd been sitting on her settee, Pela brushing Anaris' hair. They jumped up when Rissa came in.

Both eyed her warily.

Pela broke the silence. "What are you going to do with us?"

Rissa sat on the end of her bed across from them. "I can find transport so you can return home."

"No." Pela's sharp response surprised her. "I won't go back."

Anaris looked even more frightened. "Please don't," she whimpered.

With delicate probing, Rissa got their stories. Both girls had been sold by their fathers to the traffickers. Her heart twisted for them. How could a parent not appreciate the gift of life given to them? To sell their flesh and blood was unconscionable.

Rissa reined in her anger. "You have a choice where to go, what to do. Nobody will force you. Now try on these clothes, and when you're ready come down to the kitchen."

Pela stood in front of Rissa. "Why are you helping us? What's in it for you?"

"Repentance."

After swearing Merchant Graeson to secrecy, Rissa picked out two changes of clothing for each girl. Although Fortuna's girls had been generous, she thought Pela and Anaris might appreciate new clothes—especially plain undergarments. Even she looked askance at what had been provided. But Fortuna's was closer to the tavern, and Rissa hadn't wanted to leave the girls too long. Now that she knew they wouldn't run off—and possibly into danger—she felt comfortable leaving them long enough to run down several blocks to the mercantile.

"You say the ship was a slaver?" Normally, Graeson's voice boomed. Even though no one else was in the mercantile, he spoke softly.

She nodded. "Nasty bastards." When she told him how they'd treated the girls, Graeson agreed they shouldn't have anything to do with that ship and crew, if they ever returned.

"Take the clothes. No charge."

Before she could thank him, Medico Barlen came around the end of the aisle. "You're giving away merchandise? A miracle."

"Don't broadcast it," Graeson, a short, round Kruferian, huffed.

"Wouldn't think of it." Barlen winked at Rissa before sobering. "What are you going to do with the girls?"

"How much did you hear?" Rissa had thought no one was around. She must be more cautious.

"Don't worry. I'm the only one here."

"No, you're not." Fortuna stepped into view.

Rissa jumped. By the Matriarch, how did they enter without her knowing? "Maybe we should take this conversation into your office, Graeson."

"Good idea." Barlen, the colony's only medical practitioner scratched his stubby gray beard. "I can't believe traffickers are working in this system."

"They said they'd been in Vetan," Rissa said. "Apparently, they needed repairs and had to stop here. The pilot will not be giving us a five-star rating for hospitality." She explained about the pilot's reaction to what she charged him for supplies.

"Vetan?" The merchant looked worried. "Vetan isn't that far away."

Vetan's proximity had been her worry, too.

11

"What if they decide to come back?" Fortuna asked. "And not for repairs or supplies."

"We need a plan," Rissa said as she picked out some hair ribbons for Anaris and Pela. When she realized no one responded, she glanced up. "Why are you all looking at me?"

CHAPTER 2

Dillan Rusteran discovered the cure for insomnia. With his sixth yawn in the past half hour, he shoved the mining lease aside. Not for the first time, he cursed the fact that he'd chosen corporate law as a profession.

Not his choice, his father's. Until six years ago, Dillan had done everything he could to defy Boras Rusteran. Now Dillan worked for him, in a job he hated. He especially despised searching contracts for loopholes. Loopholes Boras could exploit.

He pushed away from the monstrous desk his father had gifted him when he joined the company after graduation. While Dillan appreciated the fine piece of furniture made of naurem—with its distinctive swirls and exquisite finish—from Bricaldia's rainforest, he would have preferred a less ostentatious display of wealth. He rose, put his hands to his lower back, and stretched. As he rolled his head from side to side and front to back, he eased the crick in his neck then walked to the window that took up almost the entire outside wall.

Mount Graven appeared in the distance, clouds covering the upper third. In the fog, climbing would be dangerous and thrilling. Dangerous and thrilling. Words he'd lived by for ten years until the accident. He hadn't climbed since.

Vehicles slid past the window at levels as varied as the transports themselves. Cargo freighters, single occupant skimmers, multi-passenger conveyances. A familiar Rengara 790, similar to his own, darted in and out of traffic. Dillan watched the dark red vehicle as it swooped down and landed across the street twenty floors below. He fished binocs out his desk drawer—dislodging a plexi-sheet—and trained them on the Rengara.

Dressed in the trappings of an executive—dark blue suit, brilliant white blouse, blond hair in an elegant twist—Jileena Winslott moved from the vehicle with halting steps. Where was her hover chair? Dillan raised the power and saw determination mingled with pain in her expression as she turned to say something to the tall, dark-haired man hovering a few steps away. Her spouse, Laning Servary.

Dillan understood Servary's caution. Nearly a year after being shot, Jileena had just started to walk again. Memories of her lying in a medical center bed reminded him of her desperate struggle to live then to conquer paralysis. He, Jileena, and her brother Konner had grown up together, practically siblings. Back when their fathers weren't just business partners but friends as close as brothers. As close as Konner and he.

DAMN YOU TO LEXOL'S FIRE, KONNER, FOR NOT BEING THERE FOR JILLY. His mind shouted the words he never voiced. *And damn you for not telling me you were alive for five years,* his mind whispered. Five *years* while guilt ate away inside him.

His door slammed against the wall, cutting into Dillan's thoughts. He dropped the binocs in the drawer on top of the plexi-sheet he needed to take home. His father's bulk filled the doorway. As Boras barged into the office, Dillan's assistant scurried around him.

"I'm sorry, Mr. Dillan," she said in a timid voice. "Mr. Rusteran wouldn't let me announce—"

"Don't need to announce me," Boras boomed. "I own the damn company."

And the employees.

Dillan stood behind his desk chair and forced himself not to grip the back. Sitting would put him at a disadvantage, as he'd learned the first week of his employment with Rusteran Mining. Amazing the tricks his father pulled. Or maybe not so amazing.

"It's all right, Noree," Dillan said. "Please close the door."

Boras strode to the visitor chair. A large man, from whom Dillan had gotten his height but not girth, Boras often used his size for intimidation. That had served him well during negotiations with land owners in the early years of the company. It irritated Dillan when Boras used it on his employees . . . and his son.

"You won't get those leases examined daydreaming out the window."

Dillan waited. A trick he'd learned from the master. In the ensuing silence, Boras became agitated. Finally, he threw a plexi-sheet on the desk before settling his weight into the chair. Dillan caught the sheet as it slithered across. He glanced at it then set it aside.

When he didn't say anything, Boras blustered, "That's the lease between Winslott Industries and a Sauri tribe on Galeria 7. Find a way to break it."

"It's called Galeriana now."

"What?"

"Galeria 7 was renamed Galeriana."

Boras harrumphed. "I don't care what it's called. I want to break that lease."

A disgusted Dillan stared at his father.

"Don't give me that look, boy."

Boy? He was thirty-two years old, yet his father still treated him like he was a teen.

"I didn't go to law school to help you cheat people out of their rights."

Despite his size, Boras leaped out of the chair. He slammed his palms down onto Dillan's desk and leaned forward. "I sent you to law school to enrich this company. My company. Your job is to do what I say."

And that was the crux of the matter.

"What is that?" Boras pointed to the open drawer.

"Binocs." He knew that wasn't what Boras meant.

"Not those." His father skirted the desk then yanked the plexi-sheet out of the drawer. "I asked you what this is."

Bracing himself, Dillan squared his shoulders. "Design modifications for an Agilean Speeder."

"You aren't still wasting time with this nonsense, are you?" He waved the sheet.

"My time to waste."

"Not here. Your time is my time and I don't pay you to fritter it away." With a swipe of his hand, Boras erased fifteen hours of work.

Two hours later, Dillan entered his father's office. To make a point, which he doubted his father would get, he waited to be announced first.

"Don't just stand there." In his usual gruff voice, Boras waved him in.

After closing the door behind him, Dillan stood in front of his father's desk—a more ostentatious one than his own. "I found an ambiguous item in the Winslott-Sauri Tribe lease."

Boras was all smiles. Like a manval ready to pounce on an unsuspecting chartae. "Good." He prolonged the single word in delight.

Dillan hid his disgust at the avaricious gleam in his father's eyes. How had the loving father he'd known as a child come to this? He knew when—after his mother left—but not why. Though he'd pondered the matter often, he'd be damned if he could figure out what had happened between his parents.

As he turned to leave, his father stopped him. "You did well."

Rare praise. Dillan just wish it had been for something worthwhile.

Boras scanned the notes attached to the lease. "All right then. Go to Galeria 7—or whatever it's called—and negotiate with this Sauri chief."

Dillan stood rock still. *Galeriana?* The one planet in the universe that still gave him nightmares . . . even after six years.

15

CHAPTER 3

When the episode of *Wagon Train* ended and Rissa turned off the vid player, the customers groaned. The miners and spacer crews sure did love those Terran vids. She was so tired of Westerns she promised herself she'd find a good comedy tomorrow night.

Even before her "Last call!" most of the customers started to leave, bemoaning the fact that the tavern closed at Mid-Night. They headed for the boarding houses or across the street to Fortuna's.

Only a couple of customers remained, including that no-good Nakus who groused about everything. He didn't like the food. Too salty. He didn't like the liquor. Watered down. He didn't like the vids. Too many repeats.

He slopped some of his *watered down* chokiris on her beautiful naurem bar top—the one she'd flown all the way to a remote outpost on Balderan to rescue from some idiot who didn't recognize what lay beneath grime and dirt. If Nakus ruined the finish, she would finish him.

As Kiran wiped up the mess, he glanced at the short, round Kruferian, "Need a bib?"

The former Coalition Security Chief, demoted to bouncer at Fortuna's, merely grunted and went back to slurping his drink.

Pela quit wiping down tables the customers had left and took one order from a spacer who'd come in late. Despite Rissa's assurances that she didn't need to *earn* her room and board, Pela had begged to wait tables . . . if only to spell Sophira. Rissa had relented as long as Pela kept up with her studies.

When the poor kid landed at Astron on that slaver ship, she'd only had a rudimentary education. She could read and write Universal enough to get by. After four tendays of lessons every morning, she'd advanced rapidly. Rissa couldn't be prouder.

She strolled behind the bar to Kiran. "Has Nakus paid for anything?"

"Nope," he muttered.

"Get his credits then cut him off."

Usually light on his feet, Kiran lumbered—an intimidation trick he'd perfected—over to Nakus. "Time to pay up."

"In a min." Nakus wasn't easily intimidated. "Not finished with my drink. Damn lousy liquor in this place."

Rissa rolled her eyes. "Yet you come here every night."

"Not like I have a whole lot of choices." Nakus swallowed the last few drops in his glass.

He was right about that. The only places in Astron Colony that sold liquor were Rissa's tavern and Fortuna's. An offworlder was building a tavern close to the spaceport. The miners would probably check it out, even though they and the villagers didn't much care for offworlders. Rissa wasn't worried about the competition. Her customers would return. Loyalty trumped convenience on the Rim.

"Pay up, Nakus," Kiran repeated.

"Put it on my account." The short Kruferian started to slide off the stool.

Kiran reached across the bar and grabbed the front of Nakus' shirt. "Not so fast. You don't have an account here anymore."

"Since when?" Indignation rose in his voice.

Rissa ambled closer. "Since you don't pay your bills unless I threaten to have Chief Kaminga throw you in the lock-up."

"Give a hard-working guy a break, will ya, Dix?"

"You? Hard working? Hah. And I've told you enough times my name is pronounced *Deece*. You must be hard of hearing."

"Or so stupid he can't remember," Kiran added as he released Nakus.

"I'm not going to sit here and be insulted." He slid off the stool, tripped on a rung, and landed on his well-padded rear. "I'm hurt. Lousy stools. I should sue for personal injury."

"Fat chance getting a lawyer to come here and take your case." Rissa rounded the end of the bar. "I have had enough of your bellyaching, Nakus." She grabbed the back of his belt and his collar and lifted him off the floor. "I don't need your business."

"Wait," Kiran called as she hauled the dark-skinned Kruferian toward the outer door. "He hasn't paid."

"I'll collect from Fortuna," Rissa said over her shoulder. "She'll take it out of his wages."

"You can't do that." Nakus wriggled and slapped air because his too-short arms couldn't reach her.

"I can and I will. I don't tolerate freeloaders."

Kiran strode ahead of her and opened the door. "Want me to dump his sorry ass out in the street, Boss?"

"I got it." Like hoisting a keg of ale, she hefted the Kruferian a little higher and heaved him out onto the dusty path that passed for a street.

Nakus rolled several times before scrambling to his wide, flat feet. "I'll get you for that, *Dicks*."

She was sure he deliberately mispronounced her name. "Yeah, yeah. I've heard that before, you cheapskate."

He brushed off his baggy trousers, shot her a rude gesture, and waddled across to the boardwalk in front of Fortuna's. A group of miners who'd watched his humiliation laughed and hurled insults at the little Kruferian. That only added to his indignation.

He shook his fist at her. "I mean it, *Dicks*. You haven't seen the last of me."

Rissa turned to Kiran. "I don't want him in the tavern. He's not worth the trouble."

"Agreed. I thought you've been too lenient. But, hey, you're the boss." He winked and then, with a formal bow, said, "After you, Mistress Barkeep."

As she strolled back inside, she saw Pela on the floor picking up scattered credits. The latecomer—a blue-furred Indigian—was leaning over talking to her. Apologizing, Rissa hoped. Pela was never clumsy. As the girl gathered the coins, the man stroked her rear. When she abruptly straightened, her face pale, the man slid his hand down her thigh.

"Get your hands off her!" Rissa strode to the table. "Get out."

The stranger scooted his chair back. "Didn't mean nothing."

"It's all right, Miz Rissa." Despite her words, Pela's voice trembled.

"It is not all right." Rissa put her hand on the girl's shoulder. "Everyone who comes here knows to treat my people right."

"Hey. I said I didn't mean nothing."

From his uniform, he must be an indie pilot or a crewman on a freighter.

"I told you to get out. Are you hard of hearing besides being a pung rat?"

His black mouth twisted into a mutinous expression. "Haven't finished my drink."

"You're finished. For good." Kiran stepped around Rissa and grabbed the man by the front of his shirt. Over his shoulder, he shot her a toothy grin. "My turn, Boss."

As Kiran hauled him out, the man yelled, "Hey. You can't do this to me."

"Miz Rissa said to get out," Kiran said. "You come back again and you'll regret it."

Rissa turned to Pela. "Are you all right?"

She nodded.

"What did he say to you when you were on the floor?"

"Miz Rissa, it's okay." She began to clear the table.

Diane Burton

"Stop that and look at me." When Pela did, she continued, "No, it is not okay. Did he threaten you?"

Tears filled Pela's dark eyes. "He said as soon as you left he was going to take me out back and . . . and . . ."

Rissa pulled the girl into her arms. Surprisingly, Pela didn't resist. Even though she'd been there for over four tendays, she still didn't like being held. Except now.

"I would never let that happen. Nobody will ever hurt you. You believe me, don't you?"

Pela nodded. When she began to pull away, Rissa let her go. "Why did you say it was all right? It wasn't all right what he said to you and that he touched you."

Pela ducked her head. "I didn't want to make trouble."

Rissa thought Pela had gotten past the way her father had treated her. Selling his daughter to slave traders had been the culmination of a lifetime of mental and physical abuse. Though how the girl could put that behind her when Rissa still agonized over how her own father had treated her.

Tipping up the girl's chin with her knuckle, Rissa said, "*You* weren't making trouble. He was. Anyone who mistreats my people will be thrown out and denied reentry. I do not tolerate that and neither should you."

"I know. It's just . . ."

"It's hard. I know. You deserve to be treated with dignity. We all do. Now, how did you do tonight—other than that last jerk?"

With a tenuous smile, Pela patted the front of her apron. "Very good. I should have enough to buy my own reader."

"I said you can keep mine. I hardly use it." By the time she fell into bed in the wee hours of the morning, Rissa was too tired to read.

"I know. But I want something of my own." She grabbed the half-empty glass from the table and the bowl of versarin nuts and took them to the bar.

Kiran returned, locking the tavern door behind him. "If we keep tossing out customers the way we did tonight, we won't have any left." His booming laugh echoed off the paneled walls.

"We don't need customers like that. Word will get around, as it always does." She hitched herself onto a barstool. "It's the way it was back in the early days. The miners didn't know what to make of a fem tavern owner. After I broke one man's wrist, nobody messed with me."

Pela's eyes widened. "You did?"

"She did." Kiran talked as he cleaned up. "I heard that despite a med unit, the medico said he couldn't work for three tendays. Got sent back to his homeworld."

19

The Protector

"Wow." The admiration in Pela's eyes made Rissa blush. Instead of responding, she surveyed her domain. With the exception of Nakus and the Indigian, the tavern had done well that night. It usually did when the workers from Rusteran Mines had furlough. After twenty years in the business, she didn't have to tally the credits to know.

Twenty years. By the Matriarch, that was half her life. Half her life working in bars that ranged from seedy to decent or taverns that were a lot better, then scrambling to convert a deserted warehouse into a thriving tavern. Sweat equity wasn't just a term, it had been a way of life as she'd cleared rubble a meter thick, dislodged pung rats bigger than paynzers, and remodeled the interior. She'd learned how to wield a hammer, saw with accuracy, and barter with a master electrician and plumber. Her hard work shone in the gleaming paneled walls, a floor no miners' boots could scuff, and indoor plumbing—a rarity when she opened.

Rissa seldom indulged in nostalgia. Too busy earning a living. But tonight was different. She felt entitled to a little retrospective. A little. No sense going overboard.

"You look happy," Pela said.

"Just looking at what's now mine again." Rissa grinned broadly. Kiran looked up. "So you paid off your loan?"

Rissa gave the stool a twirl. "Yep."

As she spun, the shiny wood paneling blurred, and she felt like a kid on a playground spinner. Abruptly, she stopped. A kid. She scoffed. Even as a kid, she'd never had the luxury of acting like one.

"You looked like you were having fun, Miz Rissa." Pela emptied her apron pockets on the bar top. "You shouldn't have stopped."

"Bosh. I'm too old for such nonsense."

"You're not old, Miz Rissa."

She scoffed but didn't reveal that her fortieth birthday had come and gone.

"Old is a state of mind." Kiran smoothly covered the awkward moment. "If you feel old, you are. Now me? I feel like I'm fifteen, like Pela here."

She gave him a shy smile.

"We had a good night." Kiran retrieved the cash drawer for her. Miners didn't believe in electronic credit chips. If they couldn't hold coins in their hands, the credits didn't exist.

"Next tenday will be the same when the Winslott miners come in," he said.

Rissa groaned. Only two days of respite because of the holiday. "At least they don't have furlough at the same time as Rusteran's."

"Great idea, Boss," Kiran said, "getting the supervisors to alternate furloughs."

"With the way those two teams fight, it was self-preservation." Rissa couldn't take credit for convincing the mine supervisors. She'd just gathered concerned merchants to go with her and plead their case.

Pela continued to count her tips then split them with Kiran. Best server Rissa had ever had, even better than Sophira. Not only was Pela efficient, she was honest to a fault. Sophira and Jodar were honest, too, of course. Rissa wouldn't keep either of them on if they weren't. Pela worked faster than either of her part-time servers.

Kiran nodded his thanks to Pela while Rissa took the cash drawer to a nearby table and spread out the coins to count. She didn't worry about being robbed. Kiran's presence discouraged would-be thieves.

"Is it all right if I go to bed now?" Pela asked, as she always did.

"You don't have to ask permission," Rissa said, as she always did.

The poor girl had been so brain-washed by those so-called parents that even after four tendays she was still afraid of doing something wrong. Like going to bed too soon.

Rissa put her hands on Pela's shoulders. "You are free. You can do what you want, make your own choices."

As she shifted away, the girl hung her head. "I know, Miz Rissa. I forget."

For a moment, she didn't move. Then she clasped Rissa's hands, voluntarily.

She squeezed the girl's hands gently. "It's all right. I understand. I know it's hard for you. Please believe me. You are free. Truly fr—"

Pounding on the back door interrupted. Urgent pounding and a fem calling Rissa's name.

She rushed through the kitchen and yanked open the door to the alley. Sophira, her part-time server, stumbled into the kitchen.

"My baby's gone," she cried. "Someone took my baby."

A knife jammed into Rissa's heart. *No.*

"You must help me." The fem's terror made her shiver to the point of collapse. As Rissa helped her to a stool next to the island, she cried, "I know you can. I know what you did—" She shifted her gaze to Pela.

"Of course, I'll help. Catch your breath then tell me what happened. Did you see who took the baby?"

Sophira shook her head. "I always check on her before I go to bed. That's when I saw she was gone. My baby, my sweet baby girl." She began sobbing louder.

21

A girl. Though she'd known Sophira had a girl three tendays ago, Rissa had successfully shoved the child's gender to the back of her mind. The knife in her heart twisted at the thought of another baby girl stolen.

Rissa thrust the pain away. "Where's your spouse?"

Sophira sucked in a breath. "Partorus went looking for her. He checked with our neighbors, and two boys are missing, too. They're all out searching. My baby," she wailed. "Who would take her? Why?" More sobs wracked her body.

Three children taken. Rissa had a very bad feeling. "Kiran, make the calls. Pela, stay with Sophira."

"No." Pela straightened her spine. "I'm coming with you. You'll need my help."

"You need to stay here with—"

"You said I am free to make my own choices."

Of all times for the girl to exert her free will.

Rissa lifted her wrist comm and called the traffic controller at spaceport. "Ropergor, have any ships arrived recently?"

"Yes, ma'am. Two. And another one is landing now."

"Have any left?"

"No, ma'am. Why?"

"Don't let any leave."

"I'm not sure . . ."

"Please. Make up some excuse. We might have a *situation*. One we talked about." She ended the call. "Sophira, wait here."

Sobs racked her body. "I can't stay. I have to find her."

Kiran returned carrying three bags. "I have our gear, Boss. I alerted the others."

Rissa stooped in front of Sophira. "Listen to me. If you want me to bring back your baby, you must not come. You could endanger the situation."

The fem grabbed Rissa's hands, desperation in her tight squeeze. "I'll do anything. Just find my baby."

Rissa knew exactly how she felt. "Go home. Your spouse might find her." Probably a false hope. As she unclasped their hands, she nodded to Kiran and Pela. "Let's go."

They raced to the end of the alley then casually crossed the street to the alley behind Fortuna's. As they rounded the corner of the sand-colored building, they nearly ran over a slight figure dressed as they were in baggy, multi-pocketed shirts and trousers made of coarse-spun.

Rissa smiled to herself when she saw the elegant Fortuna dressed in typical Rimmer garb. Sobering quickly at the reason they were all running through the alley, Rissa slowed down to keep pace with Fortuna.

"You changed fast," Rissa whispered.

"I just threw this on over my dress." Fortuna kept her voice low. "I can't believe this is happening. Just as you predicted."

"Seems logical with three kids missing."

"Three? I thought only a baby."

"Two boys are gone, too. Traffickers are hitting more colonies in this system. It was bound to happen here."

"I'd feel better if we had more help," Fortuna said. "Damn those people who didn't believe you."

Medico Barlen burst out the back door of his office. Apparently, he'd been asleep upstairs as his gray hair was mussed and his shirt half-undone. Kiran cleared his throat then motioned to the man to close his trousers. In the light shining through the open door, the old man's face turned red. He turned, fixed his pants, then closed the door. He gave the handle a jiggle to make sure it was locked. A wise precaution considering the drugs he stocked.

A little farther, two merchants joined them—dressed the same, carrying bags. They kept the talk to a minimum, either whispers or low voices. No sense attracting any more attention than necessary. Everything seemed to be going as planned.

"We'll be all right," Rissa said with the assurance she wished she felt. "If traffickers took the children, they won't expect any opposition. Surprise is on our side."

They circled around the spaceport, dodging wrecked spacecraft and dead skimmers. Rissa heard scurrying and shuddered at the thought of pung rats running out of the junkyard and over their feet. Over the years, she'd killed more than her share of the vermin.

Finally the group stopped and reached into their bags. They donned masks attached to hoods that completely covered their heads and necks. The two who hadn't already were rolling down their shirtsleeves. Next came the long gloves. They all wore the same attire. Other than size, there was no distinguishing one rescuer from another. Nobody for the pilot and crew to identify if they saw them.

Except for her. No mask for her. Yet.

When it looked like everyone was ready, Rissa gave Fortuna the code Traffic Controller Ropergor had given her to the back door. "Wait for me to go in through the main entrance. I'll keep the pilot occupied if he's there."

"That's not part of the plan." Kiran pulled off his hood and gloves and stuffed them in his bag, which he then slung over his shoulder. "I'm going with you."

She didn't have time to argue. If she was right about who'd stolen Sophira's baby and the two boys, they needed to move quickly.

23

Ropergor might not be able to keep any ship from leaving if Dock Master Yephos was around.

When they'd set up the plan, she wasn't sure where Yephos' loyalties lay. Would he help them or side with the freighter pilot, no matter what the cargo?

Staying close to the domed spaceport, she skirted the junkyard, ducking under windows, until she reached the boardwalk. Kiran stayed right behind her. And, to her surprise, Pela was behind him.

"You'll need my help." The girl lifted her chin in determination.

"By the Matriarch's left tit, we look like a parade." Rissa set off for the entrance.

The auto-doors grated open. Constantly blowing sand from the desert wreaked havoc with everything in the colony. As soon as there was enough space, she slipped between the doors. Pela followed, but Kiran had to wait for the doors to open more. With his longer stride, he would catch up with them quickly.

"I'm in," Rissa said into her wrist comm. She didn't stop, just kept walking through the small, empty passenger area until she reached the door to the hangar. "We don't know what we'll find. Just follow my lead. By the stars, we can't let those thieves take off."

"You're sure it's traffickers who took Sophira's baby?" Kiran said.

Rissa hesitated. "Who else? Nobody in Astron would steal children. We protect our own. We have to stop traffickers from taking them off planet."

As if she knew what she was doing, Rissa strode through the next set of auto-doors that only whooshed instead of grating like the outer ones. As Ropergor had said, only three ships were berthed, besides the old ferranite freighter owned by Rusteran Mines. That ship never left port because Rusteran was too cheap to repair the hyperdrive. He'd rather pay the berthing fee.

A cargo hauler similar to her friend Celara's was berthed next to Rusteran's freighter on the far side. On this side sat a sleek luxury yacht, a Volpian Caravel, and next to it was an unfamiliar ship—a long, dull gray Indigian transport. No markings. Since it was the closest, she headed straight for it. If it wasn't the right one, she hoped the commotion wouldn't alert the traffickers in a different ship.

Kiran yanked the back of her shirt and hauled her behind a mech's station. She was about to protest when she heard the whoosh of the hangar doors. Two distinct male voices sounded jubilant. Kiran's hearing rivaled that of a chartae.

"Easy pickings," one crowed.

"Except we nearly got caught with these two," the other said. "Who'da thought they'd start searching so soon."

Rissa peered around the tall tool chest and nearly gasped out loud. Two men each carried a limp boy under his arm. They were headed for the Indigian transport. By the Exalted One, she had to stop them. When she pulled the LZ-9 pistol out of the lower pocket of her trousers, Kiran grabbed her shoulder. He held out her hood.

"Oh, all right," she mouthed and slipped it on. The mask didn't fit well, and she had to adjust it so she could see.

He grabbed her long braid, stopping her again. After he tucked the braid inside her shirt, she shot him an angry look—angrier at herself for forgetting.

Leveling her pistol at the men, she stepped out. "Where do you think you're going?"

"What the—"

"Set the children on the floor then clasp your hands behind your heads."

The men complied. She'd set the pistol on stun, but as far as they knew, she could easily vaporize them. Before she could call Kiran and Pela to take the children, hard metal pressed against the back of her neck.

"Not so fast. Drop your weapon."

Rissa froze at the deep male voice behind her. He sounded familiar. Considering the number of people—miners, pilots, freighter crews—that came through her tavern, she had a hard time placing the man. He yanked off her hood. This time the cold metal jammed into her neck. "Who do we have here?"

The two men spun around. The taller one exclaimed, "Stars, Captain, are we glad to see you. Hey, it's the fem from the tavern."

"Take her pistol then take those kids inside the ship. We gotta get outa here. We'll take her with us and dump her out the airlock." His laugh sent frissons of fear shooting through her. Even though she knew Kiran waited in the shadows, she couldn't stop her teeth from chattering.

When the shorter male started forward, his eyes widened. The removal of the metal from her neck and the sound of a body hitting the floor told her Kiran had been right to cover her back. He zapped the two in front of her. They crumpled to the floor next to the boys.

"Thanks." She glanced over her shoulder.

A bundle of blue fur lay in a tangle of arms and legs.

"Miz Rissa." Pela came out from her hiding place. "That's—"

"Yeah. I know."

The captain of the traffickers' ship was the Indigian who'd assaulted Pela.

"Next time don't go rushing into danger," Kiran said. "My heart can't take it."

Heat burned in Rissa's cheeks. He was right. She'd been foolish to rush out like that. Definitely not the plan. She'd just been so afraid the traffickers would get away, taking not just Sophira's baby but the boys with them.

"Sorry. Let's get them tied up and out of sight."

"Yes, Boss." Kiran found electrical wire at the mech's station.

While she and Kiran trussed up the three men like holiday turkens, Pela picked up the first child—a boy about seven or eight—and carried him around the transport. Medico Barlen took the child from her. Then she raced back for the other boy, a year or so older than the first.

After she and Kiran dragged the bodies of the three men behind the mech's station, Rissa started toward the transport. Once again Kiran grabbed her braid. With a gentle tug, he said, "Be careful. And put your hood on." He and Pela had already thrown theirs on.

"No time. We have to get Sophira's baby and the other boys."

"There might be more crew. You have to stay alive. If they get you, who will protect the rest?"

As much as she hated to agree with him, Rissa put on her mask and hood then followed him around to the group that had come in through the back door. Medico Barlen was opening the hatch. Since the others crowded around, she backed up, right into the Volpian Caravel. *Sherd.* She wasn't usually that clumsy.

"Hurry," she whispered.

Dillan Rusteran jerked upright in the large bed aboard his Caravel. It took a moment to orient himself. After three tendays in space, he found it strange for his transport to be stationary. Two hours ago, Traffic Controller Ropergor had directed him to berth his ship next to a ferranite freighter with flaking orange particles around it.

After coming out of a hypergate into an asteroid field and dodging chunks of rocks bigger than his ship, Dillan had been too tired to even go down to his favorite tavern for food. Instead, he'd grabbed a snack and munched as he headed for his quarters. Normally not a slob, he'd dropped his clothes on the floor and fallen into bed.

Now he listened intently for a repeat of what had startled him out of a deep sleep. He knew every normal sound of his Volpian Caravel. And that wasn't one of them. Though the noise had come from the opposite side of the ship, he peered out the viewport at the end of his bed. Nothing besides the old freighter, its single viewport dark.

Without turning on lights, he padded naked across the corridor to the guest sleeping quarters. Staying to the left of the viewport, again he peered out. What he saw explained the bump that had awakened him.

Hooded thieves were breaking into the hold of a cargo transport.

Dillan raced back to his quarters for his wrist comm. "Ropergor, call Security. Someone's breaking into the cargo hauler in the next berth."

After a long pause, the traffic controller answered. "Thank you, sir. I'm on it."

Something in Ropergor's voice didn't sound right. During the six years since Dillan had been in Astron Colony, he'd learned a lot about body language and voice inflections. Necessary tools for an executive in his father's business. Ropergor was frightened.

Dillan threw on his clothes, sitting down momentarily to pull on the soft-soled shoes he only wore aboard ship. His boots were buried somewhere in his closet, and he wasn't about to take time to find them. Though the thieves had been careless in bumping against his ship, he was certain the six he saw would make off with his neighbor's cargo before Security arrived.

That didn't bother him as much as the fear that his ship might be their next target.

CHAPTER 4

"What in Lexol's Fire are you doing?"

Rissa turned at the strong male voice that came from the shadow at the rear of the fancy space yacht.

Sherd. We're in trouble.

At the same time, Barlen lowered the ramp into the traffickers' transport.

Rissa touched Fortuna's arm and whispered, "Take it from here. I'll deal with our audience."

As if time wasn't of the essence, she strolled toward the shadow where the male lurked. If the dock master saw her friends, they would be in a world of hurt. Languishing in Astron Lockup was not on her agenda.

The man in the shadow had spoken in Universal, his accent Bricaldian. Rissa knew better than to assume he was human. All species in the Central District spoke Universal. She expected him to step forward after announcing his presence. He didn't.

She never had to look up to most men, other than Kiran. Her size used to bother her, but since she began running a tavern on the Frontier, she was grateful for her height and strength. Still, this man made her feel small. When she looked up, her hood and mask slipped so much she couldn't see him very well. His overlong hair hung down to blend in with a heavy beard. His broad shoulders and chest made her think twice about taking him down. That and the blaster in his hand.

"Am I interrupting something?" he asked with fake casualness.

"Nah." She tried to disguise her voice and waved her hand, equally casual. "Just a little surprise party for the pilot."

"Stealing a man's cargo is hardly worthy of a party." His tone had gone from casual to harsh. "What the—"

Rissa looked over her shoulder. Pela, a child attached to both of her hands, led a parade of children to the back door of the spaceport. Kiran stood in the open doorway and waved them forward.

"Are there more?" he asked Pela who nodded.

"Is that a slave ship?" the man behind her said.

"Keep your voice down."

After leaving the children with Kiran, Pela rushed to Rissa. "They're really scared. The pilot told them slavers might try to take them away." She ducked her head and went inside.

So that was why Fortuna was taking so long—convincing kids who thought their rescuers would be worse than their captors. Rissa hurried to the cargo ramp.

"What can I do to help?" The man from the Caravel must have followed her. At least, he'd had the good sense to hide his blaster. The kids were scared enough.

"Go back to your yacht and forget you saw this. Or us." She raced inside the dark hold. By the Matriarch, the place stunk. How long had these children been locked up without proper sanitation? She shook off that thought and worried about getting them out before she and the others were caught. Who knew when the dock master might come by?

In the dim light that barely penetrated the dark hold, Fortuna whispered, "I think that's Sophira's baby." She nodded to a girl about fourteen clutching a limp bundle.

Rissa sucked in a breath. "By the Matriarch, they drugged her, like they did the boys."

"Help me make them understand we mean no harm. My Traishan is pretty rusty."

Rissa stooped in front of the knot of children in the corner. In her native language, she said, "Come with us. We'll protect you. We will not harm you, but you must come now."

The children looked to the girl holding the bundle. She didn't get up. "We're not leaving."

Rissa Dix. Dillan would recognize her voice anywhere. He couldn't believe he'd found her so soon. And in such a dangerous position. Once inside the cargo hold, he assessed the situation. Children of both sexes and a variety of races huddled in small groups against the bulkhead. They weren't moving.

In his sternest voice, and in Traishan like Rissa, he ordered, "Get out. Now. Danger."

She whirled on him. "You can't—"

Either his tone or his words had the desired effect. The children scurried around the two fems, carefully avoided him, and dashed down the ramp. He and the shorter fem followed the children to the door where a very large male motioned them to hurry.

Rissa walked up to the oldest girl. "That baby belongs to a friend of mine. I'll take her."

That was a baby the girl held? Dillan had thought it was a bundle of clothing. With obvious reluctance, the girl surrendered the infant.

Outside, four people in hoods herded the children away from the spaceport. The small fem waited with Rissa, but the huge male tapped her on the shoulder. "We have unfinished business inside."

She shook her head. "I forgot."

"I'll take the baby," the small fem said. "Do what you need to do then get out of here."

With a start, Dillan realized he knew that voice, too. The rugged clothes had thrown him. Usually, she wore slinky dresses that displayed her attributes to the best advantage. Fortuna, the owner of the best pleasure house on the Rim, baby in her arms, hurried after the group of children.

When Rissa turned around, she saw him. "I told you to go back to your ship. You do not want to get involved."

"Do not presume to tell me what to do." Without conscious thought, he'd reverted to Rusteran Mining executive. "What's the unfinished business?" he asked the big man.

"Boss?"

"His neck. Not our worry. Stars, I'm suffocating." After whipping off her hood, she strode around the transport and over to a stack of barzilium. She planted her hands on her hips. "What are we going to do with them?"

"Toss them back into their hold, where they kept the kids." The big man hauled a limp Indigian out from behind the stack of fuel. "Take this one."

"Is he dead?" Dillan asked.

With a harsh laugh, Rissa threw the blue-furred creature over her shoulder. "Don't I wish. Just stunned."

She headed toward the transport with her burden. The big man dragged out two human males, also unconscious. He hefted the larger one over his shoulder. Dillan grabbed the other, a Chellian if he wasn't mistaken, and followed.

At the transport, she dropped her burden on the floor—none too gently—to open the cargo hatch.

"I take it this is the crew?" Dillan followed her and her cohort into the hold where they dumped the bodies.

"Got it in one, Offworlder." Rissa wiped her hands on her baggy trousers.

Offworlder? She didn't recognize him. He was a tad surprised to feel hurt.

"What next?" he asked as she raised the ramp then closed the hatch.

"You go back to your ship and pretend this never happened."

"Can we trust him, Boss?"

30

"If you can't," Dillan said, "you're in a sherdload of trouble."

Her short laugh was more of a bark. "He's got a point. We could kill him and save ourselves a lot of trouble."

Rissa got a perverse delight in watching the man's expression. One part horror, two parts indecision. As in "Did she mean it?"

He cleared his throat. "I was thinking more along the lines of what are you going to do with the crew? Just leave them locked in the hold?"

"Serve them right." Her anger at the traffickers came through loud and clear. He'd have no indecision about that. "It's what they did to those poor children."

"He's got a point, Boss. We can't just leave them in there. When they wake up, they'll raise alarms then start searching the colony for us as well as for the kids. Don't forget. They know who you are."

He was right, damn it. She blew out a breath. "I'm open to suggestions."

"Let me take them off your hands." A slender, red-haired male— a Menacan, if she wasn't mistaken—strolled around the old freighter. *Sherd.* They'd been so busy talking they hadn't noticed this newcomer's approach. And there she was without her hood. At least, Kiran had left his on.

"Who are you?" Rissa said.

"Your friendly, neighborhood garbage man. Here to take out the trash." The man seemed vaguely familiar, but she couldn't place him.

He looked at the offworlder. "You have transporting capability on that Caravel?"

"Yes. Why?"

"I'll need some help."

"What are you going to do?" the offworlder asked.

"You two—" The Menacan pointed to Rissa and Kiran. "—take care of the children. And forget that I was here. Go now. What you don't know won't hurt you."

"But I—"

Kiran steered her to the side door. "He's right. We don't want to know."

Reluctantly, Rissa left.

Fortuna waylaid them in the alley behind the medico's office. "Pela took the baby to Sophira. The rest of the children are in here."

"Is the baby all right?" Rissa followed Fortuna.

Kiran entered behind them, stooping as he always did in normal dwellings. He nodded to the medico and the café owner who stood off to the side in the small room.

31

The medico assured Rissa that the children hadn't been adversely affected by whatever drug the traffickers had used. "The boys are from farms west of town. Merchant Graeson took them home."

"What are we going to do with the rest?" Fortuna asked.

Rissa rubbed her temple. She looked over at the twenty-plus children huddled in the medico's waiting room—some asleep on couches, others huddled on the floor. What *could* they do with them?

"They need food, a bath, and clean clothes," Medico Barlen said.

"Bring them to the café," Chef Nalgin said. "My spouse and I will feed them. When Graeson returns, tell him to bring clothes."

"We'll need to find out where they're from," Rissa said after Nalgin left. "And return them to their parents."

"After they've eaten, bring them to my place," Fortuna said. "I have plenty of tubs."

"But your customers will see them," Rissa protested.

"Not if I close early. I'll issue free passes to those who are waiting. They'll have time tomorrow morning before the transport from the mine arrives." She laughed. "They'll do anything for a free pass, even get up early. Have Merchant Graeson bring the clothes to my back door. I'd better go prepare my girls."

After Fortuna left, Medico Barlen looked at Rissa. "This is only a stopgap measure. What are you going to do with those children who have no homes to go back to or have good reasons not to?"

Her shoulders sagged. "I don't know." Again she rubbed her temple. She noticed Barlen had asked what *she* was going to do with the children—not *we*. As if he were distancing himself from the problem. Maybe he was.

She let out a deep sigh. "We need to warn the village." She'd tried before, and they'd ignored her. Because she couldn't give them proof without mentioning Pela and Anaris.

"How are you going to do that?" Barlen asked.

Again, he laid the problem at her feet. *Well, sherd.*

"Who are you?" Dillan asked the red-head after Rissa and her man left.

"You don't need to know." The Menacan held up his hand. "And I don't need to know who you are, either."

Dillan gave him a wary look. "I'd have more trust in a man whose name I knew."

"Then call me Quin."

"Is that your real name?"

"Does it matter?" He headed for the main hatch of the Indigian transport, the ship where the crew lay tied up in the hold. "Follow my lead out past the outer markers. I'll disable the ship and jettison the crew in escape pods. I'll need a way to get back. Only talk to Ropergor. Not the dock master."

Although he had several questions, Dillan kept them to himself. The man's plan sounded good. It wasn't murder—though that wouldn't be a bad punishment for men who trafficked in children.

From the newswaves, he knew trafficking rings traded and sold children like any other commodity, yet he'd never come across any. Not even when he and his friends had come out to the Rim to play. Shielded as he was in the Central District, trafficking was a theoretical problem. Not one he needed to deal with. Not in his backyard.

Yet here he was helping in the rescue of stolen children and the disposal of the traffickers.

In his ship's command center, he listened to Quin talk to the traffic controller, filing a bogus flight plan, readying the transport's heavy-air engine. Dillan did the same. He had second thoughts about the man's plan. But then he was already up to his eyeballs for helping Rissa and her cohorts.

Ropergor opened the dome. Quin—Dillan wondered what the man's real name was—lifted off. Two mins later, Dillan followed.

Quin took the traffickers' ship out into the main space lane between Vesteron Colony and Rhadaman City on Galeria Prime. Far enough away from Galeriana, yet eventually it would be found. Still, Dillan worried about the crew returning to punish the colonists, especially Rissa, for interfering in their business.

"Hey, Caravel. Watch for traffic. I'm going to put them into the escape pod."

"Untie them *after* you get them inside," Dillan warned.

Quin laughed. *"Good point. You aren't a dumb offworlder, after all."*

"Gee, thanks." He chuckled as he wondered what his staff would say if they heard anyone call him dumb.

Then, again, maybe this was a dumb stunt. He knew the traffickers couldn't be left on Astron. Their boss—and Dillan wasn't sure an Indigian was smart enough to mastermind a trafficking ring—would be sure to investigate. Everything he, or she, found would lead to Rissa. Did she realize what trouble she was in?

"Wake up over there. I said beam me over."

That's what he got for thinking about Rissa, worrying about her. Dillan hadn't even heard the distress signal Quin sent out before jettisoning the pod.

He activated his transporter and brought Quin aboard.

"That's done. Fastest speed back to Astron." He slouched in the copilot's seat, one leg slung over the arm. The casual pose was at odds with the man's body, which was as tightly-controlled as a coiled spring. "You can tell Ropergor you came back because you didn't like the sound of your sublight."

Dillan adjusted the engine. He wanted to return quickly to find out more about what Rissa was up to. "I can make up my own excuses, thank you very much."

"Touch-y."

"How big was that escape pod? Will they have enough air until they're rescued?"

Quin sat up straight. "Do you really care? Or are you making conversation? If it's the latter, forget it."

The ship rocked violently.

"Holy sherd! What was that?" Dillan checked his outer scanners. The traffickers' ship had exploded. Debris scattered in all directions.

"Looks like the emergency distress was real." Quin got up and stretched.

"Why did you destroy that ship?"

"Do you want their boss to figure out what those people down there did?"

As Quin walked out of the command center, Dillan called, "Did you really put those men in an escape pod?"

"You got any food?" He walked down the corridor, leaving Dillan alone at the controls, a sick feeling in his stomach.

Who was Quin? And what had he done?

* * *

"The children are fed, bathed, and clothed." Fortuna hoisted herself onto a stool at the work island in Rissa's kitchen. "My girls have them bedded down for the night."

Rissa placed a bottle of ale in front of her friend then sat across from her. Only on the Rim could a preacher's daughter be good friends with a pleasure house madam. If her father could see her now, he'd be horrified, even more upset than when he'd abandoned her on Marin 5. Serve the hypocrite right.

Fortuna took a swig of the ale made there in Astron by a couple of enterprising farmers. "With few exceptions, the kids are from Balderan."

"All right then. I know some indie pilots that regularly hit that planet. They can take the kids home." Rissa closed her eyes, glad that one large problem had been solved. She picked up her bottle of ale and let the cool, tart beverage slide down her throat.

"Not that easy." Fortuna rolled her own bottle between her hands. "They're from a homeless shelter."

"Then no one wants them back?" Rissa dropped her head on her folded arms.

"What are you going to do now?"

She lifted her head. "Why does everyone think *I* know what to do? You. Barlen, Graeson?"

Fortuna reached across and patted her hand. "Because you always come through with a plan."

"Yeah, and everyone wants me to make all the decisions." She blew out a breath. "If only they'd listened to me before."

"They'll listen to you now. You'll need to call a town meeting." With a look of chagrin, Fortuna amended, "The merchants, Barlen, and I will contact the town folk. Tomorrow morning is too soon for a meeting."

"It *is* tomorrow morning."

"Yes, I know. May we use your tavern tonight?"

Rissa nodded. Since furlough ended at Mid-Day, the miners would be gone. And her place was the largest assembly area in the colony—until the offworlder's tavern was completed near the spaceport. "Just make sure everyone knows it's an emergency."

As Fortuna got up to leave, she laid her hand on Rissa's shoulder. "It will be all right. You won't have to carry this burden all by yourself."

"What burden?" The tall man from the spaceport stood in the doorway to the bar.

"Hold it, Offworlder." Kiran held his long knife against the man's throat beneath his beard. "You'd better have a damn good reason for sneaking in here."

35

CHAPTER 5

Dillan froze. The big arm around his neck tipped his head back at a painful angle. The knife at this throat convinced him not to protest.

Rissa jumped off the stool. "Where did you come from?"

"How did you get in?" Fortuna said at the same time.

Considering his disadvantage—and the knife pressing on his throat—Dillan figured he needed a better excuse than wanting to make sure Rissa was all right.

"Kiran, release him. I think he's a friendly," Rissa said.

"Are you sure, Boss?"

When the arm around his neck fell away and the knife removed, Dillan glanced behind him. Then up. A Zebori warrior, if he wasn't mistaken, clad only in a short cloth around his waist. The big man from the spaceport. If Dillan had known the man was barefoot, he could have tromped on his foot to escape.

On second thought, the warrior probably would have slit his throat before howling about injured toes.

"Sorry, Rissa, Fortuna. Guess I should have knocked."

The three turned suspicious eyes on him. Rissa responded first. "How do you know our names?"

"Yeah, Offworlder," Kiran said. "How do you know their names?"

Dillan didn't think a funny quip, like ones he'd given them six years ago, would work this time. Not with the big Zebori looking like he wanted to gut him with that knife.

"I used to come here. A long time ago." He placed his hand over his heart. "I'm hurt, truly hurt, you don't remember." He gave the fems a wry look before glancing up at the Zebori. "Not you, of course. You weren't here then."

"By the stars, it's Rusteran!" Fortuna nearly tripped in her rush to get to him. She threw her arms around his neck and pulled down his head.

He enjoyed her enthusiastic kiss. It just wasn't the one he wanted.

She ran her fingers through his long hair then ruffled the beard he'd let grow on the trip from Bricaldia. He wondered if the barber he knew was still around. While he disentangled Fortuna's arms, Rissa sat

36

back down at the island. She did not look pleased. He could hope her tight expression was jealousy, but it probably wasn't.

Rissa sighed. "Kiran, it's okay. You can go back to bed. Thanks for being so vigilant."

"Are you sure?" Wariness stayed in the man's expression.

"I'm sure. This is one offworlder I can handle."

At Rissa's nod, Kiran thundered out through the bar. Considering the stealth with which he'd snuck up on him, Dillan figured the Zebori was making a point.

"Oh, please, let me handle him," Fortuna cooed.

The tiny fem wore a skin-tight gold dress, deeply cut in front, even deeper in back. Her blond hair was piled on top of her head in a casual twist that displayed her chain tattoo from behind her left ear down to her collarbone—a Wedoran signature for a pleasure provider. She was a beautiful fem who did nothing to turn him on, even when she kissed him again and pressed her lush body against his.

When she noticed the direction of his gaze, she huffed. "Oh, pooh. Same old, same old. I'll leave you two alone to get . . . reacquainted." She shot Rissa a look over her shoulder before sauntering through the swinging door to the bar.

Moments later, Dillan heard the outer door bang shut. Something he hadn't heard from the Zebori.

Rissa pursed her lips. "Dillan."

"Ah. You do remember me." He gave her a grin that used to make her smile.

Didn't work.

"I always remember pains in the ass."

Putting his hand on his heart, he staggered. "Ouch. You sure know how to hurt a guy."

"Go away. I've had a bad couple of hours and I'm going to bed." She walked to the alley door and opened it. "Go back where you came from."

He strolled over to the cooler and reached in for a bottle of ale, as he'd done many times in the past, then sat on a stool. "Is that anyway to treat someone who came to your aid tonight?"

While taking a long swig of the tart ale, he watched the fem who'd turned him inside out six years ago. She looked the same, although her dark hair—still skinned back into one long braid—had a few strands of gray and a few more laugh lines fanned out from her exotic dark eyes.

A blush started at her neck and rose into her high cheeks. "Thank you for helping us." She closed the door and came over to the island but didn't sit. "What happened to that ship and those men?"

He thought about what Quin had done. "Suffice it to say, they won't be bothering you or the children of Astron again."

"You killed them?" When he didn't reply immediately, she clapped her hand over her mouth. "I'm sorry. I shouldn't have said that."

"No, but then you never did think well of me."

Anger flared in the depths of her eyes. "That is not true."

"Isn't it? I recall any number of times when you called me a lazy, self-indulgent pretty boy." He gave her a wry grin. "While I didn't object to being called Pretty Boy, I didn't care for the rest."

Again her cheeks reddened. "Not just you. Your friends. You proved you weren't like them when they left, and you joined the search party for your friend."

Guilt knifed through him as it always did when he thought of that last time in Astron. This had been a stupid idea. *Why did I think she'd be happy to see me? Especially when she didn't even recognize me?* Not that he blamed her, considering his beard. It was unrealistic to think she would recognize his voice.

"I know it's late, but if you're hungry I can find something for you."

"You don't have to do that."

"Consider it a thank you for helping with the kids." She set raw vegetables and cold meat on the table. From the bread box, she took out a half loaf of jambor. While she unwrapped a couple of slices and added that to the mini-feast on the island, Dillan was already crunching away on a stalk of enfils.

Finally, she sat across from him. "When did you eat last?"

He swallowed the crisp sweet vegetable before answering. "Not sure. I kept shipboard time after leaving Bricaldia. I was surprised it was night time when I landed."

"Why did you come to Astron?"

"Konner. His sister said he was alive and well." Bitterness tinged his voice.

"She was here almost a year ago. Why did it take so long for you to come and see for yourself?"

Pride. Anger. But he wasn't going to tell her that. "How have you been? I see you have some new employees."

"Doing well." A smile curved her lips. "As of ten o'clock yesterday morning, the tavern is mine. Completely mine."

"That's great." He reached across the island with his bottle of ale. "Congratulations."

She raised her bottle and let him clink the necks. "Thanks."

"I always assumed you owned the tavern."

"I did at one time. The haboob five years ago did a lot of damage. I had to take out a loan so I could be back in business quickly."

"Haboob? That's a sandstorm, right?"

"A gigantic one that lasted five days. It blew out the windows, destroyed tables and chairs, scoured the finish off the floors and walls, besides leaving sand a half meter thick all over. I had to replace all the appliances and the well pump. Sand mucked up everything."

"Sorry to hear that. The place doesn't look like it changed." He took a swig of ale.

* * *

Rissa caught herself staring at his strong neck and the way his throat worked as he swallowed the ale. Hastily, she took a sip of her own. Six years ago, she'd tried to remember he was a kid. He wasn't one then, and he sure wasn't one now. She regretted not sending him on his way back to his ship. He made her think of things she had no business thinking of. Not with him.

"Wasn't there another sandstorm last year?" he asked.

She nodded. "I was prepared. Shutters to protect the windows and a special cover for the well pump. A small amount of sand sifted through, but no real damage. I learned the hard way to protect what is mine."

"I understand how you feel."

His expression—so serious—convinced her he did. He'd been that serious once before—when he'd lost his friend in a rock-slide up in the mountains. Even though their other friends left after a few days, Dillan stayed to help the search-and-rescue teams from neighboring colonies. When those teams gave up, he joined another team hired by Konner's father to continue the search.

His grief, compounded by survivor's guilt, had led her to comfort him. Comfort that had almost gone too far. She wasn't going to think about that time. She finished her ale and gathered the remains of Dillan's meal.

"I'd better go. I just stopped by to make sure you were all right." He walked to the alley door. "I saw several new boarding houses. Any I should stay away from?"

"You won't get a room tonight. Furlough ends tomorrow."

After a few secs, he heaved a sigh. "I'll sleep on my ship, like I've done since leaving Bricaldia. Goodnight, Rissa. It's good seeing you again."

As he walked through the alley door, she stopped him. "The room upstairs is empty."

Why did I say that? From Dillan's expression, Rissa knew she should have kept her mouth shut. He looked too pleased, like he'd just conned her. Well, his weary tone had. Now she'd have to live with the consequences of him sleeping down the hall from her.

He looked so different from the kid who used to come to Astron. He and his friends. Rich kids with nothing to do but take risks. Idiot thrill seekers.

The Dillan Rusteran standing before her was no longer tanned from the suns of the various planets he and his friends visited to climb mountains, surf in treacherous oceans, or skydive out of their luxury space yachts. From what little she could see of his face beneath the shaggy, dark-brown beard, he had the pale skin of someone who spent a lot of time indoors. Worry lines creased his forehead and fanned out from his green eyes. His shoulders were broader, and his chest had filled out. Still trim, he had a solidity about him that hadn't been there before.

This man would be sleeping under her roof. Again.

When he stared at her expectantly, she said, "You can go through the bar and use those stairs to reach the room."

"Not going to let me go up your secret staircase?" His mouth curved into a small grin.

Ah. She knew that grin. He'd charmed her—or tried to—many times in the past. She wasn't going to fall for it now.

"No. It's too close to Pela's room."

"Pela?"

"The girl who helped with the kids at the spaceport. She lives with me."

His expression grew deadly serious. "I would never mess with kids."

"I know you wouldn't," she said hastily. "Pela frightens easily. If she heard your steps, she would be terrified."

"Who is she?"

Rissa hesitated. She trusted Dillan to keep a secret, yet it wasn't her secret to share. "She's a girl who needs a safe place. Let's leave it at that."

"Sure. I understand. Does the Zebori sleep up there, too?"

"Kiran? No. His room is under the stairs. Take off your boots before you go up."

"You're joking. Not about the boots, but about a three-meter-tall Zebori sleeping under the stairs."

"Okay, you're right. The entrance to his room is under the stairs. There used to be a storeroom beyond. As you just found out, he's a light sleeper. With him here, I don't worry about break-ins." She gave him a pointed look. "Now I'm exhausted, so get along to your room before I change my mind."

He came over to her and took her shoulders. No man ever made her feel small, not like this. He did. Looking up at him, she felt almost delicate.

"What you did tonight with those children was very dangerous. And very brave."

When his thumbs rubbed her shoulders, something she hadn't felt in six years curled through her. She almost didn't recognize it.

By the Matriarch, he'd better not kiss me. Not like he did before.

CHAPTER 6

Dillan woke up to a steady thump-thump-thump. Damn, the sublight engine was acting up again. He rolled over and almost fell out of bed.

Two things hit him at the same time. He wasn't in the wide, comfortable bed in his quarters aboard ship and the thumping wasn't his sublight. Thank the stars for that. Still, it had been acting a little wonky lately. He'd have to check it out.

After dressing and taking care of his needs in the small san-fac near the stairs, he ambled down, carrying his boots in the event the big Zebori was still asleep. Although how anyone could sleep through all that thumping he had no idea. He followed the noise into the kitchen.

Rissa stood at the island kneading dough. Last night he remembered how much higher than normal the island was. She'd built it to accommodate her height. For a moment, he just watched her as she concentrated on the grayish-brown ball. More lumps sat on the flour-covered table waiting their turn. Even though he was at least a meter away, the yeasty scent hit his nose and brought back memories of the times he'd been there before. And how much he enjoyed her company. Despite her treating him like a kid.

The dark-haired teen—Pela?—worked alongside Rissa. She noticed him first. Panic crossed her strong features. In the confusion at the spaceport last night, he hadn't seen the girl clearly. Sweet Divinity, she looked like a younger version of Rissa, same dark eyes and braided hair. They could be mother and daughter.

"Good morning, sleepyhead." Rissa laughed as she turned the dough she'd been punishing into a long, loaf pan. She picked up another lump and went to work on it.

Dillan yawned. "What time is it?"

"Almost Mid-Day." When she looked up, she did a double take. "Your beard is gone."

"It itched. When I find the barber, I'll get my hair cut, too." He ran his hand across the top of his head. "It's Mid-Day? Damn. I wanted to get an early start."

Without stopping her work, she asked, "Early start on what?"

"Going into the mountains."

"Did you come here to go climbing again?"

As it had for the past six years, grief hit Dillan whenever someone mentioned his former favorite sport. He hadn't climbed since his best friend died in that freak rock-slide.

Until a year ago, he'd *thought* Konner was dead.

Rissa's dark eyes reflected guilt. She stopped kneading. "I'm sorry, Dillan. I forgot."

"Apparently, so did Konner." He didn't conceal the hurt he'd felt when he learned Konner was not only alive but had a family. "Turns out I was wrong about some things. I'll, uh, leave you to your work."

With her forearm, she wiped the sweat off her brow then went back to kneading. "Pela, you did fine. Turn that one into the next pan then get Dillan a cup of sheelonga tea."

Pela eyed him with uncertainty.

"I can get it." He sure didn't want to upset the girl. "Mugs still next to the sink?"

Rissa looked surprised that he remembered, but he remembered everything about her. She'd stayed in his mind after every trip from the time he was sixteen. Konner had teased him about being infatuated. Dillan knew it was more than infatuation. Especially after that last visit.

Pela pointed to a cupboard where he found the sheelonga. A kettle steamed on the cooker. Within a few mins, he had a nice cup of the bracing beverage.

"Would you like a piece of jambor?" Pela asked in a small voice.

"That's all right. I don't want to take you from your work." He blew on the tea before taking a sip. Just right. "The café down the street is new, isn't it? I noticed it last night."

Rissa nodded. "They serve First Meal all day long. Your miners probably slept as late as you did."

The girl smiled slightly. "Or later. It's their last half-day of furlough. The transport should come by to pick them up shortly."

"My miners?" He was a little slow catching that. Not enough sleep.

"Rusteran Mining. We'll get a short break, and then the Winslott crew will invade."

Pela snorted. "Invade is right."

"I'll leave you fems to your bread-making." He finished the tea and took the mug to the sink, rinsing it out before putting it into the sanitizer.

"Your mother taught you well," Rissa said. "Not all of my guests are as considerate."

His mother had been too busy to teach him much of anything. "Our cook taught me to clean up after myself." He headed for the swinging door.

"Don't forget your boots," Pela called after him. "Gorem snakes hide under the boardwalk."

Rissa wanted to thunk her head on the work surface. She'd screwed up mentioning mountain climbing. The boys had come every year—Dillan, Konner Winslott, and their friends. Rich boys with sleek ships and nothing to do during school holidays. At first, she'd envied them the freedom. Until she realized they were aimless, no focus except the next daredevil challenge.

When she'd been their age, her father had her working alongside him, handing out treatises and collecting donations as they wandered from place to place, planet to planet. Some freedom that.

After she heard the front door close behind Dillan, Rissa turned to Pela. "That wasn't very nice. Gorem snakes stay out in the desert."

Pela's dark eyes twinkled. "Offworlders don't know that."

"Oh, I think this offworlder does. He's been here many times."

Until that last time when his friend had been buried under a rock slide. How awful that time had been for him. Hanging from a rope and watching his friend disappear. Believing him dead.

"Is that why you let him sleep upstairs?" Pela brought her back from that dreadful time. "Because you know him?"

"He's a trust-worthy man. Does it bother you that he's there?"

Pela stopped kneading the dough. "If you trust him, I guess it's all right."

"I won't let anyone hurt you. You know that, right?"

The teen came around the island. With her flour-coated hands outstretched, she hugged Rissa. It had taken Pela so long to trust enough to touch or be touched. Rissa savored the moment.

Four tendays since they'd found her. Four tendays for her to trust. She probably had no idea how thrilled Rissa was with her hug.

"When you pulled me out of that ship, I was afraid you wanted to use me or sell me—like m-my father did. I was afraid to believe in you."

Rissa hugged her back. "I know. That must have been frightening, not knowing where they were taking you."

"And Anaris. She was so scared she cried all the time." Pela stepped away from Rissa. "Thank you for rescuing us."

Pela had chosen to stay with Rissa while Anaris wanted as far away from town as she could get. Rissa had helped her get a job in the kitchen at the Rusteran mines.

"Do you ever see Anaris?"

"Only if I go up there," Pela replied. "She's still too afraid of being captured again to come down here."

"Are you?"

A small smile curved her lips. "Kiran will slit their throats if they try."

"If who tries what?" Kiran walked into the kitchen. Since only a couple of miners had come into the tavern that morning, she'd let him sleep. After the night they'd had, the Matriarch knew how much all of them needed sleep.

Her damn internal clock—and the sun shining through open drapes—had woken her at the usual time. She'd gotten up to prepare the dough for jambor and found two customers quietly waiting on the bench outside. Too hung over from the night before, they hadn't even pounded on the door.

"If any slavers try to take me away," Pela said to Kiran. "You promised you wouldn't let them."

Kiran used his knuckles to rub the top of her head. "I keep my promises."

"I promised, too, you know." Rissa tugged on Pela's long braid that looked exactly like hers.

That evening, the tavern began to fill. She'd posted a sign on the door. "No service until after meeting." One thing she didn't want was a bunch of liquored up hot heads.

Merchant Graeson from the mercantile called for people to sit while several kept asking what this was all about. When all the tables were filled, people stood against the back wall. She hadn't realized how many would take an emergency meeting so seriously. In the past, they hadn't. Maybe word had gotten out about the slave ship.

Security Chief Kaminga walked in along with two of his deputies—a young man and a middle-aged fem. Rissa recognized the latter, Pashku. The young man was a new hire. A Rusteran Mining supervisor's son, she thought. The three spread out and stood against the back wall. With weapons in holsters at their sides, they would ensure peace. Not that Rissa expected trouble. But, as she'd found out previously, trouble had a way of sneaking up on her.

After Kiran checked outside then motioned that no more were coming, Graeson climbed up on a chair and whistled shrilly. That got everyone's attention. "We had a dangerous incident last night. Here's Rissa to tell you about it."

With a grimace she forced herself to hide, Rissa came around from behind the bar. She'd hoped Graeson would explain about the *incident*. No such luck. He'd hastily climbed down off the chair and faded into the crowd against the wall.

"Four tendays ago I warned you about—"

"This better not be about slave traders again." A short, round man from one of the farms stood. "That ain't gonna happen here."

As murmurs of agreement began, Sophira's spouse stood. "Shut up, Ramus. It can and it did. Last night."

The murmurs stopped. Silence met Partorus' announcement. "Traffickers took my baby."

The audience responded with gasps.

Another man stood. "And they tried to take my boys."

And then another. "Mine, too. If it weren't for Miz Rissa and her friends, our boys would be sold for slaves and that baby sold to rich people in the Central District."

"We should have listened to Miz Rissa last time," Sophira said.

Ramus, the short, round farmer, sat down, a stunned expression on his face. Others—town folk and farmers alike—looked at each other in surprise. When one shifted in his chair, Rissa thought she saw the red-haired Menacan who'd taken care of the traffickers with Dillan's help. Last night, she hadn't wanted to know what he did with them. She should have pressed Dillan for answers.

When the murmuring started up again, Graeson whistled. As soon as it was quiet, he climbed back up on a chair. "We also rescued twenty-one other children from the slavers' ship."

"What?" a mechanic from the spaceport shouted. "You stole a slavers' cargo? They'll come back and kill us to make an example out of what happens when you interfere."

"You've endangered all of us," someone else cried.

"What would you have us do?" Rissa said. The noise quieted down. "Leave those children to be sold as slaves or worse?"

"They ain't our kids. What do we care?" Ramus again.

"They tried to take ours," Partorus said. "We have to do something to make them stay away from Astron."

"I still say they'll come back and punish us," the mech insisted.

"No. They won't." Dillan Rusteran stood.

He'd been sitting in the back behind a couple of large men so Rissa hadn't seen him. She was surprised he'd come. The meeting didn't concern him.

"Who might you be, Offworlder?" the belligerent mechanic demanded.

"Dillan Rusteran. Rusteran Mining."

The farmer snorted. "You don't live here. This ain't your concern."

"My family's mines are here. My employees are here. So are their families. Traffickers could very well steal their wives or children. That makes this my concern."

46

The group quieted for a few secs.

"What did you mean that the slavers won't come back?" a woman said. "How do you know that?"

"We made sure they saw the error of their ways. They won't be going back to slaving. Besides, their ship exploded out in the shipping lane."

As people around her exclaimed, Rissa wondered how he knew that.

"We who?" a spaceport worker asked. "You and who else?"

"That's not the major issue," Dillan said. "Is it, Rissa?"

Quickly, before anyone asked more questions, she said, "That's right. We have to be prepared for the next time traffickers try to take our children. We need patrols, people to watch the 'port for their ships. People strong enough to send them on their way."

"Whoa, now." One of the men from town spoke up. "You're not saying we have to confront those traffickers, are you? They're dangerous."

Something inside Rissa snapped. "Aren't your children worth it? There is nothing more precious than a child. What about your daughters, wives, girlfriends? They could easily be taken, too. How dare you say this is not our problem! It's everyone's problem. When they get away with stealing one child, one baby—" Her voice cracked, but she kept going. "—they will get bolder. They'll demand payment to leave us alone. Even if we're stupid or scared enough to pay, they won't leave us alone. They'll demand more and—"

"How do you know that?" A townsman cut her off.

"She's seen it," Kiran said. "I have, too. What she says will happen."

"The point," Merchant Graeson said, "is preventing trafficking here in Astron. As Rissa said, we need people willing to help."

Again grumbling started, encouraged by Ramus, the short farmer.

Rissa signaled to Graeson who whistled. Thanks to Kiran's interruption, she'd gotten herself back in control. "All of you who don't want to help, leave. Now."

Graeson leaned toward her. "What if they all leave?"

"They won't." She knew Sophira and Partorus would stay. So would the farmers who'd almost lost their sons.

Less than half the people left. A lot more stayed than she'd expected, including many who didn't have children. With a surreptitious nod, Chief Kaminga silently sent the young deputy outside. Deputy Pashku parked herself near the exit while he remained in the middle of the back wall. Rissa thought she saw the red-haired man leave, too. Before she could look more carefully, Merchant Graeson caught her attention.

"Now what?" he asked softly.

Before she could call for order, the people, led by Partorus, took over. They organized patrols, one crafted a warning if a slave ship came in. Two mechs volunteered to alert them when a suspicious ship landed at spaceport. A small thrill went through Rissa as she watched the members of the community assume control of the situation.

When the discussion seemed to wane, Fortuna waved her hand. Even standing, like Graeson, she was too short for those in the back to see. Kiran picked her up and set her on a chair.

"We have another problem." At a few groans, she shushed them. "I have twenty-one children in my private quarters. They range in age from six to fourteen, both sexes, all human but different races. They came from a homeless shelter on Balderan. They need homes."

Silence met that announcement. Spouses looked at each other. Most people examined the table top in front of them.

Medico Barlen came to the front of the room. "The children are malnourished. They were in the cargo hold for a tenday with little to eat or drink. Thanks to Fortuna and Graeson, they are clean and have clean clothes. Nalgin and Voleya fed them at the café last night and brought more food today. The children are frightened. More frightened of us than of the slavers."

Fortuna nodded. "They are afraid *we* will use them as slaves."

Protests met that. Rissa watched the expressions on those who said nothing. "They are not free labor. If that's what you're thinking, don't take them."

"Excuse me." Pela who had been hiding behind Kiran came forward. "Miz Rissa rescued me from a slaver. She gave me a place to sleep. It was the first time I ever had a room where I felt safe. When I begged her for a job, she said I didn't have to work for her to have that room. And she even pays me for my work. She treats me like I'm her daughter. That's what she expects you to do."

She quickly hid behind Kiran again while Rissa worked very hard to keep tears from forming.

Sophira stood. "We would like to take the girl who protected our baby. We will treat her as our own daughter."

After she sat, others offered homes for the rescued children.

Medico Barlen cleared his throat. "Rissa is right. They are not free labor. Chores are all right. Every child needs to help out. But no working those children like slaves. I'm offering free medical services for them. I will also check on them periodically. If I find they are not treated properly, I will take them away from you."

48

Rissa nearly dropped her teeth. After all his dumping responsibility on her, Barlen had come through. As did others she least expected.

After the meeting broke up, Dillan came up to her. "You are quite a leader."

Heat rose in her face. "Not me. I'm no leader. The people organized themselves."

The corner of his mouth quirked. "Don't sell yourself short. You showed them the way."

"But Barlen, Graeson—"

He tapped her nose. "Accept the compliment and say, 'Why thank you, Dillan. That was so sweet.'"

"Don't push it, Rusteran."

"A little help, Boss?" Kiran called.

With the meeting over, the line for drinks stretched nearly to the back of the room. Pela had gone behind the bar taking credits as fast as Kiran poured drinks. After two hours, the crowd began to dwindle. When the stranglers finally left, Rissa helped Pela wipe down tables while Kiran took care of the bar. To her surprise, Dillan Rusteran stayed. He upended chairs and set them on the cleaned tables so the floor could be swept. With a small smile, she remembered how he'd done that before. Rather than go across the street to Fortuna's with his friends, he'd often stayed to help her. Funny the things one forgot.

When the last table was done, she stopped Pela. "I was very touched by what you said."

Pela hugged her. "You have been so good to me. Like a real mother."

For several moments they stood there, arms around each other. Though her throat was clogged with unshed tears, Rissa said, "You are like a real daughter."

Like the daughter I lost.

CHAPTER 7

Dillan awoke to thumping again. A pleasant sound, now that he knew what it was. Rissa making bread. He smiled to himself as the image of her the day before flickered through his mind—her strong hands deftly working the dough, flour on her hands, her apron, even her forehead and nose.

Sure enough, she looked the same when he entered the kitchen. He sniffed. "No bread baking?"

"You're too early, Offworlder." Pela winked. She sat at the end of the island, away from Rissa. The girl quickly returned to the reader in front of her. On a plexi-sheet next to her, she made notes with a stylus.

Rissa dumped the dough she'd been torturing into a long pan then covered it with a towel and added it to the line of pans on the counter next to the sink. She wiped her flour-covered hands on the big apron that covered her shirt and trousers. "Would you like something to eat? There's some jambor left over from yesterday."

"And mongberry jam?" By the Divine One, he sounded as eager as a young caninus. All he needed were floppy ears and a lolling tongue. Mongberry jam did that to him, especially since he hadn't had any in six years.

As she put four of the pans into the oversized oven, she nodded over her shoulder to the cooler. "Jam's in there. Give me a min to get the jambor out of the bread box."

He remembered that she had to keep food tightly closed because of the blowing sand and ever-present insects. While he got plates and mugs from the cupboard and made the tea, she sliced enough jambor for herself and Pela, too. After spreading a thick layer of mongberry jam on one slice, Rissa slid the plate across to the empty stool. He brought her some tea and refilled Pela's glass of milk.

Both looked at him in surprise.

"Your mother taught you good manners," Rissa said.

"Cook. Not my mother." He didn't bother to hide his bitterness toward the fem who'd left him behind when he was fifteen and still needed her.

Pela looked up. "What happened to your mother?"

Rissa tried to shush her.

"It's all right." He munched on the jambor smeared with sweet jam. "My mother had her own life. When I was growing up, she did good works for the less fortunate, as she called them."

"That was good, right?" Pela said. "She was helping others."

"Not when it meant she was too busy for her own child." He cleared his throat. "Water under the bridge. Even a day old, the jambor is as delicious as I remember. Same with the jam. If you sold them in Eleganza, you'd make a fortune."

"By the time either got there, they would be spoiled," Rissa said.

"Wait. Where's Eleganza?" Pela asked.

Rissa gave her a pointed look. "Now you know why geography is so important. It's on Bricaldia and is the capital of the Coalition of Planets."

"Okay, okay. I'll study harder." The girl buried her head in the reader.

"So, Rusteran, why are you up so early? Couldn't sleep?" Rissa picked up her tea and took a swallow.

"I wanted to get an early start. I'm heading up to the mines."

Rissa looked at him with a thoughtful expression. "Skimmer or zircan?"

"Skimmer. Why?"

"Good." She jumped of the stool. "I'll go with you."

He looked over the top of the mug. "You will?"

A pretty blush kissed her high cheekbones. *Kissed?* He never waxed poetic before.

"I should have asked. Sorry. May I go with you to the mines? Pela, do you mind taking care of the jambor?"

"Sure." The girl looked pleased to be given the responsibility.

Again, Rissa wiped her hands on her apron before taking it off. "Okay, that's settled. I'll just talk to Kiran and—"

"Did I say you could go with me?" Dillan struggled not to smile. He'd like nothing better than a long ride in a confined space with her.

A flustered Rissa—an emotion he hadn't seen before, even six years ago—stopped at the door to the bar. She turned to him. Uncertainty, another emotion he'd never seen, crossed her face. Maybe those emotions had been there before, but he'd been too immature to recognize them. By the Divine One, he'd been such an arrogant ass.

"Why do you want to go up to the mines?" he asked.

"To warn them about the slavers. If we keep the town safe, they may try to sneak up there. I know not many of the miners have family, but the supervisors do and—"

"It's all right. You can come."

Her smile was worth waiting for.

* * *

"That was quite an impassioned speech you gave last night," Dillan said after they'd been riding about an hour. "It sounded . . . personal."

Rissa's heart stopped. He couldn't know. It had to be a wild guess on his part.

Though they'd gotten an early start, the desert sun beat down on the high-end skimmer's bubble top. Despite the top's reflective surface and the enviro unit keeping the inside temperature cooler than outside, Rissa still felt the heat of the Galerian sun on her head and face.

Changing the subject would convince Dillan that he was onto something in her background. A secret she hadn't shared with anyone. Not even her best friend.

"I feel very strongly about traffickers of children."

"That was obvious."

"Slavers captured Kiran when he was only eight years old. They sold him to a thief in Rhadaman City who used him to wiggle through enviro ducts into jewelry stores. When he got too big, he was sold again. To an indie miner who worked a claim on Galeria 4."

"Beastly hot place," Dillan murmured. Even though they were racing at high speed, the Rengara 790 was such a quiet vehicle she easily heard him.

"I agree. Pela and another girl were destined for a prosti house on Marin 5."

"Another nasty place. And I don't mean just the planet."

Marin 5 held dreadful memories for her. Abandonment and—

She shoved the memories to the back of her mind where they belonged. "In pleasure houses, like Fortuna's, the fems choose that way of life. Not so the prosti houses." Rissa clenched her teeth to contain her anger over innocent girls like Pela forced into prostitution.

Dillan reached over and clasped her hand. "You saved her from that." After a moment, he asked, "What happened to the other girl? The one she was with?"

Uncomfortable with him holding her hand, Rissa pulled away. It generated sensations inside she didn't want to feel. Not again. So she gave him a wry grin. "You hired her."

Dillan wasn't fooled by her references to Kiran and Pela. Sure, their situations would have had an impact on Rissa. But the anguish he'd heard the night before seemed too personal. He backed off the questioning, hoping she would trust him with the truth. Some day.

"This place never changes, does it?" He waved at the surrounding vista.

"Did you expect it to? A desert is a desert. The dunes shift, the terrain changes here and there. Last year, that haboob scoured everything, even the town. Took the paint right off the buildings. Do you know Jileena Winslott? Her father is the Coalition's Chief Representative. She and the Sector's Security Chief were almost caught in it."

"I grew up with Jileena. She was Konner's pesky little sister." Dillan smiled at the recollection of her chasing after them, a skinny little kid who wanted to play with the boys.

"Of course you would know her. I'm sorry. I didn't think about your friend." Her stricken expression reminded him of how sensitive she was.

Again he reached over to squeeze her hand. Before she could jerk away as she did before, he let go.

Rissa cleared her throat. "The newswaves were full of how Hallart tried to silence her."

"He tried," Dillan said through gritted teeth. "She is one very determined fem. After her testimony, Hallart's stooge went to prison." He snorted. "Same place where ex-president Filana is incarcerated. They could share notes on what happens when that gangster sinks his teeth into his minions and they fail. I'm surprised Hallart hasn't had them eliminated."

"Is Jileena all right? I don't know her well, but I liked her when she was here."

"She's walking now. She's tougher than anyone thinks." Other memories hit him. Memories of Jileena's pale face, her lank hair on the pillow, in an Eleganza med center. Memories of her despair as Dillan sat next to her bed. Of how she eagerly awaited Laning Servary's return after she'd sent him away to eat or sleep. Of how she'd looked for Konner. And her brother never came.

Damn that man.

They reached the foothills before Mid-Day. In the cooler shade of the trees, Dillan lowered the bubble top. "Do you mind?" he asked belatedly.

Rissa leaned back in the seat and lifted her face upward. "It's fine. I was getting a little claustrophobic."

Her light-hearted laugh made him smile. She looked carefree, younger. Beautiful.

While Dillan and Mine Manager d'Arcanin holed up in the manager's office, Rissa went to the kitchen. Cook greeted her with a hug that took her breath away. Anaris, the teen who had been captured with Pela, gave her with a broad smile.

"I take it everything is going well?" Rissa asked the girl.

"Anaris is a treasure," Cook answered. "Don't know what I did before she came."

The girl blushed. "Thank you for bringing me up here, Miz Rissa. I know Pela is happy in town, but I just couldn't . . ."

Rissa patted the girl's shoulder. "I understand. It's okay."

"Mid-Day Meal is almost ready. You'll stay, won't you?" Anaris asked.

The miners ate in shifts. With Manager d'Arcanin's permission, Rissa spoke to both groups about the situation in town. The first time, Anaris gave her an anxious look until Rissa talked about the measures the townsfolk were taking. She cautioned the miners to do the same.

"We take care of our own." Manager d'Arcanin's tone brooked no argument.

After speaking to the second shift, Rissa went for a short walk with Anaris. When they were out of earshot of the kitchen, she asked, "Are you really happy here?"

"Yes, Miz Rissa," she said in that exasperated tone of teenage girls everywhere.

"Because if you're not, I will find you a better place. You do not have to stay. I will protect you."

"Miz Rissa, you say that every time you come up here." Anaris hugged her. "You don't have to worry."

Rissa realized Anaris was about to hit puberty and remembered how the Indigian had groped Pela. "The miners haven't, uh, tried anything with you?"

Anaris laughed. "Cook wouldn't let them. I heard her tell a couple of them that she'd carved them up like holiday turkens if they did. They spread the word, believe me. You don't need to worry."

Feeling better about the girl's situation, Rissa said, "Just checking."

She was still smiling ten mins later when she caught up with Dillan. "Are you ready to leave? I should return to town. Winslott miners get furlough starting tonight."

"I thought you got a couple of days respite between groups."

"Normally, yes. But every once in a while things don't work out. I'll let them know about the traffickers and they can spread the word."

"You'd better take the skimmer. I should have mentioned that I want to, uh, find Konner. I understand he lives in the caves not far from here."

The two friends would have a lot of catching up to do. Six years' worth.

He walked with her to the skimmer. "Be careful in the desert. The enviro will help, but you will feel the heat. Drink—"

"Dillan, I've lived here for over thirteen years. I know how to take care of myself." She smiled to take some of the sting out of her response. "Thank you for caring."

He pulled a long scarf out of the skimmer's storage under the passenger seat. "I've always cared about you, Rissa." As he talked, he wrapped the scarf around her head. His words and touch disconcerted her—especially when his fingers grazed her neck.

She tried to think of him as the annoying kid he'd been when he and his friends first came to mountain climb. Only this man before her was no kid. His chest had filled out. He was more muscular. He was a man and he looked at her the way a man looked at a woman he desired.

Well, that was never going to happen.

She stepped away. "How will you get back to town?"

"I'll find a way. Hold down the fort until I return." His cocky grin dissipated her thoughts about desire.

Dillan's butt was sore. Manager d'Arcanin insisted he take a zircan to the caves. Better than walking, the man had said. Dillan wasn't so sure about that. D'Arcanin warned about marauders, bandits who preyed on offworlders. Dillan's SL-247 rifle was close at hand in the saddle's scabbard, and his LZ-9 pistol rode uncomfortably against his spine. Although Rissa hadn't known, he'd gotten the weapons out of his ship before leaving Astron. Too many varmints prowled the mountains. He wasn't about to become a meal.

He'd told Rizza only part of the truth. Yes, he wanted to see Konner—since the bastard hadn't thought Dillan would want to know that he was alive. But first he had to have a talk with the Sauri chief about the lease with Winslott Industries. He had to convince Chief Sauri-Alcar to cancel the lease with Winslott and contract a new one with Rusteran.

The sleaze factor hit him every time he thought about it. Yet, if he didn't, his father wouldn't believe he'd changed from the aimless boy to a serious employee and heir to the second largest mining company in the Central District.

He remembered when his father and Konner's had been friends and business partners. Then something happened when Dillan was fifteen. None of the offspring knew what. But that was when his father changed and his mother left. The partners split and a feud began. If Adamus Winslott captured a supplier, Boras Rusteran had to capture two. If Boras discovered a mineral deposit, Adamus had to find one bigger.

Thank the Divine One the feud hadn't extended to their children.

They—he, Konner, and Jileena—had grown up together. Their homes in an affluent section of Eleganza backed to each other with a stand of trees separating the properties. They'd played hide-and-seek in those trees, often laughing at little Jilly's frustration when she couldn't find them. He and Konner conspired against her often. Age-wise, Dillan was between them. Konner, four years older; Jilly, a year younger. Konner was the big brother he'd never had and Jilly, the kid sister. He was furious with Konner for that very reason. Family stuck together. When one member was hurting—like Jilly—the others came running.

Not Konner. Apparently, Jilly being shot and paralyzed didn't mean much to him.

While Dillan was locked in his thoughts, the zirc picked its way along a rocky path, jostling him in the saddle. He hadn't ridden a zirc in six years, not since his last visit to Astron. Not since the search for his friend, his brother. The one he thought had died in a rock slide.

"Halt."

Damn. In his thought wandering, he'd rounded a corner and nearly run over a native standing on the narrow path. The bearded man was dressed in traditional Sauri garb—black scarf around his head and neck, long black robe over pants tucked into boots. He looked formidable.

At least, he spoke Universal—or maybe he only knew that one word. Dillan's Sauri speech was limited at best. Not having spoken it in over six years meant he was more than rusty. He hoped what he'd heard about the Sauri chief understanding Universal was true.

"I'm looking for Chief Sauri-Alcar," he said slowly.

"Come." The man motioned him to follow. "Leave zirc."

Dillan dismounted and tied the animal to a tenacious scrub tree that grew out of the rocks. After he removed his rifle, the Sauri took it.

"No need." Then he untied the zircan and smacked him in the rump. The zirc trotted back the way they came.

"Hey, what did you do that for?"

The Sauri shook his head. "No need for zirc, either. He return home."

Then he led Dillan down over the boulders. While the man nimbly leaped from ledge to ledge, Dillan proceeded with caution.

The story of his life now. Everything he did, he did with caution. No longer the reckless thrill-seeker. That boy was gone. Buried beneath responsibility and the desire to prove to his father that he'd changed. Konner's death had convinced him that life was more important than thrills and the adrenaline rush of taking chances.

Yet . . . Every once in a while the desire to do something more than writing new contracts and searching for ways to get out of others hit him. And he longed for that carefree feeling again.

After descending about a hundred meters below the original path, they came to a broad trail. The native took off at a good clip. Dillan jogged behind him, thanking the Divine One he ran every day at home.

Even on the trip from Bricaldia, he'd kept up his routine in the mini-gym in the hold of his ship.

When they entered the tourist cave, the native ordered him to stay before disappearing down a side tunnel not open to the public. While waiting, Dillan looked around at the petroglyphs. They had always fascinated him. The carvings told stories of the early tribes before explorers from the Central District ventured into the area. Before mining companies, like Rusteran and Winslott, had desecrated the native lands.

Desecrated? Yeah, that was the word for what they'd done. And he was one of them.

"Come." The native waved to him.

The large cavern had a series of tunnels branching off in several directions. He'd always wondered what lay beyond in the tunnels that were closed off to tourists. Following the native carrying a lighted torch, Dillan hoped to find out.

They passed alcoves and tunnels branching off in either direction. Occasionally, the man took a side tunnel then another. Still, they kept walking deeper into the mountain. If the man abandoned him, Dillan feared he would be lost forever in a maze. Maybe that was the native's intent. Dillan shook off that thought.

They entered a round room not much bigger than Dillan's living room in his apartment at home. In the shadows, a man sat on a boulder next to the wall, his head bowed. Like Dillan's guide, he was heavily-bearded. No scarf covered his dark hair worn long and tied in a queue at his neck. The light of the torch caught the gray at the man's temples. He wore a black shirt that bloused over black pants. His wide belt bristled with knives and, if Dillan wasn't mistaken, an LZ-9 laser pistol.

"Chief Sauri-Alcar, I presume." Dillan greeted him Sauri-style, fisted hand to the chest.

"Come forward, Offworlder." The man's voice was low and raspy. "Sit." He pointed to another boulder about a meter away and to the right.

"I am Dillan Ruster—"

"I know who you are, Offworlder. What do you want?"

Dillan covered his surprise by sitting on the boulder and facing the chief. The native guide had placed the flaming torch in a holder that gave the chief the advantage. While he was in the shadow, Dillan was clearly illuminated. He hated being at a disadvantage, but at least he'd gotten an audience. Beggars can't be choosers.

"I wish to talk about mining rights."

"I have spoken to your representatives before," the chief spoke quietly. "My tribe has no interest."

"Yet you leased the right to mine lambidium to Winslott Industries. Is it that you do not wish to entertain any more offers or just not those from Rusteran?"

"What do you think?"

Something in the cadence of the man's voice sounded familiar, yet Dillan was certain he'd never met the chief when he and his friends climbed in the area before.

Dillan persisted. "I believe you will find my offer interesting. All I ask is that you listen."

The man waved, king to peasant. What arrogance.

Dillan clamped down on his irritation. He was in the chief's territory. He could keep his temper under control.

"Rusteran Mining will give you better terms than your current lease with Winslott."

He wished Sauri-Alcar would look up, yet when he did, all Dillan could see were slits instead of the man's eyes and heavy brows shadowing them.

Still in a low, raspy voice, the chief said, "The lease with Winslott is unbreakable."

Dillan knew better. This was a cut-throat business, his father ensured that. Yet he almost felt dirty offering the chief a way to renege on the current lease.

"Not unbreakable. I have seen your lease, Chief. There is a way out."

After a long pause, the man stood. "You would have me break the contract? I gave Winslott my word. A man who would have me go back on my word is not one I would ever deal with. Leave. Now."

Dillan stumbled to his feet. This had not gone as planned. Still, he had to admire the chief's integrity. "If you would just listen a moment, Chief. Your tribe—"

Sauri-Alcar stepped into the light cast by the torch. "No. You listen. You sound just like your father."

The light caught the brilliant green of the man's eyes as he looked hard at Dillan.

"Konner?"

Rissa made it back to her tavern before the miners. She breathed a short sigh of relief. Kiran and Pela had been busy during her absence, especially Pela. Not only had the girl taken care of the baking, she'd even started a hearty stew from scratch. Not thawing one of the frozen stews Rissa kept on hand. Kiran had replenished the keg of ale and other beverages. Everything was ready for the influx of hungry, thirsty workers from the lambidium mines. Workers who were paid well, better than Rusteran's.

Although not as numerous as the men, fems came down from the mines also. A few were office workers, the rest miners as tough as the men. They had to be.

"The stew smells delicious." Rissa got a spoon out of a drawer. "May I?"

"Uh, sure. Wait a min, though." Pela dashed over to cooler and returned with a bottle of ale. "Okay."

Rissa gave her a sideways look before lifting the lid from the large pot. It smelled even better. She scooped up a good spoonful, blew on it then took a taste.

"Mmm. Savory, spicy, ah-ack." She dropped the lid. It banged and whirled around on the counter while she grabbed the bottle and downed half of it in two gulps. After stifling a belch, she blew out a breath. "Huh. Has a bite to it."

Pela doubled up laughing. Kiran just grinned. "Should make beverage sales go through the roof."

Pela pointed to a smaller pot. "I made a milder version. I thought it might be good to offer a choice."

Rissa put her hands on her hips. "You know none of those miners will admit wanting the mild stuff."

Pela grinned. "I know. They'll have to drink to put out the fire. Same reason we give them free *salty* nuts."

Kiran clapped her shoulder. "You have the makings of a fine barkeep. Give 'em hot and spicy, and they'll drink more."

"Not nice, you two." Rissa tried to keep from smiling. "Clever but not nice. So what still needs to be done?" She looked around to see what they'd missed.

"Not a thing. We're ready. Little miss here did all the work." Kiran smiled down at Pela.

"Then let's go down to the café and get a meal that won't burn the roof of my mouth," Rissa said. "I'm buying."

"In that case, Boss, lead on."

The three of them strolled down the boardwalk. Rissa loved this time, in between furloughs. One group of miners gone, the other not yet arrived. Peace, however short-lived. Too bad the respite wasn't longer. With the upcoming holiday, the furlough schedule had been changed to a tenday earlier.

She tucked her arm in each of theirs. What a great feeling to know she could depend on Kiran and Pela to manage the tavern for a short time. She just hadn't expected them to take on all of her jobs while she was gone over ten hours.

Only two tables were occupied when they walked into the café. Chef Nalgin hurried up to greet them. "The quiet before the storm?"

"That's right, Nally." Rissa smiled then called out, "Hi, Voleya."

His spouse in the kitchen doorway gave Rissa a quick smile then let the swinging door close behind her. Voleya had followed Nally from Chellus four years ago. While he wasn't a native Chellian, she bore the distinctive rows of spots across her forehead and along her hairline. Nally was gregarious. Because of her shyness, Voleya spent most of her time in the kitchen.

As Nally led them to a table, Rissa said, "By the way, thanks for feeding those children. You and Voleya did a great job."

"Least we could do. Two of the older boys want to be chefs. They take turns washing dishes and bussing tables." Nally grinned. "Gotta learn from the ground up."

Rissa squeezed his arm. "Thanks for taking the boys. With all the new children, I wonder if we should start a school."

"Voleya is already working on that. She wants to make sure our boys have the schooling they need. They can't wash dishes forever." After she and the others sat, he announced, "The special tonight is turken and mashed plantens."

"My favorite. I love how you fix turken," she said. "One of these days you'll have to share your secret."

Nally grinned. "And have you take away all my business?"

She grinned back. "You know I'd never do that."

Kiran interrupted with, "You'll both have to worry when that offworlder opens the tavern next to the 'port. At the rate they're building, it will be open soon."

Rissa sobered quickly. "I'm not going to worry about that until it happens. You know how people around here distrust offworlders." She handed Nally the menu she hadn't even opened. "I'll have the turken and plantens with an enfil and selba salad. Sheelonga tea to drink."

Pela and Karin ordered the same with one exception. Pela asked for milk. Moments after Nally went back to the kitchen, a server rushed out with their drinks. When Rissa looked up to thank him, she exclaimed, "Arjay. What are you doing here?"

She shoved back her chair and leapt up to give him a hug. Although the slender, blond-haired male was an android, she knew he liked to think of himself as human, with human emotions, as evidenced by the pleasure in his eyes.

Rissa looked around. "Where's Celara?"

"My Rega could not stay." He spoke with a Bricaldian accent, one he affected to appear like those he emulated. "She wanted to see you, but she and my Regus had deliveries on Magnus Prime. She knows how intensely I dislike that planet."

As she sat, Rissa shook her head. "I thought Celara and Trevarr didn't like you to call them Rega and Regus."

Arjay sighed. "It is factually correct. They do own me."

"What are you doing here at the café?"

"I offered my services. Had you been at your establishment, I would have offered mine to you. I have worked in many eateries since my—since Celara abandoned me on Magnus Prime." His mouth turned down for a moment. "I realized later that she was protecting me. But I—"

"Arjay," Nally called from the kitchen. "Come back in here and get Table 3's food while it's still hot."

"I must leave," Arjay said. "I will speak with you later, I hope."

Kiran laughed as the android hurried to the kitchen. "He never changes, does he? Yakkety-yak."

"I did not know you knew him, Miz Rissa." Pela twisted her napkin. "After I told him you went up to the mines, he left. Kiran was down in the storeroom, so I couldn't ask him. Then the ale supplier showed up, and I forgot."

"Not a problem," Rissa said. "I wish Celara had waited for me."

"Who is she?" Pela asked.

Rissa took a roll out of the basket Arjay had brought. "Celara d'Enfaden. Well, I guess she's d'Enfaden-Jovano now. My best friend ever since I opened the tavern."

"Wasn't she your supplier?" Kiran had already devoured two of the rolls and was buttering a third.

"Until that damn Trevarr Jovano spirited her away." Rissa waved her hand. "Never mind."

Kiran looked up. "I heard they're making a killing over in Willand Sector buying lathaka and selling it in the Central District."

"Lathaka? That's really expensive material, isn't it?" Pela asked. "The kind fancy dresses are made of?"

Rissa's laugh came out bitter. "Yeah. That's why they never come here. Who in this colony could afford it?"

Kiran reached over and patted her hand. "You'll get to see her. They have to come back to get that nuisance of an android."

Arjay, the nuisance android, came with their food. "You are going to love this. Roast turken and dressing with just a hint of nevele. Not too much, mind you. And mashed plantens." Arjay pointed to the fluffy pink pile. "Chef Nalgin's spouse adds just a little—"

"Arjay!" Nally hollered. "Quit talking and serve the people their food."

A subdued Arjay placed plates in front of them heaped with more food than Rissa could eat. Kiran wouldn't have any trouble disposing of it all and looking for more.

After they finished, Rissa stopped at the kitchen. "Great meal, Voleya. Nally says you're thinking about a school. When you have a chance, I'd like to hear more. I've been working with Pela, but she needs more than I can teach her."

"I will be happy to talk to you. Because we have no children of our own—" Her mouth turned down. "—I never thought about Astron not having a school. Last night, several parents expressed concern and are willing to help."

"Great. Count me in." As Arjay rushed into the kitchen, Rissa said, "After the café closes, Arjay, if you're not too tired, I could use your help at the tavern."

"Oh, goody." He clapped his hands. Then he sobered and at looked Nally. "My apologies, sir. I am very happy to work for you."

Rissa thunked the side of her head. "Too tired? I must be losing it." Arjay was an android. He didn't get tired. "Too much desert sun today."

"You must always wear head protection in the desert," Arjay intoned. "The harsh environment is hostile to humans. With extreme heat during the day and no shade—"

"Arjay, deliver the food to Table 2."

"Yes, sir. Right away, sir."

After he left, Nally gave Rissa a long look. "Are you sure you want him? He's driving me crazy with his incessant talking."

"Oh, yeah. Kiran will keep him in line."

"I can send him with you now." Nally's eyebrows lifted.

"And deprive you of his help?" Rissa smiled. "Come by after close and have a drink on me."

Voleya laughed. "He'll be too tired to even walk down to your tavern."

As Rissa strolled down the boardwalk, she heard the transport from Winslott Mines as it roared in to land. It was good that Kiran and Pela had gone on ahead. The transport disgorged its passengers outside the spaceport. If she hurried, she might avoid being trampled.

Pela met her at the back door to the tavern. Sobbing, she pointed inside.

"Look what they did!"

CHAPTER 8

"Took you long enough to recognize me." Konner Winslott stared hard.

For several secs, Dillan just stood there, royally pissed off. "Why the charade?"

"No charade. I am Chief Sauri-Alcar. That's who you came to see. Not your best friend."

"My *former* best friend would have told me he was alive instead of letting me believe I killed him."

"I assumed Jilly told you about me."

"Yeah. Funny thing. *I* assumed you would come and see me for yourself. Or at least see your sister when she lay paralyzed in a med center for five tendays after being shot by one of Hallart's men. Or while she was in rehab for another four tendays." Dillan's voice echoed in the cave. "Or even when that bastard tried to kill her by blowing up her vehicle and house."

Two Sauri natives came running out of a tunnel. They rushed at Dillan, weapons in hand. Konner said something in their language then jerked his head toward the tunnel. One spoke quickly, glancing from Konner to Dillan then back again.

After the two men retreated. Dillan breathed a sigh of relief.

"You're staying with Rissa?" Konner said. "She's had trouble at her tavern."

Panic raced through Dillan. "Trouble? What kind of trouble?"

Rissa stood on the threshold, looking at a disaster.

Pela's stew—both pots—had been thrown against the walls. The contents of every cupboard lay strewn across the floor. The one-hundred weight bag of flour, the one she'd opened that morning, dusted all. Everything from the cooler lay on top, bottles of ale broken and spilled over the flour, vegetables crushed. The entire mixture a sour mess.

Rissa staggered backward, stumbling as her boot heel caught on the small step. She righted herself by holding onto the outside of the building. Her stomach twisted then revolted at the destruction inside. She doubled over to throw up Nally's dinner. With the toe of her boot, she kicked dirt over the mess then leaned against the stone wall.

She had to go back in, had to find out what else the vandals had done. But for a moment she wanted to run away, escape from the damage to her tavern. Her life.

Straightening, she took in a deep breath. Pela stood nearby, still sobbing. From deep inside, Kiran called her name. She wasn't being fair to them by staying out in the alley. Before she stepped inside, she patted Pela's shoulder, wishing she could offer more comfort. She just didn't have any inside her. Carefully, she stepped over the gooey mess, avoided broken glass, and approached Kiran.

He stood in the doorway to the bar, his shoulders slumped. "It's worse in here."

It couldn't be. Nothing could be worse than the devastation in her kitchen.

It was.

The tap to the new keg of ale had been wrenched off. Amber liquid spilled out not just streaming into the kitchen but also lapping at the main door, where a hundred thirsty miners were about to pour in. As if that wasn't enough, bottles of hard liquor lay smashed against the back wall. The vandals must have hurled them from behind the bar and through the front window. Sand blew in, adding to the destruction.

If she hadn't leaned against the open door, she would have sunk into the stinking mess. Why would someone do this? *Who* would do it?

"You need to see something else." With reluctance, he pointed to the end of the bar.

She sloshed through the ale to see. The word "bitch" had been carved into her beautiful naurem bartop. They might just as well have carved it into her heart.

As the room began to sway, she held onto the bar to keep from falling. *Blessed Matriarch, what have I done to deserve this?*

"I called Chief Kaminga," Kiran said. "He's on his way. I told him to come in through the alley."

Kaminga. She hadn't even thought to call the Security Chief. All she thought about was the destruction to her business. She nodded, grateful for Kiran's thinking for the two of them.

To keep from crying, she sucked in a breath and got a noseful of liquor fumes. She should be grateful the vandals hadn't torched the place. With all the alcohol on the wood floor, the place would go up in flames. She made her way back to the kitchen.

"Miz Rissa, ma'am?" Kaminga called from the open alley door.

He made her feel old addressing her as *ma'am*. Astron's Chief of Security was still such a kid. Even so, he was a lot better than that lazy no-good Nakus who would have been laughing his head off before sending a deputy to take a report.

Not Kaminga. Here he was, looking almost as distressed as Pela.

"What happened?" He carefully picked his way across the kitchen to where she stood. "By the Divine One, what a mess. Who did you piss off?"

Rissa tightened her lips. Even though she knew he was right, she asked, "What makes you say that?"

"This kind of destruction wasn't just vandalism. Someone was furious." He pointed to the broken liquor bottles. "Even from here I can see the gouges in the wall. Those bottles were thrown with a lot of anger behind them."

As she listened, he pointed out other signs that this wasn't a bunch of kids having *fun*.

"Show him the bartop," Kiran said.

Rissa couldn't look at the defacement again. Instead, she pointed to the end of the bar.

Ignoring the liquor on the floor, Kaminga walked across the room. He stared for a moment, then took out his comm unit—somewhat larger than her wrist comm—and spoke quietly into it before taking a pic.

He looked back at her. "Yep, somebody is really mad at you."

Even though he was young, so very young, he'd distinguished himself as a fine investigator in other instances. At the back wall, he again used his comm and took pics to catalogue the damage. He did the same in the kitchen.

After a brief conversation with Kiran, Kaminga wanted her to accompany him to the Security Office.

"I can't leave. I need to start cleaning up this—this—" Her voice broke.

"Miz Rissa." Pela patted her shoulder, much the way Rissa had patted hers a short time before. "You go with the chief. We'll get started."

"Yeah, Boss." Kiran gave her a weak smile. "Go with Chief Kaminga. I'll put a sign on the door that we're closed."

"It's best we get your statement now." Kaminga took her elbow in a gentlemanly manner. Or he thought she was so old and feeble that she needed help.

She preferred to think he was being kind.

While her feet dragged, he strode at a quick pace down the alley to the Security Office. Once there, he took her into his office where he peppered her with questions.

"We were only gone thirty or forty mins," she said. "To the café. Everything was fine when we left."

"Did you lock the doors?"

"Of course," she snapped. "I always lock up when we leave."

He gave her a patient look. "Who found the damage? You or your employees?"

"Kiran and Pela got there first. I was, maybe, five mins behind them."

"They have keys?"

"Kiran does."

"Anyone else?"

"No."

"What about that offworlder? Rusteran. I understand he's staying with you."

Nothing got past anyone in the small village. She shook her head. "He's up in the mountains at the mines."

"And you know this . . ."

"I went up with him and left him there. He had more business, and I needed to return before the Winslott miners arrived." She leaned back in the chair and closed her eyes. The miners. Men and fems who expected the only tavern in the colony to be open.

Fortuna couldn't handle the whole contingent. They might riot. She groaned, covered her face, and doubled over. If she thought her tavern was bad, a riot would hurt all the merchants. On the newswaves, she'd seen what riots could do to a colony. Kaminga and his few deputies—

"Miz Rissa, ma'am? Are you all right?"

She straightened. "Of course I'm not all right. My livelihood has been shot to Lexol."

Kaminga cleared his throat. "I noticed no evidence of damage to the doors—street or alley. How do you think the vandals got in?"

She hadn't even considered that. "I don't know," she said slowly. "Through the front window?"

"Not big enough." Kaminga stared at her. "Have you had a problem with your employees?"

"No. Absolutely not. They couldn't have done that kind of damage. Kiran and Pela were with me."

"Except for five minutes, you said."

She shook her head. "They're as devastated as I am. I refuse to believe they did such a thing."

His comm beeped. He glanced to his right where the unit sat on his desk then looked at it more closely. "All right then. Kiran and Pela were with you. What about your part-timers?"

"Sophira? Jodar? No. They've been with me a long time. They wouldn't do such a thing."

"Have you fired anyone?"

"No. Why are you focusing on my employees?"

After he made more notes, he said, "Better to start with those who have access. Let's go on to your enemies. As I said before, who did you piss off?"

"Lately?" She wracked her brain trying to think. "You were at the meeting last night. That farmer Ramus wasn't happy with me. Oh, and I threw Nakus out the other night."

Kaminga laughed. "I heard about that. That cheapskate needed it. Anyone else?"

"There was an Indigian. I'd never seen him before. When he accosted Pela, I made him leave. Told him never to come back."

"You don't know his name?"

She shook her head then almost clapped her hand over her mouth. He was captain of the trafficking crew. The ones Dillan and the Menacan had taken care of.

"Describe him."

As she did, he made notes. When he looked up, he appeared pensive. "Besides Ramus, some other people at the meeting last night were not real happy with you."

"I know."

"I'll check out everyone. Your employees, possible enemies. I'll check with Dock Master Yefos about that Indigian. In the meantime, I'll have a deputy keep an eye on your place."

She stood. "If you don't need me for anything else, I need to get back."

He didn't get up. "You and your team deprived a ship of its cargo the other night."

Panic crept through her veins, rendering her speechless. She abruptly sat.

"I'm not supposed to know about that." His mouth quirked. "Or about that time four tendays ago. When I don't know, I can't enforce the laws. That being said, you should have called me."

"I didn't think there was enough time." A lame excuse, she knew.

"Had you called, my deputies could have arrested the captain and crew."

She shrugged. "They would have produced documents—forged documents, by the way—saying they had the right to transport the children. You know that's how they work. How they worked in other colonies, like Balderate."

His lips thinned. "This isn't Balderate Colony. I wouldn't fall for fake documents."

"I'm sorry, Chief. No disrespect, but you haven't been in the job that long and—"

67

Now he looked incensed. "I learned a lot from Chief Servary before he left. I am not the naive kid you all think I am."

"My apologies. I didn't mean—"

"Has it occurred to you that the captain and crew might have sent a message to their boss before their ship exploded? That their boss is sending *you* a message?"

A chill ran through her. "I-I hadn't thought of that?"

"Seems mighty convenient that ship blew up right after their cargo was stolen." He eyed her steadily. "Don't you think so?"

What is he implying? That I had something to do with blowing up the slave ship? Who else would think that?

She swallowed. "Chief, I don't know anything about that ship other than what I heard at the meeting last night."

He waited a few long moments, watching her. For a young man who'd been chief for less than two years, he had good interrogation techniques. And she'd thought he only wanted her statement on the vandalism of her tavern. Security Chief Kaminga had questions she couldn't, wouldn't answer. No implicating Dillan or the red-haired Menacan. Last night when she heard that the ship had exploded, she'd thought the same thing. What a coincidence that the accident—if it was an accident—happened so soon after the ship left Astron.

The *accident* had done the world a favor by ridding it of slavers. If it had been up to her, she would have planted the explosives herself. Nobody—no mother—should ever have to go through the anguish of losing her child to slavers.

Kaminga cleared his throat. "Miz Rissa, ma'am?"

By the Matriarch, how long has he been watching me?

"Sorry, Chief. I was thinking about my tavern. May I go? I need to return and help—" Her voice broke off on a sob. *What is wrong with me? I never break down.*

Kaminga came over and patted her shoulder awkwardly. "Miz Rissa, ma'am," he repeated as he stepped back. "I'm real sorry about what happened."

"Yeah, me too." She stood.

"I promise you, I'll find who did this, and they will be punished."

She'd heard promises like that before, back when she was building the tavern and *accidents* happened. Promises then, too. Promises that never panned out. Still, Kaminga meant well. "Thanks, Chief. I hope you do."

He ushered her to the alley door. At least, she didn't have to go out to the street through the main room—where prisoners were incarcerated.

Fatigue, physical from the long drive across the desert but mostly emotional from the vandalism to her tavern, made her dragged her feet. *Buck up*, she told herself as she walked to the tavern. Weariness and dread doubled the normal five-min walk.

As she approached her business—her home—several voices spilled out of the open alley door. Male and fem.

With one foot on the miniscule step, she looked in and caught her breath.

Dillan Rusteran ran behind the tribesman who led him through another maze of tunnels. Rissa was in trouble. He had to go to her.

Konner had eyed him with a sardonic grin when he'd asked—demanded—the fastest way back to Astron. "You still have it bad for her."

Not the best time to declare what was in his heart.

"A shuttle leaves for the colony shortly with the second group on furlough. You can ride back with them." When Dillan started to leave the way he'd come, Konner added, "There is a shortcut. Just don't mention your name. Considering the competition between our crews, you could start a riot."

The tribesman kept running at a pace that nearly exhausted Dillan. He hadn't even thought to ask how Konner knew or what kind of trouble Rissa was in. He just needed to get to her as fast as possible.

When they finally came out of the caves, the sunlight struck him as hard as the heat. While the inside of the tunnels was moderately cool, outside the heat sucked his remaining energy. He staggered for a moment then, seeing the waiting shuttle, dug deep into his resources and put on a burst of speed.

"No need to rush," the tribesman said as he kept pace. "Chief say wait, shuttle wait."

The pilot arched his eyebrow at Dillan as he came aboard. "Friend of Sauri-Alcar, huh? Find a seat and buckle up. Time's a-wastin' and those miners back there are rarin' to go."

Rissa couldn't believe the difference in her kitchen. She hadn't been gone that long, yet the room wasn't just clean, everything sparkled. Cleaning solution replaced the sour smell. Sophira stood at the sink, wiping down the last remnants of the disaster. Jodar, another part-timer, was scrubbing the front of the cooker.

"I checked upstairs," Sophira said. "The vandals hadn't gone up there."

In her distress over the vandalism, Rissa hadn't even thought about the second floor.

"Probably not enough time," Jodar said.

Pela and two fems, all wearing heavy mitts and carrying large, frozen blocks, scooted past Rissa.

"Mistress Rissa. You are back too soon." Arjay, Celara's AI, rushed in from the alley also carrying a bulky package twice as large as the others. "Chef Nalgin sends these with his compliments and regrets he cannot do more."

Rissa stood in a daze. "What?"

Pela set her block on the island. "Arjay put the bread on the counter. Everything will be okay, Miz Rissa. We just have to flash thaw the bread and soup, and we'll have something to feed the miners. It won't be as good as my stew." The corners of her mouth turned down for a sec. "Better than nothing, though. Go look at the tavern. We'll take care of things here."

Rissa felt as if she'd fallen down a paynzer hole. *What happened while I was gone?*

In the tavern itself, several townsfolk and a few miners were finishing up. The floor shone, as did the paneling on the walls. The gouges were still visible, though. Overturned tables had been righted and their tops were being wiped down.

After swallowing past the thickness in her throat, she asked, "What's going on?"

"Hey, Boss." Kiran waved from behind the bar. "Almost done. We thought Kaminga would keep you longer."

"You did all this?" She staggered to the nearest stool. "Who? Why?"

Medico Barlen stopped wiping a chair and strolled over to her. "As soon as we heard, we all came running." He waved to those still working. "Why is easy. Can't have our favorite tavern closed."

"*Only* tavern," she reminded him. "Why would you all do this?"

He shrugged. "We take care of our own."

"But—"

One of the Winslott miners called out, "Besides, if you're not open, where would we go?" He winked before hauling down another chair.

"Over to my place," Fortuna said over her shoulder as she backed in, guiding an anti-grav pallet through the front door. A keg of ale rode on the pallet. A miner ran to hold the heavy door for her.

She tossed her head of blond curls. "The things I do for friends."

"That's her second load, Boss. Here. Figured you might need something." Kiran handed her a glass filled with a thick brown substance. A Kruferian mudslide. Her favorite drink.

As she took a sip, he said, "I covered the carving with a mat. Tomorrow I'll sand down and refinish the top. You won't be able to see the damage when I'm done."

Unshed tears burned Rissa's eyes. She couldn't believe so many people had come to her aid. Barlen nodded then went over to help a group putting the chairs around tables.

"I can't believe this. That you all would—"

"You better believe it, girl." Leaving the pallet with Kiran, Fortuna strode—as much as a short fem could stride—over to Rissa. "You're important to us. Now get off your butt and prepare for the onslaught."

After offering free food and drinks to all who'd helped, she opened the main door. Time flew as she, Pela, Sophira, and Kiran tried to keep up with the hungry, mostly thirsty crowd. Jodar stayed in the kitchen replenishing supplies as they grew low. Voleya, followed by Arjay, came from the café. They both pitched in to help.

After two hours, there came a brief lull. Rissa knew it wouldn't last. Voleya and Jodar went home, but Arjay stayed, eager to help . . . and talk. With a *Gunsmoke* vid playing in the background, he ran a commentary on discrepancies between the program and Earth history. She needed a break.

As she sat at the kitchen island and took a breath, she thanked the Matriarch the second shuttle from Winslott Mines was late. Even though Pela and Kiran had coped with the disaster, overwhelming fatigue swamped her. She rested her head on her folded arms on the counter and closed her eyes.

Just for a moment. She'd go back into the tavern when the next batch of miners arrived.

The door to the alley burst open and slammed against the wall. "Are you all right? What happened?" Dillan Rusteran hauled her off the stool.

Dazed from being awakened so abruptly, Rissa stumbled. He caught her and held her tight against him. She blinked several times while trying to get her bearings.

"Wh-What?"

"Are you all right?" he repeated as he stroked her back.

"Miz Rissa, we need—Oh, sorry." Pela started to back out through the swinging door.

Whatever am I doing in Dillan Rusteran's arms?

Rissa pulled away. "It's all right, Pela. What do you need?" After the girl returned to the tavern with a new supply of jambor, Rissa turned on the man who'd held her. "What did you think you were doing?"

* * *

Dillan kept his disappointment hidden as he watched Rissa's temper flare. Hands fisted on her hips, eyes narrowed, lips thinned. By the stars, she looked like a warrior about to do battle. Unfortunately, the battle was with him.

Holding her for that brief moment had felt right, like she belonged in his arms. The way she had in his dreams for the past six years. Only, in his dreams, she would lift her head and wait for his kiss. What he wouldn't give for her to do that in real life.

Not going to happen now.

"I heard you were in trouble. I came as quickly as I could." He peered at her. "You're okay? Not hurt?"

She shook her head. "I'm fine. How did you get here?"

A roar of male voices came from the tavern. She glanced over her shoulder. "The second horde has arrived. I need to get back to work."

"We'll talk later," he promised. "What can I do to help?"

She gave him that look from six years ago—disbelief and cynicism. "A Rusteran serving Winslott miners? I don't think so."

She hadn't put him off before, he wasn't going to let her put him off now. He reached into a drawer under the island, grabbed a half-apron and a mini-tab for orders then strode past her into the tavern. While the noise hit him like the concussion from an explosion, he thought about her expression.

Priceless.

He'd discombobulated her.

Yes!

Now he just had to find out what kind of trouble had assailed her.

An hour later, he discovered that a gym workout hadn't prepared him for taking orders and serving rowdy miners. He hoped his employees behaved better, though he rather doubted it. Despite the blood and gore in the *Bones* vid playing on the monitors, the miners ate and drank copious amounts.

"Three ales, two chokirises, and a mudslide." After Pela gave her order, she glanced at him as he leaned against the bar. "What's the matter, Offworlder? Can't keep up?" She gave him a cheeky grin.

"Don't chase off free help, girl," Kiran said. "And you, Offworlder, don't pay any attention to her. Here's your order. Go serve." He pushed a tray toward Dillan then turned to see what the blond man called Arjay wanted.

Using skills he'd learned six years before helping out Rissa, Dillan balanced the tray overhead and threaded his way between tables to the one where six thirsty miners waited. Impatiently waited, from the looks on their faces.

"About time," one said.

"Hey, weren't you on our shuttle?" another piped up.

"Yeah, he's the reason we didn't leave on time."

Dillan ignored the chatter and delivered their drinks. His memory was getting as good a workout as his legs. As he collected credit coins, a fem joined the table. A miner from the looks of her clothes.

"Give the guy a break," she said. "If you were a friend of Sauri-Alcar, the shuttle would've waited for you."

Dillan entered "paid" for the drinks on his mini-tab then turned to the fem. "What would you like?"

A big grin creased her face as she batted her eyes at him. "A kiss?"

Dillan gave her a droll look. He'd been propositioned three times that night. "We ran out of Chellian Kisses an hour ago. Something else?"

The rest of the table guffawed. A few lewd comments followed.

"A fem can dream, can't she?" She pouted. "Not like I'd go to bed with you lunkheads. Since the kisses are gone, how about a Gover Heater?"

That was a drink he hadn't heard of. "I'll check on that."

She smirked. "You do that, big boy." As he turned to leave, she patted his rear.

"Hands off." Rissa grabbed the fem's wrist. "No one harasses my employees. You want to play slap-and-tickle, go across the street."

The fem wrenched out of Rissa's grasp. "Didn't mean nothing."

"Watch yourself." Rissa glared. "That's your only warning."

Dillan caught up with her at the bar. "I didn't need your help. I can handle myself."

She shook her head. "If I allowed her to get away with grabbing your ass, it would have signaled the others that they could do the same to Pela and Sophira."

"I'm sorry. I didn't think of that."

"No, you were thinking about how good it felt to have that fem handle you."

A quip about her *handling* him rose in Dillan's mind. Six years ago, he would have said it followed by a wink and a nudge. If he did it now, she would think he hadn't changed a bit.

"Kiran, have you ever heard of a Gover Heater?" he asked.

The big Zebori threw his head back and laughed. When he got himself under control, he said, "Let me guess. A fem ordered it."

"The Matriarch preserve us from horny fems. They're worse than the men." Rissa stalked off to the kitchen.

Sweet Divinity, he loved watching her. Her long-legged stride made him hot. Even when she was angry or disgusted, she made him hot.

Talk about horny. That had been an almost perpetual state for him around her since he was sixteen.

When he turned back to Kiran, the man was eying him suspiciously. "Don't know what you're thinking, Offworlder, but the boss lady is hands off."

"Right. Now about that Gover Heater. What's so funny?"

The bartender drizzled a green syrup over a thick white liquid then pushed the tall glass toward Dillan. "It's named after one of our moons and supposed to increase a man's, uh, libido."

Dillan raised his eyebrow. "Interesting. Why would a horny fem order one?"

A slow smile curved Kiran's mouth. "She means it for you."

CHAPTER 9

An hour later, Dillan entered the kitchen where Rissa was still berating herself for over-reacting to the fem grabbing his rear. When that Indigian touched Pela, she'd gone into protective mode. That wasn't the case with Dillan. He didn't need protecting. As he'd said, he could handle himself.

She wasn't jealous. Why would she be jealous? He meant nothing to her.

Liar.

"Hey, are you okay?" he interrupted her self-reprimand as he headed for the cooker.

She cleared her throat. "Of course. Why wouldn't I be?"

He ladled Nally's thick soup into two bowls on his tray. "You disappeared a while ago. I was concerned."

"No need. The others have everything out there under control. You don't need to help."

He set the laden tray on the island. "You can't just say, 'Thanks for your help, Dillan'?"

Ashamed at her ingratitude, she closed her eyes for a sec. When she opened them, she found him eying her with concern. Uncomfortable with his scrutiny, she murmured, "Thanks for your help."

With a wry curve to his lips, he picked up the tray. "Don't go anywhere. I'll be right back."

Where would I go? Overwhelmed by the events of the evening—ever since she returned from Last Meal at the cafe—again she rested her head on her folded arms. She shouldn't rest when the others were working.

Tears gathered behind her closed eyelids. So many people had come to her aid. Villagers and even some of the miners. She owed them more than free drinks and a meal. Cleaning up the disaster went beyond neighbors helping neighbors. Nally with food, Fortuna with liquor, Barlen and the merchants. Everyone donating their time and energy.

How can I ever repay them?

Once again, Dillan found her asleep at the island. This time he didn't wake her. He picked her up, surprised she didn't stir. As he hefted her in his arms, she snuggled into his chest. *Sweet Divinity.* Why couldn't she be this pliant while awake?

The swinging door to the bar opened and Pela strode through. If she only knew how much she imitated Rissa. Not just her long stride, she copied Rissa's mannerisms and matter-of-fact speech. She even wore her dark hair skinned back into a long braid. He wondered if that was how Rissa looked at fifteen.

"What are you doing?" Pela demanded. "What's wrong with Miz Rissa?"

Dillan shushed her. "She's exhausted. I'm putting her to bed. Would you get the devices for the stairs?"

With a wary look, Pela asked, "How do you know about the stairs?"

"I used to come here a lot." He shifted Rissa in his arms. Even with all his workouts, his arms ached. With her height, she was no lightweight. "If you don't open the door, I'll have to carry her through the tavern. She would hate that."

"She would." After she tapped the hidden button, the back wall slid open. "I'll get the one at the top."

She ran ahead of him up the stairs. Rissa didn't move. Pela even raced into Rissa's bedroom, switched on a small lamp, and turned down the covers. After he set Rissa on her bed, he unlaced her boots and put them under the bedside table.

Pela whispered, "You'd better not try anything, Offworlder."

When he looked over his shoulder, he was surprised to see a knife in the teen's hand.

"I know how to use this. You hurt Miz Rissa, and I will gut you like a mackerel."

A smile creased his face. The girl was as fierce a warrior as the fem she protected.

"She'll be more comfortable if you loosen her pants." Despite the fact that he wanted to do that, he knew both fems would be happier if he didn't.

While he closed the drapes, shutting out the light from the two moons, Pela eyed him with uncertainty before setting her knife within easy reach on the nightstand. She unhooked Rissa's trouser waistband, pulled out her shirt, then covered her. In a flash, the knife was back in her hand. "Downstairs, Offworlder."

Back in the kitchen, he said, "Do you know what a mackerel is?"

Arjay walked in as Dillan was speaking. "I know, I know." He sounded like an eager kid in a classroom. "A mackerel is a fish found in both temperate and tropical seas on Terra. They have vertical stripes on their backs and—"

Dillan shot him a quelling look, while Pela rolled her eyes. "Kiran is always threatening to gut someone like a mackerel."

"That sounds most unpleasant." Arjay peered into the soup pot. "Empty. I can thaw more if you like." His eagerness made Dillan smile.

"No." Pela still held her knife, although she kept it out of sight next to her leg. "It's almost time to close."

After Arjay left, Dillan nodded to her. "I suppose Kiran taught you how to use that?"

She looked at the knife then back at him. As if deciding he wasn't a threat, she tucked it into her boot. If he recalled correctly, that's where Rissa kept hers.

"Kiran and Miz Rissa taught me a lot of things." She eyed him warily. "So I don't have to be afraid anymore. I can take care of myself. Just remember that."

"Oh, I will."

Once again the swinging door opened. This time it slammed against the wall. Kiran strode in. "Where in Lexol's fire have you two been? Arjay says you're in here talking. We've got customers." He looked around the kitchen. "Where's Rissa?"

"She was asleep. He put her to bed."

Kiran shot him a lethal look. "And . . .?"

"It's okay, Kiran. I made sure nothing happened."

Dillan nodded. "Rissa has fine protectors with you two. She's exhausted. I should have come back with her from the mine." Ever since Konner told him Rissa was in trouble, he'd berated himself for letting her return on her own. *He* should have protected her.

"Don't tell her that," Kiran said. "She thinks she doesn't need protecting. Now get back to work, both of you. We got a lot of thirsty miners out there."

Without waiting for them, he returned to the noisy bar. "All right, all right, you mining scum. Settle down or I'll put in a Mickey Mouse vid."

With a few groans, the room quieted.

Eventually the crowd thinned out enough that Dillan was able to take a break. He leaned against the bar as Kiran cleaned up his work area.

"Are they always this rowdy?"

The big Zebori chuckled. "On the first night of furlough. There'll be fights and other such nonsense out in the street. Nothing Chief Kaminga and his crew can't handle."

Dillan nodded. "What happened today? I heard bits and pieces about vandals hitting this place?"

While Kiran explained, Dillan's temperature rose. Someone dared to violate Rissa's place? That was completely out of character for this colony. Though some inhabitants were reclusive and most went about their business, it was understood that you didn't mess with your fellow locals. Offworlders, on the other hand, were fair game.

"What is Kaminga going to do about it?"

The bartender spent an inordinate amount of time polishing a glass before speaking. "He'll investigate. Don't get me wrong. Kaminga does a great job keeping the peace. Rissa's friends will deal with this situation."

"And that means . . ."

Kiran eyed him. "What do you think it means?"

"You'll find the culprits and exact punishment?"

"You understand. I'm surprised."

"What does he understand?" Pela sidled up to him.

"Taking care of the vandals"

"You should have seen the mess." Pela went on to describe the condition they'd found upon returning from Last Meal.

Dillan looked around. Even though the miners had scuffed the floor with their workboots and left sprinklings of lambidium dust behind, he could see how clean everything was underneath. "I don't understand how you got the place ready in time."

"The townsfolk helped." Pela's enthusiasm made him smile. A little. He was more upset over the destruction.

"We take care of our own." Kiran fixed him with a fierce look. "You would do well to remember that. Two more just came in, Offworlder. Get their order then tell them we're closing in fifteen mins."

CHAPTER 10

The nightmare woke her. It used to come nightly. To the point that she hated to close her eyes. After seven years searching and coming so close to dying, she'd known it was time to let go. For her sanity as well as her physical health. Yet twenty years after losing her child, the dream still came, especially after trauma.

Disoriented, Rissa looked around. She was in bed, her room dark, yet she didn't remember coming upstairs. That never happened. She never drank so much she forgot the previous night. In fact, she didn't remember drinking at all, except for the Kruferian mudslide at the start of the evening.

The events of the day before came rushing back. The destruction in the tavern. Kiran stunned, Pela crying. Meeting with Chief Kaminga. The townsfolk coming to her aid.

Dillan.

At best, he disconcerted her. His throwing on an apron and taking orders reminded her of when he'd helped out years before. Back when he was just a kid. Even six years ago—he had to have been in his mid-twenties by then—he often worked in the tavern while his friends went off on other adventures or looked for pleasure at Fortuna's.

If she recalled correctly, he never went to Fortuna's.

She glanced at the timepiece on her nightstand. Eight-thirty? She bolted upright. Couldn't be. It was still dark. Then she realized her room-darkening drapes had been drawn across the window. She never did that, preferring to have the early morning sun wake her in time to start the jambor.

As she scrambled out of bed, she realized she'd slept in her clothes.

What had happened last night?

"What event precipitated Bricaldia and four other planets to form the Coalition?" Dillan asked Pela as she kneaded dough.

She'd asked him to test her on various subjects to prepare her for the entrance exam into an academy in Rhadaman City. Although she said she wasn't sure she wanted to leave Astron, she studied to please Rissa. He'd already covered mathematics and literature, which she'd aced. History wasn't her strong suit.

As she pushed the yeasty lump away with the heels of her hands, she appeared to be thinking. She folded the dough over then looked at him. "Give me a clue."

"The exam doesn't give clues."

She flicked flour at him. "Meanie."

He brushed the flour off his shirt. "All right. Just this once. After the war with—"

"Okay, okay. Don't tell me anymore. I remember."

"What do you remember?" A yawning Rissa stood in the doorway between the tavern and the kitchen. She looked like she'd had a bad night. Considering what happened to her tavern the day before, she had a right to look like that.

Not that she looked bad. A little rough around the edges, maybe. Dark circles under her eyes, the imprint of a wrinkle in the pillow on her right cheek, and she hadn't taken the time to re-braid her hair. Wisps straggled down her forehead and feathered her cheeks.

She looked adorable.

"Good morning, sleepyhead." Pela stopped kneading and grinned. She must have remembered how Rissa had greeted him his first morning in Astron. With her flour-covered hand, she pointed. "What's that? Is it a necklace?"

Rissa glanced down at a long chain with what looked like an argenturum pendant hanging from it. Quickly, she stuffed it inside her shirt. "What are you two doing?"

"Sit." Though curious, Dillan got up to fix her a cup of sheelonga. Her actions made it clear she wasn't going to talk about the necklace. He would be patient and maybe she'd tell him. Patience would be the death of him.

"I don't have time to sit." She looked at Pela then over at the counter next to the sink where five loaf pans sat, dough rising under the towels. "How long have you been up?"

"Since dawn." Pela dumped the dough into a pan and added it to the others.

"Sit," Dillan repeated as he cut off a slice of jambor from the leftovers.

"She likes mongberry jam," Pela said. "There's a jar in the cooler."

Rissa eyed her. "You shouldn't be making jambor. This is your study time."

"Mister Dillan's helping me. He's asking me questions he thinks will be on the exam."

"What did I say about calling me 'Mister'?" Though it was better than her sarcastic *Offworlder*.

Diane Burton

She gave him a quick smile. "I know, I know. It doesn't seem right to call you Dillan."

"She's a quick study," he told Rissa. "A whiz at math and even better in literature. History—" He wobbled his hand. "—not as good. But she's learning."

Pela pouted. "I don't see why I have to know what happened a long time ago."

"Those who don't learn from the past are doomed to repeat it." He wrinkled his forehead. "I think that's how the saying goes."

"Close enough," Rissa said. "Pela, go back to your studies. I'll finish the jambor."

"No, Miz Rissa." Her firm statement had Rissa blinking in astonishment. "I started this job, I'll finish it. Now sit down like Mister, I mean, Dillan said and have your First Meal."

He put his hands on Rissa's shoulders and steered her to the stool in front of which he'd set the tea, a plate with jambor, and the jar of jam. Though she gave a half-hearted protest, she obeyed.

"I think you two are ganging up on me." After giving them a sheepish look, she took a sip of tea. "Thank you, both of you."

"Now where were we?" he asked. "Ah, yes. The war . . .?"

With her elbow propped on the island, Rissa waved her hand. "What happened last night? And why did I sleep in my clothes?"

Pela glanced from Rissa to him. "Dillan put you to bed."

Rissa dropped her hand. "You what?"

"He carried you upstairs. I made sure he didn't try anything with you."

"With her knife," Dillan added. "Not that she needed it, mind you. *I* am a gentleman." He quirked the corner of his mouth to let her know he was mocking himself. At her astonished look, he said, "You'd fallen asleep down here."

"Yeah. You didn't even wake up when he put you in your bed." Pela hastily added, "I loosened your clothes. Not him."

Rissa's smile lit up her eyes. "Again, thank you both."

When she munched on the piece of jambor, the jam smeared the corner of her mouth. At another time, without Pela-the-Chaperone present, he would kiss her and lick it away. Since it wasn't another time, he motioned. "You have jam . . ."

After she wiped her mouth, she looked up at him. "Did you see your friend Konner yesterday?"

He'd seen Konner, all right. But his friend? That was still debatable. "I saw him. Did you know he's the Sauri tribal chief?"

"Of course," Rissa answered. "His spouse and I are friends. She gave me the recipe for the jambor. Until last year, I didn't realize he was

81

the Konner who used to come here with you and your other friends. He's changed so much."

Dillan nodded slowly. "Yes, he has changed." So much that he'd rejected his family back in Eleganza.

"Did you meet Obeya? She is so sweet. Her boys are little scamps, into everything, questioning everything and everybody."

"Little Jilly is really cute," Pela said.

Dillan's ears perked up. "Jilly?"

Pela nodded. "Obeya's baby girl. They were really worried about her and Obeya, too. They're okay now, but they both almost died, didn't they, Miz Rissa?"

Rissa, whose eyes had clouded when Pela mentioned a baby girl, just nodded.

"When was that?" he asked.

"I'm not sure." Pela wrinkled her forehead. "But it was after Baby Jilly was born. I wasn't here then, but Obeya told me. Chief Sauri-Alcar took her and the baby to a med center on Galeria Prime. They were there a long time."

"Is that right?" he asked Rissa.

Again, she nodded. "Obeya went into premature labor. Neither the Sauri medico nor Medico Barlen could help. Winslott Industries hadn't begun mining yet, and there were no ships at the spaceport. Your manager used the company ship to transport them to Rhadaman City."

"When did this happen?"

"More than half a year ago."

Dillan pondered the timing. "That would be around the time Jileena was shot."

"I think you're right," Rissa said. "Because of Winslott Industries, it was on the newswaves."

"Konner's spouse and baby are all right now?"

"Yes. As Pela said, they were in Rhadaman City for a long time."

"And they named the baby Jilly? After his sister."

That explained a lot, especially why Konner hadn't come to Bricaldia to be with Jileena when she was shot. Dillan regretted every vile thought he'd had about his friend. But why no messages? Why not explain to his family the reason he couldn't come? Why—

"You should see her, Mister—I mean, Dillan. She is so cute. Her hair is lighter than the boys and curly. But she has Obeya's dark eyes. She is just so precious."

Again, he noticed Rissa's expression. She looked like she was lightyears away. Whatever she was thinking about made her sad. He didn't think it was Konner's baby.

"How come you guys didn't invite me to the party?" A bleary-eyed Kiran, his traditional short skirt wrapped around his waist, staggered into the kitchen.

"Did we wake you?" Rissa asked. "I'm sorry. I didn't think we were that loud."

In what appeared to be mechanical moves, Kiran got a mug and fixed himself some tea. "Not loud. A nightmare woke me."

He hooked his bare foot around the rung of a stool and pulled it out. With a heaviness Dillan hadn't seen before from the big Zebori, Kiran dropped onto the stool.

Rissa reached across the corner of the island and patted his arm. "The usual one?"

Kiran nodded. "Haven't had it in several tendays."

When Pela didn't question the subject of Kiran's nightmare, Dillan knew enough to keep his mouth shut. This was private. And he was the outsider.

"How you doing, Boss?" Kiran gave her a concerned look. "Get a good night's sleep?"

"About that." She cleared her throat and looked pointedly around the worktable. "Don't ever let me sleep while you all are working."

"Actually, Boss—" Kiran winked. "—we had a party while you were snoozing."

Pela finished punishing a lump of dough and dumped it into a long loaf pan. "Speaking of parties. The naming ceremony celebration for Sophira's baby is next week. Are we closing that afternoon?"

"No."

Dillan's ears perked up at how sharply Rissa answered the girl. Very unlike her.

When a hurt look crossed Pela's features, Rissa said, "I'll stay. You can go." This time her voice was more even.

Again, Dillan noticed a sadness in Rissa's dark eyes at the mention of a baby. Ever since the meeting about slavers, he *knew* her reason for stopping them was personal. Knew it had to do with a baby. Without probing—something he wouldn't do in front of her employees—he was no closer to the reason she felt so strongly about—

Sweet Divinity. What a dunce he'd been. It was so obvious.

"Why aren't you going to the celebration, Miz Rissa? It will be fun."

Kiran shot Pela a look meant to discourage any more questions. The bartender knew something.

Rissa stood and took her dirty dishes to the sink. "I'm sure it will be. That's why you are going. It will be quiet here. I can handle things.

You go, too, Kiran. Sophira will appreciate it." As she talked, she rinsed her dishes and put them into the sanitizer rack.

After wiping her hands on a towel, she opened the hidden door to the stairs. "Since you have everything under control, Pela—" She gave the girl a quick smile. "—I'll get cleaned up for the day. And, Rusteran, you ever put me to bed again like you did last night, and we'll have serious words."

Once the door closed behind her, Dillan eyed the two. "Okay, what's going on?"

"What do you mean?" Pela put six loaf pans into the oven then, with a glass of milk in her hand, sat down at the island and let out a deep sigh. "I'm glad that part's done. I don't know how Miz Rissa does this every morning. Making jambor is hard work."

"You did a good job, little missy." Kiran gave her a toothy grin. "The boss appreciates you taking on that job and letting her sleep. Even if she doesn't always say it. And you, Offworlder, don't listen to her. You did the right thing last night. It was a rough day for her."

"Rough on all of you, I'd say. I'm sorry I wasn't here to help sooner."

"You did all right once you got here. You surprised all of us putting on that apron and serving." Kiran stood behind Pela and began rubbing her shoulders.

"A long time ago, my friends and I used to come here. We were crazy back then." He let a wistful smile quirk his mouth. "Sometimes, I stayed behind and helped Rissa. She was by herself then and tried to do everything."

Kiran nodded. "That's her problem. She tries to do everything. Never takes time for herself."

Dillan agreed. He'd seen it years ago, and she hadn't changed.

"Little missy," Kiran said in a mock stern tone, "you go on up to your room and take a nap. The offworlder and I will take care of things down here."

"But the jambor," she began. "It has to bake."

"Just tell me for how long," Dillan said. "I used to help our cook with baking. I think I can handle this."

After she left, still protesting, Dillan folded his hands on the island top. "What's with Rissa and babies?"

The big Zebori narrowed his eyes. "Not my story. You want to know, ask her. I'll be back." He headed through the doorway to the bar.

"Kiran? I care about her."

The bartender turned around. "I can see that. Some things are too private to talk about behind her back."

"I know that. I'm trying to understand her. When I was here before, I was too full of myself to see that she's experienced pain. And it has to do with traffickers." He raised his eyebrow in question.

Kiran shook his head. "She's never told me. But when she learned my story I could see she understood."

"Is that what your nightmare was about? What slavers did to you?"

For a moment, Kiran didn't say anything. "You aren't such a dumb offworlder, after all. Watch the jambor. After all Pela's hard work, don't let those loaves burn."

CHAPTER 11

As Rissa entered the kitchen, she smelled the rich, yeasty aroma of baking bread. After a quick shower and clothes change, she'd run into Pela in the upstairs hall. She heartily approved of Kiran's directive that the girl sleep. She'd done an outstanding job assuming Rissa's duties. She was grateful to all of them—Kiran, Pela, and even Dillan—for taking care of her. Even if it was hard to admit. She'd been on her own for so long, depending on no one but herself.

Accepting help did not come easy to her. Too many times, favors came with strings attached. Not that Kiran or Pela expected anything from her. She had to wonder about Dillan Rusteran's motivation, though. The man had wormed his way into her life. Again.

Still sitting at the island, he appeared so lost in his thoughts he didn't hear her come in. When the door to the stairs closed behind her, he jumped.

"Hey." He grinned. "You look all bright-eyed and bushy-tailed."

"Is that a Bricaldian description?"

"Let me get you some tea." As he busied himself making two mugs of sheelonga, despite her protests that she didn't want one, he added, "I think that's a Terran expression. I must have heard it last night on one of the vids."

She accepted the mug but didn't sit. "About last night. I appreciate your helping out."

Leaning back against the counter next to the sink, he crossed one ankle over the other. Still watching her, he took a swallow of tea. "I hope the Rusteran miners aren't as obnoxious as those from the Winslott mines."

"They're worse." She enjoyed his astonished look before grinning. "Not really. It was first day of furlough. After working two tendays straight, they like to cut loose. In another day or two, they'll settle down."

"You like what you do."

"It's a living."

He shook his head. "It's more than that. You really enjoy running the tavern."

Embarrassed at his insight, she took a sip of tea and let the bracing beverage charge through her system.

"I didn't realize when I came here before that this is more than just a job for you. Too young, too stupid, I guess."

"You were young. Still are." She let her mouth curve into a small grin. "I never thought you were stupid, though. Foolhardy, yes. A daredevil. Now your friends? They were stupid. The risks they took."

"We all took those risks."

"Do you still see them? Back in the Central District?"

"No. After Konner died—or so we thought—they were a constant reminder of what had happened to my best friend. I heard one died skydiving and another drowned off the coast of the Loren Sea on Chellus. I'm not sure what happened to the others. Don't care, either." His laugh came out more like a bark. "Stupid. Just plain stupid."

The anguish in his eyes startled her. She remembered what had happened before. And her guilt after she'd comforted him. Against her better judgment, she went to him, took his mug and set it with her own on the counter behind him. Then she did what she'd done all those years ago. She put her arms around him and held on. A shudder ran through him before he rested his forehead against hers.

As before her comfort changed into something else. When his arms encircled her waist and he drew her closer, she knew she should let go, step away. But she didn't. When he lifted his head, the anguish was gone. In its place, desire blazed from his green eyes. Desire for her.

While she hesitated, he captured her mouth. Passion she'd thought long gone overwhelmed her. She clung to him, returning his kiss, delving into his mouth for more. As if reading her mind, he slid his hand down to the base of her spine and pressed her close.

He was as aroused as she was.

By the Matriarch, she wanted him. The way she'd wanted him six years ago.

When his mouth left hers and worked its way downward, she arched her neck to give him better access. His tongue worked magic on her erratic pulse before going lower. He opened the front of her shirt and shoved it off her shoulder to reach her breast.

The cool air against her wet skin brought her back to reality. She pulled away.

"What's wrong?" His voice slurred with desire.

"For the love of quizzard, Rusteran. We're in my kitchen." Hastily, she refastened her shirt. "Anyone could walk in."

He tried to pull her back. "Let's go upstairs then."

"Stop." She shoved her loose hair behind her ears. "We can't do this."

"Do what? Make love? C'mon, Rissa. We're two consenting adults." When she pursed her lips, he dropped his arms. "At least, I thought you were consenting a few mins ago. Did I get that wrong?"

She could lie and say he'd definitely gotten it wrong. "No. Not wrong. I'm sorry. I don't usually . . ."

"You don't usually what? Get carried away? Let yourself go? You did six years ago."

"And I've regretted it ever since," she snapped.

He stared at her in stunned silence.

"You were a kid. I took advantage of you, of your grief. Just like I did this time."

"I wasn't a kid then." His eyes drilled deep into hers. "And I'm certainly no kid now."

No, he wasn't.

"You didn't take advantage of me. Not then, not now. I want you, Rissa. I've wanted you since the first time I met you." He walked to the alley door. With his hand on the lever, he stopped. "Maybe back then the seven years between us seemed like a lot. To you. It meant nothing then. It means nothing to me now."

He was wrong about their ages. He was wrong about a lot of things.

Close to eight years separated them. She'd already hit forty. Life on the Rim, especially in a desert colony, aged a fem faster than a man. To her, Dillan Rusteran was still the reckless kid who came out to the Rim to play because he had nothing better to do.

The part of her that insisted on honesty reared its head. That was no callow youth who'd just kissed her and filled her with such desire she wanted to rip off his clothes.

Dillan packed up his belongings and left the tavern. With the urgency of their kiss and her rejection, he couldn't sleep near her. It would have been too easy to tiptoe down the hall and slide into her bed. He had to wait for her to initiate the next move. He could wait.

The next morning he took the rented Rengara 790 skimmer to the Winslott mines. He had to talk to Konner. Not about the lease. About Jilly.

The mine manager insisted he wait in his office until Konner arrived. Apparently, communication existed up in the mountains. He should have guessed that, considering Konner had known about the vandalism at Rissa's tavern.

The office looked better than his own manager's. No ferranite dust coating all surfaces, or paper maps of the mines strewn around. Of course, lambidium was cleaner than ferranite, and Rusteran Mining had been on Galeriana a lot longer than Winslott Industries. Dillan walked to a window and looked out over the trees that stubbornly clung to the rocky terrain. The sun, at its zenith, beat down overhead, but the window's tinted perma-film prevented the heat from entering. He'd have to modernize his own manager's office or lose him to Winslott.

Damn, if that didn't sound like his father.

"You're back." Konner startled him.

He turned around. Konner was clad in Sauri attire. It was hard to believe this bearded stranger had been his best friend.

"Are you here to see your friend or the Sauri chief?"

"I told your manager I wanted to talk to Konner Winslott."

"That's the only reason I agreed to see you. Come." After leading him to a small conference room, Konner pulled flasks of water out of a small cooler in the corner and tossed one to him. "Sit."

Dillan decided to let his friend set the pace of the conversation.

"Your girl sure stirred up a bunch of trouble."

"She's neither a girl nor mine." Though he wanted her to be. "Your comm system is top-notch. I wondered how you knew about the vandalism."

"Miners are the biggest gossips on the planet. Is Rissa all right? She wasn't hurt?"

"No. She wasn't there when they trashed her place." He took a swig of water. Forget letting Konner set the pace. "I came to talk about Jilly."

The man slumped into a chair. "I knew you would."

"I heard about your spouse and baby. Are they all right?"

"Yes. Now."

"Why didn't you let Jilly know? She waited for you, kept asking for you."

Konner scrubbed his face. "I did. Eventually." He heaved a sigh. "I didn't take messages while we were in the med center. My spouse was fighting for her life and that of our child. I couldn't think about anything else. I didn't care about anyone else. Harsh, I know."

"You said *eventually*. So you did talk to Jilly?"

"Of course. She'd already taken over WI." He smiled. "Give that girl a lot of credit for standing up to the old man. The Divine One knows I never could."

Dillan knew how persuasive their fathers could be. Konner's determined that his son would take over the company, just like Dillan's. A bond they shared. Like Dillan, Konner had defied his father and run out to the frontier to play. Anything to avoid responsibilities their fathers demanded they shoulder.

He'd caved. Konner hadn't.

"So you're working for Uncle Boras. Doing his dirty work."

"I didn't come up here to talk about the lease. I want to ask you why you never let me know you were alive. We were best friends." He sounded like a petulant kid . . . and didn't care. He needed answers.

Konner took a long drink of water. A delaying action. "What did Jilly tell you? About what happened."

"That the natives rescued you and you'd lost your memory. I just don't understand why after it returned you didn't contact us."

"I'd made a life here. A spouse, children. I didn't want the life the Old Man scripted for me." Anguish contorted his face. "I was afraid I wasn't strong enough to defy him anymore. I didn't tell Jilly that. Ashamed, I guess. I figured if he knew I was alive, he'd get his way."

Dillan thought about how Adamus Winslott had browbeat Konner for years before the accident. "I understand. Maybe if everyone thought I was dead, I wouldn't have to make the decision to return."

With a short bark of laughter, Konner said, "We're a pair, aren't we?"

"Yeah." He stood. He'd gotten his answers. "You gonna introduce me to your family?"

Konner threw his arms around him and slapped his back. "Friends again?"

"I'm still thinking about it." Then he gave his best friend a crooked smile. "Who else would forgive you?"

"Jilly did. C'mon. Obeya and the children are waiting to meet you."

"You brought them? What if I'd brought up that lease?"

"Then you wouldn't have met them, and we'd all gone home."

Again Dillan thought about his father and the job he'd sent him to do. To Lexol with that.

At first Rissa was glad Dillan had left. But much as she wanted him to he didn't stay completely away. He helped with serving the rowdy miners each night. But he didn't sleep in the room upstairs. From overheard bits and pieces, she learned he slept aboard his ship. It was better that way. She didn't need temptation down the hall from her bedroom. Especially when her mind kept returning to that time six years ago. That time when giving comfort and sympathy had led to something else. Something she'd always regretted.

Pela had just returned from the naming ceremony celebration for Sophira's baby. She was full of descriptions of the food and gifts and how the proud parents were thrilled with the gift of holo-vid books from Rissa.

"Sophira and Partorus were really sad that you couldn't be there," Pela said. "But Sophira said she understood."

Nobody understood. Each time she heard about a baby being born, she thought of Miri. Each naming ceremony reminded her of Miri's. Every holiday made her wonder how Miri was celebrating. Were her parents kind? Did they treat her well? Were they generous and loving?

Though those thoughts brought tears to Rissa's soul, the thought that Miri's parents could be like Pela's drove daggers into her heart.

Better to harden her heart, keep her soul protected. And not think about the daughter she'd lost.

A futile effort.

". . . and that farmer whose boys were taken by the slavers sold his land to his neighbor and left for Rhadaman City." Pela was still going on about the party. After saying she wasn't hungry, she'd sat at the island and watched Kiran and Dillan eat prior to the evening rush.

Kiran looked up from the hitchen stew he'd been devouring. "What about the nasty one who kept questioning the boss? Ramus."

"He's the neighbor who bought the land." Pela hopped off her stool and went to the cooler where she pulled out a bottle of mongberry juice. "He started talking about the whole 'slaver thing' being a hoax to dump a lot of kids in our colony."

Rissa bristled. "A hoax?"

Pela nodded. "He said you started the whole scare. That you wanted publicity for your tavern because of the new one being built near the spaceport."

"What?" Kiran, Dillan, and Rissa all exclaimed at once.

"Partorus set the record straight about that," Pela said. "He even warned Ramus that if he continued to spread lies, he—Partorus—would beat him up. Then he told him to leave."

Dillan said, "I thought we were very clear at that meeting how serious the situation with slavers was."

"That Ramus has had a chip on his shoulder since he came here," Kiran said. "He's a nasty piece of work, always complaining. He's worse than Nakus about the liquor and the food. One time when I was in the mercantile, Ramus got in an argument with Graeson about the price of something and Graeson threw him out."

"What's the man's problem?" Dillan asked.

Kiran shook his head. "Some trouble he got into in the Central District. Said it was all trumped up by somebody who had it in for him. That's why he came out here. I think he just likes to stir up trouble."

A disturbing thought occurred to Rissa. She looked at Pela. "You didn't mention that you were part of the group that got those children away from the slavers, did you?"

When the girl ducked her head, Rissa knew she had. Pela was so loyal she would have leapt to Rissa's defense. But that might get her into trouble. Ramus had a big mouth.

She was about to ask more when her comm unit beeped. Chief Kaminga.

After listening, she disconnected and stood. "I have to go down to the security office. Chief Kaminga wants to talk to me."

"Does he know who the vandals are?" Pela asked. "Did he arrest them?"

"He wouldn't say." As she talked, she stripped off her apron.

Dillan rose. "I'll go with you."

"No need."

"Yes, there is, Boss," Kiran said without getting up. The man enjoyed his food. While Pela had been relaying gossip, he'd gotten a second helping of stew. "We still don't know who the vandals are. They could do something worse."

"That farmer. He even said—" Pela's voice hitched. "—you did all the damage to the tavern yourself."

While the men talked over each other, Rissa stood stunned. She couldn't believe that anyone would say such a thing.

"Makes you wonder," Dillan said, "if he's trying to divert attention from himself. Kaminga questioned him about the break-in."

"You need to go with her, Mister Dillan. Protect her."

Rissa bristled. "I don't need protection. I can take—"

"—care of yourself," he finished. "I've heard that enough times."

"I'm not going to waste time arguing." She looked at Kiran. "Take care of Pela."

"Don't worry, Boss. We'll hold down the fort."

Dillan followed Rissa down the alley. By the stars, she was glorious. Straight back, dark braid swishing, a stride that matched any man's, she made him think of an Amazon from Terran legends. The sight of her long legs and curved butt—even camouflaged by her baggy trousers—sent the same jolt through him that they had years ago. What a fem!

After watching her for a block, he drew alongside. "Trying to lose me?"

She snorted. "This place is too small to lose anyone. Keep up."

When they reached an intersection, she headed to the main street. Her boots echoed off the boardwalk as she strode to the security office. At their approach, the auto-door opened. In the large room, the entire security force had gathered along with Medico Barlen, Merchant Graeson, Dock Master Yephos, and Fortuna.

Chief Kaminga stepped forward to greet them. "Miz Rissa, Rusteran, thank you for coming." Worry and a hint of fear were etched into Kaminga's young face.

The door opened and Chef Nalgin rushed in. He looked around. "What's going on?"

"That's what I'd like to know," Graeson said. "Kaminga won't tell us."

Again the door whooshed open. Partorus—Sophira's spouse— entered, followed by two farmers. Not that nasty Ramus who'd spread lies about Rissa.

"Good, good." Sweat beaded Kaminga's forehead. "I think everyone is here. Last night, traffickers hit Marsden Colony."

Several gasps and a few "Holy sherd" followed that announcement.

Marsden, in Galeriana's southern hemisphere, was too close. Bigger than Astron and in the temperate zone, it was more attractive to settlers. And now to slavers.

Kaminga took a deep breath and went on. "They raided outlying ranches and several homes in the village itself."

"They're getting bolder," Dillan said.

The chief nodded. "I called you all here because you volunteered to protect our citizens. My security force can only do so much. We need your help."

"Of course, Chief," Rissa said. "What do you want us to do?"

"We need to put all of Astron on notice," Kaminga said.

Almost as one, the others turned to Rissa.

"We have a plan." She reminded everyone about the plan they'd drawn up at the meeting in her tavern.

Sweet Divinity, Dillan was proud of her. She issued orders better than a war-seasoned general.

"Dock Master." She eyed the rotund Yephos. "You're our first line of defense. Can you keep them from landing here?"

He shifted his sizeable weight from one foot to the other. "Well, I, uh, don't know. How can I tell what ship's a slaver and what's a legitimate cargo hauler?"

"For star's sake, Yephos," Rissa said. "You know every indie pilot in this sector."

"But—but . . ."

"The security chief at Marsden gave me the ID of the slave ship," Kaminga said. "I already sent that info to Traffic Controller Ropergor with orders not to let it land."

"What if they change their ID?" Rissa asked.

The Dock Master drew himself up. "That's illegal."

93

Rissa scoffed. "Like slaving isn't? They'll do anything, say anything to get to our people. We can't let them. Chief, can your men search every unfamiliar ship?"

"Wait, wait, wait," the Dock Master cried. "If word gets out that you're searching cargo, nobody will land here. We'll lose business. We won't get supplies. We—"

"Oh, shut up, Yephos," Rissa said. "Protecting our people is more important than cargo from unknown suppliers. What about it, Chief? Do you have enough guards, or do you need help?"

"We'll need help."

Dillan was glad to see Kaminga was smart enough to know he was out of his league. He didn't let pride keep him from admitting it. The others began to speak up, offering to go to the spaceport. Armed.

"What if they don't land at the 'port?" Partorus asked.

"Yeah," one of the farmers said. "They could land anywhere."

"Not if they're smart," the Dock Master said. "The blowing sand will get in their engines and they'll crash."

"Not if they have specially modified engines like our transports from the mines," Dillan said. "Or they could land on the leeward side of the mountain. From there, they could use skimmers to get here."

A lot of murmurs followed that.

"The important thing right now," Rissa said, "is to alert the colony and those in the outlying areas."

Partorus motioned between himself and the two farmers who'd come in with him. "We'll take care of the farms."

The others volunteered for different sections of the village.

"I'll contact the mines, both Winslott's and my own," Dillan said. "And the Sauri chief. If we're all vigilant, the slavers will have a more difficult time coming over the mountains undetected."

"Is your comm strong enough to reach the mines?" Rissa strode down the boardwalk back to her tavern.

"Yes." He grimaced as he recalled how strong the comm system was. His father had left several messages regarding Dillan's progress with negotiating a new mining lease with the Sauris. With each message, Boras Rusteran had become more agitated, more furious at his son for not responding.

Dillan knew he'd taken the coward's way out. He'd have to talk to his father. Soon.

"That's good," Rissa said. "My comm's older than dirt. It's good enough for around the village. If yours isn't strong enough, you may have to use Kaminga's. When Chief Servary was in charge of this sector, he made sure every outpost upgraded to the latest system. They can reach even the Central District."

He didn't tell her his could, too. "You should think about sending Pela up to the mines to join her friend." He held the front door to the tavern open for her. "In fact, close the tavern. You and Kiran should go up to the mines, too. For safety."

She spun around, looking appalled that he would suggest that. "What? Hide out? We have to fight. We can't allow those slavers to take any more people."

Pela rushed out from the kitchen. "What slavers? Are they here?"

"No," Rissa said quietly. "We're just trying to be prepared."

While she reassured Pela, Dillan worried about her determination to stay and fight. Pride warred with the worry. He'd always known what a strong fem she was. Fems didn't have it easy out on the Rim. Most went into subservient positions. They opened pleasure houses, not taverns.

Not Rissa. No slaving—poor choice of words—for someone else. She thrived being her own boss. And while he admired that, admired her strength of character, he feared that strength would lead to trouble.

For over two tendays, Dillan watched the citizens of Astron Colony keep vigil. Armed men strode down Main Street from the spaceport to the foothills. Every afternoon, Rissa fed the make-shift militia. She refused to listen to his warnings about making herself a target. As a member of the community, she insisted on doing her part.

But high alert became wearing. Especially when nothing happened. Freighters from Dillan's mines delivered ferranite to the mills on Menaca and deadheaded back. The smaller Winslott freighters sent lambidium to smelters in the Central District. When indie ships arrived, they were searched—whether the pilots were known or not. Most protested until they learned the reason. They gossiped—as indie pilots always did—about the increase in traffickers in other systems. In the same breath, they talked about how the gangster Hallart was spreading his influence into this sector.

Still, no slave ships arrived. Which turned out to be a good news/bad news situation. Good news that the colony was safe. Bad news that their preparedness was for naught. At least, that's how the militia groused as they ate the free food at Rissa's.

From his vantage point aboard his ship—where he continued to sleep—Dillan watched the number of guards dwindle. On his daily trips to Rissa's, he passed fewer patrols. Though many proclaimed ready to help if needed, people returned to their own lives. After the third tenday, the colony returned to normal.

Every morning before going to the tavern, he worked on modifications to his heavy-air engine, a precaution in the event he needed to get up to the mines in a hurry. No more skimmer or zircan travel. He'd done all necessary work inside the hold. Now it was time to add extra filters to the air intakes that should keep out most, if not all, the blowing sand.

He'd designed the modifications himself based on the technology of the transports as well as the skimmers. Instead of being a waste of time, as his father often said, Dillan's hobby of designing then tinkering with engines had proven to be beneficial out on the Rim. On the long trip from Eleganza, he'd had plenty of time to indulge in his favorite pastime. Plexi-sheets with his designs lay on every surface. Now he could put one of his designs into practical use.

The spaceport was quiet at that time of the morning. With no ships to work on, the mechs didn't come in unless called by the dock master. While Dillan had many tools aboard, he'd made friends with the mechanic whose workstation was nearby. Offering to pay for the use of the mech's tools helped.

For the third time in the past hour, he'd gone to the station for equipment. His mind had been wandering back to Rissa and how she was faring instead of concentrating on his work. The family cook called that thinking with your feet instead of your brain. How right she was.

"Get Dix away from the tavern."

The low voice behind him startled Dillan so much he dropped the specialized wrench down the air intake tube.

"What?" He whirled around and searched the shadows for the owner of the voice. A slight movement to the left caught his attention. "Come out where I can see you."

"I'm fine right where I am, Offworlder." The man's voice sounded familiar. "I'm only going to say this once more. She's in danger. Get her out of the colony."

Dillan's heart raced at the man's words. Rissa was in danger. He had to know more. Had to know how to protect her. "Explain."

"By organizing the colony against slavers, she's made herself a target. They don't like it when their plans are thwarted."

"Did they vandalize her tavern?"

"Quit asking questions and get moving."

"How much time do I have?"

"Very little. Don't forget that tool you dropped." The shadow moved slightly then disappeared.

Had the man not mentioned the tool, Dillan would've forgotten it. That would have wreaked havoc once his ship was airborne. He quickly fished it out and finished the job. All the while, he pondered how to get Rissa away from Astron. As he replaced the tools he'd borrowed from the mech's station, it hit him who the speaker was.

Quin. The red-haired Menacan who'd helped dispose of the three slavers.

CHAPTER 12

As Dillan raced from the 'port to the tavern, he tried to figure out how to get Rissa out of town. He couldn't tell her she was in danger. She would dig in her heels and refuse to be intimidated. He had to come up with a plan.

The few shopkeepers who were out sweeping the sand from the boardwalk in front of their businesses looked at him askance. Rarely did anyone run in the desert, even in the cool of the morning. When he burst through the alley door into the kitchen, he startled Rissa so much she spilled her tea down her front.

"Rusteran, what's wrong?"

"Let's go to Vesteron." Though he was still breathing hard from running, he managed to get the words out.

After grabbing a towel, she swiped at her skin where the tea gone inside her shirt. She yanked out the pendant, wiped it, and stuffed it back inside. "Are you crazy? I can't leave—"

"Sure you can." He looked around the kitchen. She hadn't started making jambor. "You have a tenday before the next group of miners arrive. Take a break."

"I cannot just up and leave. I have too much to do around here. What's gotten into you?"

The door to the stairs slid open. Pela walked in. "What are you guys arguing about? I could hear you all the way upstairs."

"I heard you, too." Kiran came into the kitchen, yawning and scratching his bare chest. "I'll bet the whole colony heard you, if they were awake."

"I asked Rissa to go with me to Vesteron. She could use a vacation."

"You didn't ask, Rusteran. You demanded."

Kiran nodded before fixing himself some tea. "She hasn't taken time off since . . ." He scratched the back of his head. "Was it last year you went to Balderate for the bartop?"

"The year before. That's beside the point. I can't just take off."

"Why not, Miz Rissa? You deserve to have some fun."

"How can I have fun when slavers might show up?"

Dillan had anticipated that argument. "The others will take over."

"But—"

He tapped her lips. "They know what to do if a ship lands. You don't have to take on responsibility for the entire colony."

"Yeah, Boss. Pela and me can handle the tavern. Won't be much business with the miners not here."

"Actually." Dillan paused. This was his trump card and he figured playing it would convince Rissa to leave. "I was thinking Pela would enjoy going to Vesteron. You, too, Kiran."

"Vesteron? I've never been there." Pela's large grin spoke volumes.

"But who would run the tavern?"

He still hadn't convinced her. "Close the tavern. Between the café and Fortuna's, the villagers and space crews will be well taken care of."

"C'mon, Miz Rissa. Say I can go. Please."

"Well . . ." She was softening.

Dillan turned to the bartender. "Kiran? Even been to Vesteron?"

The big man grimaced. "Yeah. Bad memories."

Oh, sherd. Not what Dillan wanted to hear.

"I can take care of things here," Kiran said. "You have a good time." He left before Rissa could protest.

"Can we go to Vesteron?" Pela was practically dancing in her excitement. "Please, Miz Rissa. I won't be any trouble."

Rissa put her arms around the girl and hugged. "You are never any trouble." She looked over Pela's head. "You win, Rusteran. I guess we can go to Vesteron. Give me a day to put things in order."

A day? Quin said they didn't have much time. "You know the point of a spontaneous vacation is to leave right away. You two pack for a tenday. I'm going to talk to Kiran."

"Not a tenday." Then Rissa modified her protest by saying, "Three days only."

While Pela regaled Rissa about all the sights she's read about and wanted to see, Dillan left the kitchen. Getting Rissa and Pela away from the colony might be enough to deter the traffickers from revenge. But what if that put Kiran in danger?

After rapping on the door under the main stairs, he ducked to enter Kiran's quarters. Inside the former storeroom, the large room bore testament to the bartender's origins. Native Zebori prints hung on the walls alongside musical instruments like flutes of varying sizes and small hand-held drums. Larger drums, some over a meter tall, rested in a corner.

Kiran, already changed into regular Rimmer attire, looked up from making his bed. "You want something, Offworlder?"

"I know you don't want to go to Vesteron, but is there somewhere you'd like to visit?"

The big Zebori straightened to his full height, his head nearly touching the ceiling. "Are you trying to say something?"

"What about your homeworld? Do you still have family on Hetropsis?"

"Two brothers. Why all this concern about me leaving?" He eyed Dillan suspiciously. "Rissa and Pela, too. What's going on?"

"I'm afraid the slavers might retaliate against Rissa. I don't want you or Pela targeted when they can't touch her."

Kiran went into warrior mode. He strode up to Dillan, grabbed the front of his shirt, and lifted him up so they were eye-to-eye. "What do you know?"

Trying to keep from choking, Dillan managed to say, "I got a warning. To get Rissa out of the colony. Let go. Please."

Unceremoniously, Kiran dropped his grip. "Who? Someone credible?"

Dillan staggered for a few secs before rubbing his throat. "Yeah. Remember the Menacan who got rid of those slavers that took Sophira's baby? He seemed real sure that something was going to happen to Rissa if she didn't leave. I can take care of the fems. I'd feel a whole lot better if you weren't around to draw the slavers' fire. If they come."

Kiran rubbed the top of his bald head. "I haven't heard from my brothers in a while. I heard on the 'waves there's been a lot of volcanic activity lately on Hetropsis. More than usual."

"You should go see if they're okay." As he turned to leave, another thought occurred. "Do you need transport?"

Kiran was already starting to pack. "An indie pilot I know is headed that way. You take care of Rissa. Pela, too."

"Can we go up to your mine, Mister Dillan, and pick up Anaris?"

Pela stood hesitantly just inside the control center of his ship. He'd finally given up on getting her to call him just Dillan. Having already contacted Traffic Controller Ropergor, Dillan was going through pre-flight.

"I already told you we can't." Rissa stood in the portal. "Dillan's ship isn't equipped to fly across the desert. The sand will damage his engine."

When Ropergor announced he was opening the dome, Dillan taxied to the turntable for launch. "Actually, I made some modifications. We could go to the mines and get your friend. As soon as we clear the dome, I'll contact the manager to have her get ready."

Pela raced up behind him and threw her arms around his neck. "Thank you, Mister Dillan. Thank you so much."

"Uh, could you let go for a moment?" He laughed. "It helps if I can breathe during launch."

"Sure thing." She stepped back.

When he glanced over his shoulder, he saw Rissa struggling not to laugh. Considering her enthusiasm, he told Pela to sit in the copilot's seat. Before taking the other seat, Rissa showed the girl how to fasten the harness that would keep her from flying around.

"I'm still not sure it's a good idea to go to Vesteron. It's so far." She buckled up.

And that was the point, though he couldn't tell her so.

Launch went smoothly and soon they were whizzing past the desert. This sure beat the long skimmer ride. In almost no time, they circled around the mountain and landed near the idle transport.

"Hurry now," Rissa instructed. "We don't want to keep Dillan waiting."

He lowered the ramp. "I need to talk to Manager d'Arcanin. Pela, you and your friend have ten mins to be back here ready to go."

As Pela raced across the landing strip, Rissa just shook her head. "Are you sure you want to take two teen girls to Vesteron? If I know those two, they won't stop talking all the way there."

"Not a problem. Do you want to come with me?"

"That's all right. You have business to discuss. I'll just walk around. Vesteron is more than a shipday away. I won't get a chance to stretch my legs."

Dillan hesitated. She should be safe away from the colony. Still, he worried that something might happen to her. "Don't go far. I don't want to have to send out a search party when we're ready to leave."

At her indignation, he laughed. "Lighten up, Dix. This is a vacation. No schedules to keep. Nowhere to be at a certain time."

When Dillan walked into d'Arcanin's office, the manager was in conference with one of the supervisors. Harraway, who'd been with Rusteran Mines since production started on Galeriana, got up to leave.

"Stay. I'll only be a min. As you know, traffickers are in this system. You should be extra vigilant."

"We are," d'Arcanin said. "Harraway here has posted more patrols around the settlement."

"Do you really think we're in danger?" Harraway asked. "Nothing's happened since that raid at Marsden Colony. Even there, they only hit a few ranches."

"I don't know," Dillan said. "Just trying to keep you all safe."

Harraway scoffed. "You just don't want production to suffer."

"That was uncalled for," Manager d'Arcanin said.

"I'm sorry you think that," Dillan said at the same time. "I do care about my employees. Without you, Rusteran Mining wouldn't exist."

Harraway didn't look convinced.

D'Arcanin put his hand on his supervisor's shoulder and guided him to the door. "Young Mister Rusteran isn't like his father." He glanced back at Dillan. "Sorry, sir. We've all gotten the impression from Senior Mister Rusteran that production is paramount."

"I understand." Dillan understood, all right. Harraway was correct. Nothing matter to Boras Rusteran like meeting production quotas. "I will explain things to my father. He's sure to see that the welfare of the employees is important."

Harraway gave him a reluctant shrug. "Yes, sir." When his boss opened the door, he looked back to Dillan. "I have a wife and daughter. I, uh, appreciate your concern for them."

After he left, d'Arcanin said, "I apologize for his attitude. Sorry to say, but that's how people up here think."

"I know. I'd hoped my presence would make a difference."

"It has, sir."

After a quick knock, the door opened again. Dillan thought Harraway had returned. Instead, Rissa hesitated in the opening. Worry etched her brow.

"Sorry for the interruption, Manager d'Arcanin." She turned to Dillan. "The girls aren't leaving with us. Anaris is too afraid to leave the area, and Pela doesn't want to go without her."

Dillan looked at the mine manager. "Is it all right for Pela to stay here for a while?"

"No, Dillan. We should return to Astron. This was not a good idea."

They couldn't go back to Astron. Not if Quin's warning came to fruition. Dillan had to quash that idea.

"Of course, your girl can stay here," d'Arcanin said. "Anaris is a hard worker. She never takes time off unless Pela comes to visit. It will do Anaris good to have some fun."

D'Arcanin to the rescue.

"But—"

"Thanks," Dillan cut off her protest. "With the extra security around here, the girls will be safe. Thank Supervisor Harraway for us."

"Rissa, we'll take care of the girls like we always do." D'Arcanin chuckled. "Besides, you'll be helping out Harraway's spouse. Ever since he issued an edict about staying within the parameter of the settlement, his daughter has been complaining that there's nothing to do. She'll enjoy the company."

After a few more protests—each weaker than the one before—Rissa finally gave in. When they reached his ship, the two girls were waiting.

"Is it okay for me to stay?" Pela asked. "Mister Dillan, I want to go to Vesteron, but I want to be with Anaris."

"You can go, Pela." The younger girl gave a half-hearted smile.

"No." Pela squared her shoulders. "We'll have fun here. When you're not working, of course."

"Manager d'Arcanin is giving you time off, Anaris," Rissa said. "He says you deserve it."

The excitement in both girls' eyes was worth leaving Pela behind. Dillan hoped that would satisfy Rissa. This was working out better than he hoped. He'd have Rissa all to himself. Maybe he could convince her he wasn't the scrawny kid who used to come to Astron to risk his life in meaningless adventures. He needed her to see that he was a grown man. A man who'd never forgotten her. Or forgot what she meant to him.

As they entered the ship's command center, Rissa hesitated. "I don't know, Dillan. Maybe we shouldn't go all the way to Vesteron. It's so far and Pela . . ."

"She'll be fine." He began pre-flight. "I think she'll have more fun with Anaris and Harraway's daughter than with us. You'd better buckle up." He pointed to the copilot's seat.

"We should go back to Astron. If there are any problems up at the mine, we could get to Pela quickly."

Dillan swiveled his seat to face her. "You're really worried about her."

"Of course. I'm responsible for her. I told her I'd keep her safe. How can I do that if we're so far away?"

"We can be back within a shipday. Almost as fast as a skimmer from Astron up to the mine. Don't worry so. Nothing's going to happen." He brought the heavy-air engine online. "With all the extra security, the traffickers aren't going to risk coming here. You know how gossipy the indie pilots are. They're sure to have spread the word about ships being searched."

Rissa pulled the safety harness into place. "You're right." Despite her words, he heard reluctance.

"You make going on vacation sound like an odious chore. Can't you just settle back and enjoy the ride?"

They lifted off and were through Galeriana's atmosphere before she spoke again. He'd noticed her white-knuckled grip on the chair arms and wondered if her reluctance to leave Astron was more than her dedication to Pela and her tavern.

"I'm sorry if I sounded ungrateful, Dillan. It's just . . . I haven't been away from the colony in a long time." She shot him a quick smile. "Other than going to Balderate for that bartop."

He switched over to the sublight engine and set a course for Vesteron Colony on Magnos Prime. "The way you were gripping the arms of the chair I thought you might fear flying."

"No. Not fear. Exactly. It brings back a lot of memories." As if afraid she'd said too much, she busied herself unbuckling the harness. "I hope you brought supplies. I'm starving."

When she started to rise, he gripped her hand. "Tell me about those memories."

After all the years he'd known her, he knew very little about her life before opening the tavern.

"They aren't good. Not worth talking about."

When she tugged, he let her go. "Can't have you starving. Nally sent that android Arjay with plenty of supplies." He led the way to the galley.

"Arjay? Did he talk your arm off?" She picked up his wrist.

"Nope. He mustn't have been around long enough. Or you weren't."

"I wasn't. I was too busy convincing you to take a vacation." He opened the small cooler. "Ah. Fruits and veggies. I really missed that on the trip from Bricaldia. Here." He began handing her the makings for a light lunch.

"Hmm," Rissa said. "Dorlap cheese. I haven't had any for quite a while. I'll have to find out who his supplier is now that Celara doesn't come here anymore."

"Celara? Arjay's owner?"

Although the galley was larger than most on a starship, they kept bumping into each other. He would go one way and sure enough she went that way, too. After the third time she apologized, he put his hands on her shoulders.

"Go sit in the lounge. I'll bring lunch when it's ready."

"But I can help."

He turned her around then slid his hands down her arms. "If we bump hips again, sweetheart, I'll have to kiss you."

"Oh, I, uh . . ."

He let go of her hands, enjoying the blush that covered her cheekbones. "Go. Now. Before I have my wicked way with you."

The man was outrageous.

Rissa never blushed. Yet her face had gotten so hot when he talked about kissing her. Not just her face, either. By the Matriarch, when he mentioned wicked ways, she'd grown hot in her fem parts.

He was such a tease. As she paced the lounge with its expensive furnishings, she told herself to remember how he used to say outrageous things just to enjoy her discomfort. Though he had the mannerisms of an executive now, she often saw the impish gleam in his eyes of the carefree, fun-loving boy.

She remembered how he used to make her laugh with his silly antics. Stars, she missed that boy. Despite a few times when he teased, he seemed so different now. So serious that lines of worry pleated his forehead. He never mentioned what he'd been doing for the past six years. From the way he talked to Manager d'Arcanin, she assumed he worked for Rusteran Mining. She remembered how he often talked about how his father wanted him to go into the family business. And how he didn't want to be his father's clone. How he wanted to do something important with his life.

"You could have sat down." Dillan interrupted her thoughts. "You keep pacing like that, you'll wear a hole in the carpet."

She spun around. "I'm sorry. I didn't—"

The silly boy was back.

"Lunch is served." With the manners of a server at a high-class restaurant, he waved at the spread on the table across the lounge.

While she was thinking about times past, he'd brought out the food. And she hadn't even heard him.

He stood behind one of the padded chairs at the table. "Come, milady. Enjoy the finest Chez Rusteran has to offer." Then as he turned the chair, he gave her a sheepish grin. "I'd pull out the chair for you, but it's bolted to the deck."

"You are being silly."

"Hey, no scolding. We're on vacation. We can be silly if we want."

Properly chastised, she sat. "I'm sorry, Dillan. I'm not sure I know how to be silly."

He sat in the chair next to her then passed the plate of cheese slices. "Didn't you do silly things as a child? A teen?"

"No." Realizing how abrupt that sounded, she added, "Maybe as a small child. My father was very strict. He would admonish my mother when she encouraged me to play. It was easier to obey him than see her get into trouble."

She took a few slices of selba and a couple of enfil sticks. As she munched the crispy vegetables in silence, she thought about her mother and her own life after the fem left. Did she give any thought to her daughter after her last visit?

"Are your parents still alive?" Dillan asked.

"I don't know. Don't care, either."

"Whoa." He held up his hands. "My turn to apologize."

"No, mine. I shouldn't have said that the way I did."

"Tell me about them."

"Why?"

"Because they made you who you are. And I want to know you better."

"Why?" she asked again.

"You know why, Rissa." His eyes darkened. In anger or desire? "I'm your friend. I want to be more."

That was desire. *Holy sherd.*

"Did you plan this trip to seduce me?" She stood, nearly tripping over the immovable chair. "Not going to happen. You can turn the ship around right now."

With a show of reluctance, he got to his feet a lot slower than she had. "Has anyone ever told you you have a suspicious mind? If you recall, I invited Pela on this trip. I certainly wouldn't seduce you or any fem in front of an impressionable teen. Now sit down and finish your meal." His tone was worthy of a high-powered executive, which of course he was.

He made her feel small. It was her own fault, she knew. She could blame years of people trying to take advantage of her—business-wise as well as on a personal level. He'd never given her reason to believe he would do the same.

"I've lost my appetite."

He sat back down. "Then stay while I finish. I hate to eat alone. Too many years of doing that when I was growing up." He flicked a gaze up at her then munched on a stalk of enfil. "My mother was always too busy with her social life. My father, too busy working. After two meals in the big dining room, sitting alone at a table that was long enough for twenty, I took my plate out to the kitchen and told Cook that was where I was eating."

"Good for you." After his revelation, she decided to stay and keep him company. She picked up a selba slice and bit into the sweet vegetable. "My mother left when I was twelve. I wanted to go with her but . . ." With a shrug, she let her voice trail off.

"I guess I shouldn't be surprised that she left you behind. That's what my mother did. Mine left when I was fifteen."

"Are we bonding over mothers who deserted their children?" She gave him a wry glance.

"Yeah, I guess we are. And how about our fathers? You've met mine, I'm sure."

"Oh, yeah. When I first opened the tavern, he told me in no uncertain terms that I was a fool. That his miners wouldn't frequent a place owned by a fem unless it was a pleasure house."

"Never any doubt about what he thinks."

From his disgusted expression, she guessed that was Rusteran's parenting method, too. "Is he still that way with you?"

"Yes." Dillan started to rise then sat down. "When I was sixteen, he laid out my life. I was to go to the university, get a law degree, then join the company."

"Is that why you came out here all those years ago? To get away from him?"

"And his demands. After each trip, coming home was worse than the time before. I didn't want to go into law. Didn't know what I wanted to do, but it sure wasn't finding loopholes for him to exploit."

"But isn't that what you do now?"

"Yeah. And I hate it."

She folded her hands on the tabletop. "Then why do it? Why did you join his company?"

"Penance, I guess."

"What are you talking about?"

"Because I survived and Konner didn't. Well, you know what I mean. I thought he was dead, and I blamed myself. It was a wake-up call. After the search-and-rescue teams gave up looking for Konner, I went home and did what my father wanted. Figured I had to make something of my life."

"Are you happy?"

"No. The reason I came out here was to convince the Sauri chief to renegotiate his lease with Winslott Industries and sign with us. To renege on his word to Winslott. Of course, I didn't know the chief was Konner. When he told me I was just like my father, it made me sick."

"From what I've learned about him, you are nothing like your father. You care about people."

"Thanks for saying that. I'm not so sure it's true. If it were, I wouldn't be ashamed of what I do." Before she could protest, he stood and began to clear the table.

When he took a pile of dishes out to the galley, she gathered the rest and followed him. "If you don't like what you do, do something else."

"Like what?"

"What do you love?" She set the dishes on the counter. "What makes you happy?"

"Coming out here. Those were the happiest times of my life. Is that pitiful or what?" While he talked, he put away the uneaten food and loaded the dishes in the sanitizer.

"Not really. You were doing what you enjoyed." She leaned her shoulder against the edge of the portal. "You can't imagine how I envied you and your friends. You had no worries. You were always laughing and having a great time."

"You envied us?"

"When I was your age, my life consisted of following my father from one colony to another as he preached repentance and salvation. It was my job to hand out literature and pass the collection plate. I saw so much hopelessness from people who needed credits more than sermons."

"But you got out of that life. You left your father, right?"

"Actually, he left me. On Marin 5. Salvation does not come to those who sin." She spun on her heel and headed through the lounge to the sleeping quarters.

He caught up with her before she entered the room she and Pela had planned to share. "He left you on Marin 5? That's the ass end of space."

"No, it's not. But you can see it from there." She tried to laugh.

"What did you mean about sinning?"

"He couldn't very well preach morality with his unmarried pregnant daughter along."

CHAPTER 13

She closed the portal to the guest quarters before he could react to her announcement. Pregnant? Her father had left her on Marin 5? Abandoned her and her unborn child?

How could a man do that? How could a father?

Dillan sat in a chair in the lounge, elbows propped on the arms, fingers steepled, pondering how little he'd known about Rissa before this trip. In the moment before she closed the portal, he'd seen such anguish in her eyes. Such vulnerability.

Rissa Dix was never vulnerable. She was a strong fem who survived on the frontier. Not just survived, flourished. Her tavern had the best reputation for integrity. Fair prices, undiluted liquor, food at a decent price. No bar fights.

She'd made a good life for herself. But at what cost?

He looked up when Rissa hesitated before entering the lounge. Her eyes were red-rimmed, her hair damp around the edges as if she'd splashed water on her face. She took a seat on the sofa across from him. "I can't unring that bell, can I?" Her mouth twisted into a wry smile.

"An odd expression."

She waved that aside. "I listen to too many Terran vids." Without looking at him, she took a deep breath. "You have questions."

"That's one of the things I've always admired about you." When she raised her eyebrow, he gave her a half-smile. "You are forthright. A person doesn't have to wonder where they stand with you."

"Are you saying I'm rude?"

"Straight forward."

"I'm not sure that's any better."

"In my opinion, it is. You aren't afraid to tackle difficult subjects."

She snorted. "If you only knew . . ."

He leaned forward. "You don't show fear. Another thing I admire about you."

"I learned the hard way. If you show fear, people will take advantage."

"I would never take advantage of you."

After she rubbed between her eyes, she looked straight into his. "I know that, Dillan. You are different now."

"Yeah. So different you didn't recognize me."

"I am sorry about that. Blame the beard and long hair. I never expected you to return to Astron. Not after you lost your friend. Besides your whole demeanor has changed." Her mouth curved slightly. "I miss that carefree boy. He was fun."

"Are we rewriting history now? You disapproved of us." When she started to argue, he cut her off. "It was quite obvious. You thought we were stupid to take risks. And you were right. We thought we were invincible."

"I didn't so much disapprove as envied. I was never that carefree. You and your friends didn't have a care in the world. You had your own ships and plenty of credits. You didn't have to worry about how you were going to make it from one day to the next. Whether you'd have enough money for rent or food or meds if your baby got sick."

"That was a convoluted way to get back to the topic that had you running away."

Indignation flashed in her dark eyes. "I did not run away."

"A strategic retreat, then? To decide how you would get me to forget what you said."

"Will you? Forget?"

He wasn't going to let her off that easily, no matter how hopeful she looked. "No."

"I didn't think so."

When she didn't say more, he prompted her. "So you got pregnant. How?"

"The usual way. Surely, you don't want the prurient details."

"I don't know." He grinned. "Maybe I'd like to hear the details. Might give me some ideas on how to seduce you."

"You don't need ideas."

His grin widened. "Really? I wondered what I was doing wrong that you haven't fallen into my bed."

Shooting him a wry look, she said, "If you only knew."

"Tell me."

"And add to your over-developed ego?"

"Once again, we've strayed from talking about the elephant in the room." He gave her a quick smile to let her know he was teasing. "See? I know some Terran expressions, too."

"I met a smooth-talking boy who convinced me he loved me until we both discovered the consequences of his not renewing his sterility injections. He couldn't get off Thesus Terce fast enough."

"He left you because *he* didn't prevent pregnancy? Were you too young to get injected?"

"I was nineteen. Old enough. Bit of a problem, though. My injection came from a faulty batch. Out here, without Coalition guidelines, meds aren't regulated. The upshot was as soon as I got pregnant, the father of my child bailed. My self-righteous father blamed me, of course. He made sure I understood why I couldn't travel with him."

"Why didn't he leave you on Thesus Terce? That's a more civilized place than Marin 5."

"He had a reputation to preserve. After all, he might return to Thesus Terce someday."

"How did you manage? Marin 5 is nothing but rocks."

"Actually, those rocks contain some minerals. Winslott Industries is mining there now. Not twenty years ago, though. He dropped me off at an outpost that didn't take him too much out of his way. Not like he had a schedule to keep. Outpost 19. The inhabitants didn't bother giving it a name. The best and worst times of my life took place there."

Wary of derailing the conversation again, he just nodded.

"I had a difficult delivery. The medico said I'd never have any more children. That made Miri so very special. My one and only child." A smile tilted her lips. "You asked why I will do anything to get rid of traffickers." She leaned forward, hands dangling between her knees. "You were right about my fight against them being personal. Traffickers stole my baby."

Dillan had been afraid of that. She'd dropped enough hints before.

"She was six tendays old. Six tendays plus three days. Her name is Miri." She gave a short laugh. "*I* named her Miri. Who knows what she's called now. They sell babies, you know. People in the Central District who can't have children of their own will pay anything."

He could tell by her strained voice that she had difficulty talking about her child so he listened, not wanting to interrupt her tale with questions. He knew there was an underground market for people who wanted children, but he'd naively thought the children came from orphanages, children who were abandoned by their natural parents. Not stolen.

A smile played on her lips. "She was so beautiful. Big round eyes as dark as the night. When she smiled, my heart would leap for joy that this wonderful gift was mine. Oh, and her hair. By the stars, she had hair. Lots of black hair."

As she paused, the smile disappeared. "I worked nights at a bar, and my landlady watched Miri. One night, men burst in, roughed up the old fem, and took Miri."

Her whole demeanor changed. She curled her legs underneath her and hunched over holding her stomach. She looked . . . fragile. So at odds with how he'd always seen her. For several moments, she didn't speak. When she did, her voice was again strained.

"I tried to follow them, but I got to the spaceport too late. They'd already left. The dock master gave me a description of the ship, even their destination. So I ran back to my room, gathered up Miri's things, and got a ride from an indie pilot. Turned out the destination was false. No surprise there. I was foolish to think I could find them."

Hopelessness clouded her eyes.

"I spent the next seven years trying to find out what happened to my child. When I ran out of credits, I worked, usually in taverns where I could get the latest gossip on the slave trade. You know indie pilots."

"Worse than old ladies at a tea party?"

Her mouth quirked before sadness crept back into her expression. "I tracked down every lead. I even went to Traish. If I couldn't find the slavers, maybe I could find her. With both her parents Traishan, I thought maybe they'd sold Miri there."

"I take it you didn't find her."

She shook her head. "Found my mother, though. Finally got to ask her why she didn't take me with her when she left. You know what she said? It wasn't worth fighting my father. *I* wasn't worth fighting for. After she left me, I vowed that I'd never leave my child behind. Nothing would keep me from taking her with me no matter what happened. After seeing my mother with her new spouse, her new family, and her beautiful house, I renewed my vow. If—no, when I found Miri, nothing would keep us apart ever again."

The despair in her eyes shredded Dillan's heart.

"I failed her. I failed my child."

When she doubled over, clutching her waist, he had to go to her. She was too fragile to hold, though he wanted to do that and more. He wanted to take her onto his lap, cradle her, let her cry on his shoulder. She wouldn't. And she would regret crying in front of him.

He sat next to her on the long sofa. Not close but near enough that she could feel his presence. Without looking at her, he said softly, "Konner's accident was my fault."

Though she straightened, she didn't turn toward him.

"It was the end of the day. Konner had wanted to quit. The others had already left to go back to your place for drinks and sex at Fortuna's. That's all they thought about back then. Thrills, booze, and sex." He made a self-disgusted noise.

Out of the corner of his eye, he noticed she wasn't hugging herself anymore. She'd let her hand drop onto the cushion a few centimeters from his. How easy it would be to clasp it. To gain and give comfort from her touch.

Instead, he kept his hand to himself. "I didn't want to leave the mountain. I dared Konner to keep going. To reach one more peak. He'd said he was too tired, but I egged him on. Questioned his manhood. He usually ignored me when I acted like a kid. Not that time. When the other guys left and we were gathering our ropes, he said his father had ordered him home, even cut off Konner's credit access. The desperation in his eyes made me want to do something that would make him forget. 'Come on, Konner. One more climb,' I'd said."

Memories of what happened next flooded back.

"I went up first. I didn't know Konner wasn't ready. I dislodged some rocks. Not enough, I thought at the time, to do any damage. I yelled down to him to look out. My warning came too late. Those few rocks dislodged more, then boulders followed. I heard Konner cry out, but by the time I looked down he was gone. Not only did I drive him to his death, I caused it."

A slight pressure on his finger made him look down. Rissa was curling her baby finger around his. He caught his breath. She'd initiated contact. He didn't dare move. She might skitter away as fast as a nervous zircan. For several secs, they sat there, only their fingers touching.

"I never told anyone all that before."

"So for five years you thought you'd killed your best friend."

She understood. She really understood.

"I did. Until Jilly came back from the Rim and told me he was alive and well. Damn, I hated him after that. He let me believe all those years . . ."

Slowly, she slipped her hand into his. "I'm sorry you had to go through all that. Is that why you never came back?"

"Partly. I returned to the university, enrolled in the program my father had laid out. In between our adventures—" He scoffed. "—I'd taken a few classes. Nothing my father wanted me to take, of course."

"What classes?"

"Design. Just to show him I wasn't his clone. After Konner's accident, I put childish resentment aside and did what I was told. I had to make my father see I was a changed man. He didn't. Not at all."

"Are you still trying to prove yourself to him?"

"How did you know?"

They didn't look at each other, just sat side-by-side.

"You want me to see that you've changed, too." By squeezing his hand, she let him know the depth of her understanding.

"You are very perceptive. I'm not the kid you used to know. I'm not reckless. I don't take risks." He blew out a breath.

"And you miss it, don't you?"

For several secs, he pondered her question. What if he answered wrong? He had to tell her the truth. If it was the wrong thing to say . . . He'd have to take that chance.

"Sometimes I miss the thrill of adventure. For the past six years, my life has been rather dull. But what do I find when I come out here? *Thieves* raiding a transport. I expected those thieves to raid my ship next. That got my heart racing. Then when I was on a visit to the mountains— and my best friend—I discovered you were in trouble. More heart racing." He didn't mention Quin's warning about her. He'd never known such fear. He was taking a big risk that she would find out and resent him for getting her away from Astron.

Her soft laugh brought him back to their conversation. "I'll try to keep you on your toes."

"Are you all right now?" he asked.

"As all right as I'll ever be." After a pause, she added, "You're a good listener. Thank you."

She released his hand and walked across the lounge to the large viewport.

When Dillan came and sat next to her, she'd feared what he would do. And feared she couldn't handle it. If he'd touched her, put his arms around her, she would've dissolved into a blubbering heap.

To her surprise, he hadn't done anything other than sit next to her. The man confused her. She'd felt totally naked in front of him. No pretenses, nothing to shield her. He'd learned her deepest secrets. At first, she couldn't look at him. Couldn't bear to see the sympathy in his eyes. She didn't want sympathy.

She wanted her child. And he seemed to sense that.

As she stood in front of the round viewport, she saw the kaleidoscope of hyperspace. The ride in Dillan's ship was so smooth she'd forgotten.

His revelation hadn't surprised her. Six years ago, she'd sensed his anguish over losing his friend. Survivor's guilt, she'd thought, never realizing how deep that guilt had cut into him. That guilt, that anguish was etched into his conscience. How did he live with himself?

The same way she lived with the guilt of not protecting her child. Her heart ached for him.

When he followed her to the viewport, she thought he would come up behind her. Even put his big hands on her shoulders. Part of her wanted that comfort. The other part—the dominant part—feared that she would break down. Like sitting on the sofa near her but not touching, he seemed to sense that she wasn't ready for comfort. He walked around her, putting a small distance between them, then leaned against the bulkhead to the left of the viewport.

"Does anyone else know about your child?"

"In Astron? Kiran suspects, but I've never told anyone. Not even Celara. If she ever finds out, she'll be hurt I never shared that with her. I couldn't. Talking about . . . Miri is not easy."

"Why did you come to Astron? Did you get a lead?"

She took a long breath then blew it out slowly. "Seven years is a long time to focus on an impossible mission. After talking to my mother, I wanted to get as far away from her and her perfect life with her perfect new family as I could. Worry for Miri had clawed at my stomach so much I collapsed in the street. Instead of going to a med center, I went to the spaceport. I walked up to the first indie pilot I saw, and asked him if I could go with him. I didn't care where he was going. Turned out it was Astron Colony."

"Whoa. Back up. You collapsed in the street?"

"Yep. Ulcers can do that, you know." She rested her forehead against the view portal. That had been such an awful time.

"Sweet Divinity, Babe."

When he reached for her, she shrunk back. "Please don't."

"Okay." He looked hurt. "What did you do?"

"Besides lying on a bunk dying?" She scoffed. "Fortuna came to the spaceport to pick up some new girls. She took one look at me and made me come with her. She took me in, nursed me, listened to my crying. Even though she didn't know why."

"I'm honored you took me into your confidence."

"As I got better, I was so tired of chasing blind leads and getting nowhere. Astron felt . . . right. Safe. So I stayed."

"Is that when stopped looking for your child?"

As she took in a breath, she shuddered. "I'll never stop. I will find her someday."

"I believe you will."

"I'm sorry you went through so much unnecessary grief over Konner. The guilt you felt for so long had to have been devastating." When he didn't respond more than a grunt, she went on. "He made his own choice to keep climbing. You might have some responsibility for goading him, but in the end he chose to continue. You can't bear all the responsibility."

"Just like it wasn't your fault traffickers grabbed your baby? You weren't even there."

In her mind, she knew he was right. But in her heart, she knew differently.

"If I'd been home, the traffickers wouldn't have taken her."

"How do you know that?"

"I would have fought them off. I wouldn't have let them take her."

"Do you seriously believe that? If they didn't hesitate to beat up an old fem, what would they have done to you? If you'd tried to fight them, they would've killed you. Life means nothing to those scum."

"Maybe."

He stepped closer. "Look at me. Ever since I helped you with those children, I researched child trafficking. I've learned more than I ever wanted to know about those in the slave trade. They are ruthless people. From the bosses to the people they hire."

Everything he said was true. Again her mind told her one thing, but her heart wasn't convinced.

He glanced at his wrist comm. "We'll be at Vesteron in three hours. You're welcome to explore the ship, take a nap, use the computer. Whatever pleases you."

"I'd like to use your computer."

He opened a set of doors in what looked like storage cabinets on the wall to her right. A dropdown shelf revealed a monitor. "You can't connect to the Central District databases while we're in hyperspace, but several have been downloaded onto the system."

After unlatching a chair next to the table, he brought it over to the monitor and relocked it to the deck. "All yours."

When she sat, he gave her his personal password.

She looked up at him. "Are you sure you trust me with that?"

"Rissa, I trust you with my life." He walked away, leaving her alone.

Swiveling around, she saw him enter the command center. His words stayed with her. He trusted her.

"Computer, search birth records. Female. Traishan. Birthdate . . ." With each filter, the number of records diminished. Still, the sheer number of entries overwhelmed her.

Dillan was right about the databases. He'd given her access to more than she could imagine. More than she'd been able to access at home. And this wasn't even—

"Are you still at it?" Dillan broke her concentration. "I'm surprised your eyes haven't fallen out of your head."

She leaned back, aware of the strain in her eyes and the ache in her neck. When she rolled her shoulders, he put his hands there.

"Relax. I'm going to give you my galaxy-famous massage."

"Galaxy famous? Oh, my."

His fingers probed a knotted muscle. At first, it hurt. But as he worked the spot, the knot eased. She moaned at the relief.

"Am I hurting you?"

"Yes, no. I mean it's wonderful. Don't stop."

For several mins, he massaged her neck and shoulders. "What you need is my famous full body massage."

At the thought of his hands all over her, she stiffened.

He blew out an exasperated breath. "That just ruined the past five mins. Relax. We don't have time for anything more than this. I came to tell you we're almost to Vesteron."

She felt foolish for thinking he was trying to get her into bed with the excuse of a massage.

"Maybe tonight," he said.

She swiveled around. "Maybe tonight what?" Almost afraid she knew.

Before walking away, he turned and gave her a cheeky grin. "That full body massage."

CHAPTER 14

Rissa raced after him into the command center. "Don't count on it, Rusteran."

"Shh. I need to contact Traffic Control. Caravel ID RM44783, requesting clearance to land." He leaned back to see her. "Sit down and buckle up."

As she slid into the copilot's seat, she marveled at the sight of the planet. Magnos Prime—especially the area around Vesteron Colony—was so green. Such a contrast to Astron's desert. And there were large expanses of water. Lakes and rivers. And an ocean.

"I can't believe how different this is from Astron."

"Haven't you ever been here before?"

Before she could answer, Traffic Control announced they were next in line to land. She waited until Dillan started the descent. "A long time ago. With my father. And then when searching for Miri." She swallowed the catch in her throat. "Is that Vesteron Colony?"

A sprawling expanse of buildings came into focus.

"Not a colony anymore. Last year, it incorporated into a city. With the influx of settlers as well as being the headquarters for Malcor Sector's Administration, it was bound to happen."

He brought the ship to a soft landing before Traffic Control directed him to a berth. Dillan taxied over to a place between a luxury yacht and a small cargo hauler that had seen better days.

Within no time, he'd grabbed their gear and ushered her out of the ship. After insisting on carrying her own bag, she slung the strap over her shoulder and proceeded down the ramp. She staggered at the sudden heat and humidity. Dillan grabbed her arm to steady her.

"Easy there. This place always hits me hard, too. It's the gravity and being in the middle of a rainforest." When he stopped to close the ramp, she leaned against the side of the ship. "Take several deep breaths. That always helps me adjust."

She did and found out he was right. It did help.

"I hope you brought lighter clothes." He gave her a quick grin. "You will sweat like crazy otherwise."

She kept up with him as he easily strode through the hangar. Or maybe he shortened his stride to match hers. "I don't own anything different. This is it." She waved at her long-sleeve shirt and trousers. "Never needed anything else."

"Then we'll stop at a mercantile and get you some clothes."

"That's not necessary. We won't be here long."

As they left the hangar and entered the main 'port, she couldn't believe all the people. Some waited on benches, others milled around, while more strode to and from waiting vessels. She couldn't wait to get outside. Too many people. It had been like this, only more so, when she went to Traish. After being on the Rim for so long with minimal people at each colony or outpost, she felt hemmed in, overwhelmed by the cacophony of so many speaking in their native tongues. Her ears hurt.

The smells were worse. The aroma of food in various kiosks that lined the corridor, the odor from the passers-by that ranged from perfumes to unwashed. She took a handkerchief out of her pocket and pretended to blow her nose. The small cloth did little to cover up the overpowering scents.

Dillan gently squeezed her elbow. "We'll be out of here in a couple of mins."

That he realized her distress surprised her. Though she thought she'd hidden her reaction, he always seemed to be attuned to her moods. She wasn't sure if she should appreciate his attention or fear it. He saw too much.

Getting away from the spaceport helped. While the heat and humidity diminished only slightly, at least the air was cleaner.

Vesteron was indeed a city, with synthcrete sidewalks and streets instead of boardwalks and dirt roads. A multitude of shops and businesses lined the walk. After leading her down three blocks then over to another, he suddenly stopped.

"I should have asked if you minded walking. After being cooped up in the ship, I find walking helps me stretch my legs. We can hire a vehicle if you want."

"I don't mind walking. You seem to know where you're going. Do you come here often?"

"We own two barzilium mines up in the mountains and another two on the southern continent. After the riots two years ago, I made a few trips out to convince the managers that fair treatment of the miners was as important as production."

"That isn't how it's been."

"I know. I'm doing my best to change the image of the all-powerful mine owner who sits in his cushy office on Bricaldia counting his money and demanding more. Ah. Here we are."

He stopped in front of an apparel shop. This was no general mercantile that sold everything from tools to housewares to serviceable unisex garments. In the windows that flanked the door, figures displayed gauzy dresses and pants cut off at the knees or higher.

"I thought you were leading us to a boarding house. I told you I don't need any clothes."

When he opened the door, cool air rushed out. It was such a welcome relief from the heat she went inside. She was so stunned by the variety of fem's clothing that she stopped and Dillan bumped into her. He slipped her tote off her shoulder then, along with his, set it in a corner.

A pretty fem with blond hair came forward. "May I help you?"

"Uh, no—"

"Yes." Dillan cut her off. "She needs clothes appropriate for the climate." He headed for a rack of short pants before turning to Rissa. "What size do you wear?"

"Size?" She shrugged. Since the unisex shirts and trousers came in three sizes—large, larger, and super large—she said, "Larger?"

The fem eyed her for a moment. "Let's take a couple of outfits to the dressing room and try them on." She grabbed three pairs of knee-length pants and from another rack, three shirts. "Come."

Rissa looked at Dillan in panic. "What did she mean try them on? I'm not stripping here in the store."

He gave her an indulgent smile. "The salesperson will take you to a private room where you can try on the clothes and see what fits. I am surprised she didn't just scan you."

The blond fem—salesperson Dillan had called her—beckoned from the back of the store. Warily, Rissa followed. Again he was right. The salesperson showed her into a room with mirrors on three walls. Stars, she looked so . . . different from the blonde in her pale green dress.

When Rissa thought the fem would leave, she didn't. She shut the door enclosing both of them. "All right now. Let's get you out of those horrid Rimmer clothes." She reached for Rissa's shirt.

"I'll remove my own clothes after you leave."

"But—"

"After you leave."

"Yes, ma'am. When something fits, open the door."

This time Rissa did the eying. "Why?"

"So I can bring more clothes in your size."

"I don't need any more clothes." Then she thought about how hot she'd been outside. "One outfit will be enough."

The salesperson smiled then left.

Rissa shrugged off her shirt and baggy trousers before realizing she should have removed her boots first. When she glanced in the mirror and saw her serviceable undergarments, she thought of the fancy, skimpy ones Fortuna's girls had donated to Pela and Anaris. Definitely not what Rissa wore. And she wasn't about to spend her hard-earned credits on something only she would see.

When Dillan talked her into a vacation in Vesteron, she hadn't envisioned shopping for clothes. After trying on and discarding pants that were too tight, she settled on a pair that fit. The shirts were another story. While her breasts weren't overlarge, the largest shirt was too tight. She closed it as best she could.

"I need a larger shirt," she said to the salesclerk as she opened the door.

Only it wasn't the salesclerk leaning against the wall. Dillan raised an eyebrow at her. "Nice."

"No, no, no." The clerk hurried up behind him. "You should not be here, sir." She turned to Rissa and examined the tags on the shirt and pants. "I know what you need and it's not larger clothes. I will be right back. You, sir, come with me."

Dillan winked at Rissa before following the disapproving fem.

Within mins, she was back with gaily colored undergarments. "These will help your clothing fit better. And your spouse will enjoy seeing you in them."

Rissa groaned. She was about to say that Dillan wasn't her spouse when the clerk said, "He told me how your clothes were lost in transit, and you had to wear that dreadful outfit. I'll take care of you, ma'am. A fem should always wear pretty things."

Flabbergasted, Rissa couldn't think of anything to say. Her silence didn't seem to faze the fem because she left quickly.

So Dillan had come up with a lie to explain why she wore Rimmer attire. He must be ashamed to be seen with her, and that's why he'd dragged her into the clothing store. For several secs, she thought about throwing on her old clothes and stomping out. Out into the heat and humidity. She reconsidered.

With reluctance, she took off her ugly—yes, she admitted they were ugly—undergarments and put on the new ones. They *were* comfortable. She looked in the mirror. And pretty. Quickly, before the salesperson opened the door, she drew on the pants and shirt. They fit better. Even the shirt.

Again, she looked in the mirror. All right, she looked better. She looked like a fem, instead of a barkeep who wore masculine clothes. That had never bothered her before. She lived in a rough colony. Only fems like the pleasure providers at Fortuna's wore such pretty clothes. One thing for sure, she never wanted to be confused with one of Fortuna's girls.

A quick rap on the door startled Rissa out of her thoughts. The salesperson called, "Come out when you're ready."

Rissa opened the door.

"Much better," the fem cooed. "I knew those colors would look good with your coloring. You're Traishan, right?" After Rissa nodded, she said, "I'll be right back with more."

"Wait," Rissa called. "I don't—"

The fem disappeared between the racks of clothes.

"That's it. I'm done." Rissa gathered up her *dreadful* clothes and started out of the little room before realizing she wasn't wearing her boots. She stuffed her feet into them and clomped out.

While she was looking around for the salesperson or where to pay for the garments she wore, Dillan approached. "Much better. You'll feel a lot cooler in those clothes. But the boots have to go." He grinned. "Too hot. Come. I found some sandals for you."

"No more, Rusteran. My boots are fine."

They weren't, but she didn't want to admit it. He was being too high-handed. Then he held up a pair of low-heeled sandals that captured the green and blue in her new shirt.

"Try them on," he said. "If you don't like them, we'll find something you do."

After making her sit, he squatted in front of her and began to unlace her boots.

"Stop that. I can do take them off."

He swatted away her hands. "Would you please not fight me on this?"

After he slipped the sandals on her, she held up one foot. The sandals fit. And looked better than her boots. When he told her to walk around, she discovered the sandals were quite comfortable. She wiggled her toes. Yes, very comfortable.

"How much are they?" she asked.

"Don't worry about that." He headed to the back of the store.

She hurried behind him. "What do you mean don't worry? What if they're so expensive I can't afford them?"

He waved that aside then called the salesperson. "Cut the tags off her garments. She'll wear them. And the sandals."

She'd never heard him use such an imperious tone before and was about to scold him when she saw how the fem reacted.

"Of course, Mister Rusteran." She removed the tags from Rissa's new pants and shirt. But when she started to open the shirt, Rissa backed up.

"My apologies, ma'am. We can take care of the undergarments in the dressing room."

When they were back in the small room, the clerk said, "Your spouse told me how shy you are. I am so sorry I didn't realize . . ." With quick efficiency, she removed those tags, too. "We are so pleased that you came here. If I can be of any more service, please let me know."

"Where do I pay for these clothes?"

The fem laughed. "Mister Rusteran has already taken care of it."

With steam coming out of her ears, Rissa strode out to find Dillan. How dare he pay for her clothes as if she were a kept fem. Or a spouse.

"You look lovely, Rissa." His smile and the pleasure in his eyes diminished her ire.

Instead of berating him in front of a salesperson, she decided to have words with him outside. After thanking the blond fem for her help, Rissa gave Dillan a haughty nod and walked out of the store. Then she had to wait for him. And wait.

When he finally came out, he was carrying their totes. Well, sherd. She'd forgotten all about the gear they'd brought from the ship. When she reached for hers, he held onto it.

"Carrying your bag will ruin your new shirt."

"About the clothes. You can't—"

"Are you comfortable?"

"Well, yes. But that's not the point. You—"

He put his hand in the middle of her back to lead her forward. "That is the point. You are not used to the climate here. With your heavy clothes, you could faint from the heat."

"I've never fainted in my life, and I'm not about to start. Astron is hot. I'm used to it."

"Not this kind of heat. It sucks all the energy out of a person. Now say 'Thanks, Dillan' and let's get something to eat. I know this lovely little café."

"Thank you. No one's ever bought clothes for me before."

He led her down a block then into an eatery named Baro's. As they entered, Rissa sighed in pleasure at the delicious aromas. The café was warm—in a good way—and inviting. A middle-aged fem with dark hair liberally sprinkled with gray greeted them.

"Mister Rusteran, you came back."

"How could I stay away, Kleema? Baro's cooking has been pulling me since we landed."

"Kleema and Baro?" Rissa said. "Celara d'Enfaden speaks well of you."

Kleema clapped her hands. "You know Celara? She was just here."

Rissa didn't want to reveal that she hadn't seen Celara in nearly a year and then missed her when she'd stopped in Astron.

"And you are?" Kleema asked.

"My apologies," Dillan said as the fem led them to a table. "This is Rissa Dix, owner of the best tavern on the Rim."

"Rissa? Celara speaks well of you, too." When they were seated, she said, "The Mid-Day special is Mindavian crepes with Baro's *secret* sauce." She winked.

"Sounds good," Dillan proclaimed.

Rissa agreed. Though she'd tasted it once, she never bought Mindavian meat for the tavern because it was too expensive. While waiting for their meal, she looked around the eatery. It must be past Mid-Day as less than half the thirty or so tables were filled.

"From the way Celara talked, I thought this place was much smaller," she said.

"It used to be about a third the size. As the colony expanded so did the café. The last time I was here, they'd just finished their third expansion. Baro is an excellent chef. He'd make a fortune if he opened a restaurant in Eleganza."

"Why doesn't he?"

"Because we're happy here." Kleema had returned with drinks and must have heard the end of their conversation.

Dillan smiled up at her. "Well, I'm happy you're here. I can't wait to taste those crepes." After the fem left, he settled back in his chair. "What would you like to see first? The sacred temples? The tallest waterfall in Malcor Sector? Shopping?"

"No shopping. Even if you're ashamed of what I wear."

His eyes widened. "Ashamed? What are you talking about?"

"You bought me clothes because you don't want to be seen with a Rimmer fem." Embarrassed that she'd blurted out her feelings, she ducked her head.

"Look at me." He tilted up her chin. "First, I'm not ashamed of you. Never. I don't care what you wear. You could go naked." He gave her a wicked smile that made her hot . . . and not because of the weather. "I could see how the climate here was getting to you. I wanted you to be comfortable."

"Yes, well." She was ashamed that she'd misjudged him. "I'm still not happy that you paid for my clothes."

"Lighten up, girl. I have more credits than I know what to do with."

"Must be nice." She didn't bother hiding her sneer.

Dillan reached across the table for her hand. "This is a vacation. I want you to be happy."

He looked so earnest, so sincere, she couldn't berate him again, especially when he changed the subject and talked about the sights they could see. Between the delicious meal, the zaloon tea that more than relaxed her, and Dillan's easy conversation, the time went by quickly. When she tried to pay for her own meal, he insisted it was his treat. She knew she should have asked more questions about the arrangements on this trip.

Before they left the café, Kleema encouraged them to return. She even hugged both of them.

Once they were outside, he led them back to the main street. "Time to find the hotel."

"Hotel? I thought we were staying at a boarding house."

"Are you going to argue every little thing with me?"

Two blocks later, he stopped at a palatial ten-story building that looked like it should be in the Central District not out on the Rim. They didn't belong there. Correction, *she* didn't belong in such a grand place. As she saw in the dress shop, Dillan had such presence he would fit in anywhere.

"I'm not sure . . ."

"Relax. You will love this place. I've stayed here before."

She pulled him aside. "Dillan, I can't afford this place."

"I can." Taking her hand, he strolled into the lobby.

"May I take your bags, sir?" A man in a black gold-trimmed uniform approached.

Dillan handed over their gear then walked to a long desk behind which stood three people—two fems and a man. The fems were talking to the people in front of them, while the man beckoned Dillan.

"Mister Rusteran, welcome back."

"Thank you, Melus. It's good to be back."

Melus consulted his computer then called the man carrying their gear. "Porter, Mr. Rusteran is staying in the Loren Sea Suite. Enjoy your stay, sir. And ma'am."

The porter led them to a conveyance where they were whisked up to a room on the top floor. As they passed doors, she noticed signs with names of waterways in the Central District—Lake Odarolo Suite, Granadia Ocean Suite, even one named Nicorama River Suite named after the river that ran through the capital city of Traish. The man opened the door for the Loren Sea Suite and ushered them in. Overwhelmed by the opulence, Rissa tried not to gawk. As soon as the porter left, she whirled on Dillan.

"This place is enormous. It's almost as big as my tavern. But where do we sleep? And don't think for a moment that we're sharing that sofa."

He laughed in a gentle manner. "Sweetheart, I would love to share your bed, but don't worry. This is a sitting room. You have your own bedroom." He opened double doors set into the wall on the left. "This is yours. Mine is across the way."

As she walked in, she marveled at the luxury—a huge bed covered by linens she'd only seen on vids and her own sanitary bigger than her bedroom.

"The closet is on the left." He pointed.

When she opened the folding doors, she exclaimed, "That man led us to the wrong room. Someone's clothes are in here. We have to leave." She started toward the door.

Dillan held her shoulders. "This *is* ours and those are your clothes."

"What?" She pulled away. "Where did they come from? How—"

"I had the owner of the dress shop pick out enough outfits for two tendays."

"Two tendays? We won't be here that long."

"I wanted to give you a choice," he said patiently. "We can send back what you don't like."

"Then you can send them all back. I don't need—"

Again he held her shoulders. "Rissa, shut up. Can't you just accept a gift?"

"Gifts come with strings."

"Not these. Not nice lodgings or meals. Not this vacation. No strings. No expectations."

"How can I believe that? This is all too much. I never should have let you talk me into leaving Astron."

When she tried to pull away again, not only didn't he let go, he pulled her close. "Rissa, Rissa, Rissa. What am I going to do with you?"

He cupped the back of her head and held her.

"I don't know." Her voice was muffled against his shoulder.

He gently created a small space between them. "Now a flirtatious fem would ask what I wanted to do with her." He gave her that boyish grin she remembered from years ago.

"I guess I'm not flirtatious."

"No, you're not. That's what I lo—like about you. You aren't afraid to speak your mind. You are upfront, no guessing what you're thinking."

He'd almost said *love*. What he *loved* about her. That couldn't be right. Must have been a slip of the tongue.

"What I'm thinking right now is that we should send those clothes back." At his disappointed look, she realized how ungrateful she sounded. "Some of the clothes. Really, Dillan, I can't wear all those."

She walked to the closet and pulled out three long dresses. "When am I ever going to wear these?"

"When we go out for Last Meal. I know you, Rissa. You won't want to go into some of the finer restaurants. You'll say you aren't dressed properly, and then we'll both miss out on a fabulous meal."

She grimaced. "You are probably right."

"What do you mean probably?" His grin was infectious. "I know I'm right."

"Conceited, too." She hung the dresses back in the closet then pulled out two pairs of short pants. "I can't wear these."

"And why not? They are perfect for going to the beach."

"Beach? I didn't notice any beaches when we were landing."

"Because they're on a secluded lake. The rainforest canopy shields it."

"Well, I'm still not wearing them." Heat burned her cheeks. "I don't use depilatory pills. You saw that salesperson. Her legs—"

"She's the shop owner."

"I don't care if she's president of the Coalition of Planets. Her legs were not hairy. Like mine." Again heat flooded her face.

"Did you hear me say the lake is secluded? Nobody will see your legs but me."

"That's still a problem."

"Not for me. I love you the way you are. Hairy legs and all." He kissed her forehead. "Let's go see those sacred temples. I hear they are really beautiful."

He left before she could protest. And he'd used the L-word. It was just an expression, she reminded herself as she used the sanitary. The way someone said they loved Galerian ale or a sunrise.

Dillan Rusteran did not love her. He couldn't.

CHAPTER 15

When Rissa entered the sitting room, Dillan sucked in a breath. "You are beautiful."

She'd coiled her braid into a sophisticated knot at the back of her head, displaying the elegance of her neck. She must have found the cosmetics the shopkeeper included with the outfits sent to the hotel. Rissa's high cheekbones glowed, her exotic eyes appeared more mysterious, and her lips looked ripe for kissing.

Down, boy. He would scare her off if he tried.

He'd been right about the color when he told the dress shop owner to select an evening dress for Rissa. With her dark hair and eyes, the cream gown was perfect against her olive skin. He admired the way the strapless dress showed off her broad shoulders and strong arms. Her toes encased in strappy sandals peeked out from under the gown.

"I'm afraid it will fall down." She tugged on the bodice.

With a chuckle, he walked toward her. "You have enough to hold it up."

The high-heeled sandals put her at eye level with him. He clasped her hand and twirled her around. The fabric crisscrossed, showing delectable glimpses of her back, then draped beautifully from her waist to the floor.

"You don't have to worry about anyone seeing your hairy legs." He gave her a teasing smile.

She swatted his arm then quickly sobered. "I'm not sure. This shows too much . . . skin."

"It does." Again he grinned. When she glared at him, he amended, "Just enough. It's perfect. *You* are perfect. We need to leave. Our reservation is in fifteen mins."

"Do we have to walk far? I'm not sure if I can walk a long way in these shoes." She stuck out her sandal-shod foot.

"Not far at all."

He escorted her out of the room and down the hall to the conveyance. Inside, she gave him an appraising glance. "You look very nice."

"This old thing?" He waved his hand over the black formal suit he'd brought from the ship on the chance that she would go along with his plans.

She deserved to be treated like a very special fem. He wanted to shower her with gifts, take her to the best places, help her see what an exceptional person she was. That he desired her no matter what she wore.

When the conveyance doors opened on the second level, he put his hand in the middle of her back to usher her out. He wanted anyone who saw this beautiful fem to know that she was his. When he threaded his fingers under the straps, he felt a shiver go through her. But she didn't pull away. Progress.

When they entered a restaurant with subdued lighting, she hesitated before stiffening her back and walking forward.

Dillan leaned close and said softly, "That's my girl. You are the most beautiful fem in the place."

With a slight turn of her head, she said equally softly, "How can you tell? It's dark."

Upon giving his name, Dillan mused at the attitude of the host. Complete deference. The Rusteran name had power in Vesteron, thanks to the mines.

After they were seated, Rissa looked around. "I've never seen so many fancy-dressed people." She grimaced as if working herself up to an unpleasant task. "You were right about the clothes. Thank you. I feel as if I belong here."

"You belong anywhere, Rissa. If you believe, everyone else will. You could have walked in here in your Rimmer coarse-spun, and everyone would have admired you."

She snorted.

"It's all a matter of attitude." He picked up the menu. "What will you have?"

After she examined the bill of fare, she looked up, panic in her eyes. "I have no idea what these dishes are," she whispered.

"Do you trust me to order for both of us?"

She breathed out a sigh. "Please."

During the meal, they talked about their excursion into the rainforest. She became more animated, less intimidated by their surroundings. Eventually, she relaxed. While discussing the hauteur of the temple guide, her throaty laugh caught the attention of a trio of men seated nearby. When they looked at her in interest, Dillan's glower made sure they understood Rissa was with him. They nodded at him in admiration.

Damn right they should.

"Is something wrong?" she asked.

"Just making sure those oglers mind their own business."

She looked around. "Who?"

One of the men raised his glass to her and smiled.

She blushed. "Oh. I see." Then she giggled. "I've never been ogled before."

"You haven't been looking. Every man who passed you today nearly tripped trying to catch your eye."

"You exaggerate." Her blush deepened.

She was such a delight to tease.

The server chose that moment to clear their plates. "Would you care to see a dessert menu?"

"Oh, no. I couldn't eat another thing."

At the same time, Dillan said, "Bring a serving of white pudding and two spoons."

After the server left, Rissa leaned forward and looked askance. "White pudding? How bland."

"Wait until you taste it."

She reached across and covered his hand. "Seriously, I couldn't eat another bite. I have never had such a rich meal."

"A taste." He flipped his hand over and squeezed her fingers. "That's all. Just a taste."

When the server returned, he carried a large scalloped bowl. Dillan enjoyed Rissa's wide-eyed look as she placed her hand in her lap to give the man room for the desert. Again she waited until the server left before speaking.

"That's enormous. It's enough for four people."

He took one of the long spoons the server had left and scooped a small portion of the creamy confection. He held it out to her. When she reached for the spoon, he shook his head. "Taste."

Though she looked mildly uncomfortable, she opened her mouth. When her lips closed over the spoon, it was Dillan's turn to feel uncomfortable. Sheer bliss crossed her features before her eyes fluttered closed. His trousers shrunk.

That was how she would look when they made love.

Rissa couldn't believe how wonderful the white pudding tasted. What a prosaic name for such a delicious treat. Eagerly, she reached for the spoon Dillan held only to have him dip it into the thick creamy dessert that held an unusual flavor. She couldn't resist taking another taste, if only to figure it out.

By the stars, the dessert tasted better than anything she'd ever had.

When she opened her eyes, she discovered Dillan was watching her, his eyes dilated with desire. *Oh, sherd.*

"What's in this?" She hoped her question would erase his lustful expression. "I can't place the flavor."

He cleared his throat and shifted in his seat. "It's, uh, zillond."

"Zillond? I'm not familiar with that."

"A nut from the zilla tree. I'm not surprised you didn't recognize it. It's so rare that it's usually only found on Bricaldia."

"Oh, my stars. If it's that rare, this must cost a fortune. You shouldn't have ordered it."

"Watching you enjoy it is worth every single credit." He dipped the spoon into the dessert and offered it to her. "Another taste?"

She rolled her eyes. "Last one. I'm so full you'll have to roll me out of here."

"It is good to see a fem enjoy my food." A slender older man in a white jacket had approached the table. He gave Dillan a short nod. "It is good to see you, Mr. Rusteran. I am pleased you returned."

Dillan stood and shook hands. "Chef, a pleasure to see you, too."

"And who is your lovely companion?"

"Chef Hesteran, may I present Rissa Dix."

She started to give him the traditional open-palm Rimmer greeting when he clasped her hand in both of his.

"A pleasure to meet a fem who appreciates my work. You must return tomorrow. I will prepare a feast that will—what is the expression?" He tapped his graying temple. "I remember. It will knock your socks off."

To hear this obviously sophisticated man use a Terran term was so amusing she laughed. "Then we must return, Dillan. I've never had my socks knocked off before."

"Good. Enjoy the rest of your meal." After he left, the chef spoke briefly to their server before returning to the kitchen.

"He looks like he belongs in the Central District," Rissa said.

"That is where he came from. He owns a chain of highly successful restaurants in Eleganza and the surrounding cities."

"Why did he come out here?" Most people came to the Rim because they either wanted an adventure or a new life. Some were even running away from something or someone.

"He wanted a challenge. And he seemed to realize that Vesteron is about to become a major hub." He signaled the server then asked for the bill.

The server smiled. "Chef already took care of it. Thank you for coming." With that, he left.

Rissa arched her eyebrow. "Chef must like you. Dinner tonight and tomorrow. Wow."

A slight flush crept up his neck. "The Rusteran Mines are important to the economy."

"Are you being modest? He likes you, not your mines."

"My father's mines." He grimaced. "Would you like anything else?"

She groaned. "Not another bite." Before she could rise, he came around to pull out her chair. "You are spoiling me, Dillan Rusteran."

"My goal in life." His silly grin made her laugh.

He said such outrageous things. She didn't believe him, of course.

The walk down the long corridor to their suite did nothing to lessen the anxiety building inside Rissa. When she'd walked out of her bedroom before dinner, desire had flared in his eyes. She feared he would act on that desire when they were alone.

To be honest, a not-so-small part of her wanted him to.

She hadn't been with a man for a very long time. The last was an indie pilot who used to come to Astron then found a more profitable route. She didn't miss *him*, but she did miss a man's arms around her and her body's release. Being self-sufficient wasn't enough. She certainly couldn't indulge in an affair with any of the colony's inhabitants. Not that she cared about the gossip. After it was over, she dreaded working with a man she'd been intimate with.

Dillan was different.

He would return to the Central District. He didn't belong out here. That was for sure. They wouldn't see each other on a day-to-day basis. Perhaps he would come back every few years. That would be enough.

"You've been quiet since we left the restaurant." He closed the door behind him.

"Thinking." She stopped in the middle of the sitting room and turned to him.

What would he do? What should *she* do? Should she just walk up to him and loop her arms around his neck? What if that wasn't what he wanted? What if she'd misinterpreted his earlier look?

As she dithered, he came to her. Desire flared in his eyes again. Relief swept through her. She wasn't mistaken.

"I, uh, had a lovely evening." She kicked off the once-comfortable sandals that were now cutting into her feet.

He slipped his arms around her waist but didn't pull her close. He just watched her. "The evening isn't over."

Oh, sweet Matriarch. The heat in his gaze. He wanted her.

His fingers traced around the crisscross straps, each touch lighting mini-fireworks inside her. He even drew his hand down below the dress to the base of her spine. The fireworks exploded. It was all she could do not to let her head loll. She wanted to tell him to do that again, but his hand went higher. When he reached the topmost strap, he traced the edge around to the front. He grazed the top of her breasts before dipping his finger into the middle.

"I knew you would look beautiful in this dress." His husky voice sent shivers through her. "I just didn't know how beautiful."

Kiss me, she silently begged. She placed her hands on his forearms, wanting to draw him closer but waiting to see what he would do. Normally she wouldn't hesitate. She could be aggressive. But it was different with Dillan. Her insecurities cried out to let him take the lead.

When he tipped her chin, she thought for sure he was going to do it. Her eyes closed in anticipation.

He dropped his arms. "Want to watch a vid?"

CHAPTER 16

Dillan chuckled at Rissa's startled expression. She'd wanted him. Almost as much as he wanted her. Yet he denied them both. A calculated move that might backfire on him. When she'd put her hands on his arms, he thought she would urge him closer. Her passivity didn't sit well with him. He wanted her to respond. Needed her to respond.

He walked over to the sofa. "Computer, play *Starship Ghost*."

"What are you doing?" She followed him. When the huge screen on the wall opposite the sofa lit up, she said, "Computer, shut down."

The screen went dark.

With as innocent expression as he could muster, he said, "It's a popular show back on Bricaldia. I thought you might enjoy it."

"I don't want to watch a vid." She hesitated in front of him.

"I'm sure I saw a deck of cards in one of the drawers while waiting for you to come out." He turned toward the lamptable next to the sofa.

She reached out and grabbed the front of his shirt. "No."

"You don't want to play cards?" Again, he tried for the innocent look.

"No games, Dillan. No vids." She pulled him close. "No teasing."

"I do love to tease you."

When he didn't put his arms around her, just let them dangle at his side, she clasped his hands and drew them around her waist. "Hold me."

All right. If he wasn't so busy following her command, he would have done a happy dance.

"As you wish." When he let his hands rest on her hips but didn't draw her closer, he enjoyed the impatience in her eyes. "I'm holding you."

"Tighter." She pressed on his back. "Like you did before."

"Like this?" He slipped his leg between hers then slid his hands down to cup her bottom. If she couldn't tell how much he wanted her, a cold shower would be necessary.

As she sighed, a shudder ran through her. Now that was more like it.

"Now kiss me."

"Yes, ma'am." He lightly touched her lips.

"Do you need an instruction manual, Rusteran? Kiss me." She clasped his face and planted a kiss that knocked his socks off.

When she let up for air, he said, "Is that the best you can do, Dix?" Then he speared his hands into the coiled bun at the back of her head and brought his mouth down on hers.

Their tongues danced while she held on.

He'd sensed her indecision earlier. As much as he'd wanted to initiate foreplay, he feared chasing her away. Not now. As he loosened the coil, pins fell to the thick carpet. Ever since he first met her, he wondered what her hair would look like loose. He was about to find out.

More pins fell then something else.

He bent down and picked up a pendant attached to a long chain. "What's this?"

"Mine." She snatched it out of his hand then slipped it over her head. As she tried to pull out her hair, it snagged on the chain.

"Let me." He moved behind her then carefully began pulling strands of her dark hair out of the links. When he got to the tangle, he gently loosened her hair until it was free. He traced the sturdy chain around until he got to the pendant that she'd tucked into the bodice of her dress.

When he tried to lift it out, she clasped the pendant. "No."

Her note of panic concerned him. "All right." Though curious, he backed off but not away. "Why was it in your hair?"

She walked away from him. At the broad window, she stopped. Her reflection in the glass revealed her distress. "It didn't look right with my dress, but I couldn't leave it behind. I've always worn it." She held the pendant, turning it over and over in her hand.

When he came up behind her, she stiffened. He rubbed the top of her shoulders with his thumbs. "I won't take it. I would just like to see what's so important to you."

"Why?"

"Because I want to know you better. Sometimes I feel like you only reveal tiny parts of yourself at a time. That you keep the rest so well hidden, I'll never really know you."

"You know more about me than anyone. You know about Miri." With her thumb, she rolled the small object in her palm. She turned to face him. Without taking it off, she held out the pendant. Made of argenturum, the round piece had tiny swirls in the center. "This is her thumbprint."

The swirls made sense now. "So tiny."

She nodded. Then she pressed the side and it opened like a locket. A hologram floated up. A laughing baby with dark hair and big eyes lay in a crib, kicking her feet and waving her hands.

"I've never shown anyone this."

He closed the pendant and pressed it back into her hand. "I am honored that you shared your daughter with me. She is beautiful. Like her mother."

The corner Rissa's mouth curved. "Thank you." She dithered for a moment. "I should go to bed."

"Alone?" He gave her a little grin that she could take in either of two ways—that he was kidding or that he was serious. He wanted her to think he was serious.

"Alone." She walked across the sitting room. When she reached the closed door of her bedroom, she turned around. "Thank you for the enjoyable day, Dillan. And for the wonderful clothes. And dinner. And—"

"No need to keep thanking me for being such a wonderful guy." This time she would have no doubt that he was kidding. "Do you think I could have a goodnight kiss?"

His hopeful puppy-dog grin produced the right effect. She laughed. Encouraged, he strode across the space, wrapped her in his arms, and dipped her in a move he'd seen on a vid and had always wanted to try on her. He laid a loud, smacking kiss on her lips before bringing her upright.

"Goodnight, sweet princess. Happy dreams." Then he spun on his heel and went into his bedroom before she could lambaste him.

A quick glance before he closed his door revealed a stunned Rissa, her mouth open.

Yes.

Dillan Rusteran was a silly boy. Rissa shook her head as she prepared for bed. His mercurial moods confused her. One moment he was passionate—and definitely not a boy. The next, he did something goofy. Then she remembered how touched he'd been when she showed him Miri's holo-pic. He'd said he was honored. She'd never shared Miri with anyone.

As she brushed her hair, she wondered why him. What was it about Dillan Rusteran that made her let down her guard? Why did she trust him when she never trusted anyone else? Not even her best friend Celara.

With practiced fingers, Rissa loosely braided her hair. Otherwise, it would be a tangled mess in the morning. Still thinking about Dillan, she went about her nightly routine then climbed into the large bed. His kiss had left her shaking. Not the silly smack on the lips, but the devastating kiss that she had to practically beg him for.

Oh, he was a sly one.

He must have realized how skittish she was, so he'd made her take the initiative. Made her? With his light caresses and tender touches, he'd just brought her to a point where she couldn't resist. Where she had to kiss him. She'd almost shoved him into his bedroom where she would have ripped his clothes off. If only her treasure hadn't fallen on the floor.

The pendant was the most precious thing she owned. Other than the holo-pics in her bedroom at home, it was all she had of her daughter.

The anguished cry jerked Dillan awake.

Before going to bed, he'd left his door slightly ajar. An invitation, if Rissa decided to wander. He didn't imagine she would. Just hoped.

"No. No."

The cry tore at his heart as he bounded out of bed and across the sitting room where a small lamp dispelled the darkness. When he yanked open the door to Rissa's bedroom, he found her moaning in distress. She thrashed in the bed, twisting the covers around her until she could barely move.

"Rissa? Sweetheart?" He sat on the edge of the bed. With soft sounds, he gently touched her shoulder. "Wake up, sweetheart. You're dreaming."

As she bolted upright, she swung out, catching him unawares. The blow to his head made him see stars.

"Get away," she cried. "You can't take her."

Careful to avoid her arm, Dillan rubbed his knuckle down her tear-stained cheek. "Rissa, wake up."

When she moaned, still in the throes of the dream, he gathered her close. No hesitation. No wondering how she would react. No worrying. He knew she needed the comfort. She clutched him, dug her fingers into his arms. As he smoothed his hand down her back and cradled her head against his shoulder, he felt her start to relax.

"There, there. That's my girl. You're okay. Just a dream."

He knew the moment she woke up. She stiffened and reared back. "Wh-What?"

From the dim light filtering in from the sitting room, he could see her confusion as she tried to process where she was.

"We're in a hotel," he said softly so as not to startle her. "In Vesteron. You were dreaming."

She scooted back against the pillows. "What are you doing here?"

"You cried out. I had to make sure you were all right."

As she shoved hair off her forehead, she eyed him. "Are you naked?"

"Almost." Out of deference to her, he'd thrown on his shorts.

"I cried out?" She closed her eyes. "I'm sorry I woke you."

"No problem." He shifted so he could prop his knee on the edge of the bed. "You were dreaming about the slavers."

She let her head fall back against the padded headboard. "Yes."

"Is that the nightmare you've had before?"

For a moment, she hesitated. "Yes."

He waited, hoping she would say more. When she didn't, he said, "Sometimes it helps to talk about bad dreams."

"Not this one."

"Especially this one." Although he was no medico, he knew all about bad dreams. "I used to wake up in a cold sweat. I'd see Konner falling, over and over again. Rocks piling on top of him. I'd see the fear in his eyes as he disappeared under the avalanche of stones. Even when Jileena told me he was alive, I still had the dream."

She clasped his hand resting on top of the coverlet. "I'm sorry."

"There were times when I was afraid to close my eyes." He hoped by relating his experience she would share hers. "I knew if I did the dream would come back."

"Yes." She took a deep breath. "I won't go back to sleep tonight."

When he got up, she gave him a look of panic. "Do you have to go? Never mind. Forget I said that."

He walked around the bed. "I'm not going anywhere. Since we're both wide awake, we might as well talk."

"Talk? You want to talk?"

After settling on top of the coverlet, he clasped his hands behind his head. "Why not?"

"Maybe I don't want to talk." Still sitting up, she leaned against the headboard.

"Okay, I will. Did you know United Suppliers is expanding into this sector?" That should be an innocuous topic. One that wouldn't remind her of the nightmare.

"I heard that. The indie pilots are afraid that will put them out of business." She scooted down until her head hit the pillow. "Pilots like my friend Celara and other cargo haulers can't compete."

They chatted about other rumors they'd heard of conglomerates expanding into the Rim. About changes in general. Both kept their heads on their pillows, neither looking at the other. Dillan wanted to give her time to get used to talking to him, used to him in her bed.

When they ran out of topics and silence stretched between them, she said, "I was there, in the dream, when the traffickers took Miri. When the one leaned over her crib, I couldn't move. I couldn't stop him from picking her up. They'd tied me to a chair. All I could do was cry." A soft sob escaped.

Dillan turned on his side. Tears were streaming down her cheeks. Once again, he gathered her into his arms. "Hush," he crooned. "Everything is all right. You aren't tied up. You can move." He cradled her head on his shoulder and just held her. "Change the dream. Hit the slaver. Slug him on the side of his head. Punch the other one. Knock him on the floor."

"I would have, you know," she muttered against the side of his neck.

"I know. They wouldn't have messed with you." While not entirely accurate—he was certain the men would have killed her if she'd intervened—he knew she needed confirmation that she was strong. That she could change the dream if it came again.

"That's probably why they waited until I was at work. My landlady was no match for them. They hit her so hard her face swelled up. I should have helped her, but I had to find Miri."

He gave her a light squeeze. "You did what you needed to do."

After several mins, she said, "Aren't you cold? You should get under the covers."

Probably not a good idea. But he did it anyway.

She turned on her side, facing him. "I'm glad you stayed, Dillan." From her small voice, he knew the nightmare still affected her. Ordinarily, she would never admit to weakness.

"As long as you need me." He patted his shoulder closest to her. "This is always yours. No strings attached."

I'm always yours.

"Good to know." Yawning broadly, she settled closer to him.

Soon her breathing deepened. While a small part of him was happy she felt comfortable enough to fall asleep with him in her bed, another part—a much large part—wanted more. He was such a selfish bastard. He wanted her to want him. And not just to keep nightmares at bay.

CHAPTER 17

Rissa awoke in a strange bed. Worse, she was sprawled across a man.

Dillan.

She'd draped her arm across his chest, her leg over his. He held her close, his arm around her shoulders. How could anything that felt so right be so wrong?

Last night's events flooded her mind. Their passionate kisses in the sitting room. Kisses that would have turned into something else. Something she wasn't ready for. Had the necklace not fallen, she might have ended up in bed with him.

Like she was now.

Except passion hadn't driven her to want him next to her. That dreadful dream. He'd been so gentle with her, so understanding. He actually knew how a nightmare tortured. He'd experienced one himself. He also knew what she needed. Just to be held. She would never have asked.

Yet she'd begged him to stay.

What a weakling she was. To be so frightened by a dream, like a child.

As she started to pull away, he tightened his hold.

"Don't go," he muttered, his voice thick with sleep.

She should leave.

"This feels right." He yawned. "Waking up with you in my arms."

"I should get up," she murmured.

"Why? Too early to get up."

The heavy drapes across the window had kept the room dark. But through the open doorway to the sitting room she could see strong morning light filled the room. Late morning light.

When he cradled her head against his chest, his steady heartbeat made a comforting sound beneath her ear. Comforting until his heart began to speed up and his body to tighten. Though she hadn't been intimate with a man in a long time, she recognized the signs. When she shifted, her knee brushed against his erection.

"Careful there, sweetheart." His turn to shift. When he did, he surprised her.

Instead of tucking her closer, he eased away. Now that was a dilemma. Or maybe not. It was what she wanted. She didn't want to be intimate with him.

Liar.

"Much as I'd like lolling around in bed with you . . ." He got up.

Huh.

"I'll order First Meal for us while you get dressed." He stopped at the doorway. "Dress comfortable. Wear your boots. We're going exploring."

And that was that. No decision making about whether to be intimate with Dillan Rusteran. He'd made the decision for her. Damn.

One of the hardest things he'd ever done was leave Rissa Dix alone. By the stars, he wanted her. After her bad dream the night before, he could have had her. Could have taken advantage of her distress. Could have kissed her until she forgot all about nightmares.

This morning while his body went into high alert, he'd felt her indecision. He could have pushed the situation. He'd even felt her disappointment when he backed away. Better to keep her off balance then take advantage. Well, that's what his conscience said. Fortunately, his conscience overruled his body's insistence.

He wasn't a kid anymore. He could control himself. Stars, he needed a cold shower.

After First Meal, he took her on a tour of the old village. New Vesteron had expanded beyond its origins. But in the old section, specialty shops were crammed together. Native wares and gaudy souvenirs sat side by side. The old mercantile still had rows upon rows of anything a miner or indie pilot might need, plus household goods and traditional Rimmer attire. Not the faux items favored by the settlers from the Central District, but shirts and trousers made of real coarse-spun.

The owner, Namil, recognized him at once. "You will want climbing equipment, sir. I changed the location due to new stock. This way."

Before Dillan could protest, Namil headed toward the back of the store. Rissa followed. With a resigned sigh, he joined the parade. He hadn't climbed since Konner's accident and wasn't interested in climbing now. To be polite, he examined the latest gear. Desire to experience the thrill of reaching a summit crept into his mind.

He set down the crampons he was examining. "I have no need for new equipment." He hoped he was vague enough. He didn't want to explain why he no longer climbed.

The mercantile owner nodded while Rissa said she wanted to see his selection of cookware. With one last longing look at the equipment,

Dillan again followed Rissa. She found a pot much larger than one she had then waffled.

"If you don't want to carry it around," he said, "we can have it delivered to the ship."

"Absolutely," Namil agreed. "Anything you purchase can be delivered. No charge."

Rissa laughed. "In that case . . ." She chose several pieces of cookware plus a few utensils. Dillan had no idea what the latter's purpose was. She also insisted on paying for her purchases.

After the mercantile, he suggested they return to the dress shop. She refused, saying she had enough clothes. Then she changed her mind and hurried down the street.

"I want to buy a couple of outfits for Pela and Anaris. They will love having something new. I wish they'd come. They would have enjoyed the sights and sounds, the foods." She laughed. "Everything. Vesteron is amazing."

While she set about choosing clothes for the girls, the owner sidled up to him. "Did she like the clothes you picked out?"

He grinned. "She says she doesn't want anything else for herself. Would you pick out a special dress for this evening? Add it to what she chooses for the girls and send it to the hotel."

The owner looked delighted. She should. He was adding much to her coffers.

"That was fun," Rissa said as they left the shop. "Pela and Anaris will love the new clothes. I'm so excited to see their faces when they see what we bought. You really shouldn't have told the owner to pick out more outfits for them."

"You didn't protest too hard." He grinned. "I'm happy to indulge them. Just as I was happy yesterday to indulge you."

"I always knew you were wealthy, Dillan. But you shouldn't waste your credits so."

"I don't consider making people happy wasteful. Now I'm famished. Let's get Mid-Day Meal."

At her suggestion, they returned to Kleema and Baro's. During the meal, she brought up climbing.

"You want to climb again." It was a flat statement, no question. "I saw how you looked at the new equipment."

She was too damn perceptive.

After taking a swallow of the fine vintage ale, he said, "I have an idea of what we can do this afternoon."

She gave him a knowing look. "You're changing the subject."

"To a more interesting one. How would you like to go up into the rainforest canopy?"

An hour later, when the guide demonstrated how they were to go up, she gaped at Dillan in panic. "No way."

"You can do it, sweetheart. I'll be right with you." He helped her into the harness then tightened the straps around her upper thighs.

"Watch it, Rusteran."

He grinned. "Oh, I am."

She swatted his shoulder. "I meant watch your hands. No funny business."

"Wouldn't think of it."

The guide checked both their harnesses then showed Rissa how to rise. After a couple of hesitant starts, she quickly got the hang of it and soon they reached the platform. As she looked around, across the top of the canopy, her eyes widened in delight.

"I can't believe what you can see up here. Oh. My. Stars."

"Thought you might like it."

"Like it. I love it. Thank you so much for bringing me up here."

"There's more to see," the guide said. "Follow me." He pushed off the platform, then using the zip-line, sailed across to another platform a hundred meters away.

Again, Rissa looked at Dillan in panic. She shook her head. "I can't."

"Sure you can. Go." He pushed her off the platform.

"You are a bas-tard." She screamed for the first ten meters then began to laugh. The guide caught her at the next platform. As soon as Dillan caught up, she grabbed his arm. "I want to do it again."

Her eyes sparkling with delight filled him with joy.

They rode the cable for several more loops until the guide said it was time to go down. He reminded Rissa how to use the brake.

She turned to Dillan. "How fast can I go?"

"As fast as you want." He gave her a smacking kiss. "Go for it, sweetheart."

She watched the guide zip down.

"Uh, I'm not sure I can go that fast."

"You know how to use the brake. The guide will catch you at the bottom."

After a tentative start and stop, she looked up at him. "Here goes." She scrunched her eyes shut then let go of the brake.

Her scream scared all the birds out of the trees.

The guide was helping her out of the harness when Dillan zipped down. As soon as he landed, she flung her arms around his neck. "That was so exciting. I thought my heart would fly out of my chest. Can we do it again?"

He looked over her head at the guide.

"I have another group to take up. You seemed to know what you're doing. You can go on your own."

They went up into the canopy three more times. Each time she zipped down her screams turned to shouts of delight. Finally, he called it quits. The setting sun brought darkness to the forest, the shadows menacing.

Worry pleated her forehead as she turned to him. "Oh, my. Can you find the way out?"

"Fine time to be thinking of that, my dear. Of course I can find the way out. It's that path over there." He pointed.

"Really? I thought it was that one over there."

"Hmm." He pretended to think about that. "You could be right. But if you're not, we could get lost and have to spend the night in the forest."

"I don't know—oh, you." She swatted his arm. "You're teasing."

"C'mon, kid." He slung his 'injured' arm around her. "I'm sure the guide left breadcrumbs to follow." Then he pointed to a small sign with an arrow.

She snorted.

As they strolled down the correct path, she said, "That was the most fun I've had in years." She paused. "In fact, I don't think I've ever had so much fun."

"I'm glad you enjoyed it."

"Is that how you felt when you climbed? That rush? That thrill?"

He smiled, remembering. "Yeah."

"Then I understand now why you risked your life on the mountains." They were almost out of the forest when she turned to him and clasped his face. "Thank you."

When she lightly kissed his mouth, it was all he could do to let her go. Throwing her down on the ground and making passionate love to her was tempting. But he would bide his time. The way he had this entire journey.

That night, after another delicious meal, they returned to the suite. Tension began to spread between them as they walked down the corridor. It heightened when he opened the door then escalated when he shut it behind them.

She stopped in the middle of the sitting room. When he came up behind her, he slid his arms around her and pulled her back against his chest.

"Did you have a good day?" he whispered before kissing the back of her ear. She'd piled her hair up in a complicated twist that made her neck so enticing.

The long, halter-type dress, a fluid green that reminded him of the rainforest, clung to her curves. All through their meal, he'd watched the fabric slid over her body every time she moved. As beautiful as it was, he wanted the dress gone.

When he pressed kisses down to her neck, she covered his hands and brought them up to her breasts. "If you say you want to watch a vid, I will hurt you."

He chuckled. "No vids."

"Good." She sighed as he massaged her breasts.

His hands slid easily over the fabric, and he felt her nipples tighten. He caressed them through the dress before sliding the plunging neckline aside, slipping his hand inside. With a small moan, she let her head fall back against him. He stroked her nipple, drew it to a peak then cupped the entire breast. She shifted her rear against him, enticing him, arousing him even more.

Without waiting for him, she turned in his arms and kissed him. Not the light kiss she'd given him before but a deep, passionate one. He'd wanted to go slow, prolong the pleasure, but she apparently didn't. When her tongue delved into his mouth, swirled around his, he slid his hands down her backless dress then cupped her bottom so he could press her closer. His erection throbbed against her mound.

Her soft moans encouraged him as did her hands along his back. She even made him step back so she could remove his jacket.

He placed his hands on her bare shoulders. "I want you. If you want me, too, we can go into my room. Otherwise, we'd better stop now."

For a moment, he thought her hesitation meant he'd pushed when he should have waited. When she pulled away, disappointment cut into him. Not even a cold shower would slake his lust. Then she grabbed his hand and drew him toward his room.

Thank the Divine One.

When she reached the side of his bed, she opened his shirt then yanked it out of his trousers. As she began to open them, he stilled her hand.

Her look of dismay excited him.

"You have on too many clothes." He reached around her neck for the closure.

"Uh, Dillan. Wait a min."

He groaned. *Please, Divine One, don't let her back off.*

"Would you, uh, turn out the light?"

"You have to be joking."

"I'm not. I want to make love with you, but I don't want you to see . . ."

"See what?"

She wrapped her arms around herself. "My body. I'm forty years old, Dillan. My boobs droop and my bottom sags. You're so young and—"

He took her hands and pulled her to him. "—and you are a strong, wonderful, beautiful fem. I don't give a damn if you're thirty or fifty. And I'll be damned if we make love in the dark. I want to see what I'm doing when I kiss every inch of you. I want to watch your face when you fly like you did in the rainforest. Now, how do I get you out of this damn thing?"

After a moment's hesitation, she undid the halter. A fiery blush bloomed on her cheeks as she dropped the two straps, revealing her beautiful breasts. Lusciously full, her dark nipples stood at attention, luring his mouth. He bent his head. With slow licks, he caressed her nipple before drawing it into his mouth. She cupped the back of his head and held him there. He tightened his hands on her hips as he switched to her other breast then gave it the attention it deserved.

To his dismay, she pushed against him. Not again. She couldn't stop now. Not with him so tight with desire. Not with her breasts glistening from his tongue. If she wanted to call a halt, he would oblige. He'd never forced a fem in his life. He would just suck it up and blame it on bad timing.

"You are killing me, girl. There is nothing wrong with your breasts, and your ass is tighter than those drums in Kiran's room. No more hesitation. Either fish or cut bait."

"What?"

"Make a decision. Drop that dress or pull it up and leave."

Her eyes widened, and he wondered if he'd gone too far. When she shimmied the dress over her hips and let it pool on the floor, he felt like he'd won a million credits. She stood there in cream-colored briefs that rode high on her hips. His body tightened in reaction to the sight of her nearly naked body. When she reached up to loosen her hair, he thought he'd died and gone to his everlasting reward. After removing her pendant and setting it on the bedside table, she shook her head to let her wavy hair hang down her back nearly to her waist. He couldn't wait to see the dark tresses spread across the pillow on his bed.

While he admired her body, she did something amazing. She straightened her spine and stared right into his eyes. The air fairly crackled with the sparks flying between them.

Again, he caressed her breasts, kneaded them, brought his head down to taste them. Her shiver prodded him to do more. He lavished kisses on her other breast then lower as he knelt in front of her. When he hooked his fingers on the edge of her briefs and drew them down her long legs, she held onto his shoulders for support.

"Now you're the one wearing too many clothes." She pushed the shirt off his shoulders. When he stood, she again reached for the opening to his trousers.

This time he didn't stop her. Until she went too slowly. He shoved off the rest of his clothes then settled her in the middle of the bed. Exactly how he imagined she'd look, her dark hair spread across the pillow, her large eyes welcoming. His imagination fell far short of reality.

When he knelt next to her, she tugged on his shoulders. "Make love to me, Dillan."

As she slept, Dillan held her close. If only he could keep her there, snuggled in, her body relaxed. He would enjoy it while he could. They had a few more days of vacation before heading back to Astron. A few days where he could enjoy her company during the day and their sweet mating at night.

No rules said they couldn't enjoy mating in the morning or Mid-Day or . . .

His comm beeped.

Without picking up the unit off the bedside table, he knew who it was. His father, demanding an update. Dillan had put him off several times, but the man wouldn't give up. Tenacious, like a caninus with a bone. He supposed that was what made his father one of the premier industrialists in the Central District.

Rissa stirred against him. He'd better answer the damn thing before the incessant beeping woke her up.

When he carefully slid out of bed, she rolled over, dragging the covers with her . . . and baring her backside. Yep, a very tight ass. It took every ounce of self-control not to trace her spine down to—

The comm vibrated in his hand. He went out into the sitting room, closing the door behind him. When he tapped the screen, he was surprised to see an anxious Kiran's impatient face.

"What's wrong?"

"Rissa needs to return. Now." Kiran proceeded to explain why.

Damn it to Lexol's Fire.

He contacted the front desk and checked out, then called Vesteron spaceport to prepare his ship for immediate departure. He went into the other bedroom and gathered Rissa's things. He knew she wouldn't take the time. *Sherd.* He hated being the bearer of bad news.

For two secs, he considered not telling her. She would hate him for it when she found out. After leaving out a change of clothes, he dropped her gear on the sofa. When he knelt on the side of the bed, she reached out for him.

"Why are you up?" Her voice, husky with sleep, sent a thrill through him. She tried to pull his head down. "Do I get a good morning kiss?"

He obliged her. One more kiss before they had to leave.

When she wanted more, he disengaged her hands from around his neck. "We need to return to Astron."

"Pela?" She bolted upright. Only his quick reflexes kept her head from smashing into his.

"Stars, no. Not Pela. It's the tavern."

She swung her legs out of bed and stood in all her naked glory. Damn. What bad timing.

"Did the vandals return?"

"No." Stars, he hated what he had to tell her. "There was a fire."

"A fire? Was anyone hurt? How much damage?" As she talked, she hunted for her clothes.

"No one was hurt." One piece of good news, at least.

"Quit dithering, Rusteran. Tell me the rest. How much damage?"

"Total. The tavern is gone."

CHAPTER 18

When Dillan tried to hold her to give her comfort, she twisted away. Her expression broke his heart. Devastation turned to stoicism. Her jaw tightened as she clenched her teeth.

"Where are my damn clothes?" She strode out of his bedroom, across the sitting room, and into her own.

Ten mins later, she came out dressed, her tangled hair clipped to the back of her neck. "Let's go."

They made record time back to Astron. During the trip, she'd said little. Each time he left the command center, he found her curled up in the corner of the sofa. Her eyes haunted.

He'd barely cut the engine upon landing when she lowered the ramp and bolted off the ship. Frustrated that he couldn't immediately follow, Dillan completed shutdown. As he left the ship, Traffic Controller Ropergor minced his way across the hangar.

"Miz Rissa knows about her tavern?"

"Obviously." Without stopping, he said, "Take care of my ship. Have it prepared to leave."

"Yes, sir. But—"

Dillan didn't wait to hear whatever Ropergor planned to say. He ran out of the spaceport. The strong smell of smoke hung in the air. Surprised that the constantly blowing wind hadn't carried it away, he realized why. The wind blew from the direction of the tavern.

People tried to stop him along the route. Medico Barlen, Merchant Graeson. He kept running. When he got to Rissa, she was surrounded by Kiran, Fortuna, and several others. She stood stoically in their midst. Shocked, alone.

The devastation of Rissa's tavern was complete. Nothing was left except the stone foundation and smoking embers. Not even the boardwalk had escaped the fire.

He worked his way between the others to her side. Ignoring the distance she affected, he put his arm around her waist. She stiffened but didn't move away. A sob ripped through her before she turned into his waiting arms.

And she cried.

For the past twelve years, her tavern had been her life. Now it was gone. Obliterated in a smoky haze.

149

Other than feeling Dillan's arm around her, she sensed nothing. She heard voices, but their words didn't penetrate. Fortuna's soft croon, Nally's concern, Kiran's rumble. She wanted them all to go away. Take their sympathy with them. Nothing they said could make this better.

If she could run away from all of them, she would. But her legs were rooted in the street. Only Dillan's arm prevented her from crumpling like a wounded animal. And like a wounded animal she wanted to lash out at whoever had done this.

Dillan shifted his hold and she was weightless, her feet no longer stuck in the dirt. He'd tucked her against him as he carried her. She had no sense of direction. No idea where he was taking her. As long as it was away from her tavern's grave, she didn't care.

Pleasant perfume replaced the acrid smoke. Fortuna's. Soon he placed her on something soft. As soon as he released her, she curled away from him. He covered her then spoke softly before placing a light kiss on her cheek.

Then all was quiet.

She was alone with her thoughts. Behind her closed eyes, she saw the wrecked tavern. The scorched rock foundation, the burned supports, the debris left by the tables, chairs, and the bartop. Her precious bartop. She'd worried how she could erase the defilement from the vandals. She didn't have to worry now.

Gone. Everything was gone.

She had nothing left of Miri. No tiny clothes, no holo-pics, nothing other than her pendant and the hologram inside.

Thank the Matriarch, she always wore the necklace.

She had to get up. She couldn't lie there and do nothing. When she rolled over, she found Dillan sitting in a chair next to the bed, watching her.

"You stayed," she said inanely.

He arched his eyebrow. "Of course, I stayed. You needed me. Where else would I be?"

She breathed out a sigh before swinging her legs off the bed. For a moment, she sat there with her eyes closed. Then she breathed out noisily. "The tavern won't get rebuilt if I lie here any longer."

He stood as she did. "There is no rush."

"Yes, there is. I have to draw up plans, line up suppliers. I—"

"You need to slow down. You've had a severe shock."

"I am not a wimpy fem, Rusteran." When she started past him, he held her shoulders.

"Accept a little comfort first. Your friends care for you very much. Let them help." He rested his cheek against hers. "Let me help."

She wrapped her arms around his waist and hung on. A shudder ran through her. "If I do, I won't be able to go on. I'll fall apart again, the way I did outside." She looked up into his brilliant green eyes. "Thank you for taking care of me. For not letting me embarrass myself."

"Don't you know yet that I'll do anything for you?" He kissed her temple then pulled back. "All right, then. Let's get started."

Security Chief Kaminga came to her at the café. He pulled out a chair, joining Dillan, Fortuna, and Kiran at a round table in the back.

"I'm real sorry, Miz Rissa. Real sorry."

If one more person said they were sorry, she would scream. She'd had about all the sympathy she could take.

"Unless you started the fire, Chief, you have nothing to be sorry about."

Dillan nudged her with his knee. "Glad you could join us, Chief. What news have you?"

"I asked the Sector Security Chief to send an arson specialist." Kaminga scratched the back of his neck. "He, uh, didn't think the fire warranted an investigation until I told him about the trafficker incidents."

Fortuna raised her eyebrow. "Do you think the fire is connected to the slavers?"

"First—" He held up one finger. "—the vandalism. And now a suspicious fire." He held up a second finger. "In my opinion, yes. They incidents are connected. We'll find who did this. They won't get away with it."

He meant well, but he hadn't even caught the vandals, and it had been over three tendays.

"I'm sure you will, Chief. Meanwhile, I'll clear out the debris and rebuild."

"You can't." At her startled look, he said, "You can't clear anything. You have to wait until the arson inspector, well, inspects and makes a report."

"From the look of those embers," Dillan said, "we'll have to wait until everything cools down."

As much as she hated to admit it, Dillan was right. So was Kaminga. But she had to do something. She couldn't just sit around, twiddling her thumbs.

After Kaminga left, Rissa let the voices swirl around her. Too often since Dillan brought her to the café, she'd zoned out thinking about her loss. The chief had to be right about the connection with the traffickers. She'd brought it on herself. She was responsible for losing everything she held dear—her home, her livelihood, her precious keepsakes of Miri.

If she hadn't rescued the girls. If she hadn't gathered the citizens. If she hadn't insisted they fight to protect their families. If she hadn't organized the patrols.

She would still have—

". . . Rissa?"

Shaking her head, she looked over at Kiran. "Sorry?"

"He asked if you wanted him to go up to the mines and get Pela," Dillan said.

Fear raked through her. "Pela? You don't think . . . ."

"No." Dillan clasped her hand. "Manager d'Arcanin and the miners will protect her and Anaris. The traffickers would be fools to try anything up there."

"But—"

He tapped his wrist comm. Within secs, he was connected to the mine manager who assured him the girls were fine. "As soon as we heard about the fire, Harraway increased patrols around the mine." He chuckled. "That Pela. She wanted to come down to the village and help. We convinced her to stay."

Rissa wondered how they'd convinced her. When Pela set her mind to something . . .

She grabbed Dillan's wrist and turned it so she could see the monitor. "You didn't lock her up, did you?"

"Of course not. Anaris and Harraway's daughter did the convincing. Don't worry about the girls."

"Keep Pela safe. Keep all the girls safe."

"We will. And, Rissa, we're really sorry about the tavern."

Yeah, we're all real sorry.

Realizing how mean-spirited that sounded, she was glad she hadn't said it out loud. Instead, she nodded and released Dillan's wrist.

When he finished the conversation, Kiran said, "Boss, I didn't mean to worry you. I checked on Pela first thing after the fire. I just thought you might want her with you."

Part of her wanted to get Pela, hold her, protect her, know she was safe. But that was selfish. The miners would protect the girls. In truth, Pela was safer away from her. Too many bad things happened around her.

"No. She should stay up there."

"Wise decision," Dillan said. "Kiran, I thought you were going to see your brothers."

"I was. I even got on a transport going to Hetropsis." He looked down at his big hands folded on top of the table. When he looked up, grief etched his features. "I tried to contact my brothers to let them know I was coming. My oldest brother's son told me they both perished during the volcanic activity three tendays ago."

"By the Matriarch, Kiran. I'm bemoaning the fact that I lost my business when you lost your brothers. I am so sorry."

He cleared his throat. "I did not know them well since the slavers took me when I was eight, and they were so much older."

"But when you were free you saw them, right?" Rissa said. "You told me you'd visited them."

"Not often. They still felt guilty that they couldn't stop the slavers." Kiran let out a deep sigh. "Even though I told them it wasn't their fault, I was a reminder of a time when they were powerless. I tried to keep in touch but . . ." He shrugged. "So that is why I did not leave. This is my home. You and Pela are my family."

She gave her bartender a small smile. "I'm glad you weren't hurt in the fire. How did you escape?"

He sat back and folded his arms across his broad chest. "That idiot android."

"Arjay? What was he doing in the tavern?"

"We, uh, were preparing a surprise for you. Ever since the vandals broke in, I've been thinking we should increase the security. Arjay was helping me put up bars on the windows. We replaced the locks with extra-secure ones. I was lucky to get them. Merchant Graeson said ever since the night Sophira's baby was kidnapped, he's had a big demand on security devices."

"I'll bet he's making a big profit, too," Fortuna scoffed.

"Could be," Kiran said. "Anyway, that chatty AI was driving me crazy, so I took him down here and convinced Nally to keep him for a while. My ears needed a rest."

"It was a good thing, too." The chatty AI stood behind Rissa with drink refills for the table. "If you had gone to bed, you'd be toast."

Rissa gasped at the crude expression.

"Now, now, Mistress Rissa." Arjay patted her shoulder. "I know that wasn't the proper way to express what could have happened to him. But that is what Kiran said. When we heard the explosion, we ran out into the street. So did most of the colony. We did our best to put out the fire, but it was an inferno. Chief Kaminga made us concentrate on preventing the fire from spreading. And—"

"That's enough." Kiran's bellow startled those few diners at the other tables. Didn't do Rissa's heart any good, either.

"No. Let him finish. I didn't know about an explosion." When the others looked down at the table, Rissa said, "What aren't you telling me?"

After a big sigh, Kiran said, "Someone saw a man running away from the fire. That's all we know for sure." He stared hard at Arjay.

"A man?" Rissa asked. "Did anyone get a description?"

Fortuna glanced at Kiran. "She's going to find out. We should be the ones who tell her. The man was short and wiry. He wore all black. But when he pushed back his hood, they said it looked like he had red hair. A Menacan."

"The man from the spaceport who helped take care of the traffickers?" Rissa asked.

"Quin?" Dillan said at the same time.

"Actually, his name is—"

"No." Kiran glared at the AI

Arjay ignored him. "His name is Quintall d'Sernin. He's my Rega's brother."

Stunned, Rissa sat back. She couldn't believe that her best friend's brother would burn down her tavern. "Celara's brother? There must be a mistake."

"It's possible," Kiran said. "I didn't see him. We only have one person's statement, and he wasn't sober."

Dear Kiran was trying to protect her. He knew how close she and Celara were.

"Now I know why he looked familiar," Rissa said. "Almost two years ago, he was here in Astron, and she came looking for him."

"This does not make sense," Dillan said. "Why would Quin help us then start the fire?"

Rissa hesitated, almost afraid to say what she knew.

While she dithered, Arjay said, "Quintall d'Sernin works for Hallart."

While the others at the table exclaimed over the connection to the gangster, Dillan shook his head. "No. That still does not make sense. If Quin works for Hallart. If he started the fire. Why would he warn me to get Rissa out of the colony?"

"He what?" Rissa stared at him.

Dillan clasped her hand. "I was working on my ship when—"

She yanked away. "I don't care where you were working. What did you mean he warned you to get me away from here?"

"Exactly that. He said to get you out of the colony right away."

"That's why you tricked me into going on vacation with you? To get me away from my tavern." She forced herself not to yell. "If I had been here—"

"If you had been in the tavern, you'd be dead. The traffickers didn't like that you'd interfered in their plans. They know you organized the town. They know you're the leader. Don't you get it? You ignored the warning when they vandalized the tavern. They want you dead."

Rissa didn't think she could take any more shocking surprises.

"Boss, he saved your life. You and Pela. Rusteran, I should have listened to you."

"Wait. You told Kiran, but you didn't tell me?" He'd tricked her. "How could you?"

Misery clouded his eyes. He knew what he'd done was wrong.

Fortuna slammed her hand on the table. "Rissa Dix, you listen to me. If he'd told you about the warning, what would you have done?" Without waiting for an answer, she rushed on. "I know what you would've done. Stayed. You'd have sat in the dark with that old double-barrel SLS-48 just waiting to blast intruders."

"Damn right I would have."

"You might have gotten off one shot." Dillan spoke patiently, as to a child.

So that's what he thought of her. That she was a child.

"Then they would have returned armed to the teeth." Anger had replaced misery in his eyes. "And we all would be having an interment ceremony for you."

"Maybe I would've listened to you. Did you think of that before making decisions for me?"

"I couldn't take that chance. I had to protect you."

"I can take care of myself, Rusteran. I don't need protecting."

"Yes, you do, boss. You wouldn't have left with him. He was trying to protect all of us. You, Pela, me. I just didn't take the warning seriously."

She regretted her outburst. "Pela. That's why you wanted to take her with us."

"Yes."

Somewhat mollified, she listened to their chatter, each trying to get her to understand why Dillan had kept the warning to himself. The fact that he tried to also protect Pela and Kiran helped. Still, she hated that he hadn't told her. That he hadn't trusted her to do what was prudent.

Prudent. She scoffed. She'd been prudent her first nineteen years and look where that got her. The one time she'd thrown caution to the wind, she'd ended up pregnant and alone. After that, prudent wasn't in her vocabulary.

"Dillan, it's been a long day for her. She needs sleep." Fortuna pushed back her chair and came around to Rissa's side. "We'll all help you, you know. You won't have to rebuild by yourself."

Her hug, along with her words, brought that awful prickling behind Rissa's eyes. She closed them tightly to hold back tears. They were all being too kind, too sympathetic. She needed to get away, to hunker down and lick her wounds.

"You can sleep at my place," Fortuna said. "Kiran already is. I have another empty room. Seems two of my girls were so freaked out by the fire, they hopped on the first ship out of Astron. Wimps."

"You can't blame them for wanting to be safe," Rissa said. "Maybe they're the smart ones."

Fortuna put her hands on her hips. "No. To make it out here on the Rim you have to be tough. You can't let adversity get you down. I know you, Rissa Dix. You don't run away. You put down roots here. You are a survivor. Like the rest of us."

Rissa rose and hugged the tiny Wedoran. The prickling behind her eyes got worse. "Thank you."

Sherd. The unshed tears had collected in her throat.

"Thanks for the offer, but Rissa's sleeping on my ship," Dillan said.

His no-nonsense tone made the rest of them stare at her. Fortuna's mouth curved up into a knowing smile, while Rissa felt her cheeks burn.

"Then get her to bed." Fortuna gave him a pointed look. "And let her sleep."

CHAPTER 19

"Are you willing to forgive me?" Dillan asked after they entered his ship.

He was surprised she'd gone with him, especially after seeing the betrayal in her eyes when she found out he hadn't told her about Quin's warning. Despite knowing how she'd react, he didn't regret not telling her.

"I don't want to talk about it. I'm going to bed."

When she entered the guest quarters, he had his answer. No forgiveness. Not yet, anyway.

He followed her. When he started to undress, she put her hands on her hips. "What are you doing?"

"Isn't it obvious?" He sat on the end of the bed to remove his boots.

"You are not sleeping in here."

After stuffing his socks into one boot, he shucked his trousers. "Okay. We can sleep in my quarters if that's what you want."

"What I want is to sleep alone."

"No, you don't." After tossing his trousers on top of his shirt on the sole chair, he loosened the opening to her new reddish-brown shirt. "You'll have nightmares."

She slapped his hands. "I don't care. I don't want you here."

"Yes, you do. You're letting pride and anger speak for you." He pulled her close. Though she stiffened, she didn't pull away. "You're angry because you think I don't respect you. That I don't trust your judgment."

"You don't."

He kissed that sweet spot behind her ear. "I do. Much more than you know. I didn't want you to worry. You don't take time for yourself. I wanted you to have a carefree time in Vesteron. If you'd known about the threat, you would have worried yourself sick."

"With good reason." She twisted her head away from his mouth.

That didn't deter him. He found a better spot for his lips, where her neck and shoulder met. With his tongue, he traced the cord running along her neck. When he reached the hollow, he nipped.

"Ouch." She reared back. "You bit me."

"Uh huh. And you liked it."

"No I didn't."

157

"Sure you did. Your heart is racing and you're shivering."

"My heart is racing because I'm angry. Besides, it's cold in here. What are you doing?"

He shoved her pants, along with the slippery briefs, off her hips. "You're wearing too many clothes, pretty as they are. Time for bed." Finally, he slipped her shirt off her shoulders and tossed it on top of his clothes.

"I don't want this, Dillan." Despite her protest, she didn't push him away. Instead, she wrapped her arms around his bare waist.

Sweet Divinity, he loved her hands on his body.

"It's all right, sweetheart. You don't have to admit it." He covered her breast.

"Please. Stop."

Dropping his hands, he stepped back. "All right." He went to the bed and turned down the covers on one side before going around to the other. "I am sleeping with you tonight. I mean that. Just sleep. If you want more, you'll have to initiate it."

By the time he got under the bed linens, she was still standing in the middle of the room, naked, a puzzled expression in her eyes.

"I don't understand you, Dillan. You get me all hot and bothered then stop."

"You asked me to stop. Simple as that." He settled his head on the pillow. "If you're cold, you should get under the covers."

She crawled into bed. "I wasn't really cold."

"I know."

"I didn't really want you to stop."

"I know."

She batted his shoulder. "Then why did you?"

"Stop means stop. I would never force you. So be careful what you say. If you want me, say so." He leaned over and pressed a light kiss on her forehead. "Now turn out the light so we can sleep."

He rolled on his side away from her. Hardest damn thing he'd ever done. In the darkness, he felt her shift around, settling into the bed. What he wouldn't give to hold her in his arms. But she had to come to him. She had to speak. When she did, it wasn't what he'd hoped for.

"I supposed you're waiting for me to apologize."

"Only if you mean it."

"You'll be waiting a long time for that."

"I'm patient." He thought about all the years he'd waited to get her into his bed. Patience and a whole lot of hoping.

"You should have told me about the warning."

"I told you why I didn't."

"You should have given me a choice. By not telling me, you took that away. You treated me like a child."

When he'd gotten into bed, he'd promised himself he wouldn't hold her unless she came to him. He ignored his intention and wrapped his arms around her.

"Sweetheart, I never meant that." When she started to protest, he tapped her lips. "I see your point. You're right. I didn't give you a choice. Be mad at me, but I'd do the same thing again. I couldn't bear to see you hurt. Or killed."

She rested her hand on his chest. "I understand. I don't like what you did, but I understand." She pinched his nipple. "Don't ever do that again."

He yelped. "Sherd. That hurt."

"If you'd had chest hair like most Rimmer men, I'd have just pulled the hair."

"Guess it's a good thing Bricaldian men don't." He stroked her bare back. At least she hadn't put on a sleep garment. She'd gotten into bed with him naked. He loved the play of her muscles along her spine. When he got to the base, he stilled his hand. He knew how much she liked it when he went lower.

But he didn't.

He'd told her she would have to tell him of her desire. As much as he wanted to make love with her, make her forget everything since he'd woken her in the Vesteron hotel, he clamped down on his libido. Patience, patience, he repeated to himself. If he said it to himself often enough, he could make it come true.

Her breathing deepened. She didn't move. Didn't take her hand from his chest or her leg from across his. Torture.

While she slept in his arms, he thought about Quin's warning and the very real possibility that he'd started the fire. The man was ruthless. Dillan was still convinced that the explosion that destroyed the slavers' ship also destroyed the men. Quin hadn't stuffed them into an escape pod. He'd exacted frontier justice.

But why, if he worked for Hallart?

Everyone in the Central Planets knew about the gangster's attempt to subvert the government by controlling ex-President Filana. And how his minions had infiltrated big corporations, including Winslott Industries. Hallart had even attempted to kill Jileena to keep her from testifying against the infiltrator.

Of course, he didn't do his own dirty work. He'd hired others to do it for him. Others like Quin.

* * *

Using his remote device, Quin d'Sernin transported aboard the old station orbiting Menaca. Coriana had chosen her trafficking base well, halfway between the Rim (supply) and the Central Planets (demand). Choosing an old station meant fewer people to notice her business. And those that lived there didn't care.

Upon rematerializing in a remote cargo bay, he disengaged the transporting mechanism on his wrist comm. He'd acquired the little device after he needed that Offworlder Rusteran when they'd taken care of the slavers captured at Astron Spaceport. Never again would he be dependent on someone else.

Quin made it a policy never to rely on anyone except himself. That was why he didn't dock his ship at the station. If the situation got nasty, he didn't trust Coriana or her crew to let him leave. Too many "accidents" could occur to his ship while docked. Better to be able to leave when he wanted to.

The dank bay smelled of mildew, oil, and the remnants of cargo long forgotten. Repeated scratching meant pung rats had found a home amidst the squalor. And that reminded him of his childhood. He pulled gloves out of his trousers pocket before climbing the vertical stairs with its rusty rungs.

That little side trip to Astron Colony three tendays ago had been full of surprises. He'd followed one of Coriana's ships there as a favor to her. She questioned the Indigian pilot's loyalty. Quin's report convinced her she had a right to be suspicious. If old Blue Fur had been loyal, he wouldn't have disappeared.

Of course it hadn't taken much to convince the pilot that Coriana had put out an execution order on him and his crew. Drifting in space in a tiny pod and watching their ship blow up made sure that once they were rescued they would reinvent themselves somewhere far, far away from her territory.

Discovering Coriana had a snitch on Astron made things difficult. It must have been recent since she appeared not to know the lost "cargo" of children had been rescued. However, she did know about Rissa Dix. He'd recognized the tavern owner even though she hadn't recognized him. That fem was a menace to herself . . . and to him.

When he got to the station's third level, he came out in a shabby, little-used section of the habitat ring. In places, the gray carpet had worn so thin the deck plating was visible. A new paint job on the scuffed and dented walls wouldn't hurt. Old cooking odors clung to the area.

He strolled leisurely, like others going to and from their quarters. He dodged a group of giggling Wedoran pleasure providers, their arms around their clients' waists. The men's hands were busy checking out what they'd purchased for an hour or more.

Quin avoided the lifts and climbed another set of stairs. This time he came out on the level the inhabitants called *Main Street*—the commerce area. There he picked up the pace, just like those going to restaurants, bars, or shops. Coriana's offices were halfway around the station from where he'd arrived.

Strolling around *Main Street*, he noted new businesses. A Volpian restaurant, three new bars, a men's clothier, and a gift shop, of all things. After his dealings with Coriana, he'd have to check out the restaurant but not just for the food. Along with manufacturing the best ships in the galaxy, Volpians were known for their ability to gather information. Getting them to release the info took tact. And credits.

Using his secure comm, he let Coriana's assistant know he was on-station. He didn't expect her to be free, and she wasn't. He asked the assistant to contact him when she was available. He would be in Toots' Bar, a watering hole frequented by indie pilots and locals alike and manned by a fellow Menacan.

When Quin entered, the noise assaulted his ears. Indies and repair crews—judging by their uniforms—plus station inhabitants crowded into every table and booth. Quin was so used to ship time, he didn't realize it was meal time on the station. Which meal was anyone's guess. Toots gave a shout of surprise as he ran out from behind the bar and hugged Quin in an enthusiastic greeting.

Mutual backslapping ensued until Toots stepped back. "Looking good there, Quin. Whatcha been up to? Come, come, have drink. How are things out in . . . wherever you been?"

"Hey, hurry up with my drink," a United Supplier mech— according to the patch on his overalls—yelled.

"Yeah, yeah, yeah." Toots gave Quin another hug then went behind the bar

Meanwhile, Quin hitched his hip on the only stool available. The fact that only a slim person could fit in the small space next to the wall had to be why it was empty. Or maybe it was the big, hairy Grungian on the next stool. Quin could put up with the stink coming off one of the Rim's outcasts since the seat gave him the perfect place to check out the crowded bar as well as whoever came in. The Grungian gave him a wary look then slammed his tankard on the bartop before leaving.

With a small sigh of relief, Quin accepted the tall glass of ale from his friend. "Looks like business is good."

"Can't complain." Toots grinned. "Ever since United Suppliers started servicing the far reaches of the Coalition, the station is getting more business. That means the bar is going great. In fact, the whole station is doing better."

"Why did they choose here not the other stations?"

"Bite your tongue, boy. We're lucky United chose us. Cheaper for them, better for us."

Quin nodded. "I noticed the new shops. Is that construction going on down the way?" He knew darn well he saw construction. He just wanted to learn more from Toots.

"Yeah. They're tearing out the section that was shut down after a barzilium freighter rammed the station three—no, four—years ago. United even built their own docking station, complete with repair bays and their own crew." As he talked, he filled drink orders. Then he leaned in close. "I heard United is expanding into the Outer Rim territories. And you know what that means. The Coalition will step up security. Might even put Hallart out of business."

Quin took a slow sip of the stout ale. "You think so? He's expanded into the Central Planets, and nothing seems to change."

Toots made a rude noise. "That's because no one knew the extent of his business. Now that it's all out in the open, Coalition Security has increased patrols, especially out here. He'll be caught. Just wait and see."

Toots better watch what he said. Hallart had a way of knowing what people were saying and then exacting punishment on those who defied him.

Quin twisted his glass. "Not too fond of him, are you?"

"His thugs tried to shake me down for protection. That's extortion and I won't do it. It's like standing up to a bully. You gotta hold your ground and they'll leave you alone."

Quin wouldn't burst his friend's bubble by mentioning how he'd interceded for Toots with his employer. Still, it wouldn't be good for Toots if it got around that he'd stood up to Hallart.

"Listen, buddy. I think you're right about standing up to bullies. But you might not want to brag about it. I heard Hallart's goons like to make examples out of those who defy their boss."

Toots punched Quin's shoulder. "You getting soft, boy? You were always the first one to wade into a fight. You never let anyone intimidate you."

Quin finished his ale. "Only those I knew I could beat. I steer well clear of gangsters and their goons. Thanks for the drink." He flipped a coin in Toots' direction.

Toots flipped it back. "On the house. Just this once. Next time I'll charge double." His laugh attracted a fem's attention as she stood in the open doorway.

Coriana attracted quite a bit of attention herself. From the top of her short, stylishly-cut hair the brilliant gray of argenturum, to her expensive sandals, the older fem exuded power. With age, a Chellian's spots faded. Not hers. He heard she'd had them enhanced. The low-cut bodice of her gray-green lathaka dress showed off those spots that extended down her neck and along the sides of her breasts. Also enhanced. He wondered if her dress came from the outrageously expensive material his sister transported.

She caught Quin's eye. With an imperious nod, she indicated that he follow her. That was a surprise. He didn't expect her to come to him. When she approached the back booth, two burly men nodded then got up—as if they'd been holding the booth for her.

"See ya later, Toots." Quin tipped a salute to his friend. "Duty calls."

"Good luck to you. You know what they say about her. She eats boys like us for First Meal."

"I'm definitely worth waiting until Last Meal." Quin was still grinning as he joined Coriana at the booth.

Of course, she'd already taken the prime position—back to the wall, looking forward. He expected nothing less. She couldn't be leader of the largest trafficking ring in three Rim sectors without knowing a few tricks.

Her one weakness was impatience, as evidenced by her tapping her fingernails on the table top. Though her nails were perfectly manicured, her hands showed her age. With all her other enhancements, he wondered why she hadn't had them done, too.

"May I get you something from the bar?" he asked before sitting down.

"No. Sit." She signaled a robo-server who quickly rolled up to the booth. "A glass of Mondavian Blue, properly chilled."

Quin asked for the less expensive Green. He never thought the Blue worth the extra credits. Besides, he hated to waste credits on something he only bought for show. He never drank with his boss or Coriana.

When he sat back in the booth, a cracked piece of the faux leather poked him near his waist. Another reason she'd chosen the seat she did. "I would have come to your office, Coriana."

"I wish to speak to you about a delicate matter."

In other words, she didn't want her staff to hear. The fem was more suspicious than he'd known. He wondered if she suspected him. Probably.

She waited while the server brought their wine then leaned forward. "You did not eliminate the threat in Astron."

"She got the message."

"A fire? Really, Quin. Couldn't you have made sure she was sleeping inside first?" Coriana's gray eyes narrowed. "I wanted her gone."

"Next time be more specific. You said you wanted her to stop interfering. She's so devastated all she'll think about is rebuilding. She won't have the energy to pursue anything else."

"No. She's tenacious. She'll want justice." Then she sat back. "She knows you were responsible. Someone saw you at the scene."

Quin frowned. He knew that's what she expected. "Too bad."

"You were sloppy."

"My boss is satisfied with my work. That's all that matters."

At the mention of his boss, she blanched. After a quick sip of her wine, her complexion returned to its former appearance. "Yes. Will you tell him I have everything under control?"

The fact that she asked rather than demanded showed her fear of his boss. Fear was good. It kept the minions in line.

"He knows. He is pleased with your expansion into Malcor Sector."

"And you will express my gratitude for your assistance?"

Quin smiled. "Already have."

She twisted the stem of her glass, watching the blue wine swirl. "I have a small matter that needs to be taken care of."

She waited for him to ask. When he didn't—he had more patience—she cleared her throat. "One of my staff is leaking information to the authorities. I want you to find out who and bring me the evidence of her betrayal."

"Her? You are certain it is a fem?" He knew damn well who was leaking info. Him.

With a tentative nod, she said, "Yes. The men wouldn't dare."

"I'll take care of it." As he started to get up, she stopped him. When she placed her hand on his, the tips of her nails dug in.

"I am not convinced the threat in Astron is neutralized."

Quin wasn't surprised she returned to Rissa Dix. He cocked his head and waited.

"I want you to eliminate her."

"Eliminate? So there is no misunderstanding this time . . ."

"All right, damn it. Kill the bitch."

His comm's vibration on the bedside table brought Dillan out of a sound sleep. Beside him, Rissa stirred. As soon as he shut off the comm, she sighed and settled down. Who is Lexol's Fire would call in the middle of the night?

He looked at the mini-monitor. A message from his father to call.

If he ignored the message, the man would send it again. And again.

With as much stealth as he could, Dillan slipped out of bed and left his quarters. On the way out, he grabbed his shirt and trousers. Feeling naked in front of his father was one thing. *Being* naked made him more vulnerable.

Fully clothed—sans underwear—he padded barefoot to the command center. Within mins, Boras Rusteran's craggy face appeared on the vid screen. Unlike Dillan, the man *was* fully dressed in a dark gray business suit. Eleganza's brilliant sunrise appeared in the window behind his father.

"Where in Lexol have you been? I'm waiting for an update." That was his father. Get right down to business, no niceties, or social chitchat.

"There have been . . . problems."

"I don't give a pung rat's ass about problems. Get me a lease to mine lambidium on Galeria 7."

"Galeriana," Dillan corrected.

Boras' face reddened. "I don't give a sherd about the name of that piece of sherd rock. I want that lease."

"The Sauri chief refuses to even consider renegotiating—"

"Convince the stupid bastard."

"The chief is Konner Winslott."

"What?"

"You heard me. Konner is Chief Sauri-Alcar."

Boras appeared to be thinking. "He's never returned to see old man Winslott. Exploit the rift between them. Get him to see—"

"No."

He reared back. "What do you mean *no?*"

"Exactly what I said. No, I will not exploit problems between Konner and his father."

"By the Divine One, you will do what I say." His face turned so red Dillan feared his father would have a stroke. "If you don't, you can look for another job."

"Fine with me. I never wanted it."

"What?"

"You heard me. I quit."

Boras blustered incoherently. "You can't quit."

"You'll have my resignation shortly." That felt so good. Something he should have done two years ago.

"You can't resign. You're my son."

"Exactly. I'm your *son*, not you."

"I'll disinherit you."

Dillan had heard that threat before, ever since he was sixteen.

"I don't want or need your credits. Or the company. It's made you a miserable old man."

"Why you ungrateful—" He broke off sputtering. "I built this company for you."

"No. You built it for yourself. I don't want it. Never did."

"You're getting it anyway." Typical Boras. Getting so worked up he reversed directions without realizing it.

"If you insist," Dillan said quietly, "I will sell it to Jileena for one credit."

Stunned, Boras opened and closed his mouth, but no words came out. Dillan couldn't believe it. He'd rendered his father speechless.

He ended the transmission.

Maybe, just maybe he would be able to go back to sleep. After ripping off his wrist comm, he shucked his clothes then got into bed.

Rissa propped herself on one elbow. "What was all that yelling?"

"Nothing." He drew her close. "Sorry I woke you. Go back to sleep."

She settled in his arms, her head resting on his chest. "Sounded like more than nothing."

"My father."

"What did he want?"

"What he always wants. My soul." At her surprised look, he added, "I quit. He isn't happy."

"What?"

"I should never have gone to work for him. I knew it when I was sixteen. The past two years convinced me I was right."

"What will you do?" She paused. "Stars, Dillan, you spent all those credits on me in Vesteron. I knew you shouldn't have."

He tapped her nose. "Sweetheart, I have more credits than I'll ever know what to do with. My grandmother encouraged me to be my own man. She left me a tidy sum so I could make a choice. I won't ever *have* to work." He rolled her under him. "Since you're awake, I can think of more important things to do than talk about my credit situation."

She wrapped her arms around his neck. "Thank you, Dillan."

"What for?"

"For not leaving last night when I told you to." She pulled his head down to kiss his lips. "You always know what I need."

"I try. The Divine One knows I try." He let her explore with her mouth, reveling in her tentative kisses along his chin then his jaw. She'd reached his ear when the comm went off again.

Without looking, he reached for the device and shut it off.

"Shouldn't you see who's calling?"

"Nope. I know. Boras Rusteran." Dillan clasped the back of her head. "Where were we?"

After another delicious mating, Rissa settled into his arms. She'd started to doze when a loud banging on the side of the ship brought both of them upright.

"This better be important." For the second time that night, Dillan threw on his trousers. He didn't bother with the shirt.

"Mister Rusteran." Banging on the hull accompanied the male voice. "Mister Rusteran, please respond."

Dillan opened the hatch. "What is so damn—"

Chief Kaminga stood outside. "Sir, is Miz Rissa here?"

Even in the midst of all the problems in the colony, Dillan had never seen Kaminga this upset. As the ramp lowered, the Security Chief hopped on.

"What is it, Chief?" She'd thrown on Dillan's discarded shirt, which swished against the middle of her thighs as she padded toward him. Her hair, all sleep tousled, made her look adorable.

"Miz Rissa, we've been trying to contact you. And Mister Rusteran." He nodded to Dillan. "Manager d'Arcanin finally called me when he couldn't contact either of you."

Rissa clutched Dillan's arm. "What's wrong?"

"A slave crew captured three girls up at the mine." Kaminga swallowed hard. "One of them was Pela."

CHAPTER 20

Rissa staggered. Only Dillan's arm around her waist kept her from collapsing. Not Pela. She couldn't lose another child. While she and Dillan made love, her Pela had been in danger.

"I don't have any details," Kaminga said. "Your manager just wanted me to contact you."

"Who else besides Pela?" Rissa let go of Dillan. "You said three girls. Anaris?"

"I'm not sure. I'm going up there to examine the scene."

As Kaminga started down the ramp, Dillan stopped him. "Come with us, Chief. It will be faster."

After telling Kaminga to wait in the lounge, Dillan led her into his quarters. He held her shoulders. "Listen to me. We will find her."

"You can't know that." She ripped off his shirt then grabbed her own clothes and threw them on. Instead of taking time to braid her hair, she wrapped a tie around it to keep it in place.

"I have no doubt. You shouldn't either. We will find Pela and the other girls."

"You should have answered your comm." As the accusation flew out of her mouth, she searched for hers. She remembered taking it off. "Where's mine?"

Dillan reached into a drawer next to the bed. He handed over her device.

"It's off. I never turn off my comm." When she stared at him, a flush shot up from his neck to his ears. Guilt. "Damn you."

In the lounge, she peppered Kaminga with questions. Though he couldn't answer any about the slavers, he did talk to her about the fire.

The fire.

She'd forgotten about it. After being so devastated by the loss of her business, not only had she forgotten, she didn't care. Pela was more important. The poor child. Snatched by traffickers. How terrified she must be.

". . . evidence of arson." Kaminga was still talking. "I am certain the investigator will verify my findings."

With a distracted wave, she said, "I'm sure he will."

"About the vandalism." Kaminga cleared his throat. "Ramus, that vocal farmer at the town meeting. He and his workers did it. Ramus said Nakus paid him to do it."

The vandalism hardly mattered, but she wasn't surprised at the perpetrators.

"Ramus and his workers are in the lock-up. Nakus disappeared. When we searched his room, I found a master key from when he was Security Chief."

That explained how the vandals got in without damaging doors or windows. Not that it mattered anymore. She only cared about finding Pela.

When Dillan called back to prepare for launch, she showed Kaminga how to buckle up. "It's only a short hop. Don't bother unbuckling." She grabbed the harness in the lounge chair and secured herself.

During prep and launch, all she could think about were the girls. After landing, she didn't wait for Dillan to shut everything down. She jumped off the ramp before it completely lowered then ran to Manager d'Arcanin's office. Supervisor Harraway was pacing and a slender fem sat in the corner quietly weeping. Another fem sat close and rubbed her shoulder.

"What happened?" Rissa demanded.

"They took my girl," Harraway shouted.

"And my Pela?" she asked. Kaminga could have gotten things wrong.

D'Arcanin nodded. "Anaris, too."

"How?"

Dillan and Kaminga came in behind her. The small office became even smaller.

"Mister Rusteran, glad you're here." D'Arcanin introduced the two fems as Harraway's spouse and his own.

"How did the traffickers get the girls?" Rissa demanded. They didn't have time for social niceties.

"They'd gone exploring in the caves," d'Arnanin said.

Dillan put his hand on Rissa's shoulder. "I thought those were off limits."

"They knew better." Harraway's grief was palpable. "My men didn't see them go beyond the perimeter. I fired them all."

His spouse clutched his hand. "It was not their fault. You hire them back."

While Harraway harrumphed, d'Arcanin went on. "My boy wanted to play with them. He's only ten, and they didn't want him hanging around. So he hid and spied on them. That's how we know what happened to the girls."

"Good thing he hid," Kaminga said. "Otherwise the slavers might have gotten him, too."

"We know." Distress filled d'Arcanin's eyes. "My boy watched three men jump the girls outside a cave. He was too scared to cry out or yell for help."

"If he had, the slavers would have caught him, too," Kaminga repeated.

"My boy said when they carried the girls off, they put bags over their heads, and the girls weren't moving. He had the good sense to follow them and saw their ship. A shuttle that barely made any noise as it lifted off."

"My men still should have noticed a ship landing and taking off."

"Did anyone contact Traffic Controller Ropergor and find out if a larger ship was in orbit?" Dillan asked.

"I did," Harraway said. "But it left orbit too quickly for identification."

"We'll find the girls." Dillan offered the same reassurance he had before. Rissa wasn't convinced. The traffickers had too large a head start. If only he hadn't turned off her comm.

"My boy is quite an artist," d'Arcanin said.

What an idiot. Rissa forced herself to choke back the words. Pela was gone, and he was bragging about his kid. *Great.* Now he was going to show pictures.

He handed over a data pad to Kaminga. "He captured the likenesses of the slavers as well as their shuttle. I'll send them to your comm, Chief."

"And mine," Dillan added.

Rissa snatched the pad from Kaminga and scrolled through the pictures. The boy *was* good. "I've seen this one—" She pointed. "—in the tavern last week. And I'm sure I've seen the others. Maybe the week before? I don't know, but they look familiar. Chief, ask the dock master."

"Miz Rissa. I know you're upset—"

"Damn right, I'm upset."

"I do know my job. Rest assured my officers and I will do everything we can to find Pela. All the girls," he hastily added.

Over her shoulder, Dillan tapped the edge of the pad. "This shuttle is from a Chellian transport. An XP-508, if I'm not mistaken. I'm sure Yephos or Ropergor can confirm that. Can you tell us anything else?"

When Harraway and d'Arcanin shook their heads, Dillan said, "We're going after them. I promise you—" He squeezed Rissa's shoulder. "—we'll find the girls. Kaminga, coming?"

"Go," he said. "I'm going to question the patrols and examine the site near the caves and where that shuttle landed. If I find out anything, I'll contact you. Answer your comm this time. Both of you."

Rissa raced ahead of Dillan back to the ship. As they approached it, she rounded on him. "Don't you ever turn off my comm again."

He rubbed the back of his neck. "I'm sorry. You were so upset by the fire, I didn't want you to be disturbed."

"You didn't even bother checking yours. You just assumed it was your father. You should have—"

"I know. You aren't saying anything I haven't said to myself ever since Kaminga showed up. I'm sorry, sweetheart. You can't know how sorry I am." Regret clouded his green eyes, etched itself on his countenance. The same regret that filled her heart.

"Do not call me sweetheart. If I was, you would respect me."

"I do respect you." He lowered the ramp.

"If you respected me, you wouldn't make decisions for me. I deserve to make my own choices." She stomped up the ramp and into the ship.

He followed her. "I promise you, Rissa, we'll get Pela and the others back. I won't let you down."

While she was still upset over what he'd done, she could understand why. His distress rivaled hers. She wouldn't think about how he'd delayed the search for Pela by not answering his comm, by hiding hers. Practicality outweighed anger . . . for the time being. He was her best chance to find Pela. He had a ship. He had contacts. It wouldn't be like before when she'd searched for Miri alone.

And she had to believe his promise. They would find the girls. They had to.

As he prepared for liftoff, she asked where they were going.

"Back to Astron."

"No. We have to follow the girls."

He swiveled around to face her. "We need more information. We don't know where that ship went. We can't just wander around space."

She slumped into the other seat. "You're right. I still feel like we should *do* something."

"We will do something. Buckle up. We're going to start with questioning the kids we rescued."

"What good will that do?" She secured her harness. "Those slavers were blown up with their ship."

He grimaced. "I know. They were part of a trafficking ring. The older kids might know more than we think. More than the crew realized they overheard. Their destination, maybe."

"I didn't think of that." Already he was helping her. The old saying about two heads being better than one applied. "We should start with the girl that Sophira and Partorus took in. In the meantime, I'm going to contact Ropergor. I want to know what he knows about their ship."

"Kaminga is going to do that."

"I know," she said. "But I have to find out for myself."

After her second try, Traffic Controller Ropergor responded. *"Mistress Rissa, I apologize for the wait. I am so sorry about Pela. She is such a sweet girl."*

"I need your help, Rope."

"Anything. What do you need?"

"Have you seen a Chellian XP-508 recently? Or its shuttle?"

"Chief Kaminga just asked me the same thing. Are you working with him?"

"Sort of. I need all the information you have on that ship."

"I told Kaminga I would get back to him with the info. As soon as I do, I will let you know what I—"

"Damn it, Rope. That's my daughter out there."

Dillan turned sharply and raised his eyebrow.

"I need that information now."

For a moment, she heard nothing but normal static. She'd taken the traffic controller aback. Would he help or stall her?

"Yes, ma'am. A shuttle from an XP-508 landed here three times."

He told her the dates, two of which coincided with when she'd seen the men. But not the third. Dillan handed her a data pad to make notes. Meanwhile, Ropergor continued.

"I detected the XP-508 in orbit two other times, but neither the ship nor the shuttle landed then."

"When?"

She noted more dates in the data pad. One of them was familiar, but she couldn't place it.

"Before you called, I contacted Marsden Colony. The traffic controller—"

"That's it. The reason I thought one time sounded familiar. That was when the slavers hit Marsden."

"Correct." Ropergor sounded disappointed. He'd discovered the information, and she'd beat him to the punch. *"I also contacted Remering Colony. They were raided by a ship that was here. I'm not sure if you remember. You brought them supplies at the last minute. They lost their passengers at another 'port but accused us of stealing them."*

When she'd rescued Pela and Anaris. So the traffickers had been at Remering, too.

"I remember. The pilot was a nasty one."

"Oh, dear," Ropergor said. *"Chief Kaminga is calling me."*

"Will you contact me when you discover anything else?" Ropergor promised then disconnected.

"Remering?" Dillan said. "I'm not familiar with that colony."

"Small population. It's in the northern hemisphere. Extreme temperatures. Half the year they're frozen in. The other half it's too hot to go outside."

"Why would anyone settle there?"

"Who knows? I heard they have a couple of weeks transitioning between the extremes where the hunting is so good they can supply Rhadaman City and half of Galeria Prime with all the meat they need. That's so profitable, they don't bother supplying small colonies like us or Marsden."

"Hearty souls to endure such extremes."

"I never thought about families in Remering, but there must be if the traffickers raided the colony. How do they know where to find children?"

"Good question. We're almost back to Astron. Take a min to jot down what we know while it's still fresh."

As soon as they landed, Ropergor walked up to them in his stiff-legged style. He often complained about his joints, which seemed to be hurting more each year.

"I have more information for you." He pulled a small data pad, similar to Dillan's, out of his trouser pocket.

Volpians were the information gatherers of the galaxy. They were smart enough to know that every commodity had a price. Rissa handed over her credit device. "Input whatever amount. I don't care how much it costs."

"Mistress Rissa, put that away." He gave her a look of affront. "I do not charge friends."

She almost asked 'Since when?' but thought better of it.

"That little Pela brings, I mean, used to bring me Mid-Day meal almost every day. I want to help find her." He consulted his pad. "I talked to every traffic controller I know in the Galeria System. I was planning to go farther afield when you called for landing. I will do so, but first I'll tell you what I know."

As he spoke, she took notes.

"You do not need to do that, Mistress Rissa. I will send this to your device."

She gave Dillan a helpless look. This pad was more sophisticated than anything she'd used before. She knew basics but not how to transfer data. He took it from her and collected Rope's information.

173

Now she had a list of all the ships that had landed at various colonies at the time of raids—though the traffic controllers couldn't tell which ships were actually slavers because of the time lapse between the ships leaving and the discovery of the missing children. Since the ships had to report destinations, she had those, too. She suspected some were false. She had dates, number of missing children, their ages, races, and genders, and where the raids had taken place—homes, orphanages, farms/ranches or colony proper.

A lot more than they had before.

After thanking Ropergor, she gave him a hug. Then she and Dillan headed outside.

"We should call Kaminga before going to Sophira's," Dillan said.

The chief, still up at the mines, had been very busy. He'd questioned d'Arcanin's boy who remembered more now that he knew he wasn't going to get into trouble.

"I talked to the security chiefs in the Galeria System and asked them to send me whatever they had about slaver raids. Then I realized I should have called Chief Plisferd in Vesteron. He is my boss, you know. I asked him to contact all the heads of security in Malcor Sector and gather their information."

"Good thinking," Rissa replied. "Will he help?"

"I have to say I wish Chief Servary was still my boss. He was much easier to talk to. Anyway, Plisferd said one of his staff had already started a database on reports of slavers and child traffickers. He said it wasn't ready to share, but I insisted we needed access."

Dillan leaned over her shoulder to see the mini-monitor on her wrist comm. "Good for you. Don't let bureaucrats keep you from getting the info you need."

Kaminga grinned broadly. "Chief Servary told me that, too. I don't have that database yet, but as soon as I do I will share it with you. The more people looking at the info the better."

"Will that get you into trouble?" Rissa asked. With him being so cooperative, she didn't want to endanger his job. She cared about the young security officer, but she was more worried about a replacement who might stonewall her.

The chief didn't look concerned. "Doesn't matter. The important thing is finding the missing girls. Who knows, we might even find other children."

Although she should care about all missing children, her main focus was on Pela. And Anaris.

"Who on your staff can get us the info you have on traffickers?" Dillan asked.

"Talk to Pashku." Kaminga looked off to the side. "I have to go. Manager d'Arcanin is giving me a ride back to Astron on the transport that's ready to leave. The miners know your tavern is . . . gone. All they can talk about is the offworlder's place that will be open in two days." He turned to the side again. "I'm coming."

After communications ended, Dillan looked at her. "I didn't realize the new tavern would be open so soon."

She gave him a wry look. "Guess I don't have to worry about the competition anymore."

"Oh, sweetheart." He gathered her in his arms. "I am so sorry about your tavern."

"I know." She stiffened. Forgiving him wouldn't be easy. "Me, too."

After giving her a quick kiss on the forehead, he let go. "We need to get out of this heat. It's Mid-Day already. Where do you want to go first? Sophira's or the security office?"

"Security Office." She strode down the street. "We need to see what they collected first so we don't duplicate."

He strode alongside her. "Good thinking. What we find might give us more ideas."

Officer Pashku was only too happy to help. "Whatever you need to find your girl. I always liked her. Sweet kid." She swiveled around to face a vid monitor. "Chief Kaminga gave me permission to let you read our reports."

"Can you send them to my data pad?" Dillan asked.

"Sure."

While Pashku transferred the data, Rissa began reading what was on the screen. The traffickers' first appearance in Astron was when she rescued Pela and Anaris. Rissa was surprised security knew about that. She hadn't told them. Possibly the dock master, especially after the pilot made such a stink about losing his *cargo*.

"I have the data," Dillan said. "You can read it later. Let's go."

He led her out the back exit. "That's Kaminga's skimmer. Pashku said we can use it while he's not here."

"It's not that far to Sophira's."

"This will save time. Get in." After she did, he added, "We're also going to talk to the boys the farmers took."

With chagrin, she knew he was right. Still, she hated sitting. Walking would have expended some of her energy and distress. Maybe even her anger over the turned-off comms.

A teary Sophira hugged her at the door. "I am so sorry about Pela. I'll do whatever I can to help."

"We want to talk to Zeka. We need to find out what she knows about the crew that took her and the other kids."

While ushering them into the small sitting room, Sophira gave her a worried look. "She doesn't like to talk about that time."

"It's important."

"Is something wrong?" Zeka came into the room, carrying the baby who must be six tendays now. The same age as Miri when she was stolen.

The usual pain knifed through her whenever she saw an infant that age.

Dillan glanced at Rissa before looking at the teen. "We'd like to ask you some questions."

At the girl's startled look, Rissa said, "You aren't in any trouble. Do you remember Pela, the girl who helped lead the children off the slave ship? She's gone and I need your help to find her."

"I don't know anything about that. I mean, Miz Sophira told me the slavers came back, and that they took some girls. But I was here. I didn't see anything."

The baby, sensing the girl's distress, began to cry. Sophira took her and told everyone to sit down. "Zeka, they rescued you. Tell them what they want to know."

Zeka looked wary but sat.

Rissa began, "I want you to think back on that time. I know it's hard. You were scared, but I need you to tell us everything that happened. Let's start with what you were doing when you were captured."

"I wasn't captured. The lady who ran the shelter gathered some of us together. She told us the men were taking us to people who wanted us and would give us new homes." She snorted. "And we all believed her."

"So they didn't take all the children at the shelter?" Dillan asked.

Zeka shook her head. "She had a list."

Rissa looked at Dillan sharply. "A list?"

Sophira said, "From what Zeka told me before, the slavers wanted certain children by age and gender."

"As if they were ordering groceries." Rissa didn't hide her disgust.

Dillan squeezed her hand. "Were you taken to the ship we found you in, or were you transferred?"

"Same ship. When they locked us in the hold, I knew we weren't going to new homes. The little kids started to cry because it was dark all the time. When the men brought us food and water, I tried to get them to give us some light. All they did was laugh."

"That must have been terrifying," Dillan said. "Now here comes the hard part. Will you close your eyes and try to remember everything they said to you or to each other?"

Zeka shuddered. "Miz Sophira, I don't want to."

Sophira shoved the baby at Rissa then sat next to Zeka and held her. In panic, Rissa had to hold onto the squirming infant. She couldn't do this. She hadn't held a baby since Miri. She never wanted to feel another infant in her arms when she couldn't hold her own.

The baby looked up at her with wide blue eyes. At least, she didn't have Miri's brown ones. She grabbed a hunk of Rissa's hair that had slipped over her shoulder. Miri used to do that, too. As the baby wiggled in excitement, Rissa clutched her to her shoulder. The little one waved her hand back and forth, yanking on Rissa's hair.

In the background, she heard Dillan asking questions and Zeka answering. But all Rissa could think about was the baby. The pain in her heart intensified. She would never hold her own daughter like this. In three tendays, Miri would be twenty, and Rissa had missed her growing up.

When the baby yanked the chain out of Rissa's shirt, she realized she had to pay more attention. The baby found the pendant. As she played with it, her tiny fingers hit the release and the hologram appeared.

Before Rissa could close the pendant, Sophira exclaimed, "What is that?"

"It's a baby," Zeka said at the same time.

"I know it's a baby." Sophira laughed. Her expression changed. "Miz Rissa. Who is that?" Her expression said she knew.

Dillan disengaged the baby's fingers, closed the pendant and tucked it inside Rissa's shirt. The baby let her displeasure at losing a plaything be known. Sophira started to take her, but Rissa shook her head.

"It's all right." She cradled the baby in her arms close to her breast. "That was my child."

"Was?" Zeka asked. "Did she die?"

Sophira tried to shush her.

"No. She was stolen by traffickers when she was about this little one's age." She walked her fingers up and down the baby's chest, even tickling her. "Hush now, little one. Play with my finger. That's right."

When she realized the others had stopped talking, she looked up. "Go on."

Dillan cleared his throat. As he asked his questions, Zeka seemed to open up more. Finally, he turned to Rissa. "I think Zeka has told us everything she knows. We can leave. Unless you'd like to stay longer."

"Uh, no." She handed the little one to Sophira then stood. "She's a beautiful baby, Sophira. What did you name her?"

"Miya Rissa."

Dillan helped Rissa into the skimmer. She hadn't spoken since discovering the name of Sophira's baby. Even when Sophira said in a sheepish tone that she'd taken a job at the new tavern, Rissa hadn't responded. Dillan had reassured Sophira that she'd done the right thing. That she needed to take care of her family.

They sped off north of the town toward the ranches dotting the landscape. How anything could grow in the soil bewildered him.

"Are you all right?"

Rissa half-turned to him. "I didn't know she'd named the baby after me."

"Didn't Pela go to the naming ceremony?"

"If she mentioned the name, I blocked it out. I never wanted to know anything about babies."

"Too many bad memories?"

"Not exactly." She stared ahead at the drab landscape. "I haven't held a baby since losing Miri. When Sophira thrust her at me, I had no choice."

He'd seen that in her face and almost stepped in to take the infant. "You could have given her back."

"And have to explain why?" She scoffed. "I ended up doing that anyway. It will be all over the village by tonight."

She was right about that. Gossip ran swiftly through the colony and the surrounding area. Anyone was fair game.

"Will that bother you?"

She let out a heavy sigh. "I used to think it would. But now I have a worse worry. Finding Pela. Did Zeka give you anything useful?"

He knew she hadn't been paying attention. Although he'd questioned Zeka, he'd kept an eye on Rissa. It only took a few mins of minor panic—which Sophira didn't see because she was concentrating on Zeka—before Rissa began to relax. When the baby grabbed her hair, she'd even smiled as she tried to pry open the tiny fingers.

But what amazed him more was when she cuddled the baby. He saw a mixture of pleasure and pain in her eyes. And longing.

"Hey, Rusteran. Are you with me? What did you get from Zeka?"

"Sorry. I got the name of the lady who runs the shelter in Balderate Colony. If she's selling homeless kids, she has to have a contact. That's a good place to start. But first let's talk to the boys." He pulled the skimmer up close to a stone farmhouse.

Like Zeka, the two boys, brothers who were eleven and twelve, didn't want to talk. With gentle prodding from the farmer and his spouse, they opened up. Dillan took notes while Rissa asked questions. Most of what they told her was a repetition of what Zeka had said. The older brother mentioned he'd seen it happen before and often hoped he'd be chosen to go to a real home. After expressing his disappointment at the cruel lie, he hastened to assure the farmer that he appreciated them taking him and his brother in.

Next, they visited a rancher who'd taken four boys. Two were old enough to question, the others too little. Or so they thought until a six-year-old said, "They were taking us to the Central District."

Dillan and Rissa looked at each other.

"How do you know?" one of the older boys asked. "I never heard that."

"That's 'cause you were always talking to Zeka. Or sleeping. I pretended to be asleep when two of them came in to check on us. The fat one said he couldn't wait until they got to this place called Manca and get rid of us."

"Manca?" Rissa said. "Is that a city you recognize?"

Dillan shook his head.

"And the skinny guy said he couldn't wait either because the stink was so awful it made him sick. Then he threw up over in a corner."

An ambiguous clue. Manca. She could search the data pad when they returned to the ship.

Back in the skimmer, he said, "That will teach us not to dismiss the little kids."

They talked to other children in the village, but didn't learn more. None mentioned Manca. Or where they were being taken. Finally, Dillan returned the chief's skimmer and they headed for his ship. As they passed Fortuna's, he had a thought. When he veered down the alley that ran behind the pleasure palace, Rissa stopped him.

"We're wasting time."

"No. We're gathering info so we aren't running around like headless turkens. The kids were here first. Remember? Fortuna's girls bathed the kids." He knocked on the back door. "The girls might remember something the kids said."

The cook took one look at Rissa and burst into tears. "We're so sorry about your tavern. What a shame. And your girl, Pela, too. Nasty business those traffickers. I'll get Miz Fortuna. Just you wait here."

After she left them in the kitchen, Rissa said softly, "I don't know if I can take any more sympathy."

"They mean well. People like you. They just don't know what else to say."

She harrumphed.

Fortuna rushed into the kitchen. "Are you okay, sweetie?" She hugged Rissa then stood back to examine her. "Rusteran, see that she gets some sleep, even if you have to tie her to the bed."

"Kinky sex." He grinned. "Sounds like fun."

Rissa batted his shoulder. "I can sleep when I'm dead. We need your help."

"Anything." Fortuna looked from her to Dillan.

Rissa spoke first. "When all your girls are free, can you get them together and ask them what they remember from the night you rescued the kids from that slaver?"

"Sure. Why?"

"They might remember something significant," Dillan said. "If they're altogether, they might jog each other's memories. We're hoping for a lead to the traffickers and, more importantly, to their boss. We have a clue. The fem who ran a homeless shelter in Balderate Colony probably sold them."

"That bitch."

"Agreed," Rissa said.

"It's possible the slavers were taking the kids to the Central District." When Fortuna opened her mouth, he added, "Don't mention that or the shelter in Balderate to your girls. No sense planting ideas."

Fortuna nodded. "Most of the girls are working right now. Is tomorrow morning too late? That's the first time they'll all be free."

"We're leaving now," Rissa said.

"No problem." Dillan pulled out his data pad and gave Fortuna the code to transmit whatever she found out.

"You two be careful." Fortuna hugged Rissa again. "You're dealing with an organized gang. The way they've been hitting the colonies lately, I wouldn't be surprised if Hallart's behind it."

A chill went through him. Hallart, again. The gangster who'd ordered the hit on Jileena to stop her from testifying against one of his minions.

"We will be careful," Rissa said. "But I'm not backing down. I don't care if I have to face Lexol himself. I will find Pela."

Fortuna reached up to hug Dillan. "Take care of my friend. Bring her back alive."

"I will," he promised.

"You'd better take care of yourself, too," Fortuna added. "If she gets tired of you, you know where to find me." She gave him a lascivious wink.

On the walk back to the 'port, Rissa asked, "Are you going to take her up on her offer?"

"Are you tired of me already?"

"Not exactly."

He stopped in the middle of the dusty street. "What do you mean *not exactly*?"

"I'm teasing. Sort of." She continued walking at her usual fast pace.

"What does *sort of* mean?"

"Give it a rest. We need to get on our way to Balderate. It's a good three-day trip."

He let her have the last word. But he still worried. She hadn't spoken about his major screw-up with the comms. Not since she'd blown up at him earlier. He prayed to the Divine One that she would eventually forgive him. The worst part? If she'd done that to him and the consequences had been as devastating, he wasn't sure he could forgive her.

"We haven't eaten all day." His stomach had been protesting for the past hour. "We should stop in at the café."

"No time." She kept striding down the street.

"Nally and his spouse fed the children. They might have learned something."

Rissa slowed down.

He pressed the advantage. "The Mid-Day rush is over. They shouldn't be too busy."

She crossed over to the boardwalk. "A quick meal then we leave."

He didn't let her see him smile. If she hadn't agreed, he would've had to force feed her on the ship. And a meal at the café had more appeal than replicated food.

The chef and his spouse were happy to join them. "Arjay can serve us," Nally said. "He's becoming a fair to middlin' line cook."

"And it keeps him from talking our ears off." Voleya laid her hand on top of Rissa's. "We were real sorry—"

Dillan saw Rissa bite her lips.

"—about Pela. Such a sweet girl."

He hoped to stave off her tears by getting to the point of their visit. "We'd like to ask you about the children you fed. The ones the traffickers captured."

"Of course," Voleya said. "What would you like to know?"

"Lunch is served," Arjay announced as he placed their meals before them with a flourish. "*Bon appetite.*"

Nally rolled his eyes. "He's been watching Terran cooking vids."

As Rissa began eating, Dillan wanted to tell her to slow down but knew that would be futile. Instead, he asked what they remembered. Arjay hovered nearby. For a change, he was silent.

"Did any of the children mention their destination?" Dillan asked.

"No," Nally replied.

"Yes," Voleya said at the same time.

Rissa put down her fork. "Where?"

"One of the little boys said he was disappointed he wouldn't get to see a station."

"A station?" Rissa asked. "Like a ranch or a farm?"

Voleya paused. "I think he meant a space station."

Nally sent Arjay along with them as they left, his arms laden with baskets of foodstuffs for their trip.

"Aren't you glad we stopped?" Dillan said. "We have enough food to last a tenday."

"I suppose. How soon can we leave? You did contact Dock Master Yephos to have the ship prepped, didn't you?" She was so anxious she reminded him of Quin, all coiled up inside, a bundle of nerves.

"You heard me call him in between the two farms. Take it easy."

The auto-doors to the spaceport grated open.

"Don't tell me to take it easy. Pela isn't your daughter." She marched on ahead.

He grabbed her elbow before she went through the doors to the hangar. "She isn't yours, either."

CHAPTER 21

Rissa whirled around, eyes blazing. "She is the closest thing I have to a daughter. I lost one because I failed to act quickly enough. I won't fail again. If you want to dillydally around, I'll hire a pilot who can get me where I need to go."

No matter what he said she wouldn't listen. The best thing was to get on their way to Balderate. They would have three shipdays to work out their problems. He hoped. Damn, the fem could be infuriating. He deserved some of her anger because of the comms. But he'd be damned to Lexol's Fire if he'd lie down and let her tromp all over him. They needed to work together to find Pela. During the trip to Balderate, they had time to figure out how to do that. They also needed to know where to go after Balderate. A space station? Stars. All planets in the Central District had at least one. Manca. Something niggled in the back of his mind. Maybe when Kaminga shared the information from the security chiefs in other colonies, something might register.

"Sir, where shall I put the food?"

Damn, he'd forgotten about Arjay. For a change, the AI hadn't yakked at all from the café to the ship.

"Just set it in the galley." Dillan pointed down the corridor. "Thanks for your help, Arjay. See yourself off the ship, okay?"

He handed his data pad to Rissa. "After you put away the food, start reading through all our notes and see if anything jumps out at you. I'm going to prepare for launch."

He knew he sounded abrupt, but he wasn't going to "waste" time being nice. She wanted to leave Astron quickly, he'd make damn sure they did.

"Mistress Rissa, you go ahead and read. I will be happy to put away the food."

"You have five mins before we launch." He headed for the command center.

"Uh, Dillan? I'm, uh . . ." Just when he thought she was going to apologize for what she'd said, she backed off. "I'll be in the lounge during launch."

That was a good place for her. He wasn't sure how long he could hold onto his temper if she sat next to him and carped about how slow his ship was.

* * *

Rissa wanted to bite her tongue.

She hadn't meant to lambaste Dillan. Part of her recognized that she was still angry with him over turning off their comms. She also realized that anxiety over Pela's fate, as well as the fire, had built up inside her so much it had to come out. Exploding at Dillan, blaming him for delaying their departure, wasn't fair.

As much as she hated to admit it, he'd been right to find out more about the traffickers before leaving Astron. Where she wanted to go off half-cocked, he was rational. She'd thought he was just plodding along while she wanted to race. Instead, he'd been gathering intelligence. She was such an idiot not to see that.

She went to the lounge. When Dillan called out to prepare for launch, she secured the harness. His ship always shot through the atmo with little disturbance, but it might not be the same this time.

Nothing was the same. Seven days ago—was it just seven?— they'd left for what he'd called a fun-filled vacation. Some fun to come home to a burned-out tavern and then losing Pela to traffickers.

If only she'd been there. If she hadn't gone on that stupid vacation, then Pela wouldn't have been up at the mine. If they hadn't gone to the mine in the first place, if she refused to let Pela stay with Anaris. She should have insisted that Pela come with her to Vesteron. If only Dillan hadn't ignored his comm, they would have gotten up to the mine sooner.

They must be through Galeriana's atmo already. He'd switched from the heavy-air to the sublight. She didn't know much about engines but could hear the difference. She braced herself for his appearance in the lounge. She would have to apologize.

But he didn't come.

She curled up in the corner of the sofa and began adding to the data pad what she knew about the traffickers from her first encounter— the crew that held Pela and Anaris. The girls had been picked up in different places. Anaris first in Balderate then Pela in nearby Penner Colony.

There was Balderate again.

Until forcing herself to slow down and recall what she knew before talking to the children, she'd forgotten Anaris was from Balderate. Was this a hub for the traffickers? She made more notes.

Still Dillan didn't come out of the command center.

She could go to him or stay in the lounge and read the info on the data pad. She stayed. As she read, she highlighted anything that struck her. Gradually, she began to see a pattern in the way the traffickers operated. The first landing at Astron had been a fluke, a leak in the hydraulics. If only those slavers had known what a can of worms they'd opened when they stopped for repairs. And what if Ropergor hadn't called her to bring food supplies? Would anyone have found the girls before the crew recaptured them? Had they not stopped at Astron, had the pilot and crew not been so obnoxious, Rissa would never have gone into that sanfac, never would have rescued the girls. And she and her friends wouldn't have been ready the second time.

"What are you doing?" Dillan demanded.

Rissa looked up from the datapad. He was standing in front of the galley. "I told you to see yourself off the ship."

"But, sir, I want to help you find Pela. She was so sweet to me—after she knew I was a friend. Please let me stay." *Arjay?*

When Rissa came up behind Dillan, he turned to her. "What are we going to do with him?"

"We can't turn around and take him back to Astron. It would waste of—"

"—time. I know. I could dump him out the airlock." Dillan winked at her.

"Sir?" Arjay's eyes grew wide. "While I am capable of existing outside the ship, I would find it very difficult to drift aimlessly. I prefer—"

Dillan blew out a breath and backed out of the portal. "Do you always talk so much?"

Arjay came forward, his head hung low. "Alas, that is what my Regus—I mean, Trevarr—says. I will endeavor to speak only when spoken to." He made a zipping motion across his lips.

Rissa almost laughed. Too many Terran vids. While Dillan dealt with their stowaway, she went back to the lounge and resumed her position in the corner of the sofa. Although she picked up the data pad, she listened to the exchange in the corridor.

"Are you capable of piloting this ship?" Dillan asked.

"Yes, sir." The AI's eagerness carried down the corridor. "I have piloted my Re—Celara's cargo hauler, an old Menacan transport with a rebuilt Chellian hyperdrive, and Trevarr's Agilean Speeder. My manufacturer's programming ensures that I am capable of piloting any civilian ship and most military ones."

"A simple yes or no would have sufficed. Go to the command center and familiarize yourself with the controls. I will be there shortly to answer any questions."

After Arjay left, Dillan came into the lounge. "How are you coming with the data?"

"Fine." She steeled herself to apologize.

"Ropergor and Kaminga got back to me. I forwarded their reports to the pad." He pointed to the device in her hand.

"Anything we didn't already know?"

"I couldn't tell. Too much information."

She cracked a smile. "Tell me about it. My eyes are crossed from reading. I want to organize the data, but it's overwhelming."

"You need sleep." When she started to protest, he held up his hand. "We both need sleep. At least a short nap. Then we can come at the data with fresh minds. And eyes." His mouth curved in a slight smile.

He was right. They couldn't *do* anything for three shipdays besides examine what they knew and what others sent them. She'd already caught herself once nodding off. When she came toward him, he didn't move.

This was it. Time to eat crow. The Terran expression seemed appropriate but odd. How did consuming an avian creature mean apologizing?

"Dillan." She took a deep breath. "I'm—"

"Choose whichever bedroom you want. I'll take the other." He stepped out of her way.

After opening the portal to the guest quarters, she turned around. The portal to his bedroom closed behind him.

Delicious aromas wafted into her room. That must have been what woke her up. Dillan must be cooking Last Meal. As she washed the sleep out of her eyes, she remembered Arjay. Like Dillan, she wondered what they were going to do with him. Maybe they should have turned around and dropped him back off at Astron. No. As she'd already pointed out, that would've wasted too much time.

When she came out to the lounge, Dillan was sitting in the large chair, repeatedly tapping the data pad.

"Did it stop working?" She took her place in the corner of the sofa, her legs drawn up.

He looked up in surprise. "You slept well, I presume."

After covering a yawn, she gave him a tentative smile. "I did. How long have you been up?"

"Two hours." He touched the pad's screen twice.

"Two hours? How long did you sleep?"

"Eight."

"Eight? That means I slept for ten hours. I never sleep that long."

Without looking up from the device, he said, "You must have needed it."

"Yes. Thank you for making me go to bed."

He gave her a pointed look.

"Uh, listen. I'm—"

"I found some new information." He tapped the pad again.

"Stop." As much as she wanted to know the new info, she had to get through this. "I need to tell you something first."

"No, you don't."

"Quit interrupting me. I'm sorry for what I said to you. I acted like a zircan's behind."

"Yes, you did."

That surprised her.

"I am sorry. You should've slapped me up the side of the head for the way I've treated you. I don't deserve your help."

After a few secs staring at her, he said, "Why didn't you tell me you were having a pity party? I would have brought the wine."

She didn't expect that from him, either. "Mondavian green or blue?"

He chuckled. "Blue, of course. It goes well with crow."

Her turn to laugh. "So you know the Terran expression, too."

"I find it appropriate. I understand crow is nasty tasting, especially the feathers." He came over to the sofa and sat next to her. "Look at this."

"Oh, good." Arjay appeared in the entry to the lounge "You are both awake. Would you like to eat Last Meal now? I have prepared a Chellian pasta dish. I followed Madam Nalgin's instructions to the letter. Utterly delicious." With a flourish, he put his fingers to his thumb then kissed them. "Or so I'm told. As you know, I am not programmed to consume food or drink."

Dillan looked at her. "I don't know about you, but I'm hungry."

"How can you even think about food?" she said. "We have all this new information to go over. Stopping to eat feels like we're wasting time."

"Are you going to fight me on everything? Along with sleep, our brains need fuel to work at optimum efficiency. Taking time to eat is not a waste of time."

Her stomach took the opportunity to make its emptiness evident. She hoped he hadn't heard the rumbling.

"See? Your body is trying to tell you something. Sure, Arjay. Go ahead and dish up. Can I assume the ship is still on course to Balderate Colony and everything is running smoothly?"

"Of course, sir. I would have told you if there were problems. What would you prefer to drink? Tea? Wine? We have Mondavian blue and green. I believe the blue would go well with Chellian pasta."

"I don't care," Rissa said. "We need to get back to work."

"The blue sounds fine." Dillan wiped his brow. "Work, work, work. That's all she thinks about, Arjay."

"Sir, she is upset."

"An understatement."

"If you will pardon my saying so, sir, I believe she needs understanding not criticism."

"Thank you, Arjay." Rissa smiled. "At least one of you understands me."

When the AI left, Dillan shook his head. "I'm seeing a different side of you, Rissa. I used to think you were level-headed, while I was the reckless, got-to-do-it-now kid."

"You *were* a reckless kid. All right, let's see what you found." She took the data pad. "Whoa. How did you do that? It's so organized."

"I'm an organized person. I look for commonalities and relationships." Then he quirked a smile. "I almost hate to admit this. While you were sleeping, Arjay asked what I was working on. He showed me how many things the device could do with data. See this screen? You can have it sort according to different parameters."

"That's amazing. I was trying to do it on my own. I feel like an idiot for not knowing."

He squeezed her hand. "I didn't know it could do that, either. Your highlights were very helpful." He brought up a different screen filled with dates and locations. "See the pattern? The raids are not random. They are slowly expanding into new territory."

"I thought I saw a pattern earlier, but I was so tired . . ." She gave him a wry look. "I know, you told me I needed sleep. I just didn't think I'd sleep for ten hours."

"Are you saying I should have woken you?"

"Yes. We have so much to do."

"And two and a half shipdays to do it. Lighten up, girl."

She made a rude sound. "I haven't been a girl for twenty years. Now can you pinpoint the locations with dates on a map?"

"Already did." He changed the screen. "What do you see?"

"Three hubs. Balderan, Menaca, and—" She peered at the screen. "Is that Marin 5?"

"Uh huh."

Marin 5. How she hated that place. Just saying the name brought back memories of being abandoned there by her father. Marin 5 was where she'd lost Miri. The ache in her heart lined up alongside the pain of losing Pela.

"Are you all right?" His gaze disconcerted her. "You're thinking of Miri, aren't you?"

She didn't want to talk about her baby.

"Dinner is served," Arjay announced.

Rissa thanked the Matriarch for the interruption. While she and Dillan were examining the data, Arjay had set the table across the lounge. She'd been so intent on the data pad that she hadn't even noticed.

The Chellian pasta was delicious, just as Arjay had proclaimed. Maybe his tagging along was a good thing. Needing to keep working with the data, she wouldn't take time to cook.

"Arjay, you are a miracle worker." She helped herself to seconds.

"Thank you. Celara says so, too. Sir, may I pour you more wine?"

"Knock yourself out." At Arjay's confused expression, he added, "Of course. Rissa?"

"No thanks. If I drink any more, my brain will get too fuzzy to think. Now, about the data. How did you get information that went back so far?"

Dillan groaned. "Back to work, huh? That database Kaminga got from his boss tracked trafficking activity going back over twenty years."

"Pardon me," Arjay said. "I accessed the Coalition central computer for adoption records that coordinated with the dates of abductions, particularly those of infants and young children. I have downloaded that data into the ship's computer."

Rissa sat back, stunned. "You could do that? You could match the date of an abduction to an adoption?"

"Of course. Is there a particular date you wish to know about?"

She had to know. "My—" She swallowed past the lump that had risen into her throat. "My daughter was abducted twenty years ago from Outpost 19 on Marin 5." She gave him the exact date.

"I will see what I can find. Was—I mean, *is* she full Traishan or a hybrid?"

"Full." The boy who abandoned her had come from Traish. "Is that important?"

"Yes. Race is listed on the adoption records. Is there anything else you can tell me?"

"She was six tendays old. Does that help?"

"Very much so. I will return when I have the information." He did an about-face worthy of a soldier.

"Considering what we know now, it's possible that those who abducted Miri worked out of Marin 5," Dillan said.

She twirled her spoon on the table. "I knew it was a dangerous place, what with the wildcat mines, pirate gangs, and outlaws, but I had no idea . . . I thought the traffickers came from, I don't know, elsewhere. Another planet." She paused. "After they took her, I followed them until I—"

He waited. That was Dillan, all patience and understanding. "Until I got sick."

Again, he waited while she remembered that black time. That time when she'd given up ever finding her child.

"I let my search eat me up inside. It nearly killed me." She cleared her throat. "I did some research years later but never turned up any information about traffickers on Marin 5."

Several thoughts hit her. What if they'd been operating out of Outpost 19? What if she knew the ringleader?

"What are you thinking about now?" Dillan asked. "You look so fierce."

She waved that aside. "Why hasn't the Coalition done something with this information? They could have tracked down the traffickers already."

"Interesting question. That was my thought, too."

"You don't think Hallart suppressed it, do you?"

Dillan leaned back in his chair. "We have to decide how to approach Jerzona."

The remnants of their meal still sat on the table between them. Every now and then, Rissa munched on a leftover vegetable. He loved watching her eat. No pretense, no protests that food would make her fat. So different from the fems on Eleganza.

"Nothing to decide. You hold down the bitch who sold those children to the traffickers, and I'll threaten to gut her with my knife."

Dillan smiled at her ruthlessness. "Bloodthirsty, aren't you?"

"You have a better idea?"

"Actually, yes. We pose as wealthy vacationers from Eleganza who heard about the good works she'd done by rescuing children from the streets."

Rissa made a rude noise. "A knife at her throat will get more information."

"And tip off everyone in the trafficking ring, who will scatter like pung rats from a sinking ship. The authorities will never find them."

"I don't care about the authorities. I just want to find Pela."

"Let's think about the bigger picture here. We have a lot of information about the ring already. We share it with the authorities, and they will organize a raid that will get them all. If we act too quickly, we'll lose them and never find Pela."

She slouched in the hard chair affixed to the decking. "You're a real spoilsport, Rusteran."

"I'm right and you know it." He grinned at her.

"Yes, damn you." She grabbed the empty bowls and took them to the galley.

After gathering their plates and the detritus of the meal, he followed her. While she scraped crumbs into the disintegrator, he put the dishes and utensils in the sanitizer. They worked in companionable silence—like an old married couple. The way he wanted them to be.

"What are you doing?" In the hall, Arjay fluttered his hands. "That is my job."

"Easy there," Dillan said. "You cooked. We clean up."

"No, no, no."

Rissa edged around Dillan. "Yes, yes, yes. You've been busy searching those databases."

"Do you need to recharge?" At the AI's expression, Dillan knew the answer. "We'll find you a place to plug in."

"That is unnecessary. I will find an empty closet."

"You don't need to hide in a closet, Arjay," Rissa said. "Dillan, any ideas?"

"Do not concern yourself for my welfare. I will go down to the engine room." As if that was settled, he scurried toward the stairs.

"Arjay, use the second guest bedroom. The one before the stairs."

"Oh, thank you, sir. That is most kind."

After he was gone, Dillan shook his head. "I don't know what to make of him. I almost believe his humble act."

"That's no act. When Celara left him behind the first time, he thought she'd abandoned him. Although he's used to her and Trevarr going off on their own without him, it makes him feel vulnerable."

"Feels? Thinks? He's an android."

"An AI that is programmed to grow. One with emotions. Celara compared him to a child whose intelligence outpaces his emotional growth. He's still learning how to adapt to our world."

"If you say so."

When she and Dillan were finished with the dishes, she wiped down the small counter and a couple of spills on the floor. He lifted her up. "You didn't need to do that."

"Better to wipe up spills right away." She tossed the cloth into the sanitizer, too, then started the cycle.

He almost hated to end the domestic chores, the only time they weren't arguing. But they needed to make plans.

Two shipdays later, they were still arguing about plans. At least, she didn't argue about where to sleep at night. She'd forgiven him about the comms. Even though they'd made love, he sensed a difference. As if her mind were elsewhere. She claimed the problem was Arjay down the corridor. Dillan wasn't convinced. She worried about Pela. With good reason.

They had to find her.

After finishing Last Meal, they sat in the lounge across from each other, Rissa in the corner of the sofa.

"I've been thinking about what you said," she began. "About the getting the whole ring. I was wrong thinking only about Pela."

"Not wrong. You were focusing on her because she means so much to you. I understand that. Let's focus on what we're going to do and say when we get to Balderate tomorrow."

"This is not a good plan. I can't act like a rich vacationer from Eleganza."

"Believe that you are and you can. Remember what's at stake. We should rehearse how we're going to extract info from the shelter manager."

She looked up. "Arjay, what's wrong?"

With lagging steps, he walked into the lounge. "I am so very sorry, Mistress Rissa. I cannot find your child."

Disappointment settled into her eyes. "I'm sure you did your best, Arjay."

He gave her a grateful look. Then his expression brightened. "May I help you rehearse? I heard your plan. I helped Celara rehearse how to convince Trevarr to return her ship. As sector administrator, he'd confiscated it, and she was most unhappy. I had to teach her the best approach, but she ignored most of my suggestions. Eventually—"

"Arjay, I think we can rehearse on our own," Rissa said more gently than Dillan would have if she'd given him a chance. The AI drove him crazy.

"How much time do we have before reaching Balderate?" Dillan asked.

"We need to travel through one more hyperlane. As soon as we enter the lane, I will recharge. We will arrive at Balderate Colony in eleven point seven hours."

As soon as Arjay left, Dillan rolled his eyes. "Divine One, save us from AIs."

"He is not that bad."

"Ri-ight. Back to our plan. We are wealthy vacationers. Remember. When in doubt, defer to me. Pretend to be a vacuous twit."

The corner of her mouth quirked. "Like Jileena Winslott used to do?"

"Yeah. She sure fooled enough people. And they all underestimated her. Even Hallart."

Hallart. The biggest, baddest gangster in the galaxy. Dillan hated what that villain had done to Jileena to stop her from testifying against his stooge who'd infiltrated her family's company. Hallart had his fingers into so many areas—racketeering, drugs, weapons—he'd even had the president of the Coalition in his pocket. Hallart had to be behind the trafficking. If they could prove that, they could bring about his downfall. Of course, they would have to find him first.

The Reptilian—who could transform into various species—had so many hideouts authorities couldn't locate them. When they did, he was gone.

For the next two hours, he and Rissa role-played. Although he tried to get her to relax and pretend, she still had difficulty acting like a Traishan elite.

"Allow me, sir." Arjay had stopped on his way to the command center.

Rissa sat on the sofa. "Go ahead, Arjay. Dillan's losing patience with me."

"No, I'm not." His tone only reinforced her statement. "Oh, all right. Just once. We should be coming out of the hyperlane soon."

"In fifteen mins and sixty-nine secs. Mistress Rissa, this is what Mister Dillan wishes you to do." He lifted his chin, stiffened his spine, then placed his hand lightly on Dillan's forearm. "I simply must have that exquisite gown," he said in a high-pitched, haughty tone. "Clerk, the wrinkles must be pressed out then deliver it to our Caravel."

With his head high, he imitated a Bricaldian fem zeroing in on a find. "Darling, that necklace is magnificent. It will match my Mondavian green gown. The lathaka I bought in that divine shop in Nicorama City. Do buy it for me, my sweet." He affected a pleading but superior expression.

"Damn, you're good, Arjay." Dillan laughed. "I think I saw that fem in a store in Eleganza."

"Actually, sir, she was at a kiosk in the central terminal at Eleganza spaceport."

From her perch on the sofa, Rissa applauded. "Do another. I'm getting what Dillan wants."

Arjay swished in a deep-kneed stride to the table next to her. Pointing, he said, "Would you look at this gaudy lamp, darling. Neldina has one. Tasteless, I must say." He sauntered to another table. "Clerk? I say, where is that fem? There you are, my dear. I must have this hat. It will protect my delicate skin from the ghastly sun." He turned to Dillan. "My darling, when you suggested this sojourn, you could have mentioned the primitive conditions."

"Okay, Arjay. Enough. I don't want her to disapprove of everything. She needs to show some enthusiasm."

Without breaking character, Arjay batted his lashes up at Dillan. "Of course, my sweet. I just adore these earrings. Such color. It changes with the light." He batted Dillan's hand. "You mustn't look at the tag. Whatever the artist is asking cannot be enough. They are priceless."

Rissa shook her head. "Perfect, Arjay. I will channel you and every haughty fem I saw on Magnos Prime." She imitated the AI's walk to Dillan. In a plummy tone, she drawled, "My precious, I do so wish to visit Madame Jerzona's children's shelter. I have heard ever so much about the good works she is performing for the underprivileged."

"Perfect. Arjay, back to the command center. Rissa, you got it." He yawned. "I've had enough role playing. I'm going to bed. Need to get my beauty sleep."

After Arjay departed, she rolled her eyes. "Don't know if I could handle you looking more beautiful . . . my darling."

"Ah hah." He played along. "You think I'm beautiful?"

"Go to bed, Rusteran. I'm going to sit out here for a while."

"Good night, Rissa." He headed for his quarters.

"Dillan?" She stopped him. "Thank you for helping me find Pela."

"It's my pleasure."

"I'm not sure I could've done this on my own. Not after what happened when I lost Miri."

"You would have done fine on your own."

"I don't think so. Your plan about being rich vacationers is a good one. I'm still not sure I will be able to pull it off."

"You will. I'm confident."

"Will you share that confidence with me? I'm afraid my acting will ruin everything. And then we'll never find Pela."

Her troubled eyes got to him. He'd known her since he was sixteen. Granted there had been gaps when he and his friends had gone off on adventures on other planets. Plus the last one of six years, when he tried to forget her. But he'd never seen her this unsure of herself. He'd always admired her strength. Now she seemed more vulnerable than ever.

"You will do fine, sweetheart. Come to bed."

"I think I'll go over the data again. Maybe I'll spot something we missed." She picked up the data pad.

That determined look discouraged him from telling her she needed sleep.

When he woke up, two hours had passed and she hadn't come to bed. She was still on the sofa, the data pad had fallen to the thickly-carpeted deck. She'd slipped down so much her head lay at an awkward angle. She needed to be in bed.

He scooped her up in his arms and carried her to his quarters. As he laid her down, she muttered, "Why are you so nice to me?"

After drawing the covers over her, he said softly, "Because I love you."

Rissa's dreams kept jarring her awake. Miri and Pela cried for her to find them while the blue-furred Indigian captain laughed. Then he morphed into the red-haired Menacan, Quin, who waved a lighted torch at the girls. Her own cries that he leave them alone could barely be heard, even by her. Each time she woke up, she found her face buried in the pillow.

At least, she didn't wake up Dillan. His heavy breathing was comforting. She didn't want him to see her shaken by nightmares again. He'd want to hold her. Although that's what she needed, she couldn't let him. She'd been half asleep when he carried her to bed. Even in her drowsy state, she'd heard what he said.

He loved her.

At first, she thought she'd dreamed it. It would have been better if that were the case. He complicated things. She didn't need complications right now. She had to find Pela then keep her safe. When she got Pela home, she wasn't letting her go. Not even to further her education. No, she'd keep the girl safe. At home.

Rissa froze. She didn't have a home anymore. The tavern was gone.

She used the corner of the sheet to wipe her eyes. No sense crying over what was done. She would rebuild the tavern. She'd make a home, a real home for Pela—not just a room over a bar. A house. People were always coming and going in Astron. She'd buy a house. Pela would enjoy helping her decorate it. They'd sit down to eat meals at a real kitchen table—not grabbing something at the island in the lulls between customers. She would hire extra staff so Pela wouldn't have to work. She would—

Who am I kidding? With the tavern gone, she had no income. She'd poured all her savings into paying off the loan.

She started from scratch before, she'd do it again.

Although she tried to go back to sleep, her mind whirled with plans. And she worried that she might never find the girl who'd come to mean so much to her. It would be just like after losing Miri. Rissa couldn't survive losing another child.

CHAPTER 22

"Rissa? Sweetheart. Time to get up."

Dillan knelt with one knee on the edge of the bed. He'd dressed in an elegant but casual outfit he'd wore in Vesteron. She had to admit he looked great.

"We just entered the Balderan System. We'll reach Balderate Colony in an hour." As he talked, he opened her closet. "I've thought about what you should wear."

After pulling out a pair of tan trousers and a blouse the deep color of an Astron sunset, he hesitated then added a cream-colored jacket. He hung the garments on the door handle then stooped to look on the floor.

"What are you looking for?"

"Shoes."

"I only have my boots and the sandals you bought on Vesteron."

"I see that." He straightened. "We'll just have to buy new shoes before we go to the shelter."

"We are not going to waste time buying shoes." When she scrambled to the edge of the bed, her sleep garment hiked up, baring her legs above her knees. She tugged it down. "Hang on. I wasn't wearing this out on the sofa."

"I know."

His smile gave her heart a little trip "How did I get into my sleep garment?"

"I put you in it. And, yes, we are going to buy you shoes. We're going to hit several shops before the shelter." He held up his hand. "All part of the plan. Remember? We're rich vacationers from the Central District. We can't go straight to the shelter without rousing suspicion."

"Damn it, Dillan. Why do you always have to be right?" She stomped into the sanitary and slammed the door.

He knocked. "Don't braid your hair. It's too distinctive."

She opened the door. "Anything else? Do you want to decide what cosmetics I should wear?"

"Not too much. Subtle. Something to highlight your—" She closed the door in his face.

When she finished dressing, she had a hard time believing what she saw in the sanitary mirror. This wasn't her. The fem staring back at her looked . . . sophisticated. She'd arranged her hair in an artful fall of curls she remembered seeing Jileena Winslott wear in a newswave. She emphasized the exotic look of her eyes—something she'd never liked, too different. But now, with the other cosmetics, she could pass for an urbane Traishan fem on vacation.

She squared her shoulders before walking out into the corridor. When she reached the command center, she hesitated. "How soon until we land?"

"Ten mins, Mistress Rissa."

Dillan glanced over his shoulder. "I was about to call—Holy sherd."

"Do I look bad?" She bit her bottom lip. Since when did she worry about how she looked? People's opinions didn't matter. Except this was for Pela.

"You look fabulous. Absolutely fabulous."

"I concur," Arjay said. "You look lovely today. However, your feet will be cold."

"The sandals are all right."

"They won't be," Dillan said.

"Mister Dillan is correct. The average temperature in Balderate Colony at this time of the year is precisely—"

"Stop." She held up her hand. "I get it. New shoes."

"Sir, traffic control wants to know our destination."

Dillan touched a couple of screens. "Balderate Traffic Control, this is Caravel ID RM44783 out of Bricaldia requesting clearance to land."

Rissa looked through the viewscreen in front of Dillan. Balderate looked much different from Astron. More greens and blues, not the rich tans, browns, and oranges of the Astron desert. She'd been there once before, to buy the bartop. The bartop now burned to a crisp.

She wasn't going to think about that.

"It's grown a lot in two years," she said.

Dillan nodded. "Ever since United Suppliers started making regular runs out to the Rim, the colonies close to the Central Planets have expanded. Better sit down and strap in."

As she pulled on the harness, she didn't bother to hide her bitterness. "United Suppliers are putting the indies out of business. I wouldn't put it past the Coalition to start annexing planets. There won't be a Rim anymore."

"Technically, Mistress, that is not correct."

Dillan chuckled. "You're right, Arjay. There will always be a Rim. The boundaries will move farther away from the Central Planets. People will leave and push farther into the unknown."

The docking area at Balderate Spaceport contained several sections depending on the type of starcraft—freighters off to the left, smaller supply ships on the right, with luxury cruisers and shuttles in the middle in a protected area. Dillan maneuvered his ship into the middle.

"Arjay, handle shutdown then stay and protect the ship."

The AI's mouth turned down. "I had hoped to go with you."

"No. I need to know the ship is safe."

"You are correct, of course. Although the spaceport security should be sufficient, it behooves us to take caution. The criminal element will consider an empty vessel, and one as luxurious as yours, a perfect target for robbery and/or mayhem. I will endeavor to—"

"Good. Lock up after us."

After they disembarked, Dillan leaned in close. "Can we leave him here?"

She smiled up at him. "He means well. Let's go." She set off at a brisk pace.

He made her slow down. "Stroll," he said softly. "We're not rushing anywhere, sweetheart."

With his hand burning its imprint into her waist, he steered her through the spaceport that was at least four times larger than Astron's. He seemed to have an innate ability to avoid the passengers hurrying to and from ships.

She faked a sweet smile. "Of course, *darling*."

He shot her a look before stopping at a gift kiosk. "Look, my sweet, at this hairclip. Wouldn't little Borina love this?" After paying for it with his credit device, he asked for directions to the shopping district.

As they left, she leaned close. "Borina?"

"And Boras. Twins. Father is so pleased."

She scoffed. "As if I'd name my children after the biggest exploiter of minerals in the Outer Rim."

"Don't forget that exploiter's employees were your best customers."

She had to give him that. "By the way, I could have told you where the shops are."

He tucked her arm in his and strolled down the walkway. Like the one in Vesteron, it was made of synthcrete, which was surprisingly comfortable to walk on. No rough boardwalks here. Or dirt streets. They hadn't been paved when she came before. Balderate made Astron look like a backwater village. And the people. Such an assortment of races and species.

"By the time we get to the shops, the owners will be eagerly waiting for us. The Rusteran name is well-known—even if we exploit."

He winked. "I'm second generation, and that means I—we have credits to spend."

She had to admit he was right. In each shop, the proprietor bent over backwards to help them. Dillan spend more credits than the tavern made in four tendays. One pair of half-boots wasn't enough. She must have one in black and dark blue, plus the brown pair she could wear out of the shop. And he paid extra to have the other boots and her sandals delivered to the ship.

In a jewelry shop, she got into the spirit.

"Oh, darling, isn't that beautiful?" She pointed to a necklace with a deep red pendant nestled inside the perma-film case that spanned half the store.

"You have a good eye, ma'am. The stone is a qatum. It's the result of volcanic activity and only found near the equator. The markings are native symbols for peace and tranquility."

"It will look lovely with your shirt," Dillan said.

"Oh." She pursed her lips. "I'm not sure."

The proprietor, knowing who he had to convince, took the necklace out of the case and held it out to her. "Try it on. Your spouse is right. It is perfect for your outfit."

After Dillan hooked it under the collar of her shirt, he straightened the necklace down the front. When his fingers grazed her breast, a tiny thrill raced through her. She couldn't react. Not in front of the proprietor, who was still talking.

"It is one of a kind. The artist never makes duplicates."

Dillan said, "We'll take it."

"Would you like to see other pieces by the artist?"

A one-of-a-kind meant expensive. Even if this was for show, she couldn't allow him to spend so much credit. "No," she said quickly, forgetting she was supposed to be rich.

"Yes. For your birthday, my sweet," Dillan said.

"My birthday was last week, *my sweet*." She pouted. "Which you forgot."

He tapped her nose. "I was waiting until we arrived here. I knew I would find exactly the right gift."

The proprietor beamed. "You heard of our reputation?"

"Renown in the Central District."

In the end, she had matching earrings that he insisted she wear along with the necklace plus another necklace and earring set made by the same artist. The proprietor beamed. He should. She almost fell over when he told Dillan the total. Without batting an eye, he held out his credit device.

Outside, while dodging passers-by, she told him no more. He ignored her and steered her into a dress shop. She couldn't believe it when he zeroed in on a sleek, iridescent-green dress. When she touched the material, she dropped it as if it burned her fingers. "Do you know what this is?" she whispered. "It's lathaka, what Celera and Trevarr are making a fortune selling. You are not buying this."

"Look, sweetheart. It's in your size. I wonder if it will be long enough."

Another proprietor fell over herself to help them. "Try it on."

"That's all right." Rissa waved her away. "We don't have time."

Dillan's insistence on shopping was driving her insane. She wanted to get to the shelter and confront the bitch that was selling children.

He squeezed her shoulder. "Of course, we do. We aren't meeting your sister until—"

"Dar-ling," she whined. "You know how upset she gets when we're late."

"Ma'am?" The fem took the exorbitantly-priced dress off the hangar. "Let me hold it up to you. I'm certain it will fit."

"Oh, all right." Rissa knew she was acting like a spoiled bitch. She hoped Dillan was satisfied. "But I'm sure we can get this in Eleganza."

Seeing a prospective sale about to slip away, the fem said, "I can assure you, this design is an original, made by a modiste here in Balderate." When she held the dress up to Rissa's shoulder, the color shimmered and shifted in the light. "Doesn't it remind you of a rainbow? And look at the deep hem. Your seamstress in Eleganza can adjust the length, if need be."

"Then we must get it." Dillan smiled. As the fem wrapped the dress in tissue, he said, "By the way, we've been hearing about a fem named Madam Jerzona who runs a shelter here for homeless children."

When the fem gave him an odd look, Rissa said, "How proud you all must be that the children are cared for. We think it's such a worthy cause, we'd like to meet her. Is the shelter far from here?"

"She is an amazing fem." The proprietor handed Dillan a bag emblazoned with the shop's logo. Although he'd sent many of their purchases to the ship, he'd kept a few, though he'd tucked the jewelry into his pocket. No sense giving a runner temptation.

"The shelter is a few streets over." The fem gave him more directions. She leaned in and spoke softly. "Sir, it is not a very . . . savory area. Perhaps you should reconsider. Or take a guard with you."

Dillan waved that aside. "I have heard Balderate is quite safe."

"It is, sir. In the business district. You will need to be alert if you proceed to the shelter."

He thanked her and agreed to be cautious.

Outside, the traffic on the walkway increased. Dillan's hand in the middle of her back made her uncomfortable, too much heat from his palm sending sensations she didn't want to feel.

"Why are you carrying those bags? You could have sent all of them to the ship."

He leaned close. "What do you think Jerzona will surmise when she sees them?"

"That you spent a lot of credits?"

"Exactly. A rich Bricaldian and his Traishan spouse who like to spend. You can be sure she'll hit us up for a donation."

She stopped at a cross street. "Don't you dare give her any credits. She sells children."

"Lower your voice," he said softly. "If you can't you control your animosity, go back to the ship."

"You have got to be kidding. I am not going back to the ship." She would have walked right into a skimmer if he hadn't pulled her back. In doing so, he dropped the bags. As she stooped to help pick them up, she caught a glimpse of a man darting into an alley behind them.

"I think someone is following us," she whispered.

"Uh huh." He took her arm as they crossed the street. "Ever since we left the spaceport."

"Are you going to do something about it?"

"Nope. Just act like you don't see him."

"But what if he tries to rob us? He knows you—we have credits."

Dillan patted the side of his jacket. "I brought an LZ-9 from the ship."

"A lot of good it will do inside your jacket."

"You'll distract him while I get it out." He grinned and kept walking.

As they got farther away from the business district, the area grew rougher. The fem had been correct to warn them. He stopped in front of a drab gray stone building. "I think we're here."

A faded sign proclaimed, "Welcome to all."

"Doesn't look very welcoming," she said. "The windows are grimy and—"

He pulled on the door. "Locked."

"Try the bell." She pointed.

A sullen girl about Anaris' age let them in. She eyed them with suspicion. "What do you want?"

The Protector

"Hello, welcome." The cheery greeting came from a large fem who bustled into the foyer. She wore a no-nonsense dark blue pantsuit, a white shirt, and half-boots that looked a lot like the pair Rissa wore. "I'm Madam Jerzona. How may I help?" She turned to the girl. "Alert Cook we have visitors."

"No, no." Rissa gritted her teeth so she wouldn't shout at the fem. Instead, she pasted on a bright smile. "Please don't fuss."

"I'm Dillan Rusteran. This is my spouse." He shook hands with Jerzona.

"Welcome. I see you found our shopping district." She smiled broadly.

"Ah, yes. My little sweetheart can't resist a bargain. I must say your merchants offer a fine selection. It's a good thing we aren't staying here long. I'll go home destitute."

When he chuckled, Jerzona's laugh echoed off the cold stone walls of the large entry. Rissa forced herself to smile. *Get on with it, Dillan. Before I do something we'll both regret.*

"I'm sure you're wondering why we're here." Dillan projected the image of the Bricaldian elite while Jerzona fawned over him. "We've heard so much about your project. What good work you're doing by taking children in off the streets and giving them food and shelter. We just had to stop by to see for ourselves."

Jerzona, of mixed heritage patted her short, curly hair that was an unnatural shade of red. "It's my mission. Those poor children were runaways or orphans. Some even were abandoned by their parents. We clothe them, give them a roof over their heads, and three good meals a day."

Then sell them to traffickers. Rissa kept her hands in her jacket pockets so she wouldn't reach out and strangle the fem until she revealed the secrets of the slave trade.

Jerzona gave her an odd look. "Is everything all right, ma'am?"

Dillan clasped Rissa's shoulder in what looked like a gentle squeeze. It wasn't. "My spouse gets very distressed by the thought of parents who don't take care of their children."

"Isn't it just dreadful?" Jerzona declared.

Not as dreadful as selling them.

"May I give you a tour?" She led them down a narrow corridor, showing off classrooms. "The children spend eight hours a day at studies. Right now they are at Mid-Day meal."

She took them to see the dining hall where thirty to forty children of various ages ate in silence. They all stopped and stared at the visitors. While the older ones looked impassive, the younger ones' eyes lit with hope.

202

"Finish eating, children." Jerzona spoke with that fake voice adults often used. "Remember we don't waste food."

Rissa wanted to shake her.

Jerzona ushered them down another hall to a staircase. "Would you like to see the sleeping quarters?"

"Of course." Dillan nodded to Rissa to follow the fem up the stairs. "How many children do you have at present?"

"Thirty-six. We can accommodate up to fifty at a time."

Rissa zeroed in on that. "How long do they stay?"

"Approximately six months. Although some have been here nearly a year. We try to find good homes for all our children." She leaned and spoke softly. "But some just cannot be placed. They were on the streets too long."

"What happens to them?" Dillan asked.

"They are apprenticed to a tradesman."

Rissa thought of Kiran and how he'd been apprenticed.

"Fifty," Dillan said. "It must cost quite a bit to keep this place running."

"The colony gives us a small stipend per child. Not enough, of course. So we depend on the generosity of donors." She gave him an eager look.

When Dillan just nodded, she opened the door to a large room with eight narrow beds. "This is the older girls' dormitory."

A girl jumped away from a window, looking guilty. "Madam Jerzona."

"Why aren't you at Mid-Day meal?"

The young teen bit her lip. "I wasn't hungry."

"Go downstairs. You mustn't be up here alone."

"Yes, ma'am." She hesitated. "I'll just use the sanitary first." She darted into a room at the far end of the dorm.

Jerzona shook her head. "She knows better." A buzzing noise came from her pocket. She pulled out a comm device. "Yes?"

"Madam Jerzona, I'm sorry to bother you. You have a vid call. I told the caller you had visitors, but she insists on speaking to you."

"I'm sorry we'll have to cut the tour short," Jerzona said.

"Oh, dear." Rissa clutched Dillan's arm. "I so wanted to see where the little children slept."

Jerzona gave a distracted wave. "Of course. Across the hall. I will see you downstairs."

After the fem rushed away, Rissa darted back into the dormitory and headed straight for the sanitary. The young teen who'd been leaning her head against a sink whirled around. When she saw Rissa was alone, she gave her an eager smile. "I'm so glad to see a fem."

"I don't understand."

"You're here to take us away, aren't you? Jerzona said you were coming today. I mean, usually it's two men. And I was so afraid."

"Explain." Dillan had come up behind her.

Tears filled the girl's eyes. "It's not you." Her shoulders slumped. "I hoped . . . I have to go." She ran past them and out the door to the hall.

Rissa turned to Dillan. "We have to get her out of here."

"How?"

"I don't know. But we can't leave her here." She leaned her forehead against his chest.

He rubbed her back. "What will we do with her? We can't take her with us. We're—"

"Is anything wrong?" Jerzona had come into the dormitory.

Dillan straightened away. "My spouse has such a tender heart. Although we have young children—twins—" He beamed. "—we lost our daughter who was about the age of the girl who was in here."

"Darling? Couldn't we adopt her?" She looked eagerly at Jerzona. "Madam, please. We would give her a good home."

"Well, uh . . . Perhaps we should talk in my office."

Once they were seated in Jerzona's office, the fem folded her hands on top of her desk. "I am sorry. That girl is leaving today."

Rissa's ears perked up. "Leaving?"

"Yes. Several good families in Vesteron City have opened their homes—"

And credit devices.

"—to our children, including the girl you saw. But we have others."

"Oh, no." Rissa touched the corner of her eye. "She looked so much like—"

"Vesteron City, you say?" Dillan raised his eyebrow. "Perhaps you could put us in touch with the family, and we—"

"I couldn't do that. We do have other girls."

"What would it take to change your mind about sending her to Vesteron?"

"Sir." Jerzona looked askance. "Are you trying to *buy* the girl?"

"Actually, I was thinking of a donation."

She cleared her throat. "A donation would certainly help with the operation of the shelter. The fine citizens of Vesteron donated twenty thousand credits to help defray the cost of a new furnace."

"Twenty thousand?" Rissa couldn't help herself. That was outrageous.

"That's for ten children."

"I know it's a lot of credits, darling, but we need to help." Rissa clutched his jacket. "I'll take back the dress you just bought. Oh, and my necklace, too." She touched the stone.

He patted her hand then looked at Jerzona. "See what I mean about a tender heart? Sweetheart, you don't need to take back the dress or the jewelry. I was teasing earlier when I said you were going to bankrupt me. Tell us about the other children."

If possible Jerzona looked more eager. "If you have your heart set on a girl, we have five, ages ten to thirteen. Would you like to see them?"

"Tell us, Madame Jerzona," Dillan said. "What does the shelter need?"

Without missing a beat, she said, "Our roof leaks. I don't know how we're going to afford a new one."

"And what does a new roof cost?" Dillan asked.

"Twelve thousand credits."

When Rissa started to sputter, Dillan stepped on her toes. "It is obvious you honor commitments, Madam Jerzona. I admire that. Although we are unable to take any girls now, I will have my assistant contact you to make financial and travel arrangements."

The fem beamed and handed him a card. "Of course. Here is my contact information."

With Jerzona thanking them profusely all the way to the front door, they finally escaped.

"Don't say anything," he whispered once they were outside. He tapped his wrist comm and requested transport to the ship. Within moments, an auto-skimmer zipped down to the curb. As soon as they were inside, it rose above the shelter then zoomed away.

"Can I talk now?" Rissa couldn't help herself. Sarcasm wasn't her usual style, but Dillan was impossible. "A shipment is going out today."

"I know. Ten children."

"Then we should have stayed close to the shelter."

"We'll watch for them at the spaceport and follow them."

"Excellent thinking."

He gave her a smug smile. "I have my moments."

The skimmer stopped and both doors opened. "Spaceport," the auto-voice said. "Passenger Terminal. Thank you."

Once they entered the hangar, Rissa and Dillan headed for their ship. As they approached, Dillan seemed very intense. And wary. His head shifted from side to side as if he were looking for someone or something. Like the slavers' ship?

They were a few meters from the Caravel when he lowered the ramp. "We'll wait inside. From the command center, we'll have a clear view of the entrance."

"Good thinking." She followed him up the ramp. When he abruptly stopped, she ran into his back.

"What are you doing here?" Dillan demanded.

Rissa looked over his shoulder. The red-haired Menacan sat in the pilot seat, his feet propped up on the console.

CHAPTER 23

Dillan eyed the LZ-9 pistol on the console next to Quin's arm. Would that deter Rissa? Of course not.

She pushed him out of her way. "Rusteran, give me your weapon."

"Is that any way to welcome a visitor?" Quin grinned.

"You burned down my tavern."

"Someone set fire to your tavern? Imagine that." He dropped his feet.

"Damn it, Dillan. Give me your pistol." She reached for his pocket.

He captured her hand. "Not yet. Let's hear what he has to say. Then you can kill him."

Quin looked at them with mock shock.

She twisted her mouth. "All right. Let's get this over with, D'Sernin. And get out of the pilot seat. That's Dillan's."

Quin didn't move, just arched his light eyebrows. "So you know who I am. Interesting."

"Why did you burn down the tavern then steal the girls? I swear if you don't tell me where Pela is, I'll gut you with my knife."

Quin gave her a questioning look. "Steal girls? Pela is missing?"

"As if you didn't know." She turned to Dillan. "All he's doing is asking questions. Give me your pistol."

Dillan steered her to the seat farthest away from Quin. He wouldn't put it past her to go for his throat with her bare hands. It was a good thing she wasn't wearing her stout boots. The ones with the knife. When she wouldn't sit, he put his hands on her shoulders and gently *helped* her then stood behind her as a precaution. They needed to find out what Quin knew. "He looks like he doesn't know about the girls."

She made a rude noise.

"Traffickers captured three girls near my Astron mine."

"And one was my Pela. Where did you take her?"

Quin held up his hands. "I don't know anything about that."

"Hah." Rissa started to get up, but Dillan kept her from rising. "I don't believe you."

"I give you my word. I know nothing about the girls."

Dillan didn't know what to think. The man seemed sincere. Still . . . "But you did destroy Rissa's tavern."

"Did you know my bartender had just left? You could have killed him."

"He and the AI went down to the café. I don't murder innocents."

Rissa clenched the arms of the chair so tightly her knuckles shown white. "So you admit you set the fire. Give me your pistol, Dillan. I mean it this time."

He patted her shoulder. "By the time I took it out of my pocket and gave it to you, he'd have shot us both."

Quin tucked the pistol into the back of his trousers. "If I'd wanted to kill you, I would have already. The fire was a warning. Just like the vandalism, which you ignored." He caught Dillan's eye. "I warned you to get her to stop meddling."

She looked up at him. "What's that supposed to mean?"

"At least you got her out of town. Did you enjoy Vesteron City?"

"How do you know we went to Vesteron?" Rissa demanded.

"Is that the important issue?" Quin blew out a breath. "Someone doesn't want you poking around. If you keep turning over rocks, you won't like what crawls out."

Dillan forced himself to grip the back of Rissa's chair when he really wanted to beat Quin senseless for the pain he'd inflicted on her. "If you know anything about Rissa, you know she's tenacious." He rubbed his temple. "Let's get back to the girls. What did you mean when you said you didn't know about traffickers grabbing them?"

"When did it happen?"

"Four days ago."

Quin slowly shook his head. "I didn't think she'd act so quickly."

"She? Who? Jerzona?"

"No. Never mind." Quin stared off in thought.

"Did you drop in for a reason? Or to gloat over destroying everything Rissa treasured?"

"It was just a building."

"Not to me."

"She poured her heart and soul into her business, and you destroyed it. Not only that, she had . . . special treasures that can never be replaced. She will never forgive you."

Quin leaned over and pulled a bag out from under the console. "You mean these?" He tossed the bag to her.

When she opened it, Dillan saw a stuffed toy panzer and baby clothing. She unwrapped them and pulled out a holo-pic. Miri. When a sob erupted, he stooped in front of her. Tears rolled down her cheeks. She quickly tucked the pic inside then looked over his shoulder.

After blinking away tears, she sniffed. "Thank you."

Dillan knew what an effort it took for her to say that. He could see it in her eyes.

"Is that enough to forgive me for destroying the tavern?" Quin stood and stretched.

"Don't push it, d'Sernin." Dillan stood, putting himself between Quin and Rissa. "You have a lot to answer for."

"Damn right, he does." Rissa got up, hip-bumping him out of her way.

"This is your last warning. Back off. Both of you. Do not interfere with the trafficking. I can't protect you anymore." The way Quin looked at her frightened Dillan.

"What do you mean protect me?"

"You were supposed to be a good girl and quit sticking your nose in where it doesn't belong." Quin shook his head. "Stubborn fem. Listen to me and listen good. There's a contract out on you."

Rissa charged forward. "What kind of contract?"

"What do you think? Coriana wants you dead."

"Rissa?" Dillan exclaimed.

"Who's Coriana?" she said at the same time.

"Ask Toots." Quin lifted his wrist. With his finger poised over a button, he looked at Dillan. "Get her off the frontier. Take her to Bricaldia. If I see her again, I'll have to kill her."

He disappeared in the haze of a transporter beam.

"That was some exit." Rissa leaned against the bulkhead.

Dillan stopped her. "Did you hear what he said?"

"Of course I did. Someone named Coriana wants me gone. I am so-o-o scared." She pretended to shiver.

Dillan grabbed her upper arms. "He meant it. *He* took the contract to kill you."

"So why didn't he?" She pulled away. "He had the perfect opportunity."

"We should go to Bricaldia. It will be safer there."

She couldn't believe him. He wanted her to run away? Leave Pela behind? Abandon her? Rissa strode down the corridor. "I'm not a quitter," she shot over her shoulder.

"No. You're foolish and headstrong."

She'd heard that before. As she changed out of her fancy clothes and into Rimmer attire, she let Dillan's words sink in. He wouldn't take her to Bricaldia against her will. Would he?

She raced to the command center. "What are you going to do?"

"Get us out of here."

As she grabbed the back of his chair to turn him around, movement outside the ship caught her eye. "Doesn't that look like the picture of the shuttle d'Arcanin's kid drew?"

Dillan stood to see. "It certainly does."

A maintenance worker directed the shuttle to a berth across from theirs.

"Wait, Dillan. Let's see who comes out."

"We should leave."

"Don't." She hated to beg. "Please."

Rissa continued to watch the shuttle. After it came to a halt, a ramp lowered and two men got out. D'Arcanin's kid had drawn the men perfectly. They were the ones who took Pela.

"They're going after more kids. Lower the ramp, Dillan. I'm going to stop those guys."

"No." He beat her to the hatch. "You are not going after them."

"They took Pela."

"And they're dangerous. Listen to me, Rissa. We can't go after them. You heard what Quin said. If you don't stop interfering, he will kill you."

She scoffed. "I don't believe that."

"You'd damn well better believe it. I saw what he did to the crew that tried to take Sophira's baby and those other kids. He blew up their ship. He said he put the men in an escape pod, but I don't believe that for a moment. The man is ruthless. And he will kill you."

"Open the damn hatch." Rissa gave Dillan her best death-stare, the one she reserved for anyone messing with her employees. He'd damn well better open the hatch, or she would hurt him. "We're losing the perfect opportunity to grab those men and find out what they did to Pela."

"And what will you do with them? Better yet, how will you grab them?"

"You'll help me."

"No. I will not help you kill yourself."

That stopped her for a moment. "I will never forgive you for that."

"Add it to my list of sins." He returned to the pilot's seat.

He spoke with such patience she wanted to slap him. She flounced over to stand close enough to the viewscreen to watch the shuttle. "As soon as they return, you get clearance from Traffic Control, and we follow them."

"Did you really not understand what Quin said? Or are you so stubborn that you're willing to risk your life?"

"What would you do if it was your daughter? Wouldn't you do everything possible to get her back?"

"Yes, I would." He took her hand. "Rissa, I don't want to fight with you. I want to find Pela, too. As well as the other girls. I can't abide the thought that they might be forced into a prosti-house or sold into slavery. I have Jerzona's info. I'll get a friend to trace my *donation*. We'll find the ringleader."

"No. Those men in the shuttle took Pela. We follow them. If they take the kids from the shelter, they're going to Vesteron. Don't you remember? That's where Jerzona said the kids were going."

He gave her an impatient look. "You really believed that load of zircan sherd? There are no *good families* who paid for a new furnace. It's the traffickers. That's what they pay her. Two thousand credits a kid. Talk about easy pickings. No grabbing kids off the streets. She delivers them in a neatly-wrapped package. And the kids think they're going to new homes, so they go willingly. What a racket."

How stupid could I get? He's right, of course. Damn it. He's always right. It was maddening. *He* was maddening. Enough to drive a fem to drink.

"Rissa, I want to find Pela. I want to crush the trafficking ring. But I don't want to lose you. And if you continue to interfere with them, I'm afraid I will."

When he rubbed her thumb, she couldn't deny the delicious sensations zinging up her arm. This was so not the time. She yanked her hand away and crossed her arms to keep from wanting more.

She rocked back on her heels then leaned forward. Maintenance people raced to some vehicles and walked to others. Auto-bots were loading fuel onto the shuttle.

"Did the ground crew load our water and fuel while we were shopping?"

"Yes." He spoke to her like a child. "I checked. Everything is topped off."

Again, she rocked. "Good. Good."

Finally, she couldn't stand still any longer. "I'm going over there. Maybe I can find something in the shuttle that will give me a clue to where they took Pela."

When she strode to the hatch, he gave an exasperated sigh. "Wait a min."

"Don't try to stop me this time." She pressed the lever that lowered the ramp.

He came up to her and held out his hand. She was about to clasp it when she saw two tiny earpieces in his palm "What's this?"

After handing her one, he stuck the other in his own ear. "I'm coming with you."

She threw her arms around his neck. "Thank you." After giving him a hard kiss, she inserted the earpiece and strode down the ramp.

"Slow down," he said in her ear. "Act like you're checking out different vessels."

"Okay, okay."

"By the way, talk softly and don't touch your ear."

She strolled around the ship next to theirs, an Agilean Speeder, sleek, fast, but built for only two. Then she crossed the wide aisle to a Volpian Cruiser next to the shuttle. She peered at the dual nacelles that made it one of the fastest mid-size passenger ships.

"Hey, what are you doing?" A maintenance worker in a green uniform rushed up to them.

"Just looking around," Dillan said. "We're thinking about getting a new ship."

"All right. Don't try to enter any, okay? We're responsible for keeping the ships berthed here secure."

So how did Quin get in our ship if you're so vigilant?

"No problem." Dillan gave the man a mock salute.

After the worker walked away, Rissa edged toward the shuttle.

"Be careful," Dillan whispered.

"Watch for the traffickers." Following an auto-bot towing an anti-grav pallet loaded with food supplies, she entered the shuttle.

They must be coming back soon. They wouldn't want food to spoil. Quickly, she examined the small cargo bay. Carefully, in case the traffickers had left someone to guard the shuttle, she slid open the hatch to the rest of the ship. Seats for ten passengers plus flight crew stations. And fortunately no guard. She scanned the instruments, looking for their destination. Instead, she found the coordinates for the mothership. *Duh.* Of course, that was their destination.

"Rissa," Dillan hissed in her ear. *"The 'bots are closing the hatch."*

"Okay, okay. Remember these coordinates. I'm afraid I'll forget." She rattled off the numbers. "That's where the mothership is."

"You need to get out of there right now."

The only way out without being seen was through the bay. No problem. There had to be a manual release. After she closed the hatch separating the cargo from the passengers, the bay was black as night in the desert.

"Rissa, They're back. Hurry."

"I'm trying." Holding onto the bulkhead on the left, she edged her way toward the hatch at the rear.

When she heard a ramp lower, she sped up . . . and tripped over a pallet the 'bots must have deliberately put in her way.

She heard children's voices and the deeper voice of the men. *For the love of quizzard, where's the rear hatch?*

After picking herself up, she ran into a wall that hadn't been there before. When she felt around, she realized the "wall" was a stack of water containers.

"Rissa, get out of there now."

As she tried to work her way around the containers, she ran into the other bulkhead.

The *wall* blocked the hatch.

"Dillan?" she whispered. "I can't get out."

"What!"

She held on to her left ear where his words just blasted out. "Don't yell." Again, she whispered. "The outer hatch is blocked."

"I can barely hear you. Speak up." And again he yelled at her.

That was it. She yanked out the earpiece and stuffed it in her pocket. She had to get out of the shuttle before it—

Oh, sherd. The pilot had just started the engine. What if someone decided to check the cargo?

So she didn't trip over any more pallets—empty or otherwise— she crawled along the wall toward the passenger area. Maybe she could find a better place to hide.

The hatchway to the passenger compartment slid open.

She flattened on the deck behind the nearest pallet of foodstuff. In the dark, nobody could see her. She hoped.

The overhead light came on.

CHAPTER 24

After his third call and no answer from Rissa, Dillan had a full-blown panic attack. *Sweet Divinity, protect her.*

Forcing himself to stay calm, he strolled back to this ship as if he had all the time in the universe. Inside, he raced to the command center and leaped into his chair. As he checked systems, he kept looking through the viewscreen, hoping—praying—to see Rissa creep out of the shuttle.

"Balderate Traffic Control," he said. "This is Caravel RM44783, ready for launch."

"Destination, Caravel RM44783?" A female traffic controller responded. She hadn't been on duty when he landed.

"Magnos Prime."

"Thank you, Caravel. You are third in the queue."

Third? Dillan clenched the edge of the control panel. That shuttle better be in front of him. He'd follow it into Lexol's Fire to get to Rissa.

Wait. He had the coordinates of the mothership.

When the shuttle pulled out of its berth, he breathed a sigh of relief. It would launch before him. He scanned the area across the aisle. He groaned in despair. No Rissa.

"Caravel RM44783, you may move into position."

Movement near a mech station caught his eye. *Rissa? Sweet Divinity, let it be Rissa.*

"Caravel RM44783, you are cleared for launch. Are you leaving?"

A mechanic walked away from the station. *Sherd.*

"Thank you, Balderate Control. Caravel RM44783 moving into position."

He followed the shuttle through Balderan's atmosphere then switched over to the sublight engine. The shuttle headed for the coordinates Rissa had given him. Keeping the shuttle in sight, Dillan set his course for Mag Prime, like he'd told Traffic Control. The mothership was straight ahead.

"Yeah." The man Rissa recognized from the tavern stood in the open hatchway and called over his shoulder. "The food and water are loaded. We'd be deep sherd if they weren't."

"I told you to look before we took off," another man said.

"You also told me to make sure the kids were buckled up." He turned off the light then slid the door closed.

While breathing a sigh of relief, Rissa heard more muffled arguing and a child crying. If she could hear that, the traffickers could hear noises from the cargo bay. Like her talking to Dillan.

The earpiece's range wouldn't extend into space. And they were in space, all right. She'd heard the sublight engine kick over. Before they got to the mothership, she had to contact Dillan.

Huddling in the corner farthest away from the door, she tapped her wrist comm. Thank the Matriarch she'd remembered to put it on when she changed clothes. The mini-screen lit up brighter than Astron's twin moons in the night sky. She cupped the device and held it close. When Dillan's startled face appeared, she whispered, "Don't speak. I'm in the cargo hold. They don't know I'm here. Nod if you're following."

A frantic Dillan nodded.

Why should he be frantic? She was the one in the enemy ship. Then she realized he was afraid for her. Her recklessness had landed her in a pot of trouble. He'd warned her and she'd ignored him.

"I'll be all right," she whispered. "Just transport me out of here."

After several long secs, Dillan whispered, *"I can't."*

She forced herself not to shout. "Explain."

"I can't beam you over. Something's interfering with the transporter. An energy shield, I think."

Sherd.

"I'm sorry, Rissa. So very sorry." His guilt was palpable through her comm.

"Not your fault. I guess we should have anticipated that. Probably the same thing on the mothership."

"Probably."

"Looks like I'm going where they're going." She forced a smile. "Hey. They might lead us right to the ringleader."

"Be careful," he whispered back. *"I love you."*

"Love you, too." She switched off the comm.

She'd just told Dillan she loved him. She needed to thunk her head against the nearest hard object, which happened to be the bulkhead. Oh, right. That would bring the traffickers running into the bay. What had possessed her to repeat his declaration? She'd wanted to reassure him, to make him stop being afraid for her.

She'd made things worse.

Dillan stared at the blank screen before tagging the source. He'd be able to find Rissa as long as she wore her comm. He just couldn't transport her. Thank the Divine One she was all right. Or as all right as one could be hiding in a cargo hold. A pressurized cargo hold.

And she'd just said she loved him. How long he'd waited to hear those words. To hear his love returned. He should be doing a happy dance. Instead, he slumped back in his seat. She'd only said it as an automatic response.

Someday, she'd say she loved him and mean it. Until then, he'd wait as he had for the past sixteen years.

The Chellian XP-508 loomed so large the shuttle looked like a toy. Could Rissa stay hidden? When they entered hyperspace, she'd be tossed around like a twig in a storm. What would they do to her if she was caught?

Scenarios—each worse than the previous one—shot through his mind.

Like seeing Konner disappear in an avalanche of rocks, Dillan watched Rissa vanish aboard a slave ship.

And he could do nothing to save her.

CHAPTER 25

The shuttle landed with a jarring thud, knocking Rissa over. They were aboard the mothership. The engine cut out and she heard excited voices calling out, "Are we there?"

She also heard the men yelling "Shut up" followed by "Release your harnesses."

Her heart ached for those children who were about to discover they'd been tricked. The cruelty of it all twisted her gut. By the Matriarch, she had to get them away from the traffickers.

Reality kicked in. They were in space and would stay in space until they got to their destination. Some place called Manca, maybe, or a space station. Didn't matter which one. She just had to figure out how to release the kids.

The hatch opened behind her.

Shielded by the water containers, she crept to the opposite end of the bay. Auto-bots wouldn't bother her. They would activate the anti-grav and tow out the pallets. She could crouch in the corner and pray that a crew member didn't see her.

"Line up. Girls to the left, boys on the right."

The order and the sounds of confused voices and shuffling easily reached Rissa in her hiding place.

"Arrange yourselves according to age. Oldest first."

More shuffling.

"When do we get to see our new parents?" a timid voice called out.

"Stupid kids," a man nearby muttered.

Wait. Nearby? What if he entered the hold?

Frantically, she looked around for a better hiding place. The auto-bots were almost finished removing the shield of water containers. As soon as they took out the last stack, she would be exposed.

On the opposite side of the hatch to the passenger area, she caught sight of the faint outline of a door. She was about to tear across the hold when a thought hit her. Symmetry. She remembered Dillan talking about the symmetry on ships. She looked up. Sure enough. With the light from the shuttle bay, she could see the door on this side. And, best of all, a recessed pull. Could she be lucky enough to find a closet big enough for her?

An auto-bot lifted the last pallet of containers. She had to move now or get caught.

When she opened the door, she nearly screamed.

"Caravel RM44783. This is Captain Dorman of the transport Freedom's Run. *Do you need assistance?*

The mothership was hailing him. That's what Dillan got for worrying about Rissa and not paying attention to what was going on around him.

Freedom's Run? Was that someone's idea of a sick joke? No freedom for those kids.

"Freedom's Run. Captain Deelan Orsgard here." *Sorry, Grandfather.* "Thanks for the offer, Captain Dorman. I thought I heard a slight fluctuation in my sublight."

"I could send one of my engineers over to give you a hand."

That was the last thing Dillan expected. He wracked his brain trying to come up with a reason to decline help.

"My AI is working on the situation as we speak. I don't want to keep you from your route, Captain." Where in Lexol was Ajay? He hadn't seen him since they first left the ship.

"No problem, Caravel. We'll be here a while. I'm waiting on two more shuttles to return."

Two more?

Forcing himself to stay calm, Dillan responded, "If my AI can't find the problem, I may take you up on your offer to send over an engineer. If you're still here, of course. Thanks. Orsgard out."

He sat back in relief. He'd convinced the mothership captain that he had a good reason for hanging around. Even if he was on the outer limits of his own sensors, he should have known the slave ship would have stronger sensors.

Dillan congratulated himself on his quick thinking. Having an AI aboard was logical. More importantly, Captain Dorman bought it.

"Arjay," Dillan called over the intraship. "I need you in the command center."

When Arjay didn't show up, he called again. He was probably recharging. Dillan didn't know enough about AIs to know whether they could hear when they were plugged in. He couldn't worry about that now. He had to warn Rissa about the extra shuttles.

If she left hers, she could be caught when the bay opened. And get sucked out into space.

Arjay, dressed in a green mechanic's uniform, yanked Rissa's arm, pulling her inside the narrow storage compartment. As soon as he shut the door behind her, darkness enveloped them. He held her in front of him, his arm around her waist. Good thing she wasn't claustrophobic.

"What are you doing here?" She turned her head slightly to whisper. "I thought you were aboard our ship."

"I am helping," the AI whispered. "I planned to contact you to let you know where the children are. Were you and Master Dillan not supposed to leave?"

She sighed. "They closed the hatch too soon. Dillan can't transport me over to his ship."

"They have an energy disrupter."

"Yeah. Found out about that. Wait. How did you know?"

Silence met her question. Finally, he said, "I hacked into their system."

"Rissa?" Dillan's face on her wrist comp lit up the cramped closet. *"You've got problems."*

"You don't know the half of it," she whispered. "Arjay is here."

"Arjay? Never mind that. Don't leave the shuttle. Two more are about to arrive."

Dillan watched two shuttles enter the mothership about two mins apart. As soon as the second one landed, the space doors closed and he could see nothing. He was so anxious with worry over the danger to Rissa he missed the first hail from the mothership.

"How's your sublight, Captain Orsgard?"

For a moment, Dillan forgot he'd taken his grandfather's name.

"My AI fixed the problem, and I'm preparing to get underway. Thanks for your offer, Captain Dorman. By the way, what's your heading?"

After a slight pause, the captain of the mothership responded, *"Mag Prime. And you?"*

"What a coincidence." Dillan faked surprise. "That's where I'm heading. Okay if I tag along. Safety in numbers and all that."

Another slight pause. *"I have another stop. You are welcome to follow until then. As you say, safety in numbers. I've never worried about pirates, but a single ship like yours would be fair game. Dorman out."*

Another stop. More kids. What a racket those people were involved in. He'd hoped to get Arjay to help track down the two names Quin had given them.

Although Arjay wasn't there to help him, Dillan knew someone who could.

As soon as Jileena's sweat-drenched face appeared on his comm screen, Dillan said, "Hello, sweetheart. Wanna run away with me?"

"Dillan, you are so silly." She sounded out of breath. *"What would my spouse say?"*

"Did I interrupt something?" He waggled his eyebrows.

"Yes. My rehab therapist is torturing me. Please keep talking and maybe she'll stop."

"You have five more mins, Madame Servary." The stern voice sounded farther away. *"You must continue."*

With a conspiratorial wink, Konner's little sister cried out, *"Save me, Dillan. She's killing me."*

"Did I not say you must not answer your comm?" A disembodied hand reached in and snatched the device then threw it onto a table. The noise as it hit and slid made Dillan winced.

"Sorry, sweetie. I'll call you back as soon as my torturer releases me." Jilly's voice was barely audible. Her cry of pain, a lot louder.

"What's going on here?" Jilly's comm was picked up then turned around. Laning Servary's dark expression filled the screen. *"Who's calling—Rusteran, what do you want?"*

"Since I can't get your spouse to run away with me, I'll ask for a favor. I need some help."

Servary chuckled. *"You never give up, do you, Dillan? I heard you were out of town."*

Dillan nodded. "In your old stomping grounds. Leaving Balderan for Mag Prime."

"Good grief. What are you doing out there?" Jilly appeared next to Servary. After wiping her face, she looped the towel around her neck. *"I'm glad that's over with for another day. Next time, sweetie, I hire the therapist. And not one from Hildy's House of Pain."*

Servary leaned down and captured Jilly's lips. Their kiss was long, passionate, and uncomfortable for Dillan. He'd always loved her, even daydreamed as a teen about marrying her. Then he'd met Rissa.

He grimaced. "Get a room, you two." When they broke apart, he explained about the trafficking.

Jilly gasped. *"That is reprehensible."*

Servary features tightened. *"What do you need?"*

"Warning. Space doors will open two minutes. Vacate the shuttle bay."

The message repeated three more times before Rissa felt a change in air pressure in her ears. Though the pressure was intense, she was grateful for Dillan's warning. Otherwise, she might have been caught out in the bay when the space doors opened.

"I do not understand why you are here, Mistress Rissa," Arjay whispered. "I had assumed you would remain aboard Mister Dillan's ship and follow the shuttle."

Although Arjay spoke softly, their proximity in the tight space meant his mouth was pressed against her head. That added to the discomfort in her ears.

"Arjay, why didn't I see you when I explored? Where were you?"

"When I heard someone coming, I hid. I did not realize it was you until later. I thought you had left the shuttle. Then when I heard you talking to Mister Dillan, I was afraid you would be angry at me for leaving the ship without permission."

"Space doors are closing."

After the reverberations from the doors locking into place, she heard the other shuttles' doors opening.

"What are we going to do, Mistress?"

"Shh," she warned Arjay.

Again the children were lined up, by sexes and ages. Only this time, more directions were given—ship level and section. That gave Rissa a better sense of where to look for the children. But what could she do with them once she found them? It wasn't like she could take them and run.

CHAPTER 26

Dillan followed the mothership but with no more contact from Rissa. He dared not call her for fear of giving away her position, wherever it was. He hoped she had enough sense to lay low until he could rescue her.

Even as he formed that thought, he knew she wouldn't hide or wait. She'd been on her own too long to wait for anyone to rescue her. Such an independent fem. Bold, take charge, stand her ground. That was his Rissa. That's what he loved about her.

During the long trip through a hyperlane—when he couldn't send or receive any communication—he slept, worked out in his mini-gym in the hold, ate replicated meals, and worried about what she was doing on the traffickers' ship. His apprehension about her safety churned his gut. Without communication, he had no way of knowing if she'd been captured . . . or killed.

Now that he'd made love with her, he didn't know what he'd do if he lost her. His life wouldn't be worth sherd.

"Where are you going, Mistress Rissa?" Arjay scurried after her as she headed for the shuttle's command center. "What if they catch you?"

With the rear hatch closed, she didn't worry about being seen. "Stay low." As soon as she slid the hatch open, she crouched below the viewscreen. "If there are cameras in the bay, we don't want them to see us."

"Would it help if I disabled the cameras?" He sounded a little too eager.

"No. Someone will come to see why, and they'll catch us for sure."

"Not if I disable all the cameras." When she looked over her shoulder, his grin was infectious.

"You can do that?"

"Of course. Although I was not programmed to hack into surveillance systems, Celara encouraged me to learn new skills."

Good for Celara. And good for me.

Rissa crawled beneath the instrument panel than sat with her knees drawn up, her arms around her shins. "Arjay, before you disable anything, can you access the camera feeds?"

"Of course. What would you like to see?" He followed her example and sat with his back against the access panel.

"Where the children are. But can you do it without the captain or communications officer noticing?"

Arjay rubbed his hands together in glee. "They'll never know I was there."

He twisted around so he could open the access panel. Within secs, her wrist comm lit up with images. Room after room contained children from toddlers to teens, some huddled in groups, others alone in corners. All with fear in their faces.

"Wait. Go back to that last room." Hope and fear mingled inside her.

"Is something wrong?"

"I'm not sure. I thought I saw . . . Yes. There she is." Though the screen was no bigger than a playing card, she could see. "My girl. Pela. She's on this ship." Relief spread through her. The traffickers hadn't sold her yet. "Where is that room?"

"Camera 21, deck 3, aft, portside, number 8."

"Okay, we have to get her out of there." She started to crawl toward the outside hatch.

"Wait." He grabbed the back of her shirt. "Two men just entered the bay."

"What are they doing?"

"They are headed this way. Hide."

Rissa scrambled toward the utility closet they'd been in before. As she left the passenger area, she looked back for Arjay and saw the access panel closing. He was safe. She'd just gotten the closet door closed when she heard the cargo hatch open.

"I still say nobody could've gotten aboard without me knowing about it," A gruff voice proclaimed.

Oh, sweet Matriarch protect us.

"We gotta search anyway. You know Captain Dorman. We do what he says, or he'll report us to *Her Majesty*." The last came out as a sneer. The other man obviously didn't like the fem in charge. "What in Lexol's—"

Lights in the bay flickered. A klaxon blared. The comm speaker boomed. "Warning, warning. Space doors will open in twenty secs. Warning."

"They shouldn't open. All the shuttles are—"

"Forget that. We gotta get outa here."

Heavy boots hitting the deck sounded as the two men ran away.

Rissa waited for the rumble of the space doors. It didn't come. She waited anyway. The hatch from the passenger area flung open, the light nearly blinding her.

"You can come out."

Rissa sagged in relief at Arjay's appearance.

"That will keep them busy." He smiled in triumph.

"You did that? The doors didn't open."

"Wait until they see what's next." He tapped the mini-screen on his comm.

"What are you doing?" She stepped out of the closet.

"Scrambling the camera feeds. And . . ." He paused, obviously pleased with himself. Lights in the bay went out. "Interfering with the lights." Which came back on.

"Attention, all hands. Report to the captain immediately. All hands to the bridge."

"Yes." Arjay pulled down his fist. "Now we'll know how many crew are aboard."

"Unless they post sentries."

"You are a killjoy," Arjay declared. "How can we have any fun?"

"Fun? You want fun? My daughter is in one of those rooms. "She will be sold into slavery or to a prosti-house if we don't rescue her in time. So will those other children. So don't talk to me of fun."

Arjay looked at her askance. "My apologies, Mistress Rissa. A poor choice of words. Oh, look. Including the captain, I count fifteen. For a ship this size, I expected more."

"Sentries," she repeated.

He concentrated on his mini-screen. "You are correct. Two sentries are positioned outside the bridge."

"Seventeen crew members—if we've seen them all." She leaned over to see Arjay's screen, which showed the men standing in loose formation. "I wish we could hear what the captain is telling them."

Arjay brightened. "He's ordering them to patrol the ship and—"

"You can hear?"

"Of course. The captain is assigning the crew different sectors."

"If they're spread out, we could take them down one at a time."

"Kill them?" Arjay looked horrified. "That is against my programming."

"To Lexol with your programming. I have to save my daughter . . . and the rest of those children."

After the fifth shipday, Dillan followed the mothership out of the lane. Movement on the comm screen caught his eye as messages scrolled down the monitor. When the messages stopped, newsfeeds began. He ignored the news and opened the message from Kaminga. Traffickers had hit three other settlements on Galeriana prior to grabbing the three up at the mines, taking a total of twenty children.

Again, they only took children. That had puzzled Dillan. Then it finally hit him. Children wouldn't fight back. They wouldn't riot or organize to escape. Diabolically clever.

He ignored the numerous messages from his father. He knew what he'd hear—more anger at Dillan's leaving the company and threats to make him return. Well, Boras wasn't going to get the response he wanted. At that moment Dillan had a higher priority. Rescuing Rissa.

When he read the text from Fortuna, he perked up. Her girls remembered the kids talking about a station. Some even said the traffickers mentioned a space station.

Laning Servary also left a message.

Toots: Menacan barkeep on Menaca Station #1, reputation for being honest and good source of gossip. Coriana Lokaran: legit import-export biz based on Menaca Station #1; biz suspected of being a front for transport of illegal goods—no proof; Chellian heritage but no record of birth on Chellus; 1st mentioned in Willand Sector as adult; 1 adult daughter. Will keep digging. Good luck. Jilly sends love.

Dillan sat back. This new information swirled around his mind. Both characters Quin mentioned were on Menaca Station #1. Could this be the space station the kids in Astron mentioned? Manca. A child's misunderstanding for Menaca? A good possibility that was the destination for the slave ship where Rissa hid.

If this Coriana was under suspicion, it was a good bet she was involved. Coalition courts might need proof. He didn't. Import-Export. That covered a multitude of sins. Were children the "goods" she transported? Could she be the trafficking ringleader?

"That's all the crew except the captain and the comm officer." Rissa shoved the unconscious man, hands and feet bound, into an escape pod. He bounced off the other two before landing on the floor. "Did you disable the comms in the pods?"

"Yes, Mistress Rissa." Arjay gave her an exasperated look. "You have asked me six times."

"Jettison the pods all at once."

"Are you certain they will not die?"

"Yes." Her turn for exasperation. "They have enough air and water for several days. They will be picked up by a passing ship." Even so, she wouldn't waste any tears on their demise if it happened. "Time to get rid of the captain."

"And comm officer."

Trust Arjay to be all inclusive.

It hadn't been easy to capture the crew, but they'd managed. Finding a laser pistol under the shuttle pilot's seat helped take down the first guard. Capturing his weapon made them more efficient. Especially once Arjay disabled the comms.

They hadn't released the children yet for fear of them either getting caught in the crossfire or being used by the guards as shields or hostages.

When they reached the portal to the bridge, she said, "Check inside, Arjay. See where the captain is."

"He's right here." The male voice came from behind them. "Weapons down."

Sherd.

After nodding to Arjay, she stooped and laid her pistol on the deck. "How did you know?"

"Kick the pistols down the corridor, then brace yourselves against the wall, hands high."

She'd failed. After all they'd done eliminating the crew, to be caught so near to the end crushed her hope of rescuing Pela and the children.

The man patted her down, searching for more weapons. Out of the corner of her eye, she could see he did the same to Arjay. Though she barely got a glimpse of the man, she knew he was the captain. Blond, heavy-set, a middle-aged Chellian with reddish spots across his forehead and down the sides of his cheeks and neck.

"Now who do we have here," he said. "You, fem, turn around. Slowly."

Rissa did as told. Though she was tall, he topped her by a few centis. If he didn't outweigh her so much, she could take him down.

"Don't even think about it," the captain said.

She affected a wide-eyed stare. "Think about what?"

"Trying to grab my weapon. Wait. I know you." He tipped his head slightly as if to eye her better.

"Mistress Rissa, don't tell him anything."

She groaned. Trust Arjay to inadvertently reveal what she wasn't going to.

The captain snapped his fingers. "Rissa. You worked at that bar on Marin 5. Outpost—now which one was it?"

"Nineteen," she said with resignation. "You remember me?"

A slow smile creased his face and he lowered his weapon. "Hard to forget a pretty fem. By the stars, what are you doing on my ship and what have you done with my crew?"

That smile. A vision of a shy young man who stuttered whenever she asked for his order. "I remember you. You worked on one of the freighters. Dar—no, Dor—Sorry, I don't remember your name." What in Lexol's Fire was she doing apologizing to the captain of a slave ship?

"Dorman. Sileas Dorman." He laughed. "Wound up owning the damn thing. Couldn't wait to leave Marin 5. What a godforsaken place. You beat me outa there by a few years. Heard you had some trouble with—" He paled. "—slavers."

Without thinking, she clasped his hand with both of hers. "Sileas, I do remember you. You were always so sweet, and you wouldn't let anyone talk nasty to me. You even beat up that guy who grabbed me. You were my hero that day."

When he blushed—and didn't jerk away—she knew she'd taken the right tack. He'd had a crush on her back on Marin 5 and still harbored feelings for her. That his weapon still rested along his thigh gave her hope.

"Sileas, they stole my baby. I left because I had to find her."
"Did you?"

Tears burned her eyes. She blinked several times. "No. And now my other daughter is aboard your ship." She squeezed his hand. "Sileas, I have to rescue her. Please, please help me."

Indecision played across his face.

Rissa clung to his hand. "You were a good man when I knew you on Marin. I know you can't have changed that much. Please, please, don't take this daughter away from me." She let a tear fall. She'd do anything to play on his sympathies. If it didn't work, she'd try something else.

Slowly, he took a step back. She'd almost had him. On impulse, she threw her arms around his neck. "Help me, Sileas. I can't bear to lose another child. It—It would destroy me."

When he wrapped his thick arms around her, his pistol dug into her back. "Rissa, I would do anything for you. But . . . If she thinks I betrayed her, she'll kill me."

"Who? Your boss?"

"Captain? What are you doing? Who are these people?"

Dorman froze. In a blur, Arjay tackled the unarmed newcomer, a small man with the shocking red hair of a Menacan. As they rolled around on the deck, they came close to the weapons she and Arjay had kicked aside. If the newcomer stretched out his arm, he would reach her pistol. He rolled Arjay beneath him and smashed a fist into the AI's face. As he prepared to hit Arjay again, the newcomer's fist stopped in mid-air. He stiffened and fell over.

In shock, Rissa looked at Dorman and the laser pistol in his hand. She couldn't believe it. Relief shot through her. He was going to help her.

Arjay scrambled up and straightened his hair. "Thank you, Captain." He rubbed his jaw. "I have never engaged in fisticuffs before. It is most unpleasant."

Dorman chuckled. "Your friend does have a way with words."

Rissa eyed the pistol in his hand. "What are you going to do now?"

"What I wanted to do twenty years ago." Dorman pulled her to him and laid a kiss on her. A hard kiss.

Still shocked over his stunning his crewmate and now him kissing her, Rissa didn't move. His erection pulsed against her. Would he demand sex for helping her? She'd thought she could do anything to save Pela and the rest of the children.

His lips softened as the kiss went on, coaxing her to respond. Her heart pounded in her ears. Could she betray Dillan? For her daughter?

Leaning into Dorman, she forced herself to respond. She could do this.

"Captain, you must release Mistress Rissa."

Again, Dorman froze. She would, too, if Arjay had pressed a laser pistol into her neck.

"You will not take advantage of her. I insist. I will not hesitate to kill you."

"Got yourself a little warrior, huh?" Dorman released her. "I only wanted a kiss. Wasn't going to take advantage."

She took his weapon, surprised at how easily he let it go. "I knew you wouldn't, Sileas," she lied. "You are an honorable man."

Arjay snorted.

"Hush," she told him. "He is. Otherwise, he would not have stunned his own man. Find something to bind his hands and feet. We need to get him into the last escape pod."

"So that's what you've done with my crew." Dorman gave her a resigned look. "You'd better stun me, to make it look good."

He'd helped her. How could she stun him?

"I'm not sure I can."

"Step aside, Mistress Rissa. I can." Arjay fired his weapon.

As Dorman slumped to the deck, Rissa cried out, "Damn it, Arjay, I wanted to question him about his boss."

"My apologies." He didn't look apologetic.

"Did you know if you had pulled the trigger against his neck, even on stun it would have killed him?"

"Of course. I feared for your life."

"Oh, for quizzard's sake. I could have handled him. We need to get these two into the pod and jettison all of them."

Hauling the Menacan into the pod was easy. Captain Dorman, not so much. Thank the Matriarch Arjay was stronger than he looked. As soon as they locked the hatch, they ran to the bridge.

"You know how to jettison the pods?" she asked Arjay.

"Yes." He tapped two places on the instrument panel. On the monitors, she saw escape pods shoot out behind and to the sides of the ship.

She breathed a sigh of relief. "All right. That's done. Now we need to release the kids. First, I need to contact Dillan."

"We have control of the slave ship."

Rissa's announcement sent a flare of relief through Dillan. "How?"

As she related what she and Arjay had done, fear replaced the relief. "Sweet Divinity, you could have been killed. Why didn't you stay hidden?"

In his wrist-comm's mini-screen, she gaped at him.

He slapped his forehead. "What am I thinking? I should have known you wouldn't hide out. Never mind. How are the kids?"

"Don't know yet. I called you first. Arjay's turning the ship around and taking us back to Astron."

"No. As long as you're this far, head for Menaca Station #1."

"Why? I think that's where the head of the trafficking ring is."

"Exactly."

"Hang on. You want me to find the boss?"

"How else are we going to capture her?"

"Her? You know the boss is a fem? How did you find out?"

"Servary. Coalition Security suspects a Chellian named Coriana—remember Quin mentioned her? She's on that space station."

She closed her eyes for a moment. *"Stars, I hate to take these kids anywhere near her. Something could happen."*

"I'm going to meet you there. I won't let anything bad happen to you or the kids. I promise." When she still looked uncertain, he added, "Trust me."

Rissa left Arjay at the helm before racing through the ship to Deck 3, where according to surveillance, she would find Pela. He'd already unlocked all the holding rooms. When she got to that level, children wandered the corridor. They were filthy and bewildered. Three older girls—none Pela or Anaris—were comforting a few young ones.

"Stop." Her sharp voice startled the children who faced her, fear in their expressions. "Where is Pela? The teen they took on—"

She was nearly bowled over by the slight figure tackling her from behind.

"Miz Rissa!" Anaris cried. "Pela said you'd save us."

Rissa hugged the small girl. "Where is she?"

"She and some of the other kids are taking the babies to the shuttle. One of the boys knows how to fly."

"By the Matriarch." Rissa tapped her wrist-comm. "Arjay, don't open the shuttle bay space doors. No matter what. Lock out the controls. I'll explain later."

She disconnected then raced down the corridor. When she realized Anaris was keeping up with her, she stopped. "Stay and get all of the kids down to the galley. Make sure they're fed."

"Yes, ma'am." Anaris hugged her around the waist before turning away.

By the time she reached the shuttle bay, Rissa was out of breath. "Arjay . . . unlock . . . the hatch . . . to the . . . shuttle bay."

"Are you all right, Mistress Rissa?"

As soon as she heard the lock disengage, she yanked open the hatch. Pela jerked away from one of the shuttles, anger in her eyes. When she saw Rissa, she handed off a baby and ran to her.

Rissa couldn't hold her tight enough. "I thought I'd lost you." Her voice cracked and tears began to fall.

Hers weren't the only ones. Pela swiped her eyes. "I knew you'd come. I knew you wouldn't let them—"

"Oh, sweet girl." She hugged Pela closer. The girl's faith humbled her.

"What's going on?" A boy about twelve stood outside the shuttle. "Aren't we leaving?"

"Gimme a min, Numius," Pela yelled back. She looked up at Rissa." He can pilot anything. He's taking the babies to Security on the nearest colony."

She put her hands on Pela's shoulders. "You all have to stay on the ship."

"No." Pela jerked away. "Not the babies. They're going to sell them."

Several kids of both genders gathered around Pela. They eyed Rissa with suspicion. From the shuttle, she could hear babies crying.

"We have a plan. We're going to one of Menaca's space stations. Trust me."

"Why should we?" one of the boys asked. "We don't know you."

"I do," Pela said. "If she says she has a plan, she's going to save us from the traffickers." She turned her attention to Rissa. "What do you want us to do?"

Again, Rissa was humbled by Pela's trust.

"Take everyone to the galley. Feed the babies then yourselves. The guards are gone. Arjay and I are the only ones here."

"Why should we trust her?" Numius stood with his arms folded across his chest. The others looked from Pela to the defiant boy.

"Because she's my mother."

CHAPTER 27

"Is that the space station?" Pela leaned over Rissa's shoulder to stare at the orbiting structure. "It doesn't look in good shape."

That was putting it mildly. The station consisted of two concentric rings with spokes emanating from a hub to the inner ring, which was connected by more spokes to the outer ring where several ships were attached. Antennas sprouted from the hub. Solar panels that stretched out on two sides of the outer ring looked like they'd been hit by approaching ships. Several panels were broken, as were three antennas.

"Maybe we should dock at the other one." She pointed to another station off in the distance.

"No," Arjay said. "This is Menacan Station #1. That's where Mister Dillan said to go." He paused. "We're being hailed."

"Space Dock Command?" Rissa asked.

"Uh, no. A fem. Coriana." He looked over at Rissa. "Do we respond?"

"Yes."

"Voice only?"

"No. I want to look that bitch in the eye and tell her she's lost this cargo. Pela, out of sight. I don't want her to see you."

The teen pouted. "I want to see her, too."

"Please, go. And close the hatch behind you."

Pela stomped out.

"Are you certain you wish to speak to this fem?" Arjay gave Rissa a worried look.

"Put her through."

The comm screen swirled then a figure appeared. As the image came into focus, Rissa gasped. "You!"

"Rusteran, we need your help. Where are you?"

Dillan had finished docking at Menacan Station #1 when Laning Servary contacted him. "Just docked at the station. What do you need?"

"Coalition Security should be there in two hours. Tell Rissa to wait for them. We can't arrest Coriana unless we catch her taking delivery."

"Are you saying Rissa has to turn the kids over to that bitch?"

"Yes."

Dillan shook his head. "She will not go along with that."

"She has to."

"I know her, Servary. She will give up her life before she gives up those kids. You can't ask her to."

"If she wants to lop off the head of this trafficking ring, she'll have to." Servary's dark eyes became almost black with intensity. *"Convince her."*

Dillan slumped back in his seat. For long moments after Servary disconnected, Dillan tried to come up with another solution, one that didn't involve Rissa surrendering the children. Finally, he called her.

She didn't answer.

Rissa signaled to Arjay to shut down communications. She couldn't believe the identity of the traffickers' ringleader. Her lungs seized. *No. No, no, no.*

As blackness crept in from the sides of her vision, Arjay called out, "Mistress Rissa? What . . ."

She sucked in air. Her heart thudded, blocking out the rest of what the AI was saying. His mouth worked, but no sound penetrated as image after image flashed through Rissa's mind. The gray-haired fem cuddling Miri, calming her when she cried, comforting Rissa when she didn't know how to soothe her baby. Bruised and distraught after Miri was stolen. Crying with Rissa.

Liar. Betrayer. Thief.

Arjay's hand on hers erased the images. "Please, talk to me."

"Coriana was my landlady at the outpost on Marin 5." The words poured out, though how she formed them she didn't know. "That wasn't her name then. Twenty years ago, she was an old fem with faded, wrinkled skin who limped and had to be helped up the stairs. Not . . ."

"She does not appear to be very old. Perhaps fifty-five or sixty."

"She stole my baby, Arjay. My Miri. When she was only six tendays old. She was taking care of her and gave her to traffickers." Rissa's stomach cramped so hard she had to bend over in the chair. "My baby. My baby."

After several secs, he said, "What shall we do? She is trying to restore communications."

Rissa straightened. "She can go straight to Lexol and rot there."

Her wrist-comm vibrated. Dillan. She couldn't talk to him. Not with her mind in such turmoil.

"Space Dock Command wants to know our intentions. Are we docking . . . or leaving?"

"I don't know. I can't think." She rubbed her temples.

Arjay swiveled his seat to face her. "You are stronger than this. You can confront her. Perhaps this is a misunderstanding. She might not be who you think she is. A relative, perhaps. Or merely someone who looks like your landlady."

She shook her head. "I'd know those Chellian eyes anywhere. It's her."

"For the sake of the children, you must talk to her. Remember what Mister Dillan said? You have to get her to acknowledge that she is in charge of the traffickers."

Arjay was right. Rissa knew it. But just talking to the fem who'd stolen Miri would be harder than anything she'd ever had to do.

"Back away from the station. Tell Space Dock Command we're having steering difficulties. Then get Coriana back. Tell her we're having problems with our comm system."

He turned back to the instrument panel. "I will have difficulty with the comm when I speak to Space Dock. Just in case Coriana has access."

"Thank you, Arjay." She patted his upper arm. "You are thinking for both of us."

After talking to Space Dock Command, he connected with Coriana. What an actor, so obsequious in his apologies. As if he were an underling, not Rissa's support and savior.

Though the words were bitter in her mouth, she too apologized for the disconnect. "Something must be interfering with our comm system."

"You appeared to recognize me?"

"I thought I did. You remind me of someone I once knew. A long time ago."

As she waved an elegant hand, the jewels in her rings caught the light and flashed. *"I thought the same thing. You do remind me of someone."* Then her expression changed. Her amber eyes narrowed. *"Where is Captain Dorman? And the crew?"*

"He is . . . indisposed. As are the others."

Coriana was not pleased. *"What did you do?"*

"I sent them on a little trip. After helping them see the error of their ways."

"Why are you on my ship?"

Rissa hardened her resolve. If Arjay could act, so could she. With a light tone, she asked, "Are you saying this is your ship?"

"You know damn well it is."

"Terrans have a saying—possession is nine-tenths of the law. I believe that applies here. I have possession. Therefore, this is my ship. Now."

The fem's expression grew so fierce, the irregular spots across her forehead stood out. *"Apparently, you do not know what you are interfering with."*

Rissa narrowed her eyes and tightened her lips. "Explain it to me."

Coriana sat back. While she appeared to be getting herself under control, Rissa examined the fem's surroundings. An office, elegantly appointed with pricey decorations. A far cry from her dingy apartment at Outpost 19.

"I knew you would be trouble. Quin said he could handle you. I knew better. You're like a caninus with a bone. Warnings wouldn't deter you."

"And how did you know that? You don't even know who I am."

"Cut the crap, Rissa Dix."

"Yes, let's . . . Rani Karr. Or is it Coriana Lokaran now?"

"Quin should have eliminated you when I told him to."

Thank the Matriarch, he hadn't obeyed. "What did you do with my daughter?"

"Finally. I wondered when you'd get around to asking."

"Do you know where she is?" Rissa forced herself to stay calm. "Where Miri is?"

Coriana gave her a smug smile. *"Of course, I do."*

"Where? Where is my daughter?"

When Coriana's eyes lit up, Rissa knew she'd lost any advantage she had. *"I have a proposition for you. You have something I want."*

"And that is?"

"You know damn well what I want. My ship and cargo."

"Yes. Let's talk about that cargo. So there's no misunderstanding, are you talking about the containers of mining equipment?"

The fem quickly covered her surprise. *"That son-of-a-bitch Dorman. He had a business on the side."*

"So the pipes and drills aren't your cargo?"

"No, damn it. The children are."

"You admit you're trafficking in children." Triumph. That had almost been too easy.

"A lot of good my admission will do you. It won't hold up in a Coalition court. Communications can be doctored."

Rissa felt blind-sided. Coriana must have seen the dismay in her expression.

"Besides, you won't deliver the recording to the authorities. I have something you want more." Now triumph shone in those amber eyes.

Coriana waited. Rissa waited. Neither ready to speak first. Both knew whoever did would lose the advantage.

"Rissa, the kids are—" Pela burst onto the bridge. "I'm sorry. I didn't think . . ."

"Is that the girl you call your daughter? Does she know how careless you are with daughters?" Coriana smirked. *"You lose them."*

"By trusting the wrong person," she snapped. "You stole my child. You sold her like a piece of chattel."

"What baby?" Pela asked.

"How does it feel to be a substitute, Pela? She took you in to replace her own child, the one she lost. Just like she lost you."

"You are a nasty fem."

Coriana laughed.

"Go," Rissa told Pela. "I'll help you with the children shortly."

"But I—"

"Go."

"Let her stay. Let her see how important she is. She and the rest of my cargo."

Rissa had a bad feeling. She glanced over her shoulder at Pela and slowly shook her head.

"Here's my offer. You want to know what happened to Miri. I want my ship and cargo. Dock my ship and release the cargo, and I will give you your daughter's whereabouts."

Hope rushed through Rissa. She could finally find Miri. All she had to do was—

"You can't," Pela cried. "You can't give the kids—us kids—to that evil bitch."

"Watch your language." What was wrong with her? So confused by the awful choice, she focused on Pela's epithet?

"You can't have your ship or cargo. No deal." She signaled to Arjay to end communication.

"You will regret that. Miri is close by. In fact, she's—"

Rissa whirled on Arjay. "Why did you cut her off?"

"You—You told me to."

Pela threw her arms around Rissa's neck. "I knew you would protect us. You'd never turn us over to her. Thank you . . . Mom."

Even Pela's comforting hug did little to console her. She'd just given up an opportunity to find her daughter. Misery like she'd never known overwhelmed her. Misery that she couldn't share. No one would understand. Arjay was an android. Pela, who'd just called her by the sweetest name—a name she never thought she'd hear—was a child. She could have no concept of what Rissa had done. Saving a shipload of children from certain slavery in exchange for her own flesh and blood.

"Mister Dillan has been calling you. He is quite insistent, but I chose not to interrupt you while talking to the Chellian."

"Pela, sweetheart." She disengaged the girl's arms from around her neck. "Look after the children, especially the babies."

"Sure." She got as far as the portal before turning around. She grinned broadly. "Mom."

Rissa gave her a weak smile in return. After the portal closed silently, she tapped her comm. "What?"

"Rissa?"

"Where are you?"

"What? I can't hear you."

"I said." She raised her voice. "Where are you?"

He wasn't on his ship, that was for sure. Bright, multi-colored lights danced behind him. The blaring of raucous music and the boisterous sounds of people talking in multiple languages nearly drowned out his voice.

"I'm on the station, in Toots' bar. Hang on while I go outside." His image bobbed on the screen as he walked. After a moment, the noise level went down but not completely. *"There. That's better. Are you okay?"* Dillan looked worried.

"What's wrong?"

"You have to turn the kids over to Coriana."

CHAPTER 28

Appalled, Rissa could only stare at Dillan. *How could he even suggest that?* "Absolutely not."

"You have to, Rissa. It's the only way the authorities can arrest her that will ensure she is convicted. Even if she admits it, a recording of her confession won't be enough."

She slumped in her chair. "Yeah, that's what she said. I'd hoped she was lying."

"You talked to her?"

Tears gathered behind her eyelids. Blinking did no good. The tears fell anyway. "She k-knows where Miri is." She swiped at her face. "Offered me a deal. Give up the kids and she'll tell me where my daughter is. How c-could I do that? I bargained away my child."

"Oh, babe. I am so sorry."

Through the mist clouding her vision, she saw the anguish in his face. It mirrored her own. Taking a deep breath, she willed herself back into control. "I made my choice."

"I know how hard that must have been." While he paused, she bit her tongue to keep from arguing. No one knew how hard it had been.

"But now you are going to change your mind."

"What? No. I can't. Pela heard me refuse."

"Servary organized a Security team to raid Coriana's headquarters. If they catch her with the children in her possession, they can bring her up on charges that will stick. The team is on the way. They just need a little more time. Can you stall?"

"How much time?"

After agonizing for ten mins, Rissa asked Arjay to contact Coriana. "My pilot needs the code to dock at your terminal."

Coriana didn't bother to hide her satisfaction. *"I knew you'd come around. So predictable."* She rattled off a series of numbers.

"I want Miri's location before I offload the children."

"You'll get it. And don't think you can launch without leaving them. My men will make certain you keep your end of the bargain."

"If you don't show up, there will be no deal."

The Chellian fem laughed. *"I don't come down to the docks."*

"Then no deal."

Her eyes narrowed. *"Why?"*

"I want to look you in the eye when you tell me why you targeted me and my baby."

"Or maybe you want to kill me." She raised a blond eyebrow.

Rissa's laugh was brittle. "Want to? Yes. But not until you tell me where she is."

"Blood thirsty, aren't you?"

"Wouldn't you be?"

"You'll be searched for weapons, you know."

"I expected that." Rissa took a deep breath. "I'll honor the bargain. My daughter's location for the children."

Coriana's gaze flickered past Rissa. At the same time, she heard a gasp. And she knew before glancing over her shoulder. Pela had heard.

"You promised," the girl cried. "You promised to take care of us. Liar!"

"Did you really expect her to choose you over her real daughter?" Coriana laughed. *"You escaped once, Pela. Don't expect to do so again."*

The connection ended.

Rissa jumped out of her seat, but Pela had already slipped away. "Wait." Rissa ran after her. "Pela, come back. Please."

"I should have known," she shot over her shoulder. "You're just like my parents."

"Let me explain. It isn't what you think."

Pela whirled around, out of breath, her face blotchy with tears and anger. "It's exactly what I think. I told those kids I trusted you. You're as bad as that fem."

"No." Rissa reached out for her.

"Don't touch me! Don't come near me again. What you did was worse than what my father did. You gave me hope. Hope for a better life. And you destroyed that."

Rissa watched helplessly as the girl who'd called her "Mom" stalked away.

Once again, her heart broke. At this rate, nothing would heal it. She held onto the corridor wall as she returned to the bridge. If she let go, she would crumple to the deck. Lead weights clung to her feet as she shuffled to the seat next to Arjay.

"I am sorry, Mistress Rissa. Perhaps it is better this way."

"Better? Better that she think I betrayed her?" She blew out a breath. "I'll give her time to cool down and then explain what's going on."

"You cannot do that." At her startled look, he said, "Coriana saw what you saw. Pela was devastated. If she knows the real reason, she couldn't hide it. She will give away the plan."

"I hadn't thought of that. How did she enter without us hearing her?"

"I did. My hearing is seventy-three percent better than yours." He gave her an apologetic look. "My programmer enhanced my vision, also. In fact, all my senses are superior."

"I guess that makes me an inferior species."

"Of course not, Mistress. I—"

"It would be best if you paid attention to where you're aiming this ship. We don't want to damage the dock."

"Line up, children. Youngest boys in front. Numius, you will lead. The older girls will carry the babies and bring up the rear."

Numius, the would-be shuttle pilot, stood at the head of the line. He sneered at her. "I knew we couldn't trust you."

Rissa glanced away. Stars, how she hated what she had to do. When she searched for Pela, she found her, Anaris, and three other young teens at the end, babies in their arms.

"You will wait here until I call for you. Arjay will give you last-min instructions."

"Whatever," the boy said. "Just get it over with."

She opened the outer hatch and lowered the ramp. Ten heavily-armed men lined either side. One of them handed his weapon to his companion and came up to her. He grabbed her upper arm and jerked her off the ramp. When she stumbled, he yanked her upright then slammed her against the side of the ship.

"Assume the position." After she raised her hands, he thrust his foot between hers to spread her legs. Looking for weapons, he felt along her sides, back and front, deliberately lingering on her breasts. But not as long as he did between her legs. When she tried to get away, he held her in place with his forearm against her back.

His violation sickened her.

Pressing her face into the ship, he said in a low voice, "Coriana said not to hurt you. But we know what you did to the crew. We're waiting for a chance to get even."

"That's enough, Jing," a fem called out. "She's not stupid enough to carry a weapon." The click-clacking of heels on synthcrete heralded her approach.

The man called Jing released Rissa with a hard shove. Again, she stumbled.

"Let me help you." His help consisted of twisting her arm behind her.

She held back a cry of pain.

"Now, now, Jing. I told you not to hurt her." Coriana Lokaran came closer. Her image on the comm screen paled in comparison to seeing her in person. She'd had rejuv done on her face. No wrinkles on that youthful skin. Her full lips were enhanced with bright coral coloring. Her blond hair, artfully arranged in an up-do had curls cascading down to her shoulders.

She looked nothing like Rissa's old landlady.

"Jing, check the ship. Count the little bastards. Dorman reported forty-seven."

"Where is my daughter?"

Coriana fluttered her hand. "In due time."

"No. Now. Or the kids don't get off."

The fem laughed. "You are no match for my men. I could have them shoot you before you take another breath."

Though fear snaked down her spine, Rissa lifted her chin. "Go ahead. I knew you wouldn't keep your word."

"The ferking airlock won't open." Jing shouted from the top of the ramp.

Coriana glared at Rissa. "Open the airlock."

"Your man can see the children. He'll verify that I kept my end of the bargain. Give me Miri's location."

"When I have the brats." She pulled a pistol out of her pocket. Though small, it was just as lethal as those held by her men. She aimed it at Rissa. "Order your pilot to open the airlock."

Rissa's comm vibrated twice against her wrist. Then three times, followed by another two vibrations. The signal that Servary's team was in place. *Thank the Matriarch.*

"Get those kids out here now," Coriana said.

"All right, all right." Rissa tapped her comm. "Arjay, release the children."

Jing got out of the way just in time. The littlest children rushed down the ramp and raced up to Coriana. Cries of "Are you our new mother?" rang throughout the docking bay as they surrounded her and Rissa. Just as Arjay instructed.

Coriana tried to disengage those who clung to her skirts and legs. "Get them away. Get them off me." In the chaos, Rissa easily captured the pistol, while Coriana's men stood there dumbfounded.

"Coalition Security! Children, hit the deck! Weapons down! Now!" The pounding of heavy boots accompanied the shouting as armed officers burst into the docking bay. "Drop those weapons! Now!"

The children did as rehearsed, flattening themselves on the floor and covering their heads. Startled by the invasion, Coriana's men dropped their guns and clasped their hands behind their necks. In all the confusion, the fem edged away.

When she realized Coriana was escaping, Rissa shoved past the Security officers. The fem glanced over her shoulder then took off running. Rissa's legs were longer and stronger. She slammed her forearm into the fem's back—the way Jing had done to her—and sent her skidding forward face down.

Rissa knelt on top of her back and grabbed a handful of blond curls. She pulled her knife out of her boot. Forcing Coriana's head back, Rissa held the blade against her neck.

"Shall we try again? Where is my daughter?"

"I don't know." She could hardly talk with her head bent back so far.

"Liar. You know. Tell me or I will slit your throat."

"Do it."

"Tempting. Very tempting."

"Better to die here than rot in prison."

"Not if I cut you slowly. Tell me where you took my baby." She flicked the blade against the edge of Coriana's ear.

She shrieked. Blood trickled down her neck.

"Where did you take my baby? Your nose is next."

"Traish. She went to Traish."

Rissa pressed the fem's face into the unclean floor. With the tip of the knife, she clipped the side of her nose.

This time, Coriana screamed while blood ran into her mouth.

"Where on Traish? It's a large planet." When the fem didn't answer, Rissa mused, "Shall I do the other side of your nose or your eyelid?"

"Nicorama City. A family named Elfors took her."

That figured. Elfors. The most common name on Traish.

"I swear I don't know where they live."

"You seem to remember more with a little help from my buddy here." Rissa waved the knife close to Coriana's eye.

"Please don't," she whimpered. "I don't know anything else. I swear. Mercy."

"Did you show those children mercy? When your people ripped them away from their families? When you loaded them like animals into cargo holds and sold them off? Where was your mercy when you stole my daughter?" Rissa re-gripped her knife. "I should gut you right now and save the Coalition the cost of a trial."

"That's enough, Rissa." Dillan. His strong arms lifted her off the whimpering fem.

"How long were you standing there?" Rissa let him hold her.

"Long enough to know that I didn't want you to kill her."

"Why not? She deserves it."

"I agree. But you will never get over taking a life."

The wicked fem scrambled to her feet . . . and into the arms of the waiting Security team.

"Coriana Lokara, you are under arrest for child trafficking." A tall fem, Hanu according to her Security ID, yanked Coriana's arms behind her and bound them.

Security questioned all of them endlessly. First her then Dillan, finally the oldest children. Rissa and Dillan made sure to stay with Pela, Anaris, and Geena Harraway during questioning. No way would they leave the girls alone. With each retelling, Rissa's anguish multiplied. Those poor, poor children. She thought she'd been angry at Coriana before. Furious didn't even come close. She wished she'd gutted the fem when she had the chance. When she said as much to Dillan, he repeated what he'd said in the cargo bay. She wouldn't want killing on her conscience.

She wasn't so sure about that.

Now, hours later, Rissa set her drink down on the bartop. "What's going to happen to the children?"

She, Dillan, and Security Officer Hanu sat at Toots' bar. Hanu had shown up to ask more questions. Still on duty, she'd gotten a non-alcoholic drink.

"My team is sorting them out. Those with families will be returned. Those who don't have parents or refuse to go home . . ." Hanu shrugged.

"They can't go back on the streets or into those orphanages." Rissa glanced through the bar's open door where three girls sat at a table.

Pela, Anaris, and Geena Harraway had colorful soft drinks and plenty of snacks in front of them. After a tearful reunion between Geena and her father via comm, Dillan promised his mine supervisor he'd bring the girl home safely. Anaris seemed stronger and less fearful after the ordeal. Pela hadn't totally forgiven Rissa, claiming she should have trusted her. True, Rissa admitted. In time, she hoped their relationship would recover.

". . . to them." Dillan had been talking and she'd completely missed what he said.

"I'm sorry. I—" Again, she was distracted by the girls out in the corridor. She hadn't protected them when they needed it. It would be a long time before her vigilance eased.

A young fem had stopped at their table. She talked to them briefly, then her shoulders slumped and she walked away. Pela jumped up so quickly her chair rocked and ran after her.

Something was wrong. She'd told the girls to stay within her line of sight.

When Rissa slid off the barstool, Dillan grabbed her arm. "What's wrong?"

"Pela." She ran out the door then after her. By the Matriarch, she couldn't lose her again. Several meters away, she and the young fem stood talking—Pela excited, the fem wary.

Rissa slowed down as she approached them. "What's going on?"

"She's looking for that evil fem," Pela said. "We told her they arrested Coriana. She's trying to find her birth parents. I told her Security would help. They'll let her look through Coriana's files, won't they?"

Officer Hanu who'd followed Rissa along with Dillan nodded. "Right now, my team is concentrating on the children from the ship. We really appreciate all the information you and your friends gave us." She smiled at Pela before nodding to Rissa. "Your AI is helping tremendously. Thanks for letting us use him. He's saving us a lot of time."

"Arjay is enjoying himself," Rissa said.

Hanu directed her attention to the young fem. "We confiscated Coriana's files and took them to our office in Jeneman City. As soon as we finish, I'll be glad to see what I can find."

Disappointment settled into the young fem's expression. "That will take a long time. I've been searching for nearly a year. When I got this far, I was sure I'd find my birth parents."

Though she stood a few centimeters taller than Pela, the two were similar. Sturdy bodies. Dark eyes and hair. While Pela's was long and in a straggly braid, the fem's was straight and sleeked back to reveal her strong cheekbones. Something about her . . .

"Let's go back to the table and sit down," Dillan said. "I'd like to hear this fem's story."

As they reached the other two girls, Officer Hanu excused herself. "I need to return to work. Give me your comm." After she input something, she returned the device to the stranger. "That's my direct contact. Send me your name and whatever info you have. I'll search the records in my spare time. Not that I'll have much of that." After nodding to the others and thanking them for their help, she strode away.

Dillan and Pela grabbed chairs from another table. When everyone sat, he said. "I think introductions are in order." He began with himself then Rissa. The girls added their names and mentioned how they'd gotten there.

"That must have been terrifying," the fem said.

"Yes and no." Pela gave Rissa a tentative smile. "I knew Mom would save us."

As relief settled over Rissa, she squeezed Pela's hand. She'd been forgiven.

"I can tell she's your mother," the fem said. "You two look alike."

Before either she or Pela could explain, Anaris said, "You didn't tell us who you are,"

"Oh, sorry." She reached out her hand to shake then raised it, palm out, in the traditional Rimmer greeting. "I'm Winty Elfors."

The name startled Rissa. She stared hard at Winty, while reminding herself that Elfors was a common name.

"Where are you from?" she asked.

"Traish. Holstrum, near the capital."

Couldn't be. A combination of excitement and apprehension rippled through her.

"When my parents died, I found my adoption papers hidden in a desk drawer. I had no idea. I wished they'd told me." Winty's mouth turned down. "That's when I decided to find my birth parents."

"How did you end up here?" Rissa asked, afraid to hope, afraid to even think this could be Miri.

"I'm going to get more drinks." Dillan stood, acting as if a planet-shattering event wasn't unfolding. Of course, he didn't know what she knew. "Winty? What can I get you?"

She smiled and pointed to Pela's glass. "That purple drink looks good."

"Oh, it is." Pela grinned. She pushed a near-empty bowl of versarin nuts toward Winty. "Have some."

"And these." Anaris pushed the other bowls of planten and veggie crisps over to her.

"Tell us your story, Winty," Rissa said as Dillan arrived with pitchers of purple and pink drinks.

Winty took a long swallow of the drink Dillan poured for her. "Thanks. I was really thirsty. Are you sure you want to know about me? You girls had quite an adventure. I'd like to hear about it."

"Later." When Rissa realized how abrupt she sounded, she softened her tone. "We'd like to hear about you first."

"Well, I started with the adoption papers and followed the trail. My father, I mean my adopted father, always said to follow the money."

Dillan smiled. "Wise words."

Rissa almost hit him for interrupting the story.

"That's what I did. I found the lawyer in Nicorama City who facilitated the adoption. Then I found out who paid him and backtracked. I'm very good at finding info on computers."

Anaris gave her a wide-eyed look. "You mean you hacked them?"

After munching a couple of nuts, Winty smiled. "Let's just say the people whose accounts I searched didn't exactly give me permission."

"Awesome," Geena Harraway said. She hadn't said much up to that point. Now she stared in admiration at Winty. "Where did you go?"

"It's felt like I've been everywhere. I ended up on Marin 5."

Rissa's heart stopped. This was too good to be true.

Dillan glanced at her and raised his eyebrow. "Nasty place, Marin 5."

"Oh, it is." Winty shivered. "I traced this fem who my sources said operated an adoption service there. Coriana Lokaran. Only she wasn't called Lokaran there."

"Rani Karr," Rissa whispered.

Winty turned on her. "Yes. How did you know?"

"I knew her then."

"Really? That was a long time ago. Before I was born." Winty laughed. "I didn't find her, but I did find her sister who didn't approve of what Rani was doing. The sister sent me to Galeria Prime. Rhadaman City. From there, I kept following clues until I ended up here. I sure hope Officer Hanu will find something about me in the files." She propped her elbows on the table. "Now you girls must tell me about your adventure."

"Wait. Why do you want to find your birth parents?" Rissa held her breath, waiting for Winty's response. Would she curse her for giving up her child? Would she berate her for not protecting her?

"I need to know what happened. At first, I wanted to know why they gave me up for adoption. Like I would understand if they were really poor and wanted me to have a better life. Then I learned what Coriana did. I couldn't believe anyone could be so cruel. I did wonder why my birth parents didn't try to find me." She waved her hand to include Rissa, Dillan, and Pela. "You three are such a happy family, you can't imagine what I've been going through."

"But we're not a family," Pela said. "And she's not really my mother. Well, she is because she loves me and I love her. And Mister—I mean Dillan—loves her and she loves him, so I guess that makes us all family."

Pela had no idea how much her words meant to Rissa. Tears formed, threatened to fall. A family. She'd called them a family.

"She rescued me from slavers. Me and Anaris. If your adopted parents were good to you, you might not want to find your birth parents.

Mine weren't very good. My father sold me to slavers and my mother let him."

"Mine, too," Anaris said in a small voice.

Winty's dark eyes clouded. "That's dreadful."

"What's worse," Pela said, "is that Mom's baby was stolen. And she really, really loved her. She couldn't help it if slavers . . ."

Tears began rolling down Rissa's face. Dillan put his arm around her, holding her close while the girls looked on in stunned silence. Sobs racked her body. All the anguish she'd felt for so many years poured out, along with her fear for Pela and despair that she'd never find Miri.

"Wh-What's wrong?" Pela cried. "I didn't mean to make you cry."

"Shh," Dillan crooned. "It's not your fault."

Rissa pulled away and grabbed some napkins from the table to wipe her face. "No. Not your fault."

"I-I don't understand." Winty eyed her strangely.

Rissa sniffed then blew her nose on the crumpled napkins. "Pela is right. My baby was stolen by slavers. She was six tendays old. My landlady was taking care of her while I worked in a bar. On Marin 5, Outpost 19."

"Outpost 19?" Winty exclaimed. "That's where—"

"Rani Karr was my landlady."

"Wow," Anaris said. "Wouldn't it be crazy if . . ." She looked back and forth from Rissa to Winty.

"My baby will be twenty-one soon. I named her Miri."

Winty/Miri shook her head. "I don't understand."

"I think you do," Dillan said quietly.

"You're my mother?"

CHAPTER 29

After the tears and laughter and hugs, Dillan suggested they move from the public concourse to his ship. Winty/Miri walked with her arm around Rissa's waist asking question after question.

He noticed Pela hanging back but not with Anaris and Geena. She seemed lost. He let the others go on ahead and walked beside her. Though she gave him a questioning look, neither spoke for several paces.

"She loves you," he said quietly.

Pela shrugged. "She's got her real daughter now."

"Are you still angry at her for turning you and the kids over to the traffickers?"

She shook her head. "I was. She did the right thing. I didn't want to admit it." She let out a deep sigh.

"So I guess you're wondering where you fit in."

"Sort of. I guess I don't even have a job anymore, what with the tavern burning down." She gave a harsh little laugh. "I don't even have a home now."

"You'll always have a home with Rissa. I know her. She'll make sure of it."

"How?"

"I don't know. We've been so focused on finding you and your friends that we haven't thought beyond that. Why don't we wait and see?"

She looped her arm around his and leaned into him. "Are you and she going to. . . you know?"

"Don't know about that either."

"You don't know much of anything, do you?" Her grin belied her words.

"Nope. Patience, my child. Everything will work out. Have a little faith in us old folks." He knuckled the top of her head, the way Kiran often did. "Go talk to your friends. I'd better lead the way or we'll all get lost."

She laughed at him then caught up with Anaris and Geena. As he strode ahead, he passed Rissa and Winty. By the stars, those two looked alike. Both wore grins, though Rissa's was broader. She looked so happy. Happier than he'd ever seen her.

A miracle, that's what it was. Rissa couldn't believe she'd finally found Miri. Here she was, laughing and talking with her. The way she'd always dreamed. How lucky she was that Miri had come to the Menacan space station looking for her at the same time she was there. What a coincidence. No, a miracle.

My daughter. Rissa wanted to pinch herself to make sure she was awake.

Dillan led them down another corridor. She marveled that he knew where he was going. Good thing no one depended on her to get to his ship.

Miri chatted about her home life on Traish. The activities she'd enjoyed as a child. Her parents had given her a good life—one Rissa with her limited formal education couldn't have. Despite losing out on all those years, she was glad good people had adopted her daughter.

Her daughter. She had two daughters now. She wanted both of them with her. As she turned to call Pela, something pierced her side. Searing hot pain. Her legs wouldn't move. *She* couldn't move. Except to drop to the floor.

Miri called out, "Help. Something's happened." As she bent over Rissa, she whispered, "Hallart says this is what happens when you interfere with his business. And this—" She twisted the blade. "—is for Coriana." The knife retracted into her sleeve.

"What's wrong?" Dillan came running.

"I don't know. She just collapsed. I'll get help." Miri tore down the corridor, brushing past the younger girls.

Rissa couldn't breathe. The agony overwhelmed her. She could only claw at Dillan's sleeve. Black edged in from the sides of her vision. With a mighty effort, she whispered, "Stop her. She . . ."

CHAPTER 30

Voices penetrated the fog in Rissa's brain. No words, just the voices. Cautious voices, worried voices. Male and fem. She tried to tell them to go away, but no words formed. Only a whimper escaped.

More voices. One male. Deep, rumbling.

She struggled to see who it was. She thought she knew. Dillan. She wanted to believe it was him. Why didn't he talk to her?

"Did you see that? Her eyelids are moving." It *was* Dillan. Only he wasn't talking to her. Who?

It took too much effort to think.

"Hey, Medico. Come back. Her baby finger moved."

"Don' shou'." Her throat hurt and the words came out raspy.

"Sweetheart, Rissa. Open your eyes, love."

"Hurz. Go 'way." No, she hadn't meant to say that. "Ss-tay."

"Let me see those beautiful brown eyes. C'mon."

"What's happening?" A different voice. Abrupt. A fem.

"She spoke. She's trying to open her eyes. I think the light is too bright."

A click and the cool air that had been blowing across her face lessened. Something hummed near her ear, then the sound diminished. After several secs, the fem said, "She's coming out of the anesthesia. Give her time. Keep the lid closed." After another click, the moving air returned. "I'll be back to check on her in an hour."

When Rissa sensed the overhead light dim, she managed to open her eyes in a slit. Not too bad. Wider hurt, but the slit wasn't bad. Dillan's image looked distorted.

"Waz hap'nin'?" She tried to swallow past the pain in her throat. "Drink. Need drink."

She heard a click, then something cold pressed against her lips. She licked them. Moisture trickled down her throat. Blessed relief. Dillan's face came into focus for a moment then distorted. The moving air returned. It felt good against her skin.

"You're in a med center on Menaca. Jeneman City. You had surgery to repair your kidney. The medicos couldn't save it. You've been in a regen unit for a day while a new one grows. You're strapped down so you don't move around. They don't want me to be here. But I couldn't leave you."

A regen unit. That's why the air came and went when the lid opened and closed. She had so many questions.

He pulled a chain out of his shirt. Miri's pendant. "I took this before you went into surgery. I was afraid it would get lost."

"Than' you. Give it."

"I can't. It's not allowed in the regen. I'll wear it until you can wear it again."

His thoughtfulness made tears form.

"M-Miri?" Would he answer truthfully or evade. She needed to know.

"Ah, yes. Winty. She's an assassin."

Rissa groaned. "No. N-Not Miri. Couldn't be."

"Oh, sweetheart. She wasn't Miri. Officer Hanu investigated. Winty—actually, Faringa Moser. She works for Hallart."

"I-I know." Her head was clearing. She remembered the last words Miri said. Wait. Not Miri. Winty. Rissa's head hurt from trying to recall what Dillan said about the fem's name. "She said Hallart wants me to know . . . what happens . . . when you interfere . . . with his business."

"Is that what she said? I saw her bend over you. I thought she was trying to find out what was wrong. Stars, girl, you gave me such a scare."

"Wasn't much fun for me either." She licked her parched lips. "More ice. Please."

He lifted the bubble top of the regen unit and placed another ice chip on her lips. "Easy does it. The medico said no drinking. It will make you sick. Faringa got away. She said she was going for help. I believed her until Pela pointed to the blood on the floor beneath you. "

"Pela. I wanted her with me. Wanted both daughters. I turned to call her—"

"That saved your life. When you turned, Faringa missed your heart and got your kidney."

"How—"

Dillan tapped her lips. "No more talking. Rest. Let the regen do its job." He stood.

"Stay with me."

"Pela is waiting for news. If I don't go out to the waiting room, she'll barge in here."

Her heavy eyes threatened to close. She gave in for a moment. "Bring her."

"Later. Maybe. If the medico agrees."

"Need her. Now."

Moments later, Pela arrived, looking frightened. She placed her hand on the bubble top. Tears streaked her cheeks. "M-Mom?"

"My sweet girl. Don't cry." Rissa wanted to reach out to her, touch her, but she couldn't.

"Dillan said you're going to be okay?" Her brown eyes, so like Rissa's own, clouded with worry.

"I will be. I promise. You're wearing the dress I got you in Vesteron. Do you like it?"

"I-I thought you were going to d-die." Tears fell. "S-So much blood." She sobbed.

"Okay, sweetheart," Dillan crooned as he took Pela into his arms. "It will be okay." Over the girl's shoulder, he gave Rissa a quick smile. "The medico says Rissa needs to rest and let the regen work. She'll be good as new in a few days."

"Get her something to eat while I sleep." Rissa closed her eyes to encourage them to leave. She wanted Dillan to stay. She needed more answers. Why did that girl pretend to be her daughter? Raising her hopes then dashing them. The cruelty of it cut through her. How did Winty, or whatever her name was, know so much? Traish, Nicorama City, Elfors, Marin 5. She knew everything. How?

Out in the corridor, Dillan held the sobbing Pela. The day before, he'd sent Anaris and Geena Harraway back to Astron on a Rusteran Mining transport. They'd been shaken by the attack on Rissa, and when told, Harraway demanded his daughter's return. Dillan couldn't blame him. If it had been his daughter, he'd have wanted her home, too.

Terrified to leave Rissa, Pela pleaded with him to let her stay. How could he refuse?

The girl's sobs hiccupped to a stop. "I'm okay." She swiped at her face. "I'm sorry I broke down."

"You had a good reason. No need to apologize." He put his hand on her shoulder. "Let's do what Rissa said and get something to eat."

"I'll join you." Security Officer Hanu came up behind him. "I have more info on Faringa Moser, and I haven't eaten since First Meal."

Dillan raised his eyebrow. It was past time for Last Meal. As they walked to the cafeteria, a place he would be glad to put behind him, Hanu asked about Rissa's condition. Pela eagerly answered then begged Hanu to tell them what she knew about the fem who tried to pass herself off as Rissa's daughter. The officer waited until they all had food in front of them.

"She's worked for Coriana Lokaran for ten years, but did freelance work for Hallart."

Dillan dropped his fork. "Ten years? Sweet Divinity, she must have been a child when she started."

"Sixteen. She's older than she looks. The straight wig, professional make-up, young voice all contributed to her disguise. She looks nothing like the holo-pic we have on file." Hanu gave him a wry look. "Otherwise, I might have recognized her."

"She fooled all of us, especially Rissa." Dillan shook his head. "The deliberate cruelty was almost worse than the vicious attack."

"All Security offices have been informed. I made sure the alert included both pics of her—the official and one from the concourse surveillance vids. After the attack, she took a circuitous route through the station until she reached an old abandoned section with no surveillance. Then she disappeared."

"How could she just disappear? Someone had to see her. What about ships? Did any leave after—" Pela's voice broke.

"Between the time of the attack and when you called for help, three ships left the station. All reputable. Even so, once we knew what happened, I sent a shuttle out to search them. The officers found nothing amiss. And no Moser. Meanwhile, my team physically searched the station as well as the vidfeed from the surveillance cameras."

"Officer? Officer Hanu." Arjay scurried up to their table. "I found something."

Several diners—med center workers and visitors alike—looked up from their meals.

Dillan shoved out a chair with his foot. "Sit. And lower your voice."

"My sincerest apologies." The AI sat. "I was too excited by what I found to remember that this is highly-sensitive information. My enthusiasm carried me a—"

"Cut to the chase," Dillan cut him off. "What did you find?"

"Please tell me Mistress Rissa is all right. I have monitored her condition, but I need to know your impression, Mister Dillan."

Pela eyed him. "You hacked the med center? Way to go, Arjay."

Hanu shot him a stern look, while Dillan gave him a quick report on Rissa. "What did you find?" he asked.

"I have determined the method Faringa Moser used to depart the station." Arjay waited, as if to heighten the drama.

Dillan glared. "If you do not explain in the next two secs, I will have you reprogrammed to serve as custodian on a garbage scow."

"Many pardons, sir. I repeatedly searched the surveillance vidfeeds, both interior and exterior."

"I do not care how you found whatever it is you found. Tell us."

"Mister Dillan, sir. I am attempting to describe my resources so you will give credence to my discovery."

Dillan nearly jumped out of his chair and throttled the android.

Arjay must have interpreted his expression correctly since he hurried on with his tale. "Quin d'Sernin."

When no one spoke, he said, "I recognized Celara's ship."

"Explain," Hanu said.

To keep Arjay from dragging out the story, Dillan said, "D'Sernin is Celara d'Enfaden-Jovano's brother. Two years ago, he stole her ship. Go on, Arjay."

"The ship, a cargo transport named *d'Enfaden's Thermopylae* but renamed *Absurdity*, which quite frankly is an absurd name for such a fine vessel as—"

"Arjay," Dillan snapped.

"The ship had been stationary beyond the Menacan marker buoy for ninety-one mins before Faringa Moser stopped to talk to Pela and her friends. Then seven point six mins after she went into the abandoned bay, she transported to his ship." He sat back in triumph.

"No one can transport that far," Hanu said.

Dillan had to agree with her skepticism.

Arjay grinned. "They can if they hopscotch—that's a Terran term, according to my Rega. Celara loves Terran vernacular. At times, I have to agree it is colorful but accu—" A threatening glance from Hanu had him swallowing quickly. "She transported from one ship to another."

"Just how did you figure that out?" Dillan was as suspicious as Hanu.

"I slowed down the speed of the vid and found a tenth of a sec flash, indicating a transport, on the ship closest to the station. One point three secs later, a flash on the next ship out. Then—"

"I get it," Dillan said. "She must have had a personal transportation device to accomplish that. If she transported to an unoccupied section of each ship—like cargo holds—the pilot and crew would never know she'd been there."

"That is correct. I was certain you would understand, sir. After she landed in d'Sernin's ship, it departed at top speed. Quin d'Sernin helped her get away."

The regen unit did its job, though none too quickly by Rissa's account. A whole tenday. All she wanted to do was go home. To Astron, the only home she knew. The home Quin d'Sernin had burned to the foundation. She had no home, no tavern. Nothing.

"That's an awful sad face this early in the morning." Dillan stood in the doorway, a tote in his hand. "Especially since you're blowing this pop stand."

She smiled at the Terran expression. "Who taught you that one?"

"I have friends in low places. The medico said you could leave. I brought you clean clothes. Unless you'd rather stay for Mid-Day Meal?"

"Throw me that bag. I can't wait to get out of here."

"Do you need help getting dressed?"

"Now there's a switch." She opened the tote. Thank the Matriarch he'd included undergarments. "Usually, you're trying to get me out of my clothes."

He waggled his eyebrows. "I suppose we could do that. But then what would the medico say if she stopped in to bid farewell?"

She shooed him out of the room and quickly got dressed. Her side was still tender, especially when she stretched to slip her camisole over her head. He'd brought the tailored slacks and the green shirt that matched his eyes. She would have preferred her Rimmer pants and shirt. They'd been thrown out because of the blood.

But then she realized she was in Jeneman City, the capital of Menaca, a Coalition planet. He didn't want her to feel embarrassed by her frontier clothes in a sophisticated town. His thoughtfulness shouldn't have surprised her.

As she closed her shirt, she automatically tucked in Miri's pendant. Dillan had returned it as soon as she came out of the regen. The med staff was not pleased, but she refused to be without it.

Pela, wearing her new yellow top and tan slacks, edged around the door.

Rissa smiled. "I knew that color would look good on you."

"I didn't thank you for all the clothes. Anaris took hers with her. She liked them, too."

"It was my pleasure to pick them out, but Dillan bought them. You should thank him."

"I will. Do you need help? He said you might not be able to buckle your shoes."

The girl needed to be needed. Needed to know that Rissa still wanted her. She smiled. "I would appreciate that."

She leaned on Pela as she walked to the door. Dillan hastily came to her other side. "A hover-chair will be here in a moment."

"I don't need it. I can walk."

"Maybe you should use the chair, Mom."

By the time an attendant guided an anti-grav chair up to her, she knew Dillan and Pela were right. Still she hated admitting weakness.

"Get in." Dillan's stern tone brooked no argument.

Giving him a look that could blister paint—she hoped—she let the attendant help her sit. The chair bounced, making her feel unstable. Reflexively, she gripped both arms before it dumped her on the floor.

Within an hour, they arrived at Dillan's ship berthed at Jeneman Spaceport. While he stowed the hover-chair, Pela helped her to the lounge. Rissa wouldn't admit he'd been right to get the chair for her. Just walking from the airlock to the sofa exhausted her.

"Can I get you something?" Pela hovered. "A snack, something to drink?"

"Prepare for launch," Dillan called over the intraship. "Pela, make sure Rissa is secure then get up here. I need your assistance."

"Go." Rissa waved at her.

Pela's eagerness showed in her skipping steps.

As he fired up the heavy air engine, Rissa closed her eyes. *Good riddance to this place.*

CHAPTER 31

Despite her protests, Dillan carried her into his quarters. After he set her down, he clasped her face. "You are going to kill me."

"I told you I could walk."

He shook his head. "Not from carrying you. I'm going to die from terror. I thought my worst fear was when the shuttle left Balderan with you trapped inside. That was nothing compared to how I felt seeing you on the floor of the cargo bay on top of Coriana, fighting with that fem. According to Servary, she's ruthless."

"I couldn't let her get away. And I was afraid once Security arrested her, I'd never find out about Miri."

"Promise me you'll never do anything that reckless again." His eyes clouded with more than worry. She'd only seen that shade of green once, the Traishan sky before a violent storm.

Because of his anxiety, she refrained from giving him a flippant response. She clasped his face between her palms, a mirror of him. "I will try my best."

When she pressed her lips to his, he pulled back. "I haven't finished yet. I have never been so frightened as when I saw your blood gushing out of your back onto the concourse floor."

"That was not my fault. I wasn't being reckless. I—"

"I know. But you scared so many years off my life, I'll be an old man too soon." He kissed the tip of her nose.

"You'll catch up with me then."

He tipped up her chin. "Are you still on about our ages?"

"Well . . ."

"Some fems find younger men attractive." He let a corner of his mouth turn up. "More staying power."

"Maybe I'm afraid I won't be able to keep up with you."

"You've been doing well so far. Why don't we wait and see how it goes?" He walked her backwards until the back of her knees hit the edge of the bed. "But not now. The medico said you'll need lots of rest."

She lay in his big bed, wide awake, waiting for him. She wanted his arms around her. She, who needed nobody, needed his comfort. Among her clothes in the tote, he'd brought her comm. She checked the time. An hour since he left. After rolling over several times, she checked again. Another hour had passed. They'd entered a hyperlane. She'd heard the switch over to the FTL engine.

Still, he didn't come.

He had nothing to do in the lane. He was avoiding her.

The light from the corridor hit her eyes. Pela's slight figure stood in the opening. "Dillan wants to know if you're ready for Last Meal."

Rissa propped herself up on her elbow. "Did I miss Mid-Day Meal?"

"You slept through it." She came farther into the room. "I'm glad we left that place."

Rissa patted the edge of the bed. "Come and sit." When she did, Rissa clasped her hand. "I'd glad, too. We should have stayed home."

In the light from the corridor, she could see tears in Pela's eyes as she crooked her knee on the bed. "I thought about that. Thought about a lot of things. How I should have gone with you and Dillan to Vesteron. But then the slavers would've gotten Anaris and Geena."

Rissa nodded. "I thought about that, too. If I'd never left Astron, I'd still have the tavern and we'd all be safe."

"Or not." Dillan came into the room. "Quin was going to burn down the tavern whether you were in Astron or not. You could have been inside and died. We don't need to rehash what we should or shouldn't have done. What happened, happened."

Pela squeezed her hand. "If it hadn't, Security would never have caught Coriana. And you never would have learned so much about the real Miri."

"She's right," Dillan said. "We have more information than ever. We can try to find her."

Rissa frowned. "If what Coriana said was true."

That night, he came to her bed. "I'll be careful. I just want to hold you."

He snugged her up against him, her back to his front. Just the way she wanted to be held. "You are strung tighter than a cable hauling barzilium up from the mine."

"Speaking of mines, how are things going with your company?"

"Not my company. My father's. His dream, not mine."

"Why did you go to work there?"

He let out a deep sigh. "After I left Astron six years ago, I was wracked by guilt. I believed my recklessness had killed Konner. I know, he wasn't really dead, but that's what I thought at the time. I couldn't go back to that life. When I came home, I told my father I'd changed. He didn't believe me. So I set about proving it to him."

"By completing your education and joining his company as a corporate lawyer," she finished. "Is that what you wanted to do?"

"No. But it was what he always wanted me to do."

"Did that job make you happy?"

"No."

"Then I'm glad you're not doing it anymore. You were right to quit." She snorted. "Here I am telling you how to live your life when I don't have one to return to. I have no home, no business. I have nothing."

"You have me. And Pela. What more do you need?"

"But I—"

"Hush. Get some sleep."

Again, she lay awake, thinking. Her mind whirled as she thought about what had happened since they left Balderan. She relived fighting with Coriana, walking so happily with Winty—Faringa, the assassin sent to make sure she never testified against the traffickers and their boss. Like an entertainment vid, Rissa saw herself with Faringa's arm around her waist. The young fem she'd thought was her long-lost daughter. The pain from the knife couldn't compare to the anguish of knowing she'd been deceived.

Dillan rolled over and threw his arm across her. After drawing her close again, he nuzzled her neck. "Can't sleep?"

"No."

"Would it help to talk about what's bothering you?"

She didn't want to talk about the attack or how she saw it behind her closed eyes. Instead, she talked about what she'd thought about during the long days and nights in the med center. "I don't know what to do about those children. The ones that were taken from the orphanages or off the streets. Do you know what happened to them?"

"Hanu said there was an organization on Menaca that shelters the homeless."

"Right. Like that orphanage in Balderate."

"No. Pela and I checked it out."

"You took Pela to one of those places? What if—"

"It was her idea. They let her wander around and talk to the kids. That girl has a built-in bullshit meter."

"A what?"

"Sorry. While you were goofing off in the med center, I hung around at the docks, talking to the indie pilots. They know all the latest expressions. Pela knows when someone isn't telling her the truth. The places we visited, while the regen did its work, were legit. The rescued kids told Hanu's team where they came from, and Coalition Security shut down all those orphanages and arrested the managers. They got even more information from Arjay. You know how he analyzed those databases? I don't know how Laning Servary got the head of Coalition Security to organize a massive strike on those involved with trafficking, but he did it."

"Then it's over?"

He snorted. "Coriana's organization is destroyed. But she was only one of many. As you discovered, she reported to Hallart. It's a good bet the other bosses report to that gangster, too."

Each day, Rissa got stronger. Dillan showed her how to use the exercise equipment in the hold. She and Pela took turns encouraging each other while Dillan kept the ship on course to Astron.

On the night before they reached Astron, she lay in bed with him. Again the fate of the children kept her awake.

"How can I help them? That organization Hanu told you about? I checked them out. They're based on the Central Planets, not on the Frontier. Children out here need protection from those who would take advantage of them. And especially protection from the traffickers."

"What are you thinking?"

"Bah." She waved her hand. "How could I do that? If I rescued them, what would I do with them? I don't even have a home."

"If you had a place, what would you do?"

"Take care of them. Teach them practical skills. Did you know Voleya is thinking about a school for the kids we rescued from that Indigian pilot and his crew? What if we had a real school?" She made a rude noise. "I can't even take care of Pela right now."

He nibbled on her ear. "If you're nice to me, maybe I'll help."

She stopped his hand that had been snaking up the edge of her sleep garment. "Don't joke."

"Who's joking?" He loomed over her. "I'll help you. All you have to do is . . ." He kissed her nose. ". . . ask."

She pushed on his shoulders until she rolled him over on his back then straddled him. "My idea would cost a lot of money."

"I have a lot of money. Ask."

"It would just be a loan. I'll find a way to pay you back."

"I will do anything for you, you know. Besides, when we're married my money will be your money."

"What?" She scrambled off him. "Married? Who said anything about getting married?"

"Me."

"Dillan Rusteran, you are out of your mind. I can't marry you."

"Why not? Neither of us is married. Quit worrying and give me a kiss."

"For the seven hundredth time, I am too old for you."

He threw his head back into the pillow and groaned. "Divine One, save me from stubborn fems. I—"

His comm vibrated on the table next to the bed. He picked it up then shut it off.

"You have to answer that," she said.

"No, I don't. It's my father. I know what he wants, and I'm not giving it to him."

She crawled across him, turned on the small lamp, and picked up the device. "He's called you—" She counted the messages. "—twenty-eight times. Did you listen to the messages?"

"Nope. Told you I know what he wants." He took the comm away from her and dropped it, none too gently, onto the table. "He even got his assistant to call me. Sixteen messages from her. I'd rather talk about this plan of yours for the children. It sounds like you'd need a fair-sized building. And staff."

"Remember what happened the last time you didn't answer your comm? At least listen to the messages."

"Are you going to be this bossy when we're married?"

"That's a moot point since I am not going to marry you. Listen to one message, at least."

The comm vibrated again.

Dillan grabbed it. "What do you want?"

"Hello to you, too." Laning Servary's voice came through loud and clear.

"Sorry, Servary. You woke me up." He gave Rissa a helpless glance.

"I'm the one who's sorry, Rusteran. I just heard about your father."

Dillan's heart tripped. "What about him?"

"By the Matriarch, didn't anyone call you?"

After Dillan went out to the lounge, Rissa got dressed and waited, giving him privacy to find out about his father. When he returned, his ravaged face told her all she needed to know. She went to him and held tight. *Sherd.* If it wasn't one of them needing comfort, it was the other. Fate had swung her fiery lance at them too many times.

"You're going back to Eleganza," she said into his bare chest.

"I have to." He blew out a long breath. "He had a stroke. The medicos claim his high-stressed job plus too much alcohol and a poor diet contributed. My announcement that I resigned pushed him over the edge."

She rubbed his back. "You don't know that."

He pulled away. "We don't lie to each other, Rissa. Don't start now. I'll drop you and Pela off in Astron, fuel up, and head for Bricaldia."

"I know. You have to leave."

"I'll be back. I promise you. I will come back."

She nodded. She knew he wouldn't.

CHAPTER 32

"So that's the new tavern," Rissa said to Pela as they walked out of the spaceport. As they'd watched Dillan leave, Pela cried enough for both of them. Rissa didn't have any tears left.

"I can't believe it's so huge." Pela stared in awe at the long synthcrete building with perma-film windows. It was twice the size of her tavern and three stories tall, reaching almost as high as the spaceport dome. Even fifteen meters away, laughter and music reached them.

"How did it get so big?" Pela continued. "We've only been gone three tendays."

"Let's go to Nally's and get Mid-Day Meal and the latest gossip."

"We'd get more gossip at Fortuna's." She winked at Rissa.

"Hey, hey, hey." Nakus stood on the wide stone walkway in front of the new tavern. "If it isn't Rissa *Dicks*. Not so high and mighty anymore."

"Mooching drinks, Nakus? I'll be sure to warn the manager."

The short, round Kruferian pointed to his chest. "*I'm* the manager. You gotta be nice to me now if you ever want a drink here."

"I'll pass." She remembered what Kaminga had told her about the vandalism. "Aren't you supposed to be in the lockup? For vandalizing my place?"

After giving her a wide-eyed innocent look, he said, "*I* didn't wreck your tavern."

"No. You just paid others to do it."

He grinned, showing stumps of brown teeth. "All a mistake. Those farmers changed their tune. Wasn't me. Kaminga had no proof I had anything to do with it." He gave Pela a long look. "Your girl can have a job here. She's pretty enough . . . for a human. Could make lots of credits if she's *nice* to the customers."

"Why you wretched piece of—" Rissa started for him.

Pela hauled on her arm. "Let's go, Mom. He's not worth it."

"Mom?" Nakus laughed. "That's a good one."

"Ignore him," Pela warned. "He only said what he did to get you angry."

Rissa slung her arm across Pela's shoulders. After a few blocks, she asked, "How did you get to be so smart?"

"Must be from my mom." She grinned broadly.

They walked down the dusty street, their feet lagging because of the sun beating down on them. As they neared the café, Pela gasped. "That's not—"

"By the Matriarch . . ."

They broke into a run, passing the café. Her tavern. How—

"Slow down, ladies. You'll get heatstroke." Merchant Graeson chuckled.

Rissa and Pela ignored him. They stopped across the side street from her tavern. Her newly rebuilt tavern.

"What? Who?" Too flabbergasted at the sight, Rissa couldn't have completed a sentence if she tried. In a large perma-film window was a sign. *Rissa's.*

Fortuna came up behind her. "Good gracious, girl. Nally was right. He said you were running like an offworlder." She took turns hugging Rissa and Pela.

Rissa could barely speak. "What happened?"

"Let's get in out of the heat." Fortuna urged them into the new building. "We had a town meeting. Since your place was gone, we had to have it outdoors. By the stars, it was hot."

The interior felt blessedly cool. Fortuna was right. They had been running like foolish offworlders. The empty room was light, airy, thanks to the large unbreakable windows. Instead of the wood paneling, the walls had been painted the color of dorlap cream. While the floors no longer gleamed from highly-polished real wood, they were a serviceable synthetic.

"Who did all this?"

The pleasure house madam put her arm around Rissa's waist and squeezed. "You have a lot of friends here, Rissa."

Several people entered. The first few in a rush, the others trickling in. Graeson, Medico Barlen, Nally and Voleya, Sophira and Partorus with Zeka carrying Baby Miya, farmers and their families, people from town. They all welcomed Rissa and Pela.

"How did you—"

"Ropergor alerted everyone that you were back." Sophira hugged her.

"Hey, Boss." Kiran picked Rissa up and twirled her around. "Glad you're home."

So many people, all looking pleased with themselves.

"You all did this?" Emotion clogged Rissa's throat. "I can't believe . . ."

"We also decided," Merchant Graeson said loudly, "that this village needs a mayor. We elected you."

Fortuna leaned in. "That's what you get for missing town meetings."

Before she could protest, others came up to her and welcomed her home, saying how much they'd missed her, and so on and so on. Her head spun at their good wishes and generosity.

They didn't stay long. Soon only Kiran, Fortuna, and Pela were left.

"I'm overwhelmed." Rissa shook her head. "Truly overwhelmed."

Pela, who'd been hugged as much as Rissa, kept looking around. "There's no bar."

Kiran knuckled Pela's head. "We weren't sure if that's what the boss wanted. We weren't even sure if you both would come back. I wouldn't after all that's happened."

"Where's that no-good Rusteran?" Fortuna demanded. "Why isn't he here?"

"He had to go back to Bricaldia," Pela said. "His father's sick."

Fortuna eyed Rissa. "He's coming back, isn't he?"

She glanced at Pela who was chatting with Kiran. She blew out a long breath. "I don't think so."

After missing Mid-Day Meal, Rissa and Pela had an early Last Meal at the café. Since the rush hadn't come yet, both Nally and Voleya sat down with them.

"I take it your apprentices are working out?" Rissa said.

Nally nodded. "And they don't talk incessantly, like that Arjay." He looked around. "Where is he, by the way?"

"He stayed on Menaca to help the authorities."

Her eyes bright with excitement, Pela leaned in. "He told Coalition Security where to find so many traffickers, the lockups were full. And, Mom, here—" She squeezed Rissa's hand. "—captured a really wicked fem who was responsible for all the kidnappings here. You should have seen Mom. She took her knife to the fem and—"

"That's enough." Rissa laughed. "Security had her surrounded. She wouldn't have gotten away."

"We heard how you rescued all those children," Voleya said. "What happened to them?"

"They're in a good place," Pela said quickly, not giving Rissa a chance. "Mister Dillan and I checked it out. It's run by good people, and the kids are happy."

"So it's all over?" Voleya asked.

Rissa shook her head. "Dillan says we got one gang. There are probably more across the Rim. We should still stay vigilant."

CHAPTER 33

"Caravel RM44783, you are cleared to land."

About time. When he last approached Astron, Dillan had clear skies and an immediate landing. This time, he'd had to wait for three other ships to land first. The delay raised his anxiety to return to Rissa. Half a Bricadian year had passed since he'd seen her last. Twenty-five of the longest tendays in his life as he fought off a hostile takeover, convinced his father to retire, and arranged the merger between Rusteran Mining and Winslott Industries. He and Jileena had even achieved the impossible. A reunion between their fathers. And his mother's return.

After eighteen years believing his spouse had cheated on him with his partner, Boras finally learned the truth. Adamus Winslott and Sarina Rusteran convinced him to listen. The fact that he lay helpless in a med center bed had more to do with it than an open mind. If only he had listened to them before. Stubborn old zircan's ass.

But if he'd listened, and believed, Sarina wouldn't have left, and Boras wouldn't have driven Dillan into a wild and reckless youth.

And he never would've met Rissa.

"I didn't think Astron would be this big," his companion said.

He surveyed the landscape around Astron Spaceport, amazed at the changes. A large structure rose up next to the 'port. The offworlder's new tavern had expanded. The village had more than doubled. Instead of three streets in both directions, eight intersected.

"It didn't used to be."

A sprawling structure south of the village caught his eye. It looked like . . . No, couldn't be. A school? Early evening shade partially covered playground equipment worthy of a Bricaldian educational institute. As he watched, children burst from the doors and clambered onto the equipment.

"That school is new." He looked more closely at the village. "Rissa rebuilt her tavern."

"Caravel RM44783, your approach is erratic." Traffic Controller Ropergor wasn't his usual pleasant self.

Sherd. He was off course and coming in too hot. "Sorry. I have it under control."

So close to seeing Rissa again, the last thing he needed was to crash and burn. If her messages were any indication, she was as eager to see him as he was to be with her again.

Traffic Control directed him to a berth. More changes. More berths, most filled. Ropergor must be too busy to come out and talk. As he left the 'port, his companion chatted nervously. After the silence of most of his trip, the past tenday had been filled with nonstop questions.

Although he wanted to race down the street, he kept pace with her. He'd wanted to bring her hover chair, but she insisted on walking. He pointed out the new businesses, as well as the old. When he called out to Merchant Graeson, the man went inside and slammed the door.

Dillan waved at Nally standing in front of his café. The chef folded his arms across his chest and glared. That was odd. Graeson had never been real friendly, but Nally had.

They finally reached the tavern. Before he fully opened the door, noise spilled out into the street. A *Firefly* vid played in the background. At the tables closest to the vid screen, Winslott miners—rather, Rusternan-Winslott miners—kept up a lively commentary on the Terrans' concept of space travel.

The tavern was filled to over-flowing. It looked like Rissa's fear of losing business to the offworlder's tavern was unfounded.

Sophira and Jodar nodded to him but didn't stop as they maneuvered between tables, trays of liquid refreshments held high. Behind the bar, Kiran filled orders for two new servers. When he glanced up, his eyes widened, and his shout could be heard all the way to the new tavern. "You bastard."

Silence descended on the place.

"You have a lot of nerve coming back, Offworlder."

As Dillan threaded his way to the bar, miners and town-folk stared at him, some curious, more with animosity. When he reached Kiran, the big Zebori grabbed the front of his shirt and lifted him off the floor.

"Where in Lexol have you been?" He tossed Dillan against the bar.

After regaining his balance, he said, "What's the matter with you? Where's Rissa? In the kitchen?"

Kiran's eyes narrowed. "Stupid offworlder, you don't know."

A crushing fear seized his chest. "Know what?"

"Need a drink here," a customer sitting at the bar called. "Quit-cher yakking and gimme another mudslide."

Without looking, Kiran called back, "You're done, Pacer. No more for you."

"What happened to Rissa? Answer me."

"She's not here. This is my tavern now." As he headed for the end of the bar, he glanced back at Dillan. "Get out of my place or I'll throw you out."

"All right. I'll go." Dillan was still confused by the big man's attitude. "Just tell me where she is."

"If you'd kept in touch, you'd know where to find her."

"She isn't here?" Leena's anxious voice came from behind him. *Sherd.* He'd forgotten about her.

"I don't know. Let's get out of here. The noise is so loud I can't think."

Once out on the boardwalk, he stopped and leaned against a post that held up the overhang. "You should sit." He pointed to a bench. "Wait here, and I'll find out where she is."

He ran across the street then around to the alley door.

"You son of a bitch." Fortuna greeted him. "Where in the galaxy have you been, you zircan's ass?"

"Hello to you, too. Where's Rissa?"

Seizing a handful of his shirt, the little madam yanked him down. *What was with people grabbing his shirt?*

"If you'd bothered to contact her, you'd know." She socked him on the nose.

Damn, that hurt. Warm liquid rolled down to his lip. When he swiped at his face, blood came away on his fingertips.

"Miz Fortuna, what did you do?" The cook stared. "Want me to get some ice?"

"Don't give this ferking idiot a thing besides a boot out the door." She spun around, her long smoky-blue dress swishing around her ankles. At the door, she paused. "And don't tell him where she is."

As soon as she left, Cook held out a wet towel. "Have you seen our new school?"

Dillan pressed the cold fabric against his upper lip and nose. "Where's Rissa?"

"Mister Dillan, I like my job." She took the towel from him. "Think."

When he went outside, Leena walked with halting steps toward him. "Was she there?"

"No. And I didn't get—" He slapped his forehead. "I think I know."

Again, he took off running before he stopped and returned to her. "I'm sorry. I knew we should have brought your hover chair. This is too much walking for you."

She squared her shoulders. "No hover chair. I was in it too damn long. Go to her. I'll catch up."

"I can't leave you be—"

She clasped his hand. "Go. You've waited too long to see her. Just point me in the right direction."

"It will be dark soon."

"All the more reason to get going."

Rissa leaned against the wall. The heat from the stone building warded off the chill of the evening. She always hated to call the children in. If she let them, they would play all night, expending pent-up energy from being cooped up during the heat of the day. Naps and exercises between classes helped some, but this was their favorite time. Hers, too. Their laughter and shouts of joy filled her with delight.

She let them play a little longer. After all they'd been through, they deserved to have some fun.

"Last Meal's ready." Pela came up alongside her.

"Let them play for three more mins."

"You are such a softie. How's your back?"

"Same old, same old." She pushed herself away from the wall. In the darkness, she saw movement. A man.

She grabbed the whistle around her neck and blew three times. "Alert! Alert! Alert!" At the same time, she reached behind her back for the MBS carbine she always carried outside.

As the children came running, Pela pulled the LZ-9 laser pistol out from the back of her trousers.

"Practice or real?" an eight-year-old said as he raced to the door.

"Doesn't matter. Pela, get them inside."

Gover, Galeriana's first moon, barely peeked over the mountains. Rissa stepped into the light, leveling the carbine at the approaching stranger. Nobody would ever hurt her children again. By the Matriarch, she'd protect them with her life.

The man stopped. "Rissa?"

Dillan held his hands out. "Rissa, it's me."

"I know who you are." She didn't lower the weapon. "What are you doing here?"

He walked toward the fem standing in the moonlit circle. The pregnant fem in the moonlight. *Sweet Divinity.* Rissa was pregnant.

"You can stop right there." Her tight voice showed no mercy.

He didn't stop. He had to come closer, hold her. The cocking of the laser carbine stopped him cold. "Sweetheart, I'm back."

"Yeah. Big deal."

"Mom, what's wrong?" Pela came out of the building, laser pistol in hand. She peered into the night. "Is that . . . "

"Uh huh."

"Would someone explain?" Dillan ignored the weapons trained on him and walked toward the small patch of light. "Why are you surprised I returned? I told you I would. And why in Lexol didn't you tell me you were pregnant?"

"Is that her?" Leena limped up behind him.

"Who's that?" Pela demanded.

Dillan put his arm around Leena's shoulder and drew her into the light. "Someone you'll want to meet. I hope you'll welcome her better than you welcomed me."

Rissa lowered her weapon slightly. "Why should we welcome you, Rusteran? You never called, never messaged. You left twenty-five tendays ago. No word for two hundred and fifty days, you bastard. Why shouldn't we be surprised when you finally showed up?"

Okay, something was very wrong.

"Is everyone here angry with you?" Leena asked.

"I think there's been a problem with communication."

"What communication?" Rissa demanded.

Yep, a real problem. He'd messaged her, and she'd messaged him in return. The fact that she'd never called him back had him worried at first, until she mentioned in a message how busy she was. He'd believed that. Now he had to wonder with whom he'd exchanged messages.

"Those are real weapons, aren't they?" Leena limped closer to him.

"Who's that?" Pela said in a snide voice. "Your new spouse?"

"What spouse?" His companion shivered.

"Do you think we could go inside?" he asked. "It's cold."

Rissa slung her weapon over her shoulder and opened the door. "Come in, Pela. He's right. It is cold out here."

After Rissa went inside, Pela glared at him. "You broke her heart. You abandoned her—just like that other guy who got her pregnant. And, by the way, she did tell you she was pregnant. I saw the message she sent. So take your girlfriend or whoever she is and leave."

When she headed for the door, he raced after her and caught it before she could lock him out. "This has gone far enough. Explanations are in order. I'll be damned if I repeat my parents' mistake."

He held the door for Leena. Together, they followed Pela into a large dining room from which came noisy chatter and laughter. No cafeteria benches there. Children of various species, races, and ages sat at cloth-covered tables, some square, others round.

As soon as he stepped into the room, silence descended like the curtain at the end of a stage play. No more laughter, no smiles. Rissa, who'd been helping a child cut his food, looked up. She motioned him to wait. At least, she didn't pull her carbine around and aim it at him in front of the kids. She talked softly to a teen. Whatever she said to the boy sent him over to cut the rest of the food.

As Rissa passed Dillan, she said, "Come."

Sweetest word he'd heard since he landed.

Her eyes flicked over Leena before leading them into a small office. Pela followed then leaned against the wall, arms crossed in front of her. After closing the door behind them, Rissa took her place behind her desk. The effect of putting a piece of furniture between them wasn't lost on him.

"You cut your hair." What an inane thing to say. Her beautiful, long hair now curled around her face, softening it. Pela had done the same. *Little Rissa.*

"Is that all you want to say?" She folded her hands on top of her desk.

"No. Let's clear the air first." He handed her his comm. "Scroll back. See my messages. Read yours."

As she read, her exotic dark eyes widened. She returned his device. "I didn't write those messages."

He rubbed the back of his neck. "I gathered that. Leena, sit."

She gave him a grateful smile.

"Who's your companion?" Rissa asked.

"Leena Colas. Leena, meet Rissa and Pela Dix."

He wondered if the irony would sink in. Colas, one of the most common surnames on Traish. Like Elfors.

"What happened to you?" Pela asked. "Why are you limping?"

Leena sat forward, looking at Rissa. "I had an accident in my skimmer. A man deliberately crashed into me and left me for dead." A small smile curved her lips. "I fooled him."

"The crash happened before I returned to Bricaldia," Dillan said. "In fact, shortly after Coriana was arrested." Again, he waited to see if it registered.

"Why did you come back?" Rissa asked.

"I told you I would. I keep my promises." He walked around the desk and stood before her. When she craned her neck to look at him, he squatted. "I'm sorry you thought I'd abandoned you. I wouldn't have hurt you for the universe. I love you."

She looked away, but not before he saw a glimpse of hope in her eyes. When he took her hand, she started to pull away then let it lay in his.

"I read the posts. The ones I didn't get. And my so-called responses." Finally, she looked into his eyes. "What's going on, Dillan? Who would do such a thing to us?"

"I can hazard a guess. One of Hallart's people. The same ones who caused Leena's crash."

"Wait a min." Pela straightened from the wall. "Why would they harm her? She's not connected to us."

"Yes, she is."

Rissa heard what Dillan said but didn't look at the young fem. She wanted to keep her eyes on him. He'd returned. Her hopes fulfilled. Yet, someone had kept his messages from her. She couldn't understand why anyone bothered. She was a nobody.

"What do you mean she's connected to us?" Pela's attitude bordered on belligerence.

Not that Rissa blamed her. The poor girl had been her staunch ally and, more importantly, her friend.

With Pela redirecting Rissa's attention, she really looked at the fem accompanying Dillan. She appeared to be too thin for her bones. Strong bones, little flesh. When she'd stood next to Dillan, she reached his shoulder—tall for a fem, even one from Traish. Dark eyes, dark hair, what little there was of it. She'd either shorn her hair for fashion or—

Rissa remembered what she'd said about a skimmer accident. When she looked closer, she saw the scars. Add that to the limp, and she concluded the fem had been seriously injured.

"You should know where I've been first," Dillan replied. "After I got my parents settled, I—"

"What do you mean *parents*?" Rissa asked. "I thought your mother walked out on you."

"She did, and now she's back." He explained about the misunderstanding. "If they'd talked things out seventeen years ago, a lot of pain would have been avoided. I don't want to make that mistake with you."

"Then get on with the story." Pela, so defiant.

"Remember what Winty/Faringa said about following the money? I asked a friend, an expert in accounting forensics, who did just that. Most of what Coriana and Faringa said was true." He stared hard at Rissa, the green in his eyes glittered with suppressed excitement. "I found Leena on Marin 5, searching for you."

The young fem was trying to hold back a grin. Rissa looked at her more closely. Yes, she could see her father in the set of the girl's jaw and a glimpse of her mother when Leena furled her brow. More, she saw a bit of herself in the tilt of her eyes.

This was her child.

But then she'd thought Winty had been Miri, and look where that led. To have her hopes elevated so high only to come crashing down had nearly crushed her. She was afraid to believe.

"Are you sure?" Her voice sounded timid. She was never timid. And yet . . .

"I've been searching for you for the past year," Leena said. "My parents—I mean the people who adopted me—told me how the adoption came about. When I turned twenty, they gave me their blessing to look for you. They'd been told you couldn't take care of me because you had too many other children. I didn't know what had happened until I met Rani Karr's—I mean Coriana's—daughter. She hated what her mother did. She's been trying to find the children and match them with their birth mothers."

"Daughter? I thought it was her sister," Pela said.

"Rani/Coriana didn't want anyone to know she had a daughter. For years, she passed the girl off as her little sister." Leena blew out a breath. "Rani's daughter followed you back to Traish then lost your trail. If Dillan hadn't found me, I'm not sure what I would've done. Except to keep looking."

Rissa listened to the story, watched the girl, and wanted to believe. Desperately wanted to believe. She wanted to hold her daughter, if this was her Miri. Fear held her back.

"You haven't said anything." Dillan stood next to the young fem while staring at Rissa. "I wouldn't have brought Leena to you if I wasn't sure. Between my forensic guy and the records Coriana's daughter showed me, I'm ninety-nine point nine percent positive Leena is your daughter."

Pela scoffed. "Ninety-nine point nine? You sound like Arjay."

"Rissa?" Dillan's question hung in the air between her and Leena.

The girl's face crumpled. "You don't believe. I'm sorry." She struggled to get up. When Dillan tried to help, she brushed him aside.

"Wait." Rissa couldn't let her go. Not yet. She rounded the desk. When she reached Leena, she hesitated. "I want to believe. Just now, you reminded me of myself when I last talked to my mother." She touched the girl's chin. "You have a lot of pride. Like me."

Leena blushed. "My parents—I mean the people who—"

"They were your parents," Rissa said. "They raised you, and they allowed you to look for me. They must have been very good people."

"They are. Can I hug you?" The hesitation and hope in Leena's expression mirrored her own.

Rissa held out her arms.

CHAPTER 34

"Have you forgiven me yet?" Dillan asked.

A perceptive Pela had left them in Rissa's office and taken Leena to see the school and meet the children. If she hadn't, Dillan was planning to find another reason to be alone with Rissa. He understood her earlier hesitation. She'd been devastated by Winty's betrayal. Fear that she'd be wrong about Leena had shown in her eyes along with reluctance to trust. She'd had to protect herself, protect her heart.

Especially her heart after what she'd believed about him.

If he could wipe away the past twenty-five tendays and spare her that hurt, he would. He could only try to make up for what she'd gone through thinking he'd abandoned her like Miri's father and her own had done. They hadn't hugged yet. She'd given him a quick kiss on the cheek to thank him for finding her daughter. Guilt prevented him from scooping her up and holding her so tight she'd believe he would never leave. The space between them might have been a crevasse. Almost too large to leap over.

Almost.

"I should have tried harder to talk to you. Called Kaminga and had him deliver a message." He wiped his face. "I didn't keep my focus on you. Instead, I let my father's company consume me."

She leaned back against the edge of her desk, half sitting. "How is he? I read on the 'waves that he retired. The biggest news around here was the merger. Was that your doing?"

"He's going to be okay. My mother will see to it." He told her about his parents' reunion. "He finally accepted that I didn't want his company. That I had my own goals. My mother and I convinced him to turn the company over to Jileena. He and her father have made their peace."

The corner of her mouth curved into the beginning of a smile, the first she'd aimed at him. When she finally accepted that Leena was her Miri, she'd beamed. Hugs, smiles, and tears between all three fems had started slowly then swelled.

"I wish you hadn't cut your hair."

With a self-conscious gesture, she touched the back of her head. "I like it like this."

"Sure. Of course." He cleared his throat. "Tell me about the baby. How soon?"

"Soon. Very soon."

"Then you were pregnant before I left." He couldn't keep the hurt out of his voice that she hadn't told him.

"I didn't know. I thought I'd gone into menopause."

"You said you couldn't have more children."

"I guess that medico was wrong."

"How do you feel about it? Happy, sad, upset?"

She bridged the gap between them then wrapped her arms around his neck. "Very, very happy. Especially now that you're here."

As he held her close, something kicked him. He jumped. "What was *that*?"

"Dillan Junior. Now kiss me. We don't have much time."

"Why? Do you have to be somewhere?" He knew she'd made a life without him, but he'd hoped to have more time with her.

"You know how I said the baby is coming soon? I think he's anxious to meet his daddy." She doubled over.

"Rissa!" He pulled her upright. "You mean *now*? What do I do? Where do we go?"

She patted his cheek. "Take me to bed."

"What! Now?"

Konner Dillan Rusteran made his appearance with a cry that brought his sisters running. Pela and Leena vied for holding him first. Rissa settled it by placing him in both their hands. She looked exhausted and happier than Dillan had ever seen her.

After Medico Barlen proclaimed the baby perfect and Rissa fine, he headed for Kiran's tavern to announce the news and celebrate. That led to a procession of friends welcoming Baby Konner with a belated nod to Dillan. Rissa's friends weren't as forgiving as she was. It would take time to convince them he'd come back to stay.

Convincing Rissa would be more difficult. While she accepted the communication problem, a bit of wariness still lingered in her eyes.

Once all the visitors left, he savored the sight of Pela sitting on the edge of Rissa's bed. Leena appeared unsure until Rissa motioned her to sit on her other side. In the middle, propped up against the headboard, his spouse-to-be held his child.

His family.

"Are you back for good?" Leave it to Pela to cut to the chase.

"I am. Is that all right with you?"

"As long as Mom wants you to stay."

Rissa smiled. "I want him to. As long as he does."

"This is where my family is. Of course I want to stay." With a quick glance at Leena, he added, "All of you are my family. As soon as possible, I want to marry Rissa, if she's willing."

The moment of truth. Would she give him that nonsense about their age difference again?

"One thing I admire about you, Rusteran. You are persistent. All the time you were gone, I thought you'd given up on me. That I'd chased you away for good. And now here you are, including my girls as if they were your own."

"Of course, they are. They're part of you. Your daughter by birth—" He nodded to Leena. "—and your daughter by choice."

Pela beamed.

Baby Konner ignored all of them and fell asleep against Rissa's breast.

"Pela, would you take the baby?" Rissa held out the sleeping infant. "Leena, would you please go with her? I'd like to talk to Dillan."

Pela smirked. "Ri-ight. Talk. C'mon, Leena. We can take a hint."

After they left, Dillan replaced Pela on the side of the bed. "I guess talk is about all we can do for a while, right?"

"Talk first. Kiss later." She picked up his hand and examined it, turning it over and running her finger down each of his. She had no idea what that was doing to him.

"If kissing is on the agenda, I can wait. I've waited for you for nearly eighteen years, Rissa. A few mins won't hurt me."

"What are your plans?"

"Marry you."

She snorted. "After that?"

"Live with you and our family."

"Will you be content with that? You aren't a man who sits around all day or lounges on a barstool. What will you do?"

"Lounging on a barstool doesn't sound like a bad idea. I may have to go to the offworlder's tavern. Kiran threatened to throw me out."

"He did? I'll talk to him. Now about the job?" she persisted.

"I have a client who likes my ideas for modifying his Agilean Speeder similar to what I did for Servary. Laning and Jileena have been touting my work ever since I returned to Bricaldia. A couple of other people are interested in what I can do for them."

"So you finally decided what you want to do when you grow up." Though she said it with a straight face, he saw the twinkle in her eyes.

"That wasn't a crack about our ages, was it? Or were you afraid I was going to mooch off you? I told you before I have more credits than I know what to do with."

"Good. Because the school needs some of those credits."

"I promised before to help you. Tell me what you need, and I'll get it. What about yourself? Pela? What do you need?"

She leaned forward, resting her hands loosely on his shoulders. "You, Dillan. All we really need is you."

Turn the page for a look at

The Pilot

The first novel in the Outer Rim Series
by Diane Burton

Now available at online retailers

The Pilot
An Outer Rim Novel

"Cargo transport, this is Coalition Security. Are you in need of assistance?"

Celara d'Enfaden raced up the vertical ladder from the hold. She leapt across a corner of the open hole in the cabin floor. Reaching under the cabinet above the aft bunk, she hit the switches that closed the hatch and started the exhaust fan. Finally, she whipped off her protective mask only to gag at the residual stench from the cargo. She took one look at the perma-film viewscreen across the bow of her starship and her heart stopped.

A Volpian cruiser nearly filled the screen. After the first hail in Universal, the deep male voice repeated the offer in different languages, even Menacan, Celera's first language.

"Arjay," she called. "We've got company."

Her boots clattered on the floor's metal plating as she raced to the cockpit. She vaulted over the arm of the pilot's chair, narrowly avoiding her copilot as he crawled out from under the instrument panel.

She hit switches to power up the sublights. It would take time to bring all systems back online—time they didn't have. "Sure hope you fixed that accelerator."

"It is only a temporary measure."

As if they had all the time in the galaxy, Arjay straightened his blond hair back into its normal perfectly-coifed appearance before brushing dust from the viridian-green uniform favored by space crews in the Central District. Ever fastidious, he refused to wear the roomy dun-colored shirt and trousers of a true indie, like she did.

"Quit primping and get us out of here."

He settled into the seat next to her. "We are leaving? They offered to help us."

"Remember what happened last time?" Her fingers flew across the instrument panel's touchpads.

Arjay's fingers flew faster. "Are they pirates?"

"Of course. Where in Lexol's Fire did they come from? And why didn't the proximity alarm go off?"

"Without further investigation, I would not know." He didn't stop his computations. "Volpian cruisers do not have shrouding capabilities. However, the ship appears new. It may be an experimental model."

A siren pierced the small cabin. "About time," she muttered before switching off the alarm.

Arjay brought the primary energizing coil online. Not for the first time she thanked the Spirits he was her copilot. He didn't need to be told what to do. That made up for his primping.

"Cargo transport. I repeat, this is Coalition Security. Identify yourself." The pirate's voice carried the ring of authority.

For a half sec, she had misgivings. What if they *were* Coalition Security? If she didn't obey, she would be in deep horse pucky. But she'd been tricked before by pirates claiming to be Coalition Security. No way were they getting her cargo. If that happened, she would be in even deeper trouble. She'd gone into serious debt to replace the cargo the first pirates stole. If she lost this load, she would lose more than her investment. Her starship was the collateral securing her loan.

She'd taken a chance shutting down in the middle-of-nowhere space to fix the sluggish sublight accelerator. But there wasn't a convenient planet—let alone a repair station—in this sector of the Rim. Pirates zeroed in on wounded prey faster than Terran jackals.

"What if they are not pirates?" Arjay said. "Their offer could be genuine. The ship might, indeed, be Coalition Security."

She grimaced. "Great minds think alike."

"That is rather frightening since mine is the superior intellect."

"Stick it in your ear, Arjay. Let's get my baby up and running. We need to haul ass."

"I am lodging a formal protest. If you must record the entertainment signals emanating from a primitive planet, please refrain from using its disgusting colloquialisms."

"Wassamadder, Arjay. You don't like Terran slang?"

As usual, she sat with her feet tucked under her in the roomy zircan leather chair built more for burly pilots than small fems. If need be, she could easily rise up on her knees to reach keypads across the instrument panel. Besides she hated dangling her feet.

Arjay, who always sat rigidly upright, continued with start-up procedures.

"What is your cargo and destination?" the pirate demanded. *"Respond or prepare to be boarded."*

"Over my dead body you'll board my ship." With the sublight engines almost back online, in another min or two they could blow this pop stand.

"It is not customary for the Coalition to disguise its Security vessels by removing identification markers," Arjay said thoughtfully. "Even so, they always use an official communications channel, which this ship is not. Consequently, I am ninety-six point three percent certain that is not Coalition Security. It could be a trap."

"Cargo transport, this is your last warning. Respond or be boarded for inspection."

The pirate vessel, which had been stationary, began moving closer.

"I lost my last load to you pirates. I am not losing another."

She shoved juice into the primary energizing coils. When her transport, *d'Enfaden's Thermopylae*, responded with lethargy, she glared at Arjay. "I thought you fixed the accelerator."

"I beg your pardon." He always got huffy when he perceived insult. "Without a fully-equipped facility, complete repair is not possible."

She smacked the control panel. "C'mon, c'mon, c'mon."

"She responds to a gentle touch," Arjay admonished. "Just like the majority of your gender." He touched two pads on the instrument panel. "You may try again. Gently."

While the Volpian cruiser steadily advanced, the accelerator hiccupped before engaging.

"You have full power," he announced with satisfaction.

The pirate ship moved in closer, aligning its docking port with hers.

"Hang onto your hat." She spiraled the agile *Thermopylae* under the belly of the cruiser. And her stomach took five secs to catch up.

His complexion, a shade darker than her fair one, turned a sickly shade of green. "You must give advanced notice before attempting to evade a ship intent on docking."

With a laugh, she goosed the sublight accelerator past standard limit. "Who said anything about *attempting* to evade?"

"You do not seriously think you can outrun a Volpian cruiser? Rega d'Enfaden, that ship can achieve speed three times faster—"

"Arjay, how long have you known me?"

The engine protested the abuse she inflicted but did not falter. The cruiser would certainly win a long-distance race with her small transport, but not a sprint. A little more time and she'd be home free.

"According to Universal Time, I have been in your service for two years, thirteen months, sixty-two days, seventy—"

She blew out an exasperated breath. "The question was rhetorical. I hate the term *Rega*. I've told you to call me Celara." They'd had this argument before. She never won.

"I could never do that. *Rega* is the proper term. You do own me."

Though technically her copilot was correct, she considered him more a companion than her property. "Okay, just a few more secs and we'll lose them."

His response came out between a rasp and a groan. "Surely, you are not going into that asteroid field."

"'Don't call me Shirley'," she quoted from a Terran vid. If she didn't need both hands to control the ship, she would've rubbed them in glee. "Those pirates won't follow."

"I recall an aphorism popular on Terra. Something about *famous last words*."

"Arjay, you are such a poop."

"Fair warning, cargo transport," the pirate said. *"Attempt to escape and we will fire on you."*

"Did he say *attempt*?" She grinned as she eased up on the throttle and dodged small asteroids at the outer edge of the field.

"Come on, Trev. You're not going in there, are you?"

Trevarr Jovano leaned forward in the pilot's chair, alert for debris. He and his friend, Laning Servary, had been on a shake-down cruise for Laning's new ship. When Trevarr had offered him the position of Chief Security Officer of Malcon Sector, he'd thrown in a newer, faster ship as incentive. He'd taken the controls a short time before sighting what he thought was a disabled cargo transport. With the way that vessel was fleeing, Trevarr was certain the pilot had something to hide.

He gave his friend a calculated smile. "He dares me to follow."

Laning chuckled. "You never could resist a challenge."

Trevarr did not ease off the accelerator of the Volpian cruiser. He just grinned.

"Glad to see the old you is back."

Laning and his cryptic remarks. "What do you mean?"

"You have been one by-the-book administrator since you got to Mag Prime."

Even though the cruiser was less agile than his personal ship, Trevarr easily dodged flying debris. His new position as Malcon Sector Administrator required him to bring order to this region of the Outer Rim. And, by the Divine One, he would fulfill his responsibility.

"Start out the way you mean to go on."

"Was that your daddy's motto or the Evil Queen's? Yeow!" Laning shrank against the copilot's seat. "You'd better not get a scratch on my new ship."

"I have asked you not to call her that." Trevarr held no hope that Laning would refrain from disparaging the President of the Coalition. "Furthermore, Chief Rep Jovano thought the term *Daddy* sickeningly sentimental."

"Never knew how lucky I was with the parents I had until I met yours. They—"

"Fire a shot across the transport's bow," Trevarr cut off the unnecessary reminder about his parents. "Show the pilot we mean business."

"Why? He's done nothing wrong."

"He is running, a sure sign of guilt. He's a smuggler. Why else would he flee?"

"Gee, I don't know. How about fear?"

"Fear of discovery of his illegal cargo is more like it. I want that ship stopped."

"You might have a point." Laning fired the lazin cannon and splintered a small asteroid in front of the transport.

The little ship easily dodged the fragments. Trevarr's frustration with the pilot's silence and failure to stop warred with admiration for the pilot's flying ability.

"Just like old times, hey, Trev? You and me together again. I've missed ya, buddy."

Trevarr would never admit how much he missed his friend. As a child, he had learned that expressing emotions was improper behavior for the heir to a political dynasty.

He dodged a rock the size of the presidential residence on Bricaldia. "Your new ship has the maneuverability of a house. I wish we had my Agilean."

"If we were in your ship, you would never have entered this asteroid field. Do you want me to fire again on that— Would you watch where you're going?"

An asteroid momentarily filled the viewscreen, obscuring the little cargo hauler. Trevarr avoided it. "Easy there, son," he mocked. "You have been out on the Frontier for eight years. I thought you would have nerves of ferranite by now. Did you get fat and complacent over in Willand Sector?"

"Hey, I resent that. So do you want me to fire or—"

"Yes, fire another round. But try not to destroy that ship under a hail of rock."

Laning grinned. "That would certainly get his attention."

About the Author

Diane Burton combines her love of mystery, adventure, science fiction and romance into writing science fiction romance. She is the author of the science fiction romance *Switched* and *Outer Rim* series plus *One Red Shoe*, a romantic suspense, and the Alex O'Hara PI mysteries. She is also a contributor to the anthology *How I Met My Husband.* Diane and her husband live in Michigan. They have two children and three grandchildren.

For more info and excerpts from her books, visit Diane's website: http://www.dianeburton.com

Connect with Diane Burton online

Blog: dianeburton.blogspot.com/
Facebook: Diane Burton Author
Twitter: @dmburton72
Pinterest: dmburton72
Goodreads: Diane Burton Author

Would you like to know when a new book is released? Sign up for Diane's newsletter. http://eepurl.com/bdHtYf